Nate

A Texas Jacks Novel

J.B. Morgan

New Cover Design by-
Front cover: Jennifer Morgan
Back cover/Spine: Blue Valley Author Services
Website: www.bluevalleyauthorservices.com

Photography- Big Stock
www.bigstockphoto.com

Revised 2017 Edits by: Heather Romanowski
Formatter: Champagne Formats
Website: www.champagneformats.com
Facebook: www.facebook.com/ChampagneFormats

Original 2016 Cover Design by: Lindsay Wolford

Original 2016 Edits by: Missed Periods Editing for Indies
Website: www.missedperiodediting.com
Facebook: www.facebook.com/missedperiodediting

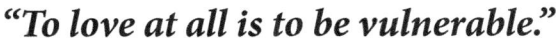

"To love at all is to be vulnerable."
C.S. Lewis

Prologue

Charlie

I'M THE CONSUMMATE SHY FRIEND OF MY GROUP, ALWAYS the one to hold back while the others have a great time. It's not that I don't know how to have fun, I'm just afraid of completely letting go.

I know that part of me holds back because I'm afraid that others will judge me. I don't dare put myself out there because I'm afraid of looking silly or messing up. I was always the girl who walked with her head down, even though my mother was constantly reminding me to walk with my head held high. In fact, my mother tells me that when I was younger, I constantly walked into walls because I focused on the ground so often. Thankfully I outgrew that phase in my life. *Mostly*.

This may contradict my shyness, but it's the absolute truth. I'm a very social person. According to my parents, I'm what some may call a 'social butterfly'. However, I'm still the girl who thinks that the good-looking guys aren't checking her out. I'm the girl secretly wishing they would, yet knowing that it's my friends who they really want. I'm not awkward or unattractive, in any obvious way. I just feel self-conscious, and I can't even explain why I feel this way. So, I just go with the flow, and try to enjoy myself as I let my friends be in the forefront, while I'm content to stay in the background.

Now I'm wondering why I can't just let go of my silly notions for once, and just join in, like everyone else around me.

I think it's about time I learned that it doesn't really matter what the world thinks of me. I need to step outside of the box, let my hair down, and have a good time. *Okay, maybe not go too crazy, but it doesn't hurt to try, right?*

Though, I do have a sneaking suspicion that tonight's my night, and something great is bound to happen. *Or so I hope, at least.* You see—my two best of friends want to head out to our favorite stomping grounds for some country dancing, and to check out the local cowboys. And I have to admit, not even I feel like passing that up. I mean *would you? Who wouldn't want to see cowboys in their tight jeans and Stetsons?*

Well, here goes nothing.

Or maybe everything.

And this is how I came to be at *Texas Jacks* when Nathan walked into my life.

Chapter One

Charlie

"**C**HARLOTTE, IS THAT YOU?" MOM CALLS OUT THE moment I step foot into the entryway of my parents' house.

"Yeah!" I holler in return, shutting the front door behind me.

The instant I'm fully ensconced into the home, the aroma of mom's cooking permeates my senses. I take an extra moment to breathe it all in, before following the scent to the source.

"Something sure smells good!" I announce, upon entry into the kitchen, where mom is busy working away on dinner preparations.

"Hey, sweetie." Mom greets me. "We're having lasagna."

Also standing in the kitchen, is my brother's fiancée, Rachel, who's slicing Mom's homemade bread at the big island.

"Hey, Charlie," she calls over her shoulder.

"Hey, Rach," I reply, as I walk over to my mom. Her back is facing me, so I wrap my arms around her middle from behind. I breathe in a whiff of her favorite perfume emanating from her turquoise blouse that is paired with black slacks.

1

The simple apron protects it. I get my lack of height from my mom, though her parents weren't that short. Her mousy brown hair is starting to grey, and it's now styled to fall just above her shoulders. She's a little softer around her curves now, after having five kids, but she's still in good shape. I let go of her waist and head over to the side counter by the phone.

"Need help with anything, Mom?" I ask as I set my purse down on the counter and head to the sink where I wash up quickly and efficiently to assist with whatever still needs to be done.

"Could you set the table?" she asks, as she starts cutting up a cucumber, which most likely will end up in a salad for tonight. "Dinner should be ready in about 20 minutes. Rachel and I have been busy cooking, so we haven't had a chance. And you know the boys," she says with an eye roll as she goes back to chopping the vegetable. "Your dad and Anson are out back, probably doing *manly* things, which makes them too busy to come inside to set the table. As for the girls, they aren't here yet. Bethany sent me a text that they're on their way, though."

The 'girls' she's referring to are my three older sisters who all live close to my parents—as does my brother. I'm the only one who moved away from my home town. I miss being close to everyone, and I hate the commute for family dinners twice a month. But, I do love having my own privacy.

"How many settings do we need tonight?" I ask her, as I open the cabinet door and reach in to pull out plates.

"How are you?" Rachel asks with a smile that shows off the cute little dimple in her left cheek. She's tall in stature with gorgeous, long-layered chocolate brown hair that's curled around her shoulders. Her lighter hazel eyes shine with happiness. Her long, coral sundress swishes around her ankles and accents her golden skin under the bright lights of the kitchen.

"At the moment, I can't complain." I reply.

"Though, I can't say anything exciting is going on in the life of Charlie Davenport," I add, realizing how boring that makes me sound. Rachel winks at me, as she starts to place slices of bread in a pretty basket that will be used for dinner.

"So, how many settings do we need tonight, Mom?" I turn my attention back to mom, reminding her I still need an answer.

"Ten. Lindsay's bringing someone home for the family to meet," Mom responds with a big smile on her face. She wants grandchildren in the worst way. *Well, at least the focus will be off of me tonight. I hope.*

Two Sundays each month my siblings and I make it a point to get together with my parents at their home for dinner. This gives us a chance to catch up with everyone's lives, enjoy each other's company, and have a really good home cooked meal. *Okay, who am I kidding?* It's mostly to appease Mom so she can dote on her 'babies' and harass us about coming home more often. Or maybe it's just me that she likes to hassle about not making an appearance more regularly. Either way, I love these dinners, and wouldn't miss them for anything. Well, I try not to at least.

"Rach, could you help me set the table, then? I'll grab the plates and silverware if you can get the glasses and napkins." And just like that, we fall into step, finishing the table before Lindsay shows up with her new boyfriend. About ten minutes later, we hear Jen shout "Ma, we're here!" I guess we wouldn't be the Davenports if we didn't always yell something out the minute we walk through the front door.

Loud—that's the word I would say best describes my big, crazy, and loving family.

Jen and Jaxon stroll into the kitchen holding hands, and

on their heels is Bethany. Mom sets down what she's doing, wipes her hands on her apron, and goes over to give all of them hugs. *Yep, Mom's a big time hugger.*

Jaxon leans down and kisses Mom on top of her head before pulling away and flashing her his brilliant smile. He wraps his arm back around my sister and tugs her closer to him. Yeah, he's swoon-worthy, and Jen's a lucky woman. She's my oldest sibling, and Jaxon's her hunky, cowboy husband. They live just a bit outside of town, where Jaxon works on their sprawling horse ranch and Jen runs the books.

I love to watch these two because they're so cute together. I'm sure I could take a page or two out of their book for my future husband. *When—or if—that ever happens.* I sigh just thinking that maybe, someday, I could be just like these two. Jen's stands proudly at a full 5'4", show casing a curvy figure, and dressed in her standard cowgirl boots and a white, knee-length, flowing sundress. It's also worth mentioning that Jaxon showed up in tight jeans, a button up black rodeo shirt, and cowboy boots.

Lindsay comes in right behind Jen and Bethany. You know, I have to give it to Lindsay—that was good timing on her part, to show up with the rest of my sisters. She's probably hoping that some of the attention would be off of her if she tagged along behind the rest of the group. Too bad for her—that's *not* going to happen. *Mom will be all over her like white on rice.*

As a burst of laughter escapes my throat, I can't help but look forward to the interrogation from my father and brother. *This should be fun*, I think to myself as I look over at Lindsay with a grin on my face.

Lindsay shoots me the evil eye and then looks back over to Mom, who's making her way to them with a big smile on her face. Lindsay hugs mom, then introduces the tall, attractive blond standing next to her. "Mom, this is Greg, and this is my mom, Natalie."

Greg reaches a hand out to mom, murmuring, "It's a pleasure to meet you."

"We're pleased to meet you too, Greg. Welcome to our home." Mom says, gesturing towards Dad as he walks over to shake Greg's hand. "This old, handsome man is my husband, James." And not surprisingly, Mom decides to hug Greg instead of shaking his hand. That's my mom for you—all loving and affectionate, no matter whom you are.

I have to admit that this new guy is handsome. If I had to guess, I would say he's probably around six feet tall, which is the same height as my brother, and close to my dad's as well. He's got broad shoulders, lean in a muscular way, and has a good tan going on. He looks clean cut with his khaki pants, white striped polo, and tan Sperry's. And then there's Lindsay, looking cute in her knee-length, pale yellow sundress.

Wait a minute, what's going on here? Is Bethany in a dress, too? I look over at my sister, only to realize that yes, she's sporting a navy blue sundress. What is this? *Did Mom and I not get the memo to put on a dress for tonight?* Not that I love dresses that much, but come on! If I had known that Lindsay was bringing home a man, I wouldn't have come over in my butt-hugging Wrangler jeans and a nice blouse. I would have tried to look a little nicer.

"Heads up, big sis," I whisper to Bethany. "When you decide to bring someone home, a little warning would be nice, please and thank you."

"Well, that would require me to have to choose between Cash and Ty. When I figure it out, I'll make sure I send out an announcement to the national media," she whispers back, and then laughs at me before sticking out her tongue.

I take in Bethany's appearance and reflect for a moment

on how strikingly beautiful she is. All of us girls inherited my mom's fair complexion, curvy figure, and lovely features. Bethany, standing at 5'7", is the tallest of the girls. She has brown hair with blonde highlights that goes halfway down her back, and blue eyes. I can see why she would have the attention of two guys at the moment.

"Yeah, yeah, laugh it up, buttercup. One of these days—" I trail off, deciding to drop the subject. I'm supposed to be flying under the radar here—not attracting unwanted questions. I shoot her a grin instead and turn my head back to the new man in our sister's life, but not before I catch Jen and Jaxon grinning at me.

Uh-oh...I don't think I want to even go there with these two. I might love their relationship, but I'm the last one looking for love advice. That would require me to actually find someone first.

"Don't worry, you'll be the first to know when I sign up for one of those television dating shows in search of a husband. Then you can shower me with all of the advice you want."

"How are you supposed to rope a guy in when you don't put yourself out there, Charlie?" Jen challenges.

"Well, thanks for *that* mood killer," I say over a nervous bubble of laughter and look back to Lindsay.

Jaxon touches my arm, letting me know not to take any offense, and that they love me, and want the best for me. I sigh. "I'm sorry. I'm just tired of being hassled. Can we just get through one sister's man at a time?" I semi plead, giving a meaningful glance Bethany's way and sending an apologetic look over to Jen.

Watching Lindsay's man make the rounds of meeting my family, he looks like he could be a good fit. Lindsay matches his height perfectly at 5'5", not too short or too tall. My sister looks good standing next to him, with her blondish-brown loose curls, creamy complexion, and generous curves in all the right places. But I guess we will see if their personalities complement each other when we sit down for dinner.

Looking over at Lindsay, I see that she's smiling from ear to ear, and I can't recall the last time I've seen her so happy about someone. The thought makes me feel warm and fuzzy on the inside. I'm such a hopeless romantic. Although, I'm still hoping that all of the attention will be off of me tonight. If I'm lucky, they'll pester Bethany about finally settling down before they include me in the inquisition. She's older than I am, so naturally it should be her turn, right? *Go in pecking order? Oldest to youngest is best, I say.*

"Greg, this is my sister, Charlotte," Lindsay introduces as I shyly hold out my hand to shake his—which is so big that it completely dwarfs mine.

"It's nice to finally meet you, and the rest of your family. Lindsay talks so much about you all, I feel like I already know everyone," Greg says through a grin and kind, knowing eyes. *Hmm.* I wonder exactly what she's told him about this crazy family of ours. Though, I have a feeling he knows all about our antics, and Dad's obsession with being Mr. Competitive with any type of game, since he always has to win.

"It's nice to meet you, too." I reply.

"All right, everyone's here, so let's head to the table before dinner gets cold." Mom announces as she starts herding us like cattle to the dining room.

No one has to ask me twice to be seated. I look forward to coming home, as I miss Mom's hearty meals. She usually out does herself every time we get together, but who's complaining? As I sit down next to Jennifer, my stomach starts to growl. Jaxon sits on the other side of her, where he lays his hand on her thigh, and then winks at me. He really is a good guy, and is very sweet to my sister. She couldn't have picked anyone better, in my opinion. He's got a funny sense of humor, beautiful, piercing ice blue eyes, sandy brown hair, a golden-brown complexion from being outside at his job most days, nice muscle definition, and he towers over me. But then again, all the men in this family tower over me, and it looks like Greg will be the next in line to make me feel more like a tiny shrimp, being only 5'2" and all.

"Greg, how did you meet my daughter?" I hear my dad ask matter of factly, which draws my attention to him. I look down the long table to where he is sitting at the head, and notice the laugh lines around his eyes with his face in profile, hiding behind his glasses. His hair has become more salt and pepper in color, probably thanks to us kids and all of our shenanigans. He's staring Greg down like he's on trial and my dad's the judge, jury, and executioner. I find this funny, since we all know Dad's a big pushover, but don't get him started when it comes to games, or sports. Growing up, we used to hate playing board games as a family once we learned that Dad *never* loses. Now, as adults, we try to team up against him and overthrow his victory. It doesn't happen often, but there have been times when we've beaten him, which makes him call for a rematch, right then and there. He really can't stand losing.

Looking over at Greg, I see that he has Lindsay curled up under his long, toned arm, and she's resting her head on his right shoulder with a tiny, knowing smile on her face.

"I met Lindsay at work." Greg smiles warmly down at Lindsay, before turning his eyes back to my dad. "I had to come to her side of the building for a business meeting, and noticed that she was a bit caught up," he tells Dad through a chuckle. He tries fighting a smile, as his lips start to rise up on the left side. Lindsay automatically blushes, as she tries to sneakily pull her lips in between her teeth to hide her embarrassment. There's obviously a story behind their meeting.

"Oh? And how's that?" Anson pipes up, wanting to get the dirt on our sister. Most likely so he can tease her for the rest of her life. You know brothers, always up for some good embarrassing stories to blackmail you with later.

Anson is an awesome brother and our biggest protector, but don't give him any ammunition to use against you. He will exploit it for all it's worth. He's quite the comedian, but is a big softy, like our dad. In addition to personality, he inherited our dad's good looks, height, and hazel eyes. He works hard, but can be found down at the beach on the weekends, trying to catch a wave. Giving his skin a golden brown color from the sun.

"Don't you dare tell him, Greg!" Lindsay laughs. No way does she want any fodder for our brother to rib her with later.

"Oh come on, we won't laugh," Bethany says with a conspiratorial wink thrown our way. *Oh yeah, like that will stop us from howling like hyenas at our poor sister.*

"Nope, we would never laugh or make fun of you. Our lips are zipped," Rachel throws in, zipping her lips with her right thumb and pointer finger.

"All right, everyone, settle down. Let Greg share his story, and we promise, Lindsay, we won't laugh. No matter what. *Right* children?" *Mom, ever the diplomat and peacemaker.*

Jen's light brown eyes meet my deep blue ones on an exaggerated roll, and we share a laugh before we look back at my sister and Greg.

"Fine. You want to know what happened? I'll tell you what happened," Lindsay finally gives in. "I had my arms full of documents that I needed for our meeting. I was trying to juggle the papers, my bottled water, and send a text to my assistant, all at the same time. I didn't want to be late, so I was multitasking. Anyway, I wasn't paying attention to where I was walking, and snagged my high heel on the area rug next to this ridiculously big potted plant that we have in the hall. And that's when—"

"She tripped, but managed to not go down for the count," Greg smoothly cuts in with a straight face, though I can tell he's trying hard to stay composed. "Instead, she ended up being smacked in the face by the fronds on this big palm tree as she passed by it. It caught her hair, and it snapped her head back a bit, causing everything in her hands to drop to the ground. I decided to be the knight in shining armor and tried to help her get untangled." He says as he tries to quell his laughter that we all know is ready to burst forth.

"Oh, is that what you call yourself? It's more like the harbinger of bad luck, since you managed to get my earring caught up in the palm leaves, too," my sister shakes her head at him. "One of my earrings was almost ripped out of my ear, and the leaves smacked me in the face, again!" She all but dares him to say otherwise. He wisely keeps his mouth shut, grins at her, then squeezes her tightly with his right arm and kisses the top of her head. She darts her eyes at the rest of us, challenging us not to laugh, and that's when we all lose it. Even Greg can't hold his laughter back any longer.

What does she expect from us? She grew up with us, she should know how we were going to react to that story. We can't help it! I laugh until my left side is aching and my ragged breathing matches my family's.

"Well, I think its romantic how you met. You'll have a great story to tell your children one day," Mom sounds hopeful as she tries to come to Linday's defense. She tries valiantly to keep a straight face, but we all burst out laughing again.

"So, Charlotte oh Charlotte, how's *your* dating life going?" Lindsay turns the tables on me, with a wicked grin. *So much for flying under the radar.* That question sends all eyes skidding my way, as everyone starts to calm down.

"Yeah, what plant-face says—what's up, Charlie?" Anson snickers while taking a dig at our sister.

"Oh, real mature, Anson McPantson." Lindsay retorts, using his old nickname from the time that someone dared to pants him in elementary school.

I can't help it; I burst out laughing all over again at his nickname for her. I'm thinking she won't be living that one down for a while. "Oh come on, you all know I'm way too busy for a dating life right now." I remind them, after I calm down from the hilarity of the prior moments. "I'm working hard, and I'm happy. Why do I need a man, anyway?" I ask, turning to Bethany. I bug my eyes out at her for moral support.

Do you think she backs me up? *Nope.* She just laughs and shakes her head, saying, "Don't look at me on this one, little sis. I've got enough men-trouble on my hands to deal with."

"Traitor."

The next logical choice is to look to Rachel. She's been dating my brother for well over a year. They have been engaged for the last six months, and have yet to tie the knot. Normally, she has my back, but it looks like tonight they all plan to get in on the action. So I change the subject and turn the tables on them instead.

"So, Rachel, how's that wedding planning coming along? Shouldn't it be a shotgun wedding now? I mean—you did say something about the color baby blue, right? Or was it soft pink?" I smile sweetly at my brother and soon to be sister-in-law, all while holding back a giggle.

That gets the instant reaction I'm looking for from my mom. "Oops," I say with a sly smile. Every one stares at me, as they have no idea what to say.

Before my mom can get a word in edgewise, I look over at Jaxon and Jen.

"What about you guys? Don't you have a bun in the oven yet? Throw me a bone here. You've been married for three years now. I think it's time you pay your family dues and pop out a kid already."

"Oh, and Bethany—don't think you're off the hook with two men!"

Then I look over to my dad and smile, because we all know I'm his favorite kid, and add, "So, Dad, how about the Red Sox? Damn those Yankees for beating them again."

This automatically sets my Dad off. Now my family is in a feeding frenzy of chaos, and I just sit back and enjoy the show. Watching Mom freak out on my sisters for not having kids yet, tying the knot, or settling down with one man already. The men dig into the baseball conversation, and just like that, score one for the little people.

I may be shy when it comes to men and being out with my friends, but it's a whole different ballgame when it comes to my family.

Chapter Two

Nate

ON SUNDAYS, THE TRACK AND I BECOME ONE, AND my soul is free to soar. When everyone's at church, like today, I'm out here, finding my peace and solitude. Letting the fear of love and loss become a forgotten memory, buried so deep it would be a miracle if you could find a trace of it at all. This is the place I come to forget. To lose myself in the high of the adrenaline rush I get from being on my bike.

People feel the need to go to church to fellowship with others, uplift their spirits, and commune with their God. For me, the track is the place I come to commune with nature, and to worship what I long to do throughout the workweek. Out here, I'm fellowshipping in my own way, along with the others who come to ride. It's the one place that calms my soul, and lets me be free from the pain and memories.

Today, and here of all places, those painful memories come flooding back to me, especially while I'm sitting on the tailgate of her truck. They're the kind that take you prisoner and hold you down, then twist you up so tight you can't breathe, right before they pierce you straight through the heart. My eyes start sting a bit, and I know it's not from the sun's bright rays on this warm summer day. *No, it's definitely not from that.* It's the thought of sitting here on the edge of the truck that she gave me before she passed away. It's become a part of me, as this track has, and it's the one physical thing I have left that was hers. So I give it the utmost care I possibly can, willing it to last me a lifetime so that I won't ever have to part with it. With *her.*

I squeeze my eyes shut, attempting to force the memories of her to recede to where they came from, just as I hear gravel kicking up on the road in front of me. I blink them open in time to see Holt and Tucker pull in next to my Ford. *Perfect timing.* A few minutes longer, and I would have given up on riding today and headed home. That's the one thing you don't want while out on the track—*a distraction.* One small miscalculation could lead to a life altering injury.

"About time you two knuckleheads showed up!" I holler as they climb out of Holt's truck, trying to cover up the emotional turmoil I was under.

Rolling his eyes, Tucker walks past me and smacks the back of my head. "Keep your boots on, we weren't *that* late. Did you think we stood you up for someone hotter than you?"

"It wouldn't be the first time." I chuckle.

Riding is something that means more to me than it does to them. Sure, they love the feel of the high they get from riding. But for me, it's something else altogether. Sometimes I wonder if they just come out to ride so they can show off for the women that the track seems to attract. Or for bragging rights they can use when picking women up while we're out at *Texas Jacks.* Still, it's just not the same for them as it is for me.

"Why are you just standing there? Are you communing with the ground, or do you plan to get a move on sometime today so we can ride?" Holt throws a jab at my abs as he walks by.

"What is this, pick on Nate day?"

"Oh, didn't you know? It's National Beat on Your Friend Day." Tucker laughs while scanning the track, then looks over to where the women like to hang out to watch the riders.

"Seriously, man, get your head on straight. Forget the bike bunnies and focus. I'm not playing nurse to your ugly mug if you get hurt, or hauling your butt to the hospital." I smack Tucker on the back of the head, and I would be lying if I didn't say that didn't feel good.

I laugh as I jump out of arm's reach when he tries to tackle me. I know, we sound like a bunch of high school teens when we're far from it, being in our early to mid-twenties. *But hey, boys will always be boys.* There's a part of us that will never grow up, no matter how hard some women out there pray that we will. *What's the purpose of life if you can't enjoy it by having a lot of fun?* We can be serious when we need to be, but having fun is a lot better. Otherwise, the heaviness of reality and memories can sneak up on you, forcing you to a place you'd rather leave buried under a rock. It's not that I don't want to remember her; I just can't handle the sadness and pain it brings with those memories, knowing that I'll never see her again in this lifetime.

Is there something else out there? Did she go to a better place than here on this Earth?

I have no idea.

I don't know what to think. I just know I don't want to think about it—*at all.*

"I'm not looking for bike bunnies," Tucker scowls at me. "I'm trying to see if Lisa showed up or not. Ever since I dumped her, I swear she's stalking me. She still hasn't clued in that I'm never putting a ring on her finger. Anyway, I'm just hoping to make it out onto the track without a scene." He looks over there one last time, and then heads off to the tailgate of Holt's truck and where the ramp that Holt set up is, while Tucker was looking for Lisa.

"Chill out. I'm just making sure we're all focused." I turn to my other friend. "Holt, you good to ride, or do I need to smack you around, too? I could free up the rest of those cobwebs left over from high school."

"Ha, I'd like to see you try." Holt laughs at me.

"You forget that I know where you sleep, and it's not that far of a walk from my room to yours. Or maybe you forgot about that one time in college, when Tucker and I jumped you from the big oak tree on your path to English class." Tucker high-fives me as he's walking by with his bike towards the track, laughing.

"You know, I still owe you two stooges for that. You made me drop my backpack when I jumped and screamed like a girl. I thought I was on the verge of a heart attack."

I just laugh at him and start wheeling my own dirt bike out to the track calling out, "Good luck with that!" over my shoulder.

Lisa's a pretty girl, and she seemed nice enough, but she really just wanted one thing—good old Tuck-boy. In high school, she was quiet, laid back, and rather smart—even a little shy. The girl doesn't have a single mean bone in her body. Or so we used to think. I know one thing for sure—she has it bad, and it appears she can't let go of Tucker. Heck, she's wanted him since freshman year of high school. He finally decided to take her out not too long ago, and then ended up dating her for two months. It all seemed to be going well for a time, until she started dropping hints about moving in together. That was a big red flag for Tucker. Living together, settling down with a wife and then kids isn't on his list of life plans. He would probably still be dating her if she hadn't gotten that serious on him. Although, he had to know it was coming, since she's been after him for so long. She made Tucker her life mission until she finally landed him.

Why can't women be content to just date us and not worry about lifelong plans? Eventually, it all goes south from there, and then you have to break her heart. After that, it's really downhill when you have to hear about it from her friends, and your friends' girlfriends, or other people in town. That's the awful part about living in a smallish community. Everyone knows everyone, and judgments pass easily, whether you were actually the bad guy or not. Or, you have to deal with the pitying looks when you lose a loved one and can't seem to move on from it.

Great, just what I need—my head filled with more distractions.

Getting a grip on my thoughts, I make my way to the starting line of the track, park my bike next to Tucker's, and suit up with the proper gear to protect my body.

Once I'm dressed, I look out at the track that's calling my name and begging me to take it on. It's the biggest dragon in the kingdom, and I'm the only one who can slay it with my sword. I take in a cleansing breath, calming myself down, and then let it go slowly. I do this a few times while Holt pushes his bike up next to mine.

It's time to get this show on the road.

Climbing on to my bike and starting it up, I feel it rumble under me, letting the excitement for what's about to come wash over me. I clear my head, knowing it's time to let go of everything and everyone invading my thoughts and just focusing on myself, the road, and the jumps ahead.

I look over at the guys and give them each a thumbs-up before taking off.

Chapter Three

Charlie

IT'S 7 PM, AND I'M TRYING TO DECIDE WHAT TO WEAR—but I have no idea what to throw together. A denim skirt, paired with a blouse and my cowgirl boots? Or my butt hugging jeans, cowboy belt buckle, boots, and a cute t-shirt? I don't have the slightest clue. And where are my partners-in-crime? Why didn't we agree to all get ready at one place? They know how fashion-challenged I am. Okay, maybe not completely. But still, I need someone's opinion as I tear apart my wardrobe. And what about my hair—up or down? If only I were guy, I would be done and out the door in ten minutes flat.

The time is ticking by late into the evening as I finally decide to put on my knee-length denim skirt, the one without the back pockets. I grab my favorite black, short-sleeved blouse that ties at the top and gathers around the scooped neckline and the arms, then ribs around the waist. It has pink flowers and small pink diamonds in between that go down the front on both sides. I slip it over my head. Then I pull on a pair of black socks, followed by my black boots. I carefully flat iron my shoulder-length chocolate-brown hair, spritz on some Beautiful perfume, and put in my gold hoop earrings. I apply some light makeup next, and check my purse for the necessities I'll need for a night out. I pull out my ID and money, slipping them into the front pocket of my skirt.

I hear a knock at my front door, and I know that it's Halley and Naomi. They have a key, but knock out of courtesy so they don't scare me to death.

I make it into the hallway just as they come waltzing in.

"So, how do I look?" They both look me over while giving me appreciative smiles, and Halley even whistles.

I'm certain my cheeks are a bit pink from their antics, and they crack up when they notice how embarrassed I am.

I have to admit that they're both looking good in their painted-on jeans, belt buckles, and boots, each paired with her own cute blouse. Although, they're the smart ones, as I notice that they put their hair up. I've been out with them before, and it does get hot and sweaty in the bar, especially while out on the dance floor. *Hmm.* I'm rethinking the hair option as I head towards the bathroom.

However, Naomi clotheslines me at the hall entrance with a straight-armed maneuver and starts hustling us towards the front door instead, ordering, "Get a move on, ladies! I don't want to miss my favorite dances." *Looks like my hair will be staying down tonight.*

Halley decides to drive, so we all climb in to her black Chevy. As I get close to the back of her truck, I notice a new sticker on her rear window and read aloud, "*Q: What is the difference between a Ford and a porcupine? A: Porcupines have pricks on the outside,*" which causes all three of us to bust up laughing. This puts us in a whacky mood as we pull out of the parking lot and head out to the highway, toward *Texas Jacks.*

Nate

There's not much to do in Vacaville on a Friday night, so you'll most likely find us at *Texas Jacks* shooting pool, grabbing a few drinks, and watching the local girls dance. The bar and dance club is a popular place to be. It draws crowds in from the surrounding towns and cities, as far out as Sacramento. They also play a great mix of music. There's a little something for everyone there, even the folks who are not so 'country.'

Texas Jacks is where the guys and I go to unwind from a long week of work. If we aren't there, we're probably fishing, camping, racing our dirt bikes, or sitting around the house relaxing and shooting the breeze. And okay, I admit it—you might even catch us playing video games from time to time. However, you'll more than likely find us at the dirt track, if not here.

Tonight, Tucker, Holt, and I have managed to grab a table upstairs, where we settle in with our drinks and check out the women on the dance floor. Once we get the lay of the land, we'll probably go shoot a few rounds of pool, and maybe take a turn or two on the dance floor with some lucky lady.

I sit back and relax while taking in the crowd, checking out what the night has in store for us. I spot a few regulars hanging around on the first level, and some on the dance floor. I like that about this place—you can come in here and see a lot of the same faces, in a sea of nameless others. The out-of-towners seem to flock here to tie one on or for a hook-up, while the locals come to play pool, unwind on the dance floor, and meet up with old friends. As I look out over the second level railing, I see a few girls I've known since high school out on the dance floor, kicking it up and having a good time.

Even though I like to come here to have fun, I never troll

the bar for women just for a 'good time.' *That's not my style.* I've dated a few women in my life, but I'm not a serial dater. I like to think that I'm a bit picky in this department, so while I may be known to dance with the girls who are brave enough to ask, I don't give out my number, or ask for theirs in return. If I see the same girl again on another night, I won't hesitate to dance with her or strike up a conversation. But that's all it will be, because I leave it all here at *Texas Jacks* when I go home at the end of the night. Maybe one day, if the right woman came along, I wouldn't hesitate to stake my claim. But I haven't met her yet.

I kick Tucker in the foot. "Hey Tuck, you up to hitting the track tomorrow for a race?"

We may like doing a lot of other things, but dirt bike racing is the singular thing that I *love*. I almost feel like a junkie at times, as I can't get enough of the high I feel from it. When I'm out on the track, I don't have to think of the sorrows or problems that bounce around in my head at any given time. I can go out there and be free to soar, to let go to my heart's content. I only have to worry about the next sharp turn, the speed of my bike making my body hum, or the next jump that sends butterflies crashing around in my stomach. Just thinking about it makes me want to go out there now. Too bad it's too late in the evening—otherwise, I would ditch this place and head out there right now.

I already know that Tucker is going to take me up on going to the track tomorrow. After catching sight of Lisa the time before last, when the three of us were there, he bailed on me. I don't blame him, but he still owes me a race, and I'm ready to cash in on it. I live for these races, so any time I can get out there, I'm all over it.

Tucker looks at me with a smirk on his face. "Who do you think you're talking to? I'll be out there at the finish line, waiting for the twenty bucks you'll owe me when I leave your sorry butt behind, choking on the dust I kick up."

Holt laughs as he slaps him on the back for his cocky, yet predictable, comment.

"Fine, we'll see who's eating dirt and coughing up money when it's all said and done. Just make sure you stick around this time and leave your, 'I have to mow my mom's yard' excuse at the starting line." I say, laughing at him. I can't resist messing with him, even though he would do anything to help his single mother out.

Holt looks up when Sarah, a redheaded beauty, saunters up to our table. "Hey boys," she says, giving Holt a sly smile. She's a local we see from time to time out here, and she loves two-stepping with him. I'm pretty sure she would probably like to do more than just dance. However, Holt's not interested in her in that way. She's a great person; he's just not looking at the moment.

"Holt, you ready to hit the dance floor yet? I asked DJ Jeff to put on a two-step number next, if you're up for it," she murmurs as she slips one of her arms around his shoulders.

Holt slips his arm around her waist, "Sure thing, honey. Let's show these amateurs how it's really done." He gives her a quick squeeze as he stands up. "Lead the way, sweet thing."

And off they go, leaving Tucker and I to talk about our plans for tomorrow.

We arrive at *Texas Jacks* around 8:20, and judging by the full parking lot, the place is busy tonight. We end up parking further away than we had hoped, so it looks like the front door bouncer, Dave, will be walking us out tonight. We make our way past the long line towards the front. We don't have to stand in line with the rest of the crowd, since Naomi is good friends with Dave. After we hand over our money, he stamps our hands and in we go.

The music pumping out of the speakers is pretty loud, which makes it hard to talk. Shortly upon entry, I see an empty table on the lower level by the dance floor, so I tug on Halley's shirt and point to the spot. Once she catches on, I lead us that way without uttering a word.

Halley and Naomi make a beeline to the bar, after placing their jackets on the backs of the chairs. I take in my surroundings after settling into my seat, getting a feel for what's going on and checking out the crowd. I recognize a few of the regulars as they wave to me, and I smile back politely.

The bar is busy, too, as I see Naomi give up and head out to the dance floor. Looking over my shoulder, I catch Halley still waiting to be served. I don't think she minds, though; she's already found a hot-looking guy to chat with. I turn my head back in time to see a couple of other girls we know come over and sit down. We make polite small talk, and they start talking about some cowboys they've been eyeing for about a half hour now.

Eventually, Halley makes it back to us, sans hot guy, and puts our drinks on the table. Just as she goes to sit down, her favorite song comes on, and she jumps to her feet, ready to hit the dance floor. Unfortunately for me, she starts pulling me with her. I don't want to dance with her for two reasons: one, I'm not that great of a dancer, and two, she may embarrass me on this one. The embarrassment would only be due to my shy nature.

I note an older song by Tracy Byrd come on as I also hear the DJ spit out, "Come on, ladies! Time to shake what your mamas gave you." It's a fun, get up and start moving kind of song.

So here's my dilemma: when the chorus to *Watermelon Crawl* comes on, Halley may or may not grab her own 'watermelons' to emphasize their greatness. The last thing I need is unwanted attention from some of the men out here on the dance floor. But, I see that I have no choice as she has a good grip on me, leaving a couple of our other friends, who stopped by for a chat, to watch our table. With a roll of my eyes, off we go to do the Watermelon Crawl.

Nate

Tucker, Holt, and I are still upstairs at our table, watching everyone on the dance floor as the song, *Watermelon Crawl*, starts to play. As I scan the dance floor, I notice a really good looking woman, with blonde hair, making her way up the stairs, dragging her friend with her. I watch them make their way to the front of the railing and start to dance. Although, good looking girl's friend isn't really doing much but swaying a bit to the music.

When the chorus comes on, I about choke on my drink when the hot girl grabs her 'watermelons,' giving them a bit of a squeeze when she hears, "watermelons on the vine," and says something at the same time. I think she's singing the words to the chorus, but I can't be sure.

I look over to Holt and Tucker, wondering if I was the only one to see what just happened. Though—it would seem they hadn't as both are giving me funny looks.

"Hey, man, you good? Or do I need to bust out my mouth-to-mouth skills?" Tucker eye's me with a mix of amusement and concern.

I point to the ladies and say, "If that hot girl stops grabbing her 'watermelons,' I won't need your mad skills. Check out the blonde with the long ponytail over her shoulder, and the brunette next to her."

They both turn their heads to the side so they can look out at the dance floor over the railing. I catch their eyes widening a bit as they see the same 'dance move' I just witnessed. Tucker chuckles, while Holt sports a big grin on his face. The other woman seems a bit embarrassed, maybe, but it's hard to tell up here. By the way she darts her eyes around the dance floor, then looks up to where we're sitting, I'm thinking that's an affirmative.

But it's in that moment, when she looks up at our table, that I notice just how beautiful she is. I'm also struck by an unexpected feeling as I watch her, feeling like I need to meet this woman who seems to be captivating my attention. Instead, I decide it's best to stay in my seat, content to watch for now—safely hidden in the shadows.

The guys and I watch awhile longer before she finally makes her way off the dance floor. I watch her the whole way back to her seat, as much as I can. She seems to be sitting with a few other girls, and now it looks like the bouncer, Dave, has made his way over to her chair. He wraps an arm around her, spiking my curiosity, and I wonder if there's something going on between them, or if they're just friends.

I turn to my right, where Holt is sitting, and he seems to be staring at the blonde. "Hey Holt, have you ever seen those ladies in here before?" *If he has, how is it that I've missed them? Was I that blind?*

Maybe our paths just haven't aligned until tonight.

"The blonde one and her dark-haired friend to the left are in here all the time. I've only seen the brunette a few random times," he tells me.

I look at both Holt and Tucker and ask, "What do you either of you know about her and Dave? Is there something going on there?"

They both just look at me and shake their heads. *Well, it looks like I'll be heading downstairs for another drink and a round of pool.* As luck would have it, their table is pretty close to the pool area. This will allow me to scope out the situation, and get a better look at her.

It's time to check out the competition, and find out who this little lady is.

Chapter Four

Charlie

HALLEY, NAOMI, AND I ARE SITTING AT THE TABLE when a slow song comes on, and two guys approach them to dance. They readily accept, leaving me to watch over the table. I'm relieved when I don't get asked to dance. I prefer to sit here and people watch, checking out which couples have hooked up, and seeing others have a good time. While watching a couple flirt off to the right side of the dance floor, I notice movement from the corner of my eye. I look over my shoulder, where the most handsome man I think I've ever seen appears in my line of sight.

I barely register his two friends following behind him down the stairs as I blatantly stare at him. Quickly, before he notices, I turn my head back towards the dance floor. However, I can still see him out of the corner of my eye. My eyes trail behind him as he slowly makes a path to the bar, noting how tall he is as I carefully scan his body, from his boots to the top of his dark head. He makes it over to the bar with his laidback, easy paced walk, and leans against the bar top. He looks over the side of his shoulder, and pasted on his tan, rugged face is a killer smile aimed right at me, as if he knows I've been watching him all along. I quickly duck my chin down and hide a small smile as my cheeks tint with red, knowing I've been caught in the act of gawking.

I look up again after a few short minutes, but his back is now facing me as he's ordering a drink. While I have the chance, I check out his appearance a little more. He's wearing dark jeans, black boots, and a blue and green plaid, long sleeved button up shirt. I'm pretty sure that through my dazed stare earlier I noticed that he had on a big, silver belt buckle, as well.

I slowly avert my eyes to scan the pool tables for his friends. *They couldn't have gone too far.* Sure enough, I find them fairly close to our table. The dirty blond one is looking my way with a knowing smirk on his face, basically telling me that he busted me checking out Mr. Tall and Handsome at the bar. I give him a small smile and look back to the dance floor to see where my friends have gone off to. That's when I feel someone's eyes on me. I slowly turn around, and guess what? I was right—only, he's not where I thought he was. Now he's standing just a few inches behind me, with a grin on his face. I gulp, then meet his eyes and give him a timid smile back when he asks, "May I?"

I watch as he points to the chair directly across from me. I don't say anything, but stare at him.

Nate

Well, if I've learned one thing—besides the fact that this woman is beautiful—it would seem that she's shy, as well. That's refreshing, for a change. I don't mind putting in the legwork to get to know her better.

Setting my drink on the table, I pull a chair out and plant myself in it, sitting across from her so I don't come off too strongly at first. I reach across the table and offer her my hand. "This is the part where I introduce myself and you smile, and then you agree to take a spin on the dance floor with me." I give her a reassuring smile. "I'm Nathan, by the way. So, darlin', may I ask what *your* name is?"

She continues to sit there, staring at me like a deer in head lights.

"I laid it on a little too thick, right?" I grin at her. I watch as she blinks, then slowly the left side of her mouth curves up into a small grin in response.

Looks I'll be pulling out all the stops with this one, if she lets me. Finally, she reaches her hand across the table and takes my larger hand in her small, daintier one, giving it a firm shake before pulling it back and tucking it neatly in her lap.

"My name's Charlotte," she replies shyly, "and I would love to dance with you, but I'm saving this table while my friends are out dancing."

Well, will just have to see about that.

I look over my left shoulder at my friends, who are now looking our way, and smile, nodding my head slightly to Charlotte. With the single gesture, I'm basically letting them know I will be foregoing our game to talk to Charlotte until one of her friends gets back. Then I plan to whisk her out onto the floor, preferably with some helpful prodding from the other girls.

Charlie

Oh my gosh. *Now what? Why did my friends have to ditch me?* I need back up. I wish I could send out a signal to them saying: *MAY DAY! MAY DAY! Sinking ship! S-O-S.* But no such luck, as they don't have ESP. It's not like I don't want Nathan sitting with me, or his hand touching mine, making my body flush with excitement. But I'm nervous as a newborn colt, and I don't know what to do. *I'm in panic-mode here.*

Okay, it's not like I don't *totally* know what to do; I just don't know how to properly go about doing it without looking like a big dork. I decide, on a deep breath, that I'd better say something, so I don't come across as rude by not speaking to this good-looking man. But before I can, he continues to break the ice for me.

"So, tell me, Charlotte, what's a pretty girl like you doing all alone tonight?"

Oh, smooth one, Nathan, trying to see if I'm single.

"Unless there *is* someone coming later to take over this chair? I don't want to overstep my bounds and presume anything." He tilts his head towards the front doors of *Texas Jacks*, and then looks back at me, waiting for an answer.

"Oh. No, you're fine. I don't plan on meeting up with anyone, and I don't have a boyfriend, if that's what you're asking." *Why am I rambling? Pull it together, woman. You're a 21-year old woman, not a freshman in high school.* Surely, this shouldn't be so hard. "Is that what you wanted to know?"

Oh my gosh, I can't believe I just said that out loud. But then again, it did make Nathan's lips quirk up in a small smile, so what the heck. I decide to throw caution to the wind and shyly smile back at him.

"Well now, you've caught me," he laughs. "You can't

blame a guy for trying. And yes, little one, that's exactly what I wanted to know. Care to tell me why the spot hasn't been filled yet?"

Oh, come on! I'm no good at this. Avoiding eye contact with Nathan is the best way to go here, so I take a slow perusal of the dance floor, desperately trying to find my friends. *Someone has to come back to the table sometime soon, right? They wouldn't dare leave their wingman behind, would they?*

Oh, who am I kidding, they probably saw Nathan sitting here and left me to fend for myself. Problem is, I think I might crash and burn this plane before it even taxis out for takeoff. I silently groan.

I know I made a resolution about coming out tonight, and that was to finally put myself out there and take a chance. Nathan just landed himself at the end of that rope, and I'm going to grab on and pull myself up, praying for strength along the way. After all, he wouldn't be sitting here, talking to me if he didn't want to pursue something, right? Most guys would have walked away by now. I should know—it's happened plenty of times before when I've clammed up.

Here goes nothing.

Or maybe, for once, it could be something.

"Well, um—I'm not really sure why it hasn't been filled. I mean, umm—it's not like I wouldn't want it to be." The statement comes falling out of my mouth nervously. "I guess I just haven't found the right man yet?" I finish lamely, while tucking a good amount of hair behind my ear and ducking my head down. I can't look at his face. I'm totally crashing and burning—there are one too many *umm*'s in that first sentence. I'm just not a smooth talker. Maybe I never will be.

I feel deflated when he doesn't respond, causing me to wonder if I've just scared him off. Glancing back up, I look right into his eyes and realize that they are almost the color of coal, they're so dark. Then I look down to his lips, and he's smiling at me so sweetly, I want to melt in my chair.

"I'm sorry if I'm making you feel uncomfortable. Do you want me to leave you alone?" he hesitantly asks, with his brows furrowed.

"No!" I all but yell, causing my face to flame up with heat. "I mean, it's fine. You don't have to go. I'm just no good at this, and I'm not used to guys sticking around this long to talk to me, if we're being honest here." I duck my head again as that embarrassing remark departs my lips, without permission from my brain.

Reaching across the table, he lightly takes my hand in his again, sending a tingling sensation up my arm. "Relax and take a breath. I just want to get to know you. And you still owe me a dance, by the way." He gives my hand a little squeeze before pulling it away.

"Oh? And when did we make *that* date?" I tease back. Phew, some of the spunk I use at home has decided to make its way to the forefront tonight. *Thank heavens for siblings who like to tease you.*

Nathan is full-on grinning at me now, making butterflies dance all over the place inside my belly.

"A date, huh? I didn't realize we had tipped the scales here."

"Oh, well, I didn't mean an actual date," I stumble over my words in embarrassment. *What was I thinking?* Now he thinks I'm coming on to him, and assuming that there would be a date in the cards. *Where's a plant I can hide behind until it's time to leave?*

"If a date is what you wanted, why didn't you just say so in the first place?" he teases back with a wink and a big smirk on his face.

Just as I'm about to reply, I'm saved by, "Hey Nate, are

these seats taken?"

Off to the right side of me are his two friends, looking at us with goofy grins on their faces. *Oh lovely, more hunky men to add to the mix.* They must have over heard our flirting banter.

Where the heck are my friends, anyway?

Nate

Poor little Charlotte. She looks so cute sitting here, squirming in her chair now that the guys have shown up. I would have said it was good timing earlier to help ease the tension of her shyness, but not so much now. We were just starting to get somewhere when she let a little feistiness show. I'm determined to bring that back out. *For now, though, I'll just have to bide my time.*

"Tucker, Holt, this is Charlotte. Charlotte, meet two buddies of mine." I nod towards the guys.

"Charlotte, nice to meet you." Tucker holds his hand out to shake hers. She timidly places hers in his for a quick shake, then snatches her hand back quickly, like she's afraid to get burned.

"We thought we would come over here and save you from the likes of this guy." Holt teases, with a lopsided grin and winks at her, causing her cheeks to blush slightly.

"Charlotte here was just asking me out on a date. We haven't even had our first dance yet, and I've already scored a date. She's a fast worker, this one. I say you two better watch it—she's a tiger." Winking over at Charlotte, I cause her face to deepen further with heat. I can't help teasing her. She's so cute, and I know it isn't an act. She really does seem to have a hard time with attention.

I know the guys heard our conversation when they walked up to the table, so why not just get it out of the way now before it becomes more awkward?

"We leave you alone for a few songs, and what happens when we come back? You start collecting men. What is this, *Charlie's Angels*?" Charlotte's blonde friend—the one with the watermelon moves—asks with a big, fat grin.

"Hello, Ladies. You must be Charlotte's good-looking friend we saw earlier on the dance floor. Nice *watermelon* moves you have." Holt says to the blonde, like he's the big bad wolf and he's about to eat her up.

Blondie laughs and sticks out her hand to Holt. "I'm Halley, and this is Naomi. We're Charlie's close friends. And you are?" she asks, looking over at Tucker.

"I'm Tucker, and the big bad wolf over there is Holt. And Prince Charming over here is Nathan. Charlotte was just asking him out on a date."

At the mention of a date, Blondie's eyebrows shoot way up. *Way to go, Tucker!* I scowl over in his direction. I don't need them—or her friends, for that matter—to scare Charlotte away, or embarrass her further before I have a chance to dance with her.

This place just became too crowded.

"Charlotte, what do you say to that dance now? It looks like we're outnumbered, so we'd better make a clean getaway." The smile she gives me, and the relief that washes over her face, is enough to make me get out of the chair, walk over to her, gently grab her hand, and lead her to the dance floor before anyone else can take a jab or ask annoying questions.

We make it out on to the dance floor just in time for a slow song. "It must be fate," I joke to Charlotte once we find a good spot close to the middle of the dance floor, far away from prying eyes.

"It's more like really good timing, with lots of luck." She quips back at me, making me smile.

Keeping hold of her hand, I lead her to stand in front of me. I place my other hand on her waist, while bringing her free hand to my shoulder. I gently pull her into me a little more, so there's only a slight space separating our bodies from touching. I tuck our adjoined hands in between us and rest them on my chest, over my heart. Then I start to find our rhythm to the slow song with this blue eyed, brown haired beauty.

"Thank you for saving me back there. I don't think I could have handled an interrogation from my friends. I think I can stave that off for a little while longer, like maybe the car ride home," she chuckles.

Wanting to feel more of her, I draw her body closer to mine using the arm around her waist to pull her in, eliminating that last bit of distance between us. I can feel both of our heartbeats pitter against our joined hands as her left arm hesitantly leaves my shoulder to circle around my neck. I know I'm making her slightly uncomfortable, but for some reason, I can't manage to stop the urge of needing to feel her closer, and wanting to hold her against me.

"I heard your friends call you Charlie earlier. What's your preference? Or would you rather I stick with Charlotte?" I ask her on a quiet inhale of breath, smelling the scent of her hair and skin that's right under my nose, all while loving the fact that she's short and feels secure in my arms.

I have no idea what's gotten in to me. I just barely met Charlotte, and I'm letting my emotions run rampant. Not that I can't be the sweet, caring, and doting boyfriend-type. However, this girl pulls at my heartstrings a little harder than she should for just meeting me, and way more than any other woman I've met before her ever has.

I look down at her as she quietly contemplates allowing me to use her nickname, as if it might be too intimate for me to call her that. Finally, she says, "You can call me Charlie," causing me to smile above her head.

"Charlie it is, little one."

Earlier, Charlie had said that we might have had lots of luck when the slow song came on, saving the day between us and our friends. I'm starting to think that she's right, as two more slow songs come on right after the first one ends, allowing me to hold on to her petite body a little longer. It's either that, or someone tipped the DJ to play an extra one, which works out perfectly for me. Charlie finally let down her guard by the second song, and tentatively laid her head on my chest. She's been quiet for most of our time on the dance floor, which allows me a little peace while blocking out everyone else around us but Charlie.

"I never did ask you—" Charlie startles me from my thoughts, raising her head as she hesitates before saying what's on her mind. "Are you seeing anyone? I never asked, and here I am dancing with you with my head on your chest. I just—I just thought that maybe—well, maybe I was crossing the line by doing that." And now she's really embarrassed by her actions and words.

"I wouldn't be out here with the town's prettiest lady, holding her intimately, if I was seeing someone—causally or seriously." I'm hoping for gentleness with that statement, as to not further embarrass her, yet also letting her know that I'm not that kind of guy, and how I don't want to be anywhere else but here. "So the answer to your question, little one, is no."

"I'm sorry. That probably came out rude, or like an accusation. I just felt dumb for not asking you earlier, and you can never tell with some of the guys who come here."

"Don't worry about it, Charlie. You had every right to ask. After all, it was only fair, since I asked you earlier if you were seeing someone. I'm not offended in any way, and I wouldn't want to be anywhere else but right here with you."

Feeling her inhale and then exhale, she rests her head back on my chest as I hear, "Good." If I could pull her in any closer, I would, but it's not possible, as we are as close as we can be with our hands still between us.

Quietly sighing, I wonder what makes her so special that I have to know her. I guess only time will tell, if I dare to go there. Then again, I'm scared that I actually want her to know more about me, and vice versa. And if I really want to stop being a coward with myself, then I already know that the answers to my rambling thoughts are a definite yes to wanting to know her better.

Only one more question remains: how far will I allow this to go?

Charlie

Nathan keeps a strong hold on my hand as he leads me off the dance floor and back to the curious eyes of our friends. I can only imagine what they were talking about while we were away. At this point, I'm ready to go home. I've had a good night so far, and I loved being in the muscular arms of Nathan. *Why let them ruin it with questions that, no doubt, they're waiting to ambush us with?* Sighing, I take a seat by Naomi, and to no surprise, our wonderful friends have left a seat open for Nathan to occupy, which just happens to be next to mine. *How convenient*. And do you think he's let go of my hand for one second? *Nope*.

Feeling happy, I turn my head to the side, trying to hide my secret little smile. In the process of turning my head, I notice his friends. Holt and Tucker both raise an eyebrow at Nathan. *Oh, the mischievous grins they give him*. He must have given them some kind of signal, because they're no longer looking inquisitive or teasing, and have gone back to talking to Naomi and Halley by the time I turn my head back to the group.

We sit at the table for another hour and a half talking, and a few times getting up to dance. The dancing was mainly Halley and Naomi, accompanied by Holt and Tucker. I don't mind, though. I prefer to sit and watch—especially now that I have someone else at my side to keep me company. During that time, Nathan has either held my hand, or kept his on my thigh, causing me to shiver as goose bumps form from the touch of his hand. Feeling his fingers lightly brush my leg above my knee sends a thrill down my spine. Part of me, during those times, thought that I should remove his hand. But then I would talk myself out of it, remembering that I made a promise to myself to be more open and less shy tonight. Also, I couldn't deny how good his hand felt, either.

All around, it's been a win-win situation, if you ask me.

The night is wearing on, and it's getting late. Even though I've had three cokes, I'm tired. We've been here going on three hours, and I've had a long week with work. Meeting Nathan and his friends has been a lot of fun, but dancing with Nathan was definitely the highlight of my night. I'm ready to go home, hit the pillow, and let Nathan invade my dreams.

Motioning to me, Naomi asks if I'm ready to settle up and head out. Giving her a smile, I reply, "I do believe my glass slipper is about to turn into a pumpkin if we don't get going soon." At that, Nathan squeezes my hand, giving me a cute, lazy smile.

"Are you sure you ladies have to leave already?" Tucker asks.

"Unfortunately, we do. I have too much to do tomorrow, and I need to sleep so I don't waste the day away. We also all came together, so it's best that we stick together when we leave. It's smart and safer that way. Plus, we have to walk a bit to our truck," I tell him. *Could I sound any more ridiculous?* I shouldn't be allowed around good-looking men. It's like my brain and mouth keep feeding the ramble meter.

"Perfect, we should get going ourselves. We'll walk you out, and to your truck. We might even be parked close to each other." Holt tells us with a charming smile, which seems to widen a little more when he looks at Halley.

"Holt's right, Tuck. We should get going, unless you plan on backing out of tomorrow? Or did you forget already?" Nathan ribs Tucker with a cocky grin, while I'm wondering what's up with tomorrow and secretly wishing I could go along.

"Look here, cowboy. I'm not backing out, and no way am I losing more money to you, either. So get that stupid smile off your face." Tucker fires back.

"I feel like I've been watching a comedy act between the Three Stooges all night. Don't you think, ladies?" Halley asks Naomi and I with a teasing smile, making us laugh. *Leave it to her*. She's a straight-forward person, and doesn't mind saying what she thinks when she wants to.

"Woman! You did not just go there." Holt holds his hand over his heart, like she's wounded him, or his pride—or both. It's all an act with this guy. You can tell he's a big ham who loves attention, and eats it up. From what I've seen of him so far, he's a perfect match for Halley. They are both witty and blunt people. I have to wonder if he has a serious side to him, or if he's one big jokester. I also wonder, for her sake, if he's a player.

I don't know much about Tucker, though. He clearly keeps up with the best of them, and he's just as good looking as Holt is. I saw how the women in this place kept eyeballing our table when the guys decided to stick around. Especially this one redhead, who couldn't keep the pout off her lips every time she looked at Holt. *I'm not stupid. I know we got the men that a lot of the women want.* Our table felt like it had one giant target on it, and the weapon of choice tonight would be the daggers in the other women's eyes. Funny thing is, the men didn't even notice, or seem to care. They seemed happy and content to be where they were. *So, the question is, what the heck are they doing with us? It's not like we aren't a catch or anything, but don't they want these other women, too?*

I'm not saying that all the women here were being horrible with their looks. Just a few zoned in on us, especially the redhead. I have a feeling she could be trouble down the road. *I sure hope not, though.* I'm not one who loves drama, and Halley wouldn't have a problem speaking up in a confrontation. I think it was more jealousy than anything hateful with these women, and I try to let the feeling of impending doom go.

Sighing to myself, I realize that I'm lapsing back into being insecure as I feel Nathan's hand in mine. He's giving it a squeeze while his eyes shoot me a questioning look.

"You okay there, Charlie? You seem to have disappeared for a minute. Are we that boring? The Two Stooges aren't entertaining enough?" He chuckles, bumping my hip with his side. I notice that he left himself out of the comedy group, which makes me give him a soft smile.

"Oh, she found your secret out, Nate. Now she knows what a bump on a log you are. She just took a trip in time through snoozeville, and realized that she has to get out while she can before she sleeps through your relationship." Holt cracks himself up at my expense.

"Yeah, real funny, Curly," Nathan throws back at him, cracking the rest of the group up. "How old are you, again?"

"*Curly.* I like it. I think that's your new name, babe." Halley taunts Holt.

At this point, we're close to the exit, and Holt decides to chase Halley out the front door, right past Dave.

Dave stops us, pulling me in for a big hug, and forcing Nathan to let go of my hand. I automatically miss the heat and strength of his hand surrounding mine. I know Dave means well, and after all, he looks after us when we're here. So I can't blame him for giving me a hug, which is habit for him. He lets me go and hugs Naomi, then releases her, too.

"You ladies need an escort out to the lot? I can get Tim to come up here and take over for a few," he says while eyeing Tucker, but more specifically, Nathan. Okay, what's *that* all about?

"No, we're good. Nathan, Tucker, and Holt are walking us out. Thanks, Dave. You're the best. Always looking out for us and making sure we're good," Naomi says, saving us from what felt like an awkward situation coming on.

"Are you sure? Charlie?" Dave asks, looking at me. He's holding my eyes for a minute longer than usual. "It's no bother. I do it every time you ladies come out. It's really not a problem. And do you even know these guys?" he asks, looking dubiously at Nathan. "No offense, Nate. I know you're a good guy, but I doubt the ladies know you well enough to know that."

Wow. Dave seems to be in overprotective mode right now.

"It's okay, Dave," I say, laying my hand on his arm. "They're really good guys, so I'm not worried. It seems like you know them pretty well. That just endorsed my approval for them walking us to our truck even more. Thanks!" I say it with a smile that I hope will ease his mind and let us go without any more issues.

He lets out a long breath. "Sure. Yeah, they are pretty good guys. I'm just being overprotective. You know me." He smiles, sounding a little deflated. The weird tension in the air evaporates as he lets us go with one more hug, saying good-bye, and to be safe driving home.

Chapter Five

Nate

I WRAP MY ARM AROUND CHARLIE AS WE WALK OUT THE front door, letting Dave know she's mine tonight. As for his comments, I'm not fired up about whatever he was trying to insinuate about me.

The next time I come out to *Texas Jacks*, Dave and I will be having chat on that subject. As for Charlie, she said she didn't have a boyfriend, but she didn't mention that Dave was into her. Either she has no clue, or she chooses to ignore it. And for some reason, either way, I don't like it.

I keep Charlie wrapped under my arm, making sure she's close to me, as we walk through the parking lot. Thankfully, as it turns out—the girls are parked only a few cars away from ours. Even though I'm not ready to let go of Charlie yet, I know I need to as it's late, and I really need to get sleep before tomorrow morning at the track.

We walk over to my truck and stop as we notice that Halley is laughing herself silly. I raise my eyebrows at Holt and he just points to the sticker on the back of the truck, which Charlie reads out loud.

"That's not a leak. My Ford's just marking its territory."

"You know what 'Ford' stands for right?" she asks, and before I can answer, she says, "Fix or Repair Daily." Halley laughs again.

"Woman, you need some new jokes. Want to know how to remedy that?" Holt teases, as he bounces his eyebrows up and down at her.

"Oh this should be good." She mutters under her breath.

"You do know I can still hear you, right?" he smirks at her.

"So? What's your brilliant response going to be, hmm?" she chuckles.

"Babe, I just wanted your number. Is that a crime?"

"I don't know. It could be, since it *is* you asking for it, after all." We all laugh at her comeback.

"You wound me." He lays a hand over his heart.

"I'm not just a 'call for a good time only' kind of lady, you know. How do I know you're not just a player?" Well, she's not wrong as Holt usually is a player. I smile at him, waiting to see how he'll play this.

"That's the thing. You won't know, unless you give it to me so you can find out."

"Maybe you should have to work for it." she teases.

"Oh geez, already. *I'll* give you her number if you two stop gagging me with your flirting." Naomi jumps into the conversation, cracking us all up.

"Well, who knew you had it in you all of this time, you little firecracker!" Tucker appreciatively sizes Naomi up; giving her one of his cheesy grins he uses when he hits on women.

"Oh, it's always there, just lying in wait to go boom." Charlie says as she laughs.

"That's right, and don't you all forget it." Naomi quips back with a smirk on her face.

The exchange reminds me of the cliché line, *it's always the quiet ones*…But that can't be true, because Charlie is much quieter than Naomi. However, you can tell there's a fire burning behind those green eyes of hers, just waiting to blow up into a full-on inferno. I bet she's one of those people who are slow to anger; however, once she hits her mark, she combusts. *Tuck better watch out with this one.*

Rolling her eyes, Halley looks at Holt. "Fair warning, you'd better not add my number to your black book either, mister! So far, I like you, and I would like to keep it that way."

He snatches her phone out of the back pocket of her jeans and starts typing in his contact information.

"So, Miss July, can I have your number, too?" Tucker winks at Naomi, and surprisingly, she blushes. Even more surprisingly, she actually fishes through her small purse, finding her phone, and hands it over. *Interesting.*

Leaning down, I whisper in Charlie's ear, "Let's ditch the crazies and head to your truck." She smiles up at me and we head off towards the girls' truck without a glance back to the beeping phones behind us.

I lean up against the truck that Charlie stops in front of and pull her over next to me. I want to reach out and touch her. Instead I just let her lean slightly up against me and the tailgate. I've already crossed so many physical lines tonight with embracing her on the dance floor, holding her hand practically all night, resting my hand on her thigh, and at the end, wrapping my arm around her. I think I've hit the limit on the touchy-feely meter. Though, I must admit, I'm surprised she let me touch her so much for being so shy. So here I am, trying to practice self-restraint so I don't scare her off.

"So, what were you all talking about earlier, when you mentioned tomorrow?" she asks me, though it seems like she's not sure it's her place to ask.

"The guys and I like to ride out on the dirt track with our dirt bikes. We usually spend a lot of time out there, or here at *Texas Jacks* on the weekends, if we can manage it. Sundays are another story though, since that's the one day I make sure to ride."

"Why Sundays? What's so special about that day?"

"Honestly, I'm not sure. It's just the one day I live for, and I make sure I'm there religiously. What about you? Is there one thing you do out of habit that you never break?"

"Yes. Twice a month, also on Sundays, I drive up to Sacramento and spend time with my family. We have family dinners, and I never break the tradition, if I can help it."

Hearing the love in her voice makes me melancholy where my own family is concerned. I can't recall the last time we've had a family meal of any kind together. Maybe I need to be the one to break the barrier, and check in with my sister and dad.

"Nathan, are you okay?" Charlie asks, reaching up to touch my arm. "You looked a little sad." I look down into her big express blue eyes that are shining with concern at the moment.

"I'm fine, little one. Just thinking about my family, is all. We don't get together very often, so I was thinking that I should probably check in with them. That's all. No big deal." I smile, trying to play it off as best as I can. No need to delve into places I don't want to, or ruin one of the best nights I've had in a really long time, outside of the track.

"By the way, Charlie, you can call me Nate. It's what my friends call me."

"I like calling you Nathan, to be honest. But, maybe—" she trails off.

"*Maybe*—as in, the next time you see me, you'll give Nate a try?" I playfully tease her.

"Maybe." She murmurs back, resting her head on my arm.

Feeling the need to break the tension even more, I decide

to go for broke by asking her for something I usually don't do while I'm here. "So, what do you think—should we follow the lead of our friends and exchange numbers, too?"

"I don't like to give my number out, especially to someone I just met." She ducks her head, but not before I see her worrying her lip between her teeth.

"You know, I usually don't ask the women I meet here for their numbers, nor do I give mine out. So, how about this instead…The next time I see you here, I'll ask you again?" I can respect Charlie for not handing out her number. I've already pushed her as far as she could handle, apparently.

"Oh. Okay. Yeah, I think that would be a good idea." She awkwardly stumbles over her reply, giving me a shy but hopeful look, too.

The gang shows up at the truck just then, and I let it go. I'm not going to push for it, but I won't lie that it sucks I didn't get her number tonight, either.

"Nate, didn't you see my sticker?" Halley asks.

I turn around to see her window sticker, as Tucker reads out loud,

"Q: What is the difference between a Ford and a porcupine? A: Porcupines have pricks on the outside."

"Fitting, wouldn't you say?" she asks, while smirking at Holt.

"Oh, you're a funny one, aren't you, woman?" Holt says, shaking his head. I know he finds it funny, but he won't let a Chevy owner get the best of him and his Ford.

"Time to say goodnight to the ladies. We can't let Charlie ruin a good pair of boots by letting them turn into a pumpkin now, can we? What would that say about us as gentleman?" I say to the guys.

"Ha! No one's ever accused me of being a gentleman." Holt winks over at Halley, who just laughs at him and rolls her eyes.

On that note, Halley and Naomi head to the front of the truck, as Halley clicks her remote to unlock it. They climb in as I walk Charlie over to the passenger side, and because I can't help it this time, I wrap my arms around her, lifting her off the ground. I reach out to open the door, and then set her in the backseat.

Leaning in, I place a light kiss on her cheek, whispering in her ear, "Goodnight, Charlie. It was a pleasure to meet you. I hope to see you again real soon." Then I close her door and walk away.

Charlie

On the drive home, I can't stop thinking of Nathan. *Nate.* The way he kissed my cheek and whispered in my ear before he left. The way he held my hand most of the night, and when we danced. *When was the last time I let my guard down that much when it came to a man?*

"Charlie." Halley calls my name, pulling me out of my happy trance. Looking up, I see that we're outside of my complex, and both of my friends are staring at me.

"Why didn't you give Nathan your phone number?" Halley wants to know.

They're looking at me like I've lost my marbles in crazy-town.

I'm perplexed as to how they knew that. "How did you know?"

"We heard part of your conversation, but didn't want to

ruin the mood, so we tried to hang back until we couldn't resist coming over there." Naomi bugs her eyes out at me.

"Really? " I sigh. "Do you not remember which friend you're talking to? You know I don't give out my number, nor do I ask for a guy for his. The real question is, why are you looking at me like I'm nuts?"

"He was really into you, and I know for a fact you were feeling it, too. I can't recall the last time you let a guy get close to you so fast." Halley gives me a pointed look. "He seemed like a really sweet guy, and his friends may be goofballs, but they were a fun group to be around. When have you ever let a man dote all over you that way? I would hate for you to lose out on a great dating opportunity here."

"Charlie, we understand that you're shy when it comes to men, but it is okay to step out of your comfort zone here. Even Dave said he was cool. We don't want to push you—we just thought this could be a guy you could afford to get to know better. Really, we want you to be happy, and to stop being the girl on the sidelines." Naomi gently tells me. Apparently, she's taking a different approach than Halley is on this.

Before I can get a word in, Halley has more to say on my inability to let men in. "You have to take chances, Charlotte. How are you supposed to ever settle down when you won't even give up a thing as small as a phone number?"

"Look," I say, cutting them both off before they can get any deeper into my issues. "First of all, why are you marrying me off before I even have a date with this guy? Second, I like Nathan, and I would like to see him again. However, I think it's okay to know him through *Texas Jacks* first, before handing out my number. If you'd both waited to hear me out, I would have told you sooner. He's asking me again for my number the next time we meet. When the night is over, and we've had more time together, I'll give it to him then." Blowing air deeply out of my lungs, I continue. "I already decided to take a chance and not let life pass me by anymore. I know I'm young, but I feel like I'm holding back too much, and I want to step outside of my comfort zone, as Naomi stated. However, I don't need anyone pushing me. Let's just take this nice and slow, and let the chips land where they may, shall we?"

Now they're both staring at me with mixed emotions washing over their faces. Finally, raising her left eyebrow and giving me a big, lopsided grin, Halley asks, "When were you going to let us in on the big secret, you sneaky woman? And— what prompted you to finally cross over to the dark side?" she laughs.

Relief wash over me, knowing the tension has been broken. I don't like confrontations, especially with my friends.

"Honestly? I'm not one hundred-percent positive, but I think it stems from my siblings and parents. Going to family dinners and watching them with their partners, it makes me feel left out. They're happy and in love, and naturally I want that, too. Then there's you two, always having fun and meeting new guys. You have a life, and I feel like I'm on a boring car ride, enjoying the pretty scenery from the confines of the inside, but never getting out and truly experiencing it. For once, I wanted to know what it was like to take a leap of faith. Nathan seemed like the right guy to jump with."

"Well I, for one, am excited to add some men to our circle of friends. I'm seeing exciting times ahead for this group, and I can't wait for the good times to roll," Halley happily states. "But more importantly, Charlie, we are happy for you in taking this giant step. Remember, we will always be here to hold your hand. We're your sisters from other misters, and we don't let sisters fall," she reminds me with a wink. We've always been there for each other, through life's many ups and downs.

"By the way, thanks for the surprise intervention," I shake my head at them. "I know you mean well. However, I've got this." I smile saucily at them, then turn the handle on the door and push out of the truck.

They wait, watching to make sure I've gotten inside my apartment before pulling out of the lot to head to their own place.

Making sure the apartment is secure for the night, I head to my room to change into pajamas before going to the bathroom to wash my face and brush my teeth. I return to my room, flipping the light switch off as I make my way to the bed and climb in. After pulling the covers up to my neck, I snuggle deeper into them, trying to find a comfortable position to sleep in. Turning onto my right side, curling up in an S-shape, I rest my hands under my cheek as my heavy eyes finally start to close, allowing visions of Nathan to play through my thoughts. Before sleep finally claims me, I think of how I hope Nathan stars in my dreams tonight.

Nate

The guys and I make it uneventfully back to our house, ready to crash for the night.

I'm heading down the hall to my room when Holt stops me. "What's up with you and Charlie? Did you get her number?" he asks, stifling a yawn.

Sighing, I rub a hand through my hair. "No," I tell him honestly. "She didn't give it to me, as much as I wanted it. She didn't ask for mine, either."

Tucker's now standing in the doorway of his room,

overhearing our conversation. Raising his eyebrows in shock, he asks, "Seriously? After she practically let you in her lap, she didn't throw you a lifeline with her number? That's messed up, dude." Tucker lets out a chuckle, but I know he feels bad for me, too.

"You were different with her tonight. The last time you were really into someone like that, would've been back when you dated Heather Morgan. Right around the time your mom—" Holt trails off, making for an awkward moment.

Deciding to let it go, I'm determined to push past his words. "Yes, she turned me down, and yes—it sucked, but she did promise I could have it the next time we saw each other. And, if I recall right, you both were able to get her friends' numbers. Which means you now have the access to make it happen," I remind them with a grin.

A smile plays at the corners of Holt's lips, at the idea, as he slowly nods. "Darn straight I got that saucy woman's number. I have no doubt we'll be seeing them again. If you want, I can get Charlie's number for you. All you have to do is say the word, and I'm on it. Besides, I wouldn't put it past Halley to freely give it out. I get the impression she's already planning your wedding," he says, cracking himself up along with Tucker.

"You're laughing now, but with Halley's speech, I'm pretty sure she's not a ship passing in the night. So, you better not screw this one up."

"Chill out. If you really plan on getting serious with Charlie," Tucker says seriously. "Then we won't screw it up."

"I really don't know what I'm doing. She's different, and I want to get to know her better. That, I know for sure. Otherwise, I can't promise anything—and yet, I can't get her out of my head, either. So I'm taking a chance, and seeing what happens. That's my plan for now."

The guys share a look between them, but I let that go, too. I don't want to think too deeply about what this could mean, and it doesn't matter, anyway. We barely know each other, so for now, their point is moot. *At least that's what I tell myself.* And with that thought, I'm ready to put my mind to rest, content with the possibility of Charlie dancing through my dreams.

"Let's not get too serious or carried away here. I'm heading to bed. Just make sure you set a plan in motion with the girls, and let me know where to be," I tell Holt. "By the way, thanks. I appreciate it."

"Goodnight, John-boy." Holt calls over his shoulder as he walks away to his room.

"Goodnight, Jim Bob." I toss at Tucker, continuing down the hall to mine.

"Goodnight Ben," he says to Holt. "Wait a minute," he continues, stopping us both for a moment. "Why do I always get stuck with Jim Bob? That makes me sound like a freaking hillbilly." He sounds peeved, and we just laugh at him, closing our doors behind us.

Sometimes we really are childish. Case in point: our Walton's bedtime routine.

Chapter Six

Charlie

The week passes by at a snail's pace, and the only thing on my brain is Nathan. Somehow, I'm able to function normally at work and interact with my friends, but my nights are spent dreaming of Nathan.

Thursday starts off decently enough, but I wish the hands of time would speed up so I can see him again.

I'm sitting at the reception desk that I'm in charge of when my cell phone alerts me to a text message. Good thing we don't get in trouble at work by having our cell phones out. The place I work for is pretty lax, as long as you don't abuse their generosity and follow the rules.

Picking it up, I see that it's just my mom, wishing me a good day and telling me she loves me. She also reminds me about the family dinner coming up again soon—*like I would forget*. I reply with the same sentiments and get back to work, silently regretting not giving Nathan my number. I've contemplated the reasons I never gave it to him in the first place, and my only conclusion is that, basically, I was a big chicken. No other ways around it. I hate that I didn't jump at the chance; however, I can't just change in a blink of an eye. After only a few short hours of knowing him, I had already pushed the limits on my comfort zone. Maybe if he hadn't been so touchy-feely that night and had asked for my number instead, I would have given it to him. Then again, I wouldn't take back those moments over the exchange of a few numbers. So back to work I go, trudging along, as there's no point in going over it more. *It is what it is.*

I work for a family medical practice here in town, as Dr. Blankenship's medical receptionist. We tend to see a lot of elderly patients and children. The patients are really sweet and friendly, and the staff is like a second family to me, so I can't complain. Sometimes, the older women bring in homemade food for Dr. B as a thank you for his medical care. Truly, this is a great place to work. The staff is upbeat and positive, and that makes a difference in the patients' overall wellness and care.

By lunchtime, I'm ready to ditch this place—as much as I love working for Dr. Blankenship, I'm ready to call it a day and sleep until it's Friday night. I really can't wait to see Nathan again, but I need to pull myself together. I'm sure he's not sitting at his job—whatever it is—pining over me. I need to get a grip. Maybe I'll work on *that* after lunch.

I'm usually the last to go to lunch, as I finish checking patients out and scheduling future appointments. When it's time to head out, I turn the phones over to an answering service during our lunch hour. If there's an emergency, the staff can give Dr. B a call right away without the patient waiting for us to get back.

I'm starving, and need food pronto. As I'm walking to my car, my phone buzzes in my hand. Looking down, I see that I have a new text from Halley.

Halley: Are you off to lunch yet?
Charlie: Yes. Just left the office and heading to my car.
Halley: Want to meet up?

Charlie: Sure. Mexican sound good?
Halley: Yep! Meet me at Freebirds World Burrito. I'm headed out there now.
Charlie: Sounds good, see you shortly.

I get into my blue Honda and pull out of the lot, headed towards *Freebirds* and Halley.

Nate

It's Thursday afternoon, nearing lunch hour, and the guys and I will be knocking off soon to go eat. I have no idea what their plans are, but as for me, I've decided to check in with my family. I'm long overdue for a visit. Today seems as good a day as any to stop by and show my face.

Holt, Tucker, and I all work at the same construction company, where we mainly build houses. We've been working for Jim Cates, at *B&B Builders*, for three years now. Jim is a cool guy, a longtime friend of Holt's dad, and he knows our vision for the near future. He's genuinely interested in helping us make our dreams a reality, and goes about doing so by showing us all sides of the business.

Our goal is to someday have our own company, and that is why we all live together now. We purchased the home we live in so that we could pool all of our resources together and save the money needed to build our company.

We're currently working on a big project, building 30 new homes for *B&B*. We just happen to be building in a subdivision that's close to my childhood home, which was the deciding factor for me to stop by and check in. I have a little bit of time to go by the house and see how everyone is before I need to get back to the site. My dad works from his home office a couple days a week, so at least he should be there.

"Hey, you ready to blow this place and grab some lunch?" Tucker semi-shouts as he and Holt make their way over to me.

"I'm actually going to head over to see my dad and check in. I've been slacking on that a lot lately. What about you guys? Any plans?"

"Not really. I sent Halley a text to see what she's doing. She's supposed to have lunch with Charlie today and make a plan for this weekend to meet up with us." Holt says, double-checking his phone for an update. "But she hasn't responded back about it yet."

"Do you really think it's going to be that hard to convince her to come out?" I didn't get that vibe from her last weekend. I thought she wanted to see us—*me*—again.

"I really don't think it will take that much convincing. She seemed to be into you, especially for being super shy. I don't think you have anything to worry about." Tucker tries to reassure me, but you never know. Sometimes people can surprise you with who they really are.

Holt looks down at his phone again when it dings. Reading the text, he smiles, looking back up at Tucker. "Have any lunch plans?"

"No. Why?"

"You do now. Halley says she's meeting Charlie at *Freebirds*. Feel like burritos?"

"Sure, why not? Food is food, and I don't care where we go. I'm freaking starving right now."

"Good. You ready to surprise the ladies and crash their lunch date?"

"I'm definitely game. Let's get a move on already before

I start eating dirt." Tucker says, as he heads towards Holt's truck.

"Hey, are you sure you don't want to tag along and see the pretty little mouse?" Holt taunts me.

"Man, you guys suck, you know that?" I grumpily reply before scrubbing a hand down my face. "As much as I want to see her, I can't. I really need to check in if I want to have a fun-filled weekend. I would go after work, but I'll be too beat and much dirtier. It's best to get it over and done with now, rather than later." I tell him, letting out a long breath.

"Fine, suit yourself. Enjoy lunch, and tell your pops we said hi." He says as he starts to walk away. "Oh, and kiss that sister of yours on the cheek, and make sure you tell her it's from me, too." Holt taunts me. I try to sock him in the arm, but he sees it coming and easily dances out of my way. He's a big flirt, and doesn't really mean anything by it. Carianna is practically a sister to both of the guys. Holt just likes to get under my skin whenever he can. Although, right now, I believe he's trying to lighten my mood before I head home.

"Don't have too much fun without me, and make sure you tell Charlie that tomorrow night her dance card will be full, with only my name on it."

"Aye aye, Captain!" Holt says, giving me a mock salute. "See you in less than an hour. Chin up, man." He says, slapping me on the back as he leaves me to go have lunch with my girl.

What a day. Can't time just speed up so I can get to the part where I'm holding Charlie in my arms, swaying to the slow beat of some sappy country song?

Charlie

"How's work today?" I ask Halley before taking a really big bite of my burrito. This place is awesome, and I'm so dang hungry, I'm surprised I didn't order two of everything.

"It's going okay, nothing special or major at the moment. Although, the weather is awesome, so I would rather be at the beach. Or hanging at your pool would work, too."

"How's 'Kyle the Pest' being these days?" He doesn't seem to get that Halley isn't interested. He feels that if he keeps being persistent, she will eventually cave and accept at least one pity date with him. Although, it wouldn't be a hardship, seeing as he's a good-looking guy. Why he's so fixated on Halley is beyond me, though. You would think he would take a couple of 'no's' from her as a hint, then move on. However, the rejection only seems to egg him on further in pursing her.

"Don't even get me started on him right now. It's the same old garbage as usual. He asks, I say no, he thinks I'm playing hard to get, and the cycle starts all over." She says, waving her hands at me in a shooing action. "Enough about him, let's talk about what our plans are for the weekend. What are you doing?"

"I plan to relax and swim a few laps in the pool. What about you?"

"I'm thinking we need a night out dancing again. I had a blast last weekend, and I want to see the guys again. What do you say?" she asks in a giddy, hopeful way.

"What about Naomi? Is she up for going, too?"

"Of course! I think she really liked Tucker, so she's definitely on board to see them again." Halley wiggles her eyebrows at me before taking a drink of her soda.

"Fancy meeting you here, you saucy woman," we hear

Holt say as he stands over Halley, looking down at her with a sexy grin on his face.

"Of all the places, in all of the burrito joints, in the entire world, you had to walk into mine." Halley deadpans while looking up into Holt's eyes and carefree, smiling face.

"Babe, you have to know I would follow you anywhere." He shamelessly flirts back.

"So—what are you two doing here? Stalking much?" she asks with a tiny smile playing on her lips.

"Hey, it's your fault for texting Holt where you would be. You had to know after last weekend that he's head over heels in love with you. He would kiss your feet if you asked. I bet he would even let you paint his nails and curl his hair," Tucker teases both of them.

Holt replies sarcastically, "Aren't you hilarious, Jim Bob." He turns back to Halley. "What? We were hungry, and decided to stop by. Is it a crime that two handsome men wanted to eat lunch with two hot babes?"

Rolling her eyes, Halley smiles sweetly at them. "Well, when you put it *that* way, how can a girl resist the likes of you two? Go ahead, pull up two chairs, cowboy, before my food gets cold."

"Yes ma'am." Holt mockingly tips his nonexistent cowboy hat at her.

"Where's your little firecracker friend, Miss July?" Tucker looks around the restaurant like Naomi might appear out of thin air.

"She's at work, like every other red-blooded American. You should have sent her a text to meet you for lunch."

"Hey, I didn't realize I was coming here until the last minute, when I was roped into spying on Charlie for Nate." Tucker states with mischief written all over his face, at the same time triggering my curiosity.

"Spying?" asks Halley.

"We aren't here to spy for Nate," Holt corrects. "However, he was pretty bummed to be missing out on seeing Charlie," his eyes sparkle with a hint of humor. "Once he knew we were coming to see you both for lunch."

"Why didn't he come?" I wonder out loud.

"He had family stuff to take care of. He did however, leave an important message for me to pass on to you though," Holt says, wagging his eyebrows.

"Oh yeah? What is it?" I ask, trying *not* to sound too eager at what his response would be.

"That he would see you tomorrow night, and your dance card would be full with one name on it—his." Holt says, watching to see what my reaction will be to this news.

On the inside, I'm giddy; butterflies are swimming around, and my heart races. On the outside, I try to remain cool and collected. However, when I look back up, three faces are staring back at me with probing eyes.

With a small smile, I reply cool as a cucumber, "Guess I'll just have to fulfill that request now, won't I?"

"'Atta girl." Tucker says, widely grinning over at the other two.

"Well, Tuck-boy," Holt slaps Tucker on the back. "We'd best get something to eat and leave these pretty ladies alone. We need to grab lunch to go as to make it back to work on time." Looking back at Halley, he says, "And you, woman, I'll text you for the details later. Until then," he reaches over and grabs her hand, eyes locked on hers, as he places a kiss on her knuckles whispering huskily, "later, babe."

"Later, ladies." Tucker echoes in a deep sexy voice as he walks over to the counter to place an order to go.

"Oh. My. Gosh. Those two—" Halley sighs as she fans her flushed cheeks with her hand.

"Pull it together, *woman*." I snap my fingers in front of her face. "Time to get back to work. The clock is ticking, and we're wasting time." I say while getting up to throw my trash away. "We need to meet up after work with Naomi to make plans for tomorrow night. I'll text you later to let you know when I'm off work."

"Okay, sounds good." Halley sounds as if she's in a daze.

"Earth to Halley!" I wave my hand in her face, this time. "Come back to me." I chuckle.

"Right. I'm with you." She shakes her head, then checks one more time over her shoulder to where the guys went. "I'll get Naomi on board. She's going to be so upset that she missed Tucker today." Halley giggles as she gathers up her belongings.

"Maybe." As I really don't know for sure one way or the other if she would be, yet. "I'll catch you later." I tell her, then look over and see the guys grabbing their orders. "See you later, boys!" I call over my shoulder as I saunter out of the restaurant.

Nate

"How did it go with your dad?" Tucker asks me as we're putting things away for the night at the job site.

"Not bad. He was actually working from home when I dropped in, and Carianna had stopped by for lunch in between classes. I think they were both surprised to see me. Unfortunately it had to be a short visit, but it was a pleasant one at the same time."

"I'm glad it went well. Do you plan on stopping in again

now that we're working close to the house?" asks Holt. "If you do, next time, I'd like to tag along and see your family. It's been awhile for us too, you know," he hesitates for a moment, and I know why but don't want to acknowledge it. "That is—if you're cool with it, and all seems good on the home front."

"Yeah, that's fine, Holt, I don't mind." I reply, hoping to get passed this conversation as fast as I can so I can move on. "Honestly, I would actually prefer if you guys tagged along. It would certainly make it easier, and less awkward. Next time, I'll plan it better so I can give you plenty of notice when I decide to head that way again. Anyway, enough heavy stuff. I want to know how lunch was."

"Oh, you know—Charlie was cute as ever, and good old Tuck had her convinced we were there to spy on her for you," Holt laughs.

"Great. This is what I get when you two are sent to the front lines. So, what's the plan? Are they meeting up with us tomorrow night?"

"You insult me," Tucker acts as if he's wounded. "I'm the king of smoothness."

"Yes, Casanova, you can simmer down. The girls are cool, and we didn't scare your mouse off—yet." Holt gives me a wicked looking smirk, making me want to kick his legs out from under him to wipe it off his face.

"Good. I'm glad you didn't screw it up." I chuckle; glad that they didn't really ruin it for me. "Let's get out of here. I'm definitely ready to grab something to eat. Pizza, anybody?"

With a couple of head nods, we head off toward the lot where our trucks are, together.

As I follow the guys out, I smile and think to myself, *one more day until I get to see Charlie again.*

Chapter Seven

Charlie

F RIDAY NIGHT HAS FINALLY ARRIVED, AND I'M definitely ready to get it started. I've been excited all day about seeing the guys again, especially Nathan. I don't know how I survived my half-day of work at the reception desk. Luckily, I was able to go swimming and lay out by the pool after I left the office. Sleeping under the sun's rays was relaxing, and helped to speed up time.

Halley and Naomi showed up for dinner, which consisted of chicken salad sandwiches and fruit. Truthfully, that was all I could stomach, with my nerves being frayed. I didn't want to eat something heavy, and it was too warm out to cook. So, easy and cool it was.

The night before, the girls and I sat around their living room, eating pizza and frozen yogurt, making plans for tonight. It was decided that they would come over after work, since they both had a full day, to get ready and have dinner. Then we would head over to *Texas Jacks* in one car, in case one of us wanted to hitch a ride home with one of the guys. I'm thinking the girls and Nathan's friends cooked up this little plan, trying to get Nathan and me together again.

Before long we're back at *Texas Jacks*, passing through

the lot. I don't see Nate's truck, which leaves me feeling a bit disappointed. I had hoped he would be here first. Sighing, I keep reminding myself that it's no big deal; his friends said he would be here, so he will be. I just need to relax and know that he'll show up at some point. Until then, I'm sure the girls and I can make our own fun while we wait.

Nate

Pulling into the lot of *Texas Jacks*, I note that the girls have arrived before us. That's fine by me; it gives me a chance to find her, instead of her searching for us.

I woke up this morning in a great mood, which in turn made the rest of my day at work turn out well. It also helped the day go faster, knowing that I would see Charlie later. Though, time did slow down over the last few hours before leaving to meet up with the ladies, as my anticipation to see Charlie grew stronger.

The first thing I notice upon entering the doors of *Texas Jacks* is one very absent person—Dave. I have never been here on a night he hasn't been working the door. Instead, Tim seems to be the man in charge at the moment. It may not seem like a big deal, but for some reason, I want to know where he is. After last week, I got the impression that he was really into Charlie, and tried to stake somewhat of a claim when we were leaving.

"What's up, man?" I ask Tim with chin lift.

"I see you got stuck with the boring job tonight. I guess this means you won't be inside, scoping out the women." Tucker heckles Tim.

The guys and I chuckle, knowing how Tim is, and that being at the front door is the last place he wants to be. He might be able to see the women walk through the door, but that's as far as it goes for him tonight.

"So, where's Dave? Does he have the night off or what?" Holt asks.

"I'm only filling in for Dave while he's on a break. No way am I going to babysit the door the whole night," Tim replies.

"I bet Dave's scamming on your action inside," Tucker laughs.

"Dude, that's not even funny. I wouldn't worry about Dave, anyway," he nods his head towards the next set of doors. "He's inside with three hot chicks. He went on break the minute they walked in. They even waited for him before heading inside, so it's safe to say my game is all good when it comes to Dave." Tim says without even realizing that all three of us are staring at him with hard eyes. I bet we're all thinking the same thing, and hoping it's not the same three women we're here to see. Since we already know that Dave is friendly with them, I'm sure I'm right.

"Oh, is he now? And exactly who might they be?" Holt immediately responds, trying to sound as causal and friendly as he can through a forced, lopsided grin. Meanwhile, I see his left hand forming a fist by his side.

"One's blonde, and the other two are brunettes." Tim raises his eyebrows while looking at Holt, "What's it to you, anyway?"

"No, it's cool. I'm just curious how Dave got so lucky, is all. I want to know how he's got so much game, being stuck at the door all the time," Holt smoothly replies.

"What do you say, gentlemen? I think we should drop in on Dave, and see if he's willing to share." Tucker says, although he looks none too thrilled, either.

"Sounds good to me," Holt replies, looking through Tim and over to me, nodding his head before pushing through the last set of doors to the inside of the club.

Charlie

Tonight, Dave decided to take a break when we came through the doors, which he never does. Normally, he just stops by at some point in the evening to check on us, and then at the end of the night, he walks us out. I think he has a bit of a crush on Naomi, though sometimes I think he may even like me, too. I can't tell. He's definitely not obvious about it.

"So, Dave, what's shaking with you lately? Any new babes you have on your hook?" Halley playfully nudges Dave, who happens to be standing between her and I at the table we're sitting at.

Dave looks over at Naomi, then shyly at me before responding, "No. However, there is one person I'm interested in. I'm just not sure she knows it yet."

"Maybe she doesn't have a clue. What have you done to let her know you're even interested in her?" Halley counters back.

This is not my area of expertise, so I keep quiet and let the girls hold up our end of the conversation.

"Dave, you just have to be bold and flat out ask her to go on a date with you. Is she a regular here?" Naomi asks.

"Yes. I see her from time to time with her friends," he says, looking over at me, and then back to the girls.

Okay, why did he just look at me? "Sorry, Dave. I'm not

good with this stuff, so you won't be getting any advice from me." I nervously laugh as he simply gives me a small smile.

"She's not joking, either. She's definitely not good at reading the signs. You're barking up the wrong tree there." Naomi laughs, causing me to shoot her a *thanks a lot* look, even if it is true.

"Well, I think we need to help this poor guy out, don't you, ladies?" Halley tries to rally us up to help in this new found cause for the poor guy.

"No, it's okay." Dave sounds a bit panicked. I scrunch my forehead together, trying to figure out why. "I'm sure I can manage to ask a woman out on my own. Thanks, though," he tries to stop this train wreck of an idea from completely forming in their minds.

"Dave, seriously, we can help you score a date. Just point her out the next time she's here, and—"

Quickly cutting her off, he says, "No, really, I'm good. I'm just slower at this kind of thing than most guys. Especially the guys you ladies were hanging with last week. Speaking of which, what's the deal with them? I didn't realize you all knew each other."

Wait, doesn't he like Naomi? That's the impression I get. If so, then what's his deal? He's known her a long time, and has had plenty of chances to ask her out.

"We just met last week, actually." Halley says, bringing my attention back to the conversation. "I've seen them in here before, but we've never talked. It wasn't until Nate made a play for Charlie that we even met," Halley answers for us with a mischievous little grin on her face.

What the heck was that for? I give her a questioning look and she just smiles brighter, shaking her head at me like I'm clueless.

"*Woman!*" We hear as we look over towards Halley,

seeing the guys bearing down on us.

"Don't you *woman* me, Curly!" Halley fires back at Holt, causing him to smile, knowing that he's got her.

"Don't you know how to check your phone?" Holt asks, having moved off to her left side, staring down at her.

Standing behind Holt is Tucker, who's looking over at Naomi, and then there's Nathan. However, it's not me he's looking at. It's Dave.

"Dave." He states gruffly.

"Nate. What's up? I didn't expect to see you in here tonight. How's it going, man?" Dave greets, turning around to acknowledge Tucker and Nate.

"We have a date." Nathan casually replies, watching for what seems like a reaction from Dave.

Dave looks hopeful when he asks, "Oh? Who's your date? Anyone I know?"

"We *all* have a date, and you're holding it up, to be honest." Tucker cuts in, staring Dave down.

Raising my eyebrows, I look over to Naomi. She only glances back with a small shrug of her shoulders. Shaking my head, I look back over to the guys.

Nathan moves around Dave to my right, and wraps his left arm around my shoulders, effectively bringing me closer to him before he places a kiss on the crown of my head. He lets me go slightly while still keeping his arm loosely around me. Raising my head to look up at him, I see that he's looking down at me with a sweet smile on his full lips, causing me to smile back at him and feeling those butterflies all over again.

"You see, we're actually here to meet *these* three lovely ladies," Holt smiles at each of us before bringing his attention back to Dave. "We appreciate you hanging out with them, keeping them company and warding off the other prowling men until we got here," he continues, trying to cut out the weird tension that surrounds the men.

"Oh. Yeah, sure. No problem. It was a pleasure, ladies. I won't hold you up further, and I'm sure my break is up now anyway. I'll check in later with you. Have a good time." Dave says, looking a tad mournful before he gives me a sideways glance, and then smiles over at Halley and Naomi while leaving our area.

Nate

Watching Dave around Charlie irritates me. I'm normally not the possessive type, and I'm certainly not one to go all cave-man, like Holt. However, I didn't like the looks he was giving my girl.

"Was that necessary?" Halley's narrowed eyes zero in on Holt, her eyebrows creasing.

"What? We're on a date, and he was holding it up. Why are you looking at me like that, woman?"

"Oh, so you felt the need to go all territorial on the poor guy?" she shoots back, obviously irritated with him.

"He wasn't even doing anything but talking with us. He was telling us about some girl he likes that hangs out here, and how he's slow about asking her out." Naomi fills them in before the room explodes with the two hot heads sitting across from us.

"Is that so? And who was he referring to?" Tucker asks, looking pointedly at me. However, his question is meant for the girls.

"Who knows? You Neanderthals interrupted before we could find out," Halley huffs out.

"Hey, don't throw me in to that statement. I didn't do anything to rile anyone up." I say, defending myself.

"Why don't we just turn down the hormone levels and take a breather? I thought we were out to have fun, not size anyone up with petty jealousies." Charlie surprises us all with that statement.

That's my quiet little one, I think before giving her shoulders a squeeze.

"Well, what are you all standing around for? Pull up a chair and sit awhile." Charlie tells us, and we proceed to do what the little lady instructed.

Before the night is over, we're laughing and having a great time. Dave makes an appearance once more, looking a bit dejected to see us still sitting with the girls before heading back to his post. The girls are in rare form tonight, and all the while I'm sitting here, holding on to Charlie's hand again, thinking about the promise of finally getting her number before we leave the parking lot.

Charlie happens to catch me smiling to myself and asks, "What's that smile for, cowboy?"

"Oh, it's *cowboy* now, is it?" I tease her back.

"Yes, and I'm wondering what that smile's all about. Care to share?"

"Nope." Staring into her beautiful blue eyes, I tell her, "You'll just have to wait and find out."

"I think we need to get going before these two love birds make us gag," I hear Tucker say.

"There's always one bad apple that has to ruin it for the others." I say and look over to Tucker, while he gives me an all too pleased smile. Shaking my head, I turn back to Charlie. "Well, little one, let's head out to the lot. The others can catch up. I do believe we have some unfinished business to attend to."

Not even giving her a second to think, I pull her out of her chair and lead her out of the club, leaving the others to catch up in a few minutes.

I walk Charlie over to my truck and lean up against it, like I did last time, guiding her to stand in front of me as I slowly move my hands down to her hips. I draw her forward until our foreheads are touching, and I quietly ask, "Did you have a good time tonight, sweetheart?"

She softly replies, "Yes, thanks to you."

"Why is that?" I want to hear her say the words out loud to me.

"You kept my dance card full all night." She says with a little grin on her face, which I find attractive.

"So, you weren't upset that I monopolized all of your time and attention from the male population?"

She laughs and shakes her head. "You didn't hear me complaining, did you?"

"Not one complaint came from these sweet lips." I say, lightly running a finger across her full, pouty bottom lip, causing her cheeks to blush and her chest to inhale sharply. Tipping her face up until she's looking into my eyes, I ask her, "Charlie, can I have your number?"

Charlie

I'm standing here staring into Nathan's eyes, thinking he's about to ask me to kiss him and he... *asks for my number?*

"What?" I ask stupidly.

He chuckles. "I'm asking you for your number, sweetheart.

That's our unfinished business. Remember? You did promise me that the next time we met you would give it to me."

"Oh. Yes. You're right." I say, stumbling over my words. *Great.* He gets me all flustered, and now I can't even form a sentence correctly.

"Charlie, it's okay. If you're not comfortable or ready, I can wait until you are."

"It's okay. I was just thrown off there for a minute." I tell him honestly before looking down at his boots like they're the best things since chocolate before taking the plunge and admitting, "I want you to have my number. I was actually thinking this week how I had wished I'd given it to you last week."

"It's okay that you didn't. Even though I really wanted it, I'm glad you made me wait this whole week. It was worth it." He admits, causing me to look back up, searching his eyes for the truth in that statement. "Really, *you're* worth it. Honestly. I feel like I'm in uncharted territory with you, Charlie. I barely know you, yet I can't stop thinking about you. I find that I'm dancing through this, making up the moves as I go."

"That makes two of us. Honestly, I don't even know what I'm doing. I feel so out of place, but I can't get you off my mind, either." Shyly looking into his eyes, I admit to him, "I barely know you, too, Nate. However, I really like you, and want to get to know you better. It's not like I haven't dated, it's just been a really long time. I'm not sure what I'm supposed to do. Sometimes I feel like I want to do all the things couples do in public—like holding hands—but then I'm afraid that it's too fast for me. But I don't want to be afraid anymore, either."

"I get that you're vulnerable, and I'll try to take things slowly. There's no pressure here, little one. You're in good hands with me, promise. If slow is what you want, then I'm willing to do that. However, I reserve the right to kiss you or hold your hand at any given time." He says with a teasing grin. I can't help it; I smile back, and nod my head, trying not to let my hormones over take my body.

He places a kiss on my forehead and says in a husky voice, "Don't worry, sweetheart. When I kiss your sweet lips for the first time, it will be worth the wait."

By the time Nathan hugs me and kisses my cheek one more time, I'm left in a daze of happiness. I know I'll sleep well tonight.

Chapter Eight

Nate

THREE DAYS. THAT'S HOW LONG IT'S BEEN SINCE I'VE seen Charlie. She's all that I can think about lately, which makes no sense. *Since when do I get all worked up about a little slip of a woman?* Yet, I can't deny it. She's on my mind more often than not.

Bang. Bang. Bang.

The pounding on the bathroom door brings me back from my Charlie-induced fog, startling me. My hand slips while I'm shaving my face, causing me to nick my cheek.

"Keep your pants on!" I yell at the offender on the other side of the door.

"If I had some on, maybe I would. But some of us have a job to get to, while others hog the bathroom!" Holt yells through the door. "I hope you have yours on. I'm coming in, and I'm not all fired up for a full moon." I hear, right before the door knob twists, and Holt's blond head appears around the door before he admits the rest of his body in.

"You build things for a living – go build your own bathroom." I grumpily mumble at him through the bathroom mirror.

"Are you PMSing?" he quirks his left eyebrow at me with a small grin on his face. "Or is this all due to that sweet little mouse you seemed all tied up in knots over?"

"No." I lie, going back to applying toilet paper to the fresh wound, trying to staunch the blood flow on my left cheek, so I can finish wiping the rest of the shaving cream off of my face.

"Uh-huh. Right. So, what's the problem? Still wishing you had gone in for that kiss?" he taunts as he makes himself at home, sitting on the toilet lid.

"I did kiss her."

"Oh, right. I forgot—cheek kisses count now. What base would you call that? Half way to first?" he laughs.

"Don't you have a job to get to?"

"Touchy. Do you want me to run to the mini-mart for Midol?"

"I'm just wondering when you're going to get your own bathroom so we can stop having these morning tea and cookie chats."

Tucker makes his way into the bathroom, yawning.

"What's this? Are we having a bonding moment, or an intervention on kissing skills?"

"Nope." Holt reaches into the medicine cabinet for his toothbrush, as he scratches his chest. "Just need to get ready for work. I'm not the one who wimped out on a kissing a chick."

"I did kiss her." I remind them.

"Cheeks don't cut it, man." Holt says around a mouth full of tooth paste.

"So, as fun as this has been, are we all driving into work together?" I ask, a bit testily. I really don't want to delve into what I did or didn't do with Charlie, or let on to the fact that she occupies my whole head.

"Sure, get the heck out of the bathroom already so we can hit the road in 15." Holt replies, totally unfazed by my attitude this morning.

"Great. I'll update my Facebook status." I quip, as I remove myself from their presence.

"Don't worry. I know exactly what he needs. A little dose of his favorite new flavor, and Nate will be good as new." I hear Holt say to Tucker right before I round the corner to the front room.

I think it's time to chill out, and the only way that's going to happen is to either stop whatever this is with Charlie, or send her a text so no one gets hurt today.

Charlie

"Hey. Do you want to grab dinner with us?" Naomi asks, the moment I answer my cell.

I just locked up after work and was heading to my car when she called. "Sure. Where do you want to meet? I'm starving!"

"We thought *Merchant & Main Grill* sounded good. Are you game?"

"I'm game for anything at this point, and I haven't been there in a while, so yeah, I'll totally meet you there. I'm just heading to my car now. Should I drive straight over?"

"Yep! We'll all meet you there in about 15 minutes."

"Wait. What do you mean we'll *all* meet you there? Who else is tagging along?" I'm baffled as to who else she could be talking about.

"The Three Stooges, of course. Who else?"

"Right." *Why I wouldn't get that on my own is beyond me.*

"All right. I'll see you in a few minutes, then."

I end the call, wondering why I didn't get a message from Nate about tonight, or even a personal invite from him.

I slip into my blue Honda and click on my seat belt, before firing up the engine and head to the restaurant.

Nate

"Holt and I are headed out to *Merchant & Main Grill* if you want to join us. The girls are meeting us there, too." Tucker tells me the minute he walks out of his bedroom. "I just got off the phone with Naomi, and she promised to get Charlie on board."

"Sure. Give me a few moments to clean up, and then we can head out." I tell him, as I head back to my room and change out of my sweats.

We called it quits early on the project we were working on, which allowed us to come home and clean up at a decent time. I didn't have any plans to go anywhere once I got in. The only things on my mind were phoning in a pizza, and calling Charlie. Though, phoning Charlie was on the back burner, seeing as she was at work. Thankfully, Tucker just killed two birds with one stone, as there was no way I was going to turn that offer down. *Food and Charlie?* I'm in, one hundred percent.

A few minutes later, we climb into my truck and head towards *M and M*.

We find the ladies shortly after arriving, and pull up seats next to each of them. I automatically reach out and take Charlie's hand in mine, placing it on my thigh.

Looking up at me, I wink at her as she asks, "How was your day?"

"Good. Though, it would have been better if I could have seen your pretty face all day long. Instead, I had to endure the looks of the motley crew sitting next to your friends." I nod towards Holt and Tucker as Charlie giggles, bumping her shoulder into mine.

"Well, I'm glad you no longer have to wear your 'beer goggles' to face them." She jokes at the expense of the guys.

"Look here, Squirt. Tucker and I are the best looking things at work. Don't let Nate fool you, we cause traffic jams all day long." Holt winks, as he wraps his arm around Halley. "Halley would know. Right, babe?"

She rolls her eyes. "Sure. If that's what you want to tell yourself." She winks over at Charlie. "Though, I think the hottest guy sitting at this table right now would be Nate. Right Charlie?" Earning herself a big grin from Charlie and a frown from Holt.

Now I'm laughing at Holt's expression, as I hold my hands up in surrender. "Don't even look at me. She's with you. Though, she is right. The girls just can't help themselves when I'm around."

Charlie

Ever since I gave Nathan my number, we've been talking, or texting each other, with every free moment that we had. I know, I wasn't playing it very cool, or slow for that matter, but there's just something about Nate that draws me in to him completely. I love talking to him, or being in his presence and I just can't help myself. I don't think there's a woman with a brain in her head who would want to avoid all things that are Nathan.

I've been waiting all week for tonight. We're supposed to go out on our first *real* date. I don't count last Friday, when we all met up for dancing. Tonight, it's just the two of us.

I was glad that today was a half-day at work. I didn't think I could have survived the work day without messing something up. I was too distracted with excitement about my impending date, to really even think straight, or fully do my job. Luckily, I made it through without any major screw-ups before I rushed home to find an outfit.

I still can't believe I'm actually going out with this nice, good-looking guy.

So, here I sit on my closet floor, in the middle of the day, trying to determine what to wear. I'm not even sure what we're doing, as he never told me. *Should I dress up? Go semi-dressy, or semi-casual?* I'm driving myself crazy, and I can't even call my friends, since they're all at work.

After another half hour of trying to choose something, I give up. Picking my phone up off the floor, I decide to shoot Nathan a text instead. He's the only one who can really help me with the matter at hand.

Charlie: Any hints as to what I should wear tonight?

I set the phone back down after a few moments, know-ing he's on a jobsite and can't jump every time I send him a message. I start pawing through my clothes again. I decide that maybe I would be fine wearing jeans and a dressy blouse. Maybe I could pair the outfit with sexy heels—though I'm sure I'll have to bug Halley for a pair. Just as I'm thinking it would be worth sending a text to Halley, my phone chimes with a text.

I look down and automatically my whole face burns with embarrassment as I read his response.

Nate: Anything you want…or a bikini. ;)

Charlie: Umm…I'm not even sure what to say to that.

Nate: Nothing to say, babe.

Charlie: Then again, I wouldn't know, since someone won't tell me what our plans are for later.

Nate: Be prepared…for anything.

Charlie: Isn't that part of the Boy Scout motto?

Nate: Who ever said I was a Boy Scout?

Charlie: Are you sure your name is Nathan?

Nate: I never claimed to be Nate, either.

Charlie: So, let me guess. I've got one of the other Stooges on the other end of Nathan's phone. Right?

Nate: Oh, a wise guy, huh? And who's to say you aren't talking to Nate right now?

Charlie: If I were to call you right now, who would I get?

I wait for a response, but all I get is radio silence. *Just as I thought, one of the guys messing around with Nathan's phone. Typical of the Stooges.* Giving up, I vow to stick to the items of clothing I've laid out, deciding against the heels. *Who needs to fall and break a leg on their first date? So,* it's flats for this short chick. Too bad. Heels would have put me in a closer proximity to his kissable lips.

The phone rings a while later, flashing Nathan's phone number.

"Hey, cowboy." I greet Nathan as soon as I answer.

"Hey, short stuff," he replies.

Nate

"Since when did I become short stuff? I thought I was your little one?" She sounds confused at my change of nicknames for her.

"You are, and you're my short stuff, too." I reassure her, not realizing that she liked me calling her little one over the last week or so. "The guys and I could come up with cuter names for your pint-size all day long, if that appeases you." I tease her as the guys chuckle around me, nodding their heads in agreement.

"Great. You just gave the Stooges more ammunition against my size!" She sounds appalled by my revelation. "I'll be the brunt of all of their short jokes now," she pouts.

"Don't worry, sweetheart. It just means they think the world of you. Speaking of the Stooges," I start, as I take notice that Holt and Tucker are starting to slowly back away from me. Frowning, I wonder what that's all about. But then I turn my attention back to Charlie. "I hear you tried to reach me?" I'm worried something's come up and she has to cancel on me. Although, that wasn't the impression I got from Holt when he said he talked to her earlier. Still, her reaching out to me first has me overly curious. Normally, I make all of the first moves.

There's a pregnant pause in the conversation, as I'm waiting for her to let me in on why she needed to talk to me.

"I'm guessing you weren't fully briefed on our conversation then." She states.

"Uh, no. Holt didn't really say much of anything." Narrowing my eyes at my friends, I see that they're now too far away for me to say anything without her knowing. "Is something wrong? We are still on for tonight, right?" I quietly inhale, and then slowly exhale, wondering to myself if that came out as desperate as I thought it sounded.

"Oh, we're still on for tonight," she assures me. "I was just texting you to see what I should wear. Though, the response I got wasn't what I was expecting." Now she sounds a bit shy and unsure.

"Okay. And exactly what did they say?" Now I'm more suspicious as to what was said to get shy Charlie on the other end all of a sudden. "Did they give away our date?" If those punks ruined this, there *will* be hell to pay. I love a little thing called instant karma—though only when it comes to those two knuckleheads.

"No, no, it was nothing like that." She tries to reassure me. *What did they say to her?*

"Okay. Mind telling me what happened?"

"Maybe you should just read your text messages. That should explain it all."

Great, now I have to wait until we end the call to find out. I'm thinking it's a good thing the guys took off. I should have known better than to leave my phone lying around. With Holt and Tucker, you never know what they'll do, especially when it comes to my cell phone. Add Charlie into the mix, and that spells trouble—*for me.*

"I'll be sure to do that, just as soon as we hang up," I mumble into the phone. "As for what to wear," I say, getting us back on track, "make sure to dress warm and comfortable, but that's all of the clues you're getting out of me, little one." I playfully warn her. No way am I giving up my well-laid plans.

"But, what if I'm overdressed? Or under dressed, for that matter?" I can tell she's back to being nervous.

"Charlie, you never have to worry about being dressed inappropriately. You, my little one, are always dressed per-fectly. Now, stop biting your lip, because I'm not there to kiss those lips I love to stare at, and stop worrying yourself sick. I want you to say goodbye, then hang up, and find the best date outfit to wear with a cowboy. I'll be there in an hour to pick you up. Can you do that for me?"

"I can do that," she's says on a sigh, but I can tell she's also back to being the sweet Charlie I have come to like so much in the short time we've know each other.

"Sounds good, sweetheart. See you in a while." Then I hang up before she can say anything else.

Chapter Nine

Charlie

I'M REALLY NERVOUS ABOUT TONIGHT'S DATE. BUT AT the same time, I'm beyond excited. I haven't told my family about Nathan yet. *That's the last thing I want to do.* I can imagine the hours of teasing they will unleash upon me. Then, there's my mom who have me married off with eight babies, a mini-van, and a white picket fence. *Yeah, time to move on to other thoughts*, I start to think when I hear a knock at the front door, making my insides twist in knots.

On shaky legs, I make my way to the front door to let Nathan in. My giddiness ratchets up a notch as he stands there with a crooked grin on his handsome face. Just looking at him, and seeing how pleased he is at the sight of me, helps to uncoil the knots that had my stomach in jitters all day. I step back out of the way and let him in.

"Hey, beautiful."

"Hi," barely passes my lips on a breath.

"What did I tell you?" he says, as he checks me out, from head to toe and slowly back up again, a satisfied smile prominent on his face. "You look perfect, just like I knew you would." He reaches out and pulls me into a quick embrace, and then lets me go shortly after. "You ready, little one?"

"As ready as I'll ever be." I try for a flirty response, but fail. So I quickly grab my purse, jacket, and keys off the couch before turning back to Nathan. "Where to, cowboy?" The second flirty response is a charm, right? I hope so.

Can he tell how giddy I feel?

"Cowboy. I really like when you call me that."

"Good." I murmur as we step out onto the landing in front of my door so I can lock up. Then I boldly reach out to take his hand and lead us to the parking lot. I'm sure he can feel the slight tremor that's taken up residence in my hand, as I'm trying for assertiveness and hoping to calm my nerves. I'm trying to let go of shyness, as much as I dare—for the moment anyway. After all, it's only our first real date of being alone together.

He helps me up into his 275 Ford extended cab, with his hands on my waist, when it hits me. *This is our first date. Alone.* This will be our first time without the guys acting as comic relief, or the girls as my safety net. As he shuts the passenger door and rounds the front of the truck, I start to wonder if he feels just as nervous as I am. As he climbs into the main cab of the truck, I pray I can overcome the awkwardness I'm feeling.

Does he feel it, too?

"Feel free to change the station to whatever you want." He winks at me, before he puts the truck into drive and pulls out of the parking lot. "Feel free to make yourself at home whenever you're in my truck."

I sit over on my side of the truck, with this big, gaping, void in between our seats. It's awkward already, and I have no idea what to do next, so I reach my hand out to the radio, searching for my favorite country station before settling back into the nice, semi-cushy, leather seats. I'm still striving for calmness and confidence, which I'm lacking in both departments for the time being.

"Are you okay all the way over there?" I hear, as he pulls me out of my thoughts.

"Peachy." I give him a tentative smile that I know spikes his curiosity.

"Any reason you're practically hugging the door?" He chuckles.

"Sorry," I give him a sheepish look. "Just a little nervous, I guess."

"No need to be, I'm not planning to bite." I sneak a glance at him to see he's got that crooked grin on his face again. "Probably. I can't make any promises though," he teases.

Too ease some of the tension I'm feeling, I decide to ask about the details of our date.

"Sorry, you'll just have to be patient until the ride is over, little one."

"One thing you should know about me—patience isn't my strong suit."

He laughs, probably thinking that I'm joking. He would change his tune if he got anywhere near my siblings.

"You feel it too, right?" I suddenly feel the urge to ask.

"Feel what?" His eyebrows pull inward, as he looks over at me with a confused glance.

"How different this feels. You know, without our friends here?"

"You know what would help remedy that?" his voice holds a bit of amusement in it, and something else I'm studiously trying to ignore as I calm my traitorous heart down.

I'm afraid to ask but I can't help myself, and fall for the bait—hook, line and sinker. "What?" I softly ask just as Keith Urban's Sweet Thing comes on the radio.

"If you scooted that cute rear of yours across the bench seat and sat right next to me. I don't like the distance sitting between us," he says as he pats the spot right next to him.

I swallow hard and decide that no harm could come by just sitting next to him, and who am I kidding? I would regret it if I didn't go for it. So I scoot over and latch the lap belt around my body as he pulls me snuggly against his side, leaving his arm around my shoulders. *A girl could totally get used to this.*

"I know you're nervous to be alone with me for the first time," he states in a low voice. "I really wish you wouldn't be." He gives my shoulder a light squeeze."I really like you. And as far as I can tell, you like me, I hope." He chuckles and playfully bumps my other shoulder with his. "I'm trying to make this date special for you, and it would help me out if you could relax and pretend you like it—or me for that matter." He wiggles his brows at me, causing me to giggle.

"Tell me about your day," he changes the subject with small talk, easing us out of the seriousness of feelings.

"Are you trying to distract me? More than you already are?" I nudge him with my shoulder.

"If I wanted to distract you," he murmurs softly. "I would find better methods than talking."

He keeps a loose hold on me, while I decide to throw more caution to the wind and relax further into him. We have a pleasant, run of the mill, conversation about our day as we drive through town and out into the country.

Nate

Eventually, I pull up to a nice-looking iron fence with the ranch's brand on the front. I park and hop out of the truck to open the gate, then get back in and drive through. I get out one more time to close it then take us down a long and dusty dirt road. Soon we come to a stop, and I park us as close as I can to a big, man-made pond.

"Where are we?" Charlie asks, as I watch her survey our surroundings from the window.

"We're on a friend's ranch out in Dixon. She let us have use of her property for our picnic."

"It's beautiful." I can hear the awe in her voice as she looks out the window, and I fully agree with her assessment. It really is a beautiful piece of property full of green grass, different types of colorful flowers, big shady trees, and some land-scaped rock areas around the clean, blue colored pond. It's the perfect setting for our picnic, as it's peaceful back here—with no interruptions from our nosey friends or loud music from the DJ.

"Calissa, the owner of this ranch, is a good friend of mine. We grew up together, and went to the same schools. Though, she doesn't get out much—especially to *Texas Jacks.*"

"Why is that?"

"She's busy with the ranch, her horses, and lately it seems like something else is up, but she won't talk about it. I've been too distracted myself to really be a nosey friend and pry." I give her a pointed look so she knows exactly which distraction I'm talking about. She blushes and turns her head, but I still catch that small smile that pulls at her full lips.

"So, you brought me all the way out here for a picnic?" She's trying to use the same 'distraction' tactic I used on her, and I let her have her way.

"Anything for a pretty lady." I open the door and hop out, before she has time to respond, then reach up and offer my services to help her down. *Like that's a hardship*, I smile inwardly. I love it when she has to depend on me to get in and out of my truck. Any opportunity to get my hands on her, I fully plan to take advantage of.

I help her down and then close the door before taking her hand and walking us around the truck, towards the pond. There's a blanket already spread out with a basket sitting on it. All around the blanket are strategically placed mason jars that hold battery operated candles in them for when the sun goes down. They're already turned on, so as not to ruin the mood for later. I lead her over to the blanket and help her sit, then go back to the truck. In the back, I have more blankets and a bouquet of flowers for her.

I can feel her eyes on me the entire time as I make my way back to her, with one hand behind my back holding the fresh flowers. I drop the extra blankets off to the side and sink to my knees, bringing out the bouquet. Her eyes widen in surprise, then light up with excitement when she gushes over the beautiful gift. I watch her bring them to her nose, smelling the intoxicating fragrance.

Placing the bundle on the blanket, she leans over on her knees, bringing a hand to my shoulder to balance her as she gives me a peck on the cheek. We stay in this position for a few moments longer, as we stare into each other's eyes, before she retreats to her original seating position. I really wanted to take her into my arms right then and kiss the day lights out of her—which I fully plan to do before this date is over.

"I love Stargazer Lilies. How did you know?"

"I didn't. But I'm glad I do now. Besides, I couldn't resist the smell of their perfume, so I had to get them for you."

"Thank you. They really are beautiful."

"Beautiful flowers for a truly beautiful woman."

"My oldest sister, Jennifer, grows them out on her property. I love going to her house and being able to walk past, breathing in the wonderful aroma. It's one of my favorite things when I go out to see her family." She smiles fondly at the memories running through her mind.

I'm not ready to delve into the topic of family, just yet, so I move us along to the topic of dinner. "Are you hungry? I asked Leti, Calissa's cook, to make us her specialty." I pull the basket in between us. "I couldn't resist sharing my favorites with you. Really, it would be too selfish to keep it all to myself." I playfully tell her, loving the laugh I receive in return.

As I pull each dish out, I name them off as I go. "Grilled buffalo chicken sandwiches, potato salad, watermelon, and lemonade. Though, I hope you save room for dessert, as she made her chocolate coconut mound bar brownies." I lick my lips. "I hope you've brought your appetite!"

"I don't know if I can out eat you," she teases. "However, I did bring a healthy appetite. Everything sounds delicious, and that sandwich—it really smells good, too."

We sit across from each other, enjoying the scenery, the food, and each other's company in a comfortable silence as we eat. It would seem that Charlie has finally let her guard all the way down.

I realize how much I like being with Charlie as I sit on my side of the blanket gazing over at her. The sun is starting to set, and we've been sitting here for quite some time making small talk, but nothing really important enough to care about.

"It's strange, isn't it?" I ask her.

"What's strange?"

"Being able to sit here with you in this peaceful place, you know—without the whole gang around being loud and crazy."

"You mean, there's no one to cut the tension with?" She giggles.

"Okay, fine, you were right. But I'll deny it if you ever tell the guys I said that!"

"What, you think the shy girl would be such a tattle-tale?" batting her eyelashes with fake innocence, but I bet anything that she's far from that when it comes to this subject.

"Why do I not believe you?" I laugh when she makes her best shocked face.

"I have no idea what you mean by that." She turns her face to the side, biting her lip.

"Uh-huh. Sure." I knock her foot with my own. "Why are you sitting all the way over on the other side of the blanket?" I raise an eyebrow at her, trying to help her tumble over that line she's not sure how to cross. That's fine though. I have no problem going for what I want.

"Me? I think it's *you* who's on the wrong side."

"Are you asking what I think you're asking?" I'm comfortably leaning back on my elbows, propped up so I can have a good view of her.

"Umm—I'm not sure. What do you think I'm asking?" Now she just seems confused.

Leaning over, I hold out my hand for her to grab on to. She looks me straight in the eye as she latches on with determine confidence. She's still sitting on her knees as I stare back at her, waiting to see what she will do. She gives me a small smile, as she tucks a strand of hair behind her ear. So, I decide for her, and pull her down to lie partially on my chest, leaving her no choice but to lay her head against me. We end up fully lying down on the blanket, staring up into the sky.

After sometime of just listening to the still-quietness of the area that surrounds us, while enjoying each other's warmth, I roll to the side, gently pushing her away. She startles for a moment, then slowly sits up.

"Sorry," I murmur, as I turn her around then plant her between my legs. I wrap one arm about her, leaning her into me, as the other arm steadies my weight on the blanket.

"Let's watch the sun set, beautiful." I whisper into her ear, feeling her body shudder against me. "Cold?"

"*No*," she faintly whispers. I hold her a little tighter as we watch the sun go down. As it starts to grow darker, the glow from the mason jars start to filter through the night, making for an intimate ambience. I'll have to remember to thank Calissa for being so romantically inclined to add that detail.

"This is really nice, and peaceful," she sighs. "It's great to be able to enjoy the beauty of this ranch with exceptional company. Thank you, Nate, for thinking of this date. I'm having a wonderful time."

"You're not so bad yourself, short stuff." I give her another squeeze.

"What do you think our friends are up to?"

"Probably trying to figure out where we went, and why we're not answering our phones or hanging out at *Texas Jacks*." I feel her silent laughter as her body shakes against my chest.

"They're going to bombard us the moment we step back into the center of their worlds, you know. Neither one of us is going to get out unscathed."

"I wouldn't worry about them, sweetheart. Right now, it's just you and I, and I really want to dance with you."

Charlie doesn't even hesitate as pops up then reaches down to pull me to my feet.

"What will we dance to? Are you going to serenade me?" she asks full of mirth.

I laugh hard at that one. "Trust me, you don't want that. If you want to save your ears, and not have any nearby animals whine, then you'll have to make do with the truck's radio."

I snatch up my keys from the blanket and walk over to the truck, opening the door so I can start her up. I find the right CD and slide it into a slot in the dashboard. I key up the perfect song, and then flip on the headlights so we have a spotlight to dance in before making my way back to Charlie.

She's just standing there, watching me as I slowly make it back to her side. The moment I reach her, I gently haul her up against my chest and wrap both arms around her waist, causing her to circle her arms around my neck. Just a Kiss by Lady Antebellum starts playing, as I lean my chin against the top of her head and sway our bodies to the beat of the song.

This song couldn't be any more fitting for Charlie and me at the moment, in not wanting to push things too far—yet always being caught up in the moment with each other. I'll be content with just a kiss—that's the truth of the matter. I've been waiting patiently for the right moment.

Tonight has been perfect, though I really should have made a better attempt to get to know more about her life, or share more about me. My heart's just not into discussing the family hoopla at the moment. I really just want to be with her and share these kinds of moments before I get too deep into a potential relationship.

We dance for a while, listening to the different slow songs on the mixed CD I had made for tonight. She seems content to stay in my arms just the way we are, and I love every single moment of her body pressed against mine.

She pulls away slightly and looks up at me at the same time I dip my head down to take in her beautiful blue eyes. When I do, I see her face is filled with so much emotion, that I can't take it anymore. I have to kiss this woman with every fiber of my being. I start to lower my lips to her pretty plump ones, but stop just a hairs breadth away from kissing her.

"Charlie, I'm going to kiss you now," I gruffly whisper, giving her a chance to back out. After all, I did promise to go slow with her, and tonight I've done a few things that wouldn't be considered slow. She blinks once, then twice, and finally, ever so slowly, closes her eyes and tilts her face towards mine. That's all the permission I need as I crash my lips into hers.

The moment our lips collide, I feel that instant connection we have, but overwhelmingly so. Being lost in the pleasurable sensation of my mind and body, I was unaware of the moment that I started backing her up towards the truck. I push her up against the hood, lifting her up until her back is fully pressed on top, all while I continue to devour her luscious lips.

This kiss—there are no words for it. I now know what it's like to get lost in the moment with her sweet mouth. It's powerful, and possibly heartbreaking. I believe this woman could either mend my heart or break it, and I don't know which one terrifies me more.

Charlie

The moment my back dips onto the hood of his truck, my heartbeat kicks into overtime. I've been waiting for this moment to happen, and now it feels so surreal to have Nate kissing me. This is such a heady feeling, and it's in this moment that I know, without a shadow of a doubt, that he possesses my heart.

I hold him firmly to me while he feasts upon my lips, like he can't get enough. He pulls me tighter to his body, causing my legs to instinctively go around his waist, holding on for dear life while he kisses me senseless. There's strong chemistry between us, and I know he has to feel it, too.

He pulls back from our amazing kiss to gaze into my eyes. I can only stare back at him in a daze, while my lips feel tingly and thoroughly used. I run my hands through his hair, trying to sort out my thoughts. But only one keeps circling through my mind: *How far is Nathan willing to go to hold on to this connection we can't run from?*

I see a play of emotions dance all over his face as he waits for my reaction to the best kiss I've ever experienced in my adult life. There's only one thing to say here.

"Wow."

I slowly smile up at him as I bring one finger to my lips, feeling how plump and swollen they are. He just smiles back, like he's on top of the world.

Chapter Ten

Charlie

I WAKE UP FROM A FOGGY, DREAM-INDUCED STATE TO THE annoying sound of my cell phone vibrating across the top of my dresser. I had planned to sleep in, so I had set it to vibrate and promptly passed out with Nathan on my mind and a smile on my well-kissed lips.

Now, I'm awakened by the irritating clatter of my phone bouncing around and worse of all—I'm pulled away from my dream starring Nathan. I already know it's either Halley or Naomi on the other end. I should be glad it's the phone rather than pounding on my front door, or worse—both of them jumping on my bed to wake me up, since they both can get into my apartment. Sighing, I roll over and drag my body from the warmth of my bed to answer it against my will. If I don't, they'll keep calling—or just show up—so I might as well get this over with.

"No. You can't come over, and no, I'm not going to be a part of your torture session of questions." Yep, that's how I groggily answered the phone.

I hear chuckling on the other end of the line. "Why do I have a feeling you're not Halley or Naomi?" I groan and pull the phone away from my ear, squinting to see that it's Nate's number. *Great. Just put me out of my misery now*!

"Good morning to you, too, little one. Expecting an interrogation so soon, are you?" he says in my ear as I crawl back to bed and flop back down.

"Do you *not* know my friends? I'm surprised they're not here in my apartment, screaming the walls down already." I roll onto my side and snuggle back into the warmth of my covers.

"Oh, I'm sure they'll be calling shortly. I just heard the guys talking to them on speaker phone. I'm pretty sure they're on their way over to kidnap you for breakfast. And for the goods on last night, which was perfect, by the way." I can hear a smile in voice.

I can't help the big, silly smile that forms as I hear him say the date was perfect.

"So, the reason I called was to tell you thank you, again, for being my date last night. The guys have been harassing me all morning for details."

Yesterday's date pops up into my mind going over the details of that *hot* kiss.

"I have things to do today, but I couldn't get on with my day until I heard your voice," he continues.

"So basically, what you're saying is, your day is now complete because of me? You're welcome." I laugh into the phone.

"Yeah, yeah, yeah, smarty pants. Keep that up, and no more kisses for you." He teasingly threatens.

"As if you could refrain," I tease. "You can't wait for the next one to happen. Just like me!"

"Is that so?" I hear the smugness in his tone. *Shoot*. I shouldn't have given him that key piece of information.

"Hey, just trying to feed your ego. Someone has to!" I grin to myself for that one.

"You're playing with fire, woman." He chuckles. "Are you free later tonight? I thought we could hang out at *Texas Jacks*. Maybe even get you out on the dance floor for a bit of two-stepping. What do you say?"

"Sure, if you plan for me to trample on your toes—count me in! Do you want me to meet you there?"

"What? Why would I want to meet the prettiest girl in town at T.J.'s? No. I pick my girl up—she doesn't meet me anywhere. Just make sure you're ready at eight, wearing a sexy jean skirt and your boots."

"Are jean skirts even considered sexy?" I scrunch my nose at the thought.

"If it's hugging *your* curves, it is." His tone is flirty and husky.

"And will you be wearing your butt-hugging jeans?" I can't help but giggle as I say that. It seems a little crazy to say it, but it feels good—this flirting thing. "It would be a crime if you didn't. I need something to keep me motivated for when I run into Halley and Naomi in a little while. You know, in case I feel like strangling them, instead I'll picture your sinful-looking butt."

"*Charlotte Davenport*!" He bursts out laughing. I hear the phone muffle a bit, then I hear him yelling to the guys, "You won't believe the things Charlie's saying to me right now. I think she needs to see one of the local pastors!"

"Oh shush! I can hear you, by the way, and I'm not even that religious!" I roll my eyes, even though he can't see it.

"I think an alien came and spirited Charlie away if she won't see a pastor," he continues talking to the guys. "She's talking about my sinful butt."

"I think it's time for me to go." My eyes are watering from his banter as I laugh myself silly.

"Charlie, you've definitely shocked me. Where's my shy

girl? I think your feisty side is coming out," he says appreciatively. "Are you going to treat me to more of that later?" he hopefully asks.

"If you came to dinner at my parents', then yes, I would. Though, it wouldn't be flirty."

"Fine, fine. I'll stop. Promise." I can tell that the tone he's using is still playful, but a little more subdued. *What did I say?*

"I'll be ready at eight. Until then, try to keep your mind focused on your day before you wind up in a ditch."

"Yes, ma'am. See you soon, short stuff." He hangs up first.

I toss the phone on the bed and pull the covers up over my face. I really want a few more hours of shut-eye before I have to face the firing squad.

"Charlotte Davenport!" I hear a short while later, but really—according to the clock—it's only been like 45 minutes. Groaning, I roll over and look up to see my two best friends standing over me.

"Wake up, you hard-sleeping rock!" Halley pulls back the covers. "Time to get up. I can't believe you've kept us in the dark until now!"

"This is exciting, Charlie!" Naomi chimes in. "You've officially gone on your very first date, like ever!" She's practically jumping up and down. She isn't really, but she looks like she wants to.

"It was not my first date, come on—I've been on quite a few in the past." I remind them both as I sit up, running my hand over my hair and tucking some stragglers behind my ear. "Remember there was Sheldon my junior year of high school, and Phil at the end of senior year. Then there were Khalid, Art, and Bill during our freshman year of college." I rub the sleep out of my eyes.

"Okay, fine, but the high school boys don't really count, and the college guys were only a few dates each. So, I'm not counting them because none of them were serious," says Halley.

"How can you tell that this one's different?" I ask, because really, I want to know.

"I see the way he looks at you, and vice versa. Let's not forget that the guys told us earlier all about how he can't stop smiling. It's a whole new ballgame, sister!" she says.

I climb out of bed and stretch all of my limbs, yawning really big before making my way into the kitchen, knowing they'll follow as I go. "I hope you ladies brought me some cocoa and donuts, or something else to eat. I'm starving!" I call over my shoulder.

"We figured as much. We really wanted to take you out to eat, but then we considered the time, and knew we wouldn't make it out 'til lunchtime. So, ta-dah! Here we are." Naomi says, grinning from ear to ear at me. "Now, grab your drink and the breakfast sandwich we brought you and spill the beans, already! We're dying over here for the hot goss!"

I give her a funny look. "*Hot goss*?" scrunching my nose at that stupid word. "Do you mean, gossip? And who even says that? Never mind, I don't want to know. It was probably some ridiculous celeb. Moving on—" *Well, I guess it's in for a penny, in for a pound.* Time to rip the old Band-Aid off by getting it over with straight out of the gate.

I look each one in the eye, seeing how anxious they are to hear what happened. "We kissed."

Crickets.

No one makes a sound for like a full five seconds before they both are high-fiving the other. "Well? What are you waiting for?" Halley asks as she's pushing me into the recliner, right before they both make themselves at home on the couch. "Was it sweet? Was it straight up hot as sin? Don't leave your girls hanging!"

"Best kiss ever! Does that work for you?" They both stare at me with wide eyes. "Really though, the date was very sweet," I say, as I tuck my stockinged feet up and under me on the chair. "He had a picnic set up and waiting for us at his friend's ranch in Dixon. We talked a little, ate dinner, watched the sunset, and danced in the truck's headlights as our spotlight. He even had mason jars with candles burning in them for a romantic setting. Then, he told me he was going to kiss me right before he slammed his lips on to mine."

"Wow." Naomi whispers and eyes dreamy looking. "Who knew Nate was so romantic like that!"

"I'm impressed." Halley says, as she regards the happy look on my face. "Did he walk you to your door and kiss you one last time?"

"He walked me to the door and kissed me on the cheek before we said goodnight. He waited until I had my door locked before he left." I tell them, as I sip my hot cocoa.

"Any future plans?" Naomi asks.

"Yes, as a matter of fact." I say right before I take a big whopping bite of my sandwich. *Mmm, so good.* It's a bacon, egg, and cheese croissant. "He's taking me out tonight to T.J.'s."

They look at each other, then both break out into knowing smiles.

"What?" I ask suspiciously, around another bite of my sandwich.

"Oh, I'm sure his friends will be there, too. That means we should all go and hang out." Halley says, with her own secret smile. I narrow my eyes at her.

"Halley, is there something you want to share with the rest of the class?" I have a suspicion that she and Holt have something going on, but it has yet to be confirmed.

"Trust me, if there was, you both would be the first to

know. For now, it's all fun, harmless flirting when we run into them or via texts. Holt hasn't asked me out yet. I think he may be a bit of a player. You know, every group has to have at least one, and I think he's our group's playa–playa." She gives a saucy wink and a bit of an over done laugh. *Mmm–hmm, sure.* I thought she was developing feelings for him. "Anyway, enough of that arrogant hothead. Time to move on to something fun to do until it's time to hang out with the guys later."

"Whoa. Back the train up. Who says we're all hanging out later? Nathan asked *me* out. He's also picking me up tonight."

"No need to get in a tizzy. We're going to show up on our own and hang out with the other guys, if you want to join us. No pressure. Don't worry, we would never infringe on your date. We like Nate too much to interfere. We're all for Operation Nate the Great." I cringe once I hear the silly name they came up with. *Great. Well, what can I do?* They are my best friends, and they both want the best for me.

"Fine," I give in. "What did we want to do today?"

"Well," Naomi slowly draws out the word, "we were thinking that we wanted to check out the race track. You know, the one that Tucker is always at." They both laugh.

"Why are you two laughing? What did I miss?"

"Oh, just his crazy ex-girlfriend, Lisa." Halley rolls her eyes.

"Wait, when did you run into her?" I don't recall having a conversation about them meeting his ex, or going to the track.

"Well, you've been busy and preoccupied with Nate. I guess it just slipped our minds." Naomi looks a bit guilty for not sharing their outing with me. "We went out there the other day, as he invited us to come chill with him. Though, now I wonder if it was to help scare off his ex?" Naomi fills me in, but is now contemplating his real motives.

"Maybe he really did want to hang out and it had nothing to do with her. Don't over think it." Halley warns her. "Remember, this is Tucker were talking about," she laughs. "It's not complicated like that with him."

"Yeah, I know. I just had a doubtful thought there for a moment. You're right," Naomi assures us. But now I want to know more about this woman.

"Why, is she crazy? Is she stalkerish?" I raise an eyebrow, trying to figure out what the looks on their faces are all about.

"Yes!" It's Naomi's turn to groan as she flops back against the couch. "She's a crazy bike bunny who wants Tucker to marry her. She totally doesn't take a hint, either."

"Last time we were out there, he pretended he didn't hear her when she was practically screaming out his name," Halley explains. "He was trying to hide from her every chance he got. At one point, she got up all close and personal with him, trying to hold on to his biceps. She was falling all over him, and he couldn't get away fast enough. He kept giving us looks, but all we could do was laugh behind our hands."

"It's not like we could pull the piranha off of him. She really didn't appreciate the fact that we were both there, and she didn't believe that both of us were his friends, even though Holt was hanging with us. You should see her, with her orange glow tan, bleached out hair, and long nails. She's a typical cliché."

"Poor Tucker. I can't see him dating someone who looks like that." I say, making a face at the thought that orange skin on anyone is not attractive.

"Well, she didn't used to look like that. She was a lot prettier. I saw a photo of her online. We teased the heck out of Tucker about it until he pulled up photos on Facebook to prove that she wasn't always a toxic color," says Naomi on a laugh.

"What's that look for, Charlie?" Naomi narrows her eyes on me.

I wince, knowing I've been caught. Sighing, I decide to air out my worries. "Do you think that Nathan has any girls like that in his dating past? I know he is always at the track too, and it makes me wonder if he was into the bike bunnies." *Great, now I'm stressing out over something stupid.*

"The past is the past, hon," Halley gently reminds me. "You can't worry about something that won't affect you now and something you can't change if he did. It's past tense. If you're truly worried, why don't you come down with us to the track and check it out? See the guys and what goes on down there. It's fun, and to be honest, I can't see him paying attention to any of the ladies while he's there. I'm sure he's too focused on his bike and the track." She reassures me.

I nod my head slowly, as I think about what she says. So far, Nathan seems like the type who wouldn't lie, or try to make every girl feel special just to do so. "You're right, I'm just being silly. Okay. Let's do it." I clap my hands with a hint of giddiness to see what this passion of his is all about, but mostly, it's because I hope he'll be there.

"Sweet!" Halley jumps up from her spot on the couch. "Go get ready," she pulls me out of my chair and starts pushing me down the hall. "They plan to go down there in an hour." Well, someone is in a hurry to get us down there. I think someone is just as excited as I am to see 'her' man.

Nate

The guys and I are all sitting around, watching other riders use the track. There's a large group of us catching up—both guys and girls. Though, we're all on the lookout for crazy Lisa. Everyone at the track knows to warn us the moment they see her.

We've been here close to an hour when I see three familiar ladies stroll into my line of sight. Holt's too busy chatting up one of the bike bunnies, and Tucker's talking with some of the guys, so they have no clue who's making their way towards us. I stay where I'm sitting with the goofiest grin on my face. I really wasn't expecting to see her until later tonight. *Why didn't I think about bringing her out here sooner?* The other two had been out here before and seemed to fit in just fine. Sometimes I can be dense, I suppose. This is my place to just *be*. It should have occurred to me to share it with her, too. Unless, deep down, I knew I wasn't ready for that.

At any rate, it's too late now because she's here and she looks worried as she watches the other girls walking around in cut-off short shorts and bikini tops. I watch her making some faces at the chicks as they walk by, causing me to bite my lip so I don't ruin it with my laughter. I love watching her reactions. Then she looks out at the track in time to watch a few riders fly by on their bikes. Now she looks like she's ready to throw up. I see Halley nudge her and point in our direction. The instant she sees me, she lights up like the sky on the Fourth of July.

That knocks me off kilter for a moment before I stand up, waiting for them to make their way to us. The moment she's within reaching distance, I lift her up into my arms, giving her a bone-crushing hug as I swing her around. Setting her back on her feet, but not letting go of her, I ask, "What are you doing out here, short stuff? I thought we were meeting up later."

"Well, we were. Umm—I mean, we still are. The girls

wanted to come hang out, and invited me along. Though, now I might regret it if you take to the track. I'm not so sure I like that part just yet." She worries her lip until I pluck it out from under her teeth and lean down to nip her bottom lip, and then kiss the sting. She smiles up at me, and then buries her face into my chest. I shake with silent laughter, hugging her a little more. "I thought you would be happy to see me." She says it a bit too cautiously.

"Believe me, I'm happy you're here. I was just asking myself why I didn't think of it first."

"Well, well, well. Who do we have here?" One of the girls who's always trying to catch my attention wanders over, eyeing up all three of the girls. "I've seen the two of you around," she nods to Halley and Naomi. "I haven't seen *you* around, sweetheart." She focuses her glare back on Charlie as she checks her out and seems to find her lacking. That chafes me, but I'm not going to say anything just yet, unless she gets too catty.

I feel Charlie tense up at the use of the nickname I call her and watch her face as she scrutinizes the other woman right back. "And who might you be?" she asks a bit too sweetly. I can tell Charlie is not a fan. That's good, because neither am I. This chick wants the cowboy who wears the biggest buckle. She knows most of us race in competitions, whether it's on the track or participating in rodeos.

"Shelly, sweetie. How long have you've known Nate?" She narrows her eyes at Charlie, then at me. "I don't recall ever seeing you here before."

"Now that's not any of your concern," I decide to enter the conversation so it can't sprout feet and take off into the unknown. "Why don't you go find Chase? I hear he's slotted to win the next race when he goes to nationals." I see her eye twitch a bit, but other than that, she doesn't show any other emotion towards what she just learned.

"Nate, I don't know why you're always trying to brush me off. You know you're the only man I want," she scans my body from top to bottom, then back again until they land on my lips. She licks hers then looks back into my eyes seductively. "Anyway, I see you're busy now, but later, when you send your little groupie home, give me a call. You still have my number, right?" She smiles up at me all sugary sweet, then runs her hand over my arm before she flounces off in a different direction than the one she came in.

Charlie starts to pull away, but I hold on to her so she can't escape. "Charlotte, don't let her get to you. She's just trying to rile you up, and see? It's working. There's nothing going on there. There hasn't been, nor will ever be. She's an annoyance who tries her hardest to get my attention. Don't let her get yours." I kiss the top of her head and look over to see Tucker and Holt, as they silently stood by, watching the exchange.

"Shelly was tame compared to Lisa, don't you think, Naomi?" Halley winks at me, trying to break up the tension.

"Lisa?" We hear Tucker groan. "Please don't tell me you saw her on your way in." His eyes dart all over the place.

"Relax, big guy, we didn't see her." Naomi reassures him. He takes a deep breath in and then lets it out as he swings an arm around Naomi, pulling her into him and nuzzling her cheek.

I feel my eyebrows rise at the show of intimate affection he's showering on her. *When did this happen?* I clear my throat, grabbing his attention before he smiles over at me sheepishly, but he never lets her go. *Interesting.* I think we need a guy's night. I look down at Charlie and raise an eyebrow to see if she knows anything. She just shakes her head, letting me know she's just as clueless.

"Ladies, glad you could come out to watch us ride. Why don't we get you set up in a prime spot?" Holt decides to take control of the situation before anything else can happen. He looks at Halley, who's watching his every move. He winks at her and holds out his arm for her to tuck around so he can escort her to their seats.

"Before you ask," Charlie speaks in a low voice for my ears only, "there's supposedly nothing but flirting going on with Holt and Halley. Though, I get the impression she's more into him than she lets on."

"I figured as much. I feel like he likes her more than he realizes. Time will only tell, I suppose. We should definitely stay out of it, though." I warn her quietly.

"I'm inclined to follow your advice. She's always been our wild one. It would take a lot to tame her. Though, I wonder if she just met her match?" she continues to quietly speculate, but no way am I touching that thought with a ten-foot pole. I lead her off in the direction of our friends so she can watch me in my element. Though, I would be lying if I said I wasn't nervous to have her here.

We get the girls situated, and then roll our bikes out and prepare to spend a lot of time flying in the wind. I look back over at Charlie and motion for her to come over. I watch her as she walks over to me, admiring her jean skirt, green t-shirt, and cowboy boots. Her hair is up in a ponytail, and she's wearing a ball cap. She's too sexy for her own good, and what I love about Charlie is, she has no idea that men think that about her. *I plan to keep that my little secret.*

When she gets close to me, I pull her between my legs and loop my arms loosely around her back. I kiss the top of her head, and then tip her chin up to look at me. "How're you doing?"

"I'm good," she smiles up at me. "Though, I'm worried

about you getting on this bike." She says as she reaches behind me and runs her hand over the seat. "Are you sure this is safe?"

"Sweetheart, I know what I'm doing. It's why I called you over here before I head out. I needed to hold you one more time so I could clear my head. My only worry is you sitting by yourself and some knucklehead or bike bunny coming over to bother you. Plus," I start to say, as I give her the once-over look I love to do, "you looking the way you do," I bite my lip, shaking my head, "that's distracting all on its own."

"Sorry." She bites her lip again and gives me a shy look. "I guess I should have planned my outfit better, huh?"

"Nah, I like it. I just don't want *others* to like it!" I give her a scorching kiss in front of our audience so they know she's mine. I'm also hoping it does the trick of centering my mind enough to focus on my bike, my body, and the track. I hear catcalls and whistles coming from the peanut gallery behind Charlie, but I couldn't care less. This, right here, in my arms, is exactly what I need at the moment. All too soon I release her perky mouth and kiss her softly, one last time. Looking down at her, I see she's in a bit of a daze, but she looks happy and calm. I give her one last hug before gently pushing her away.

"One of these days, I'm going to get you on a bike and show you how to ride."

She shakes her head, and laughs as she slowly walks away from me, backwards. She gives me a flirty wink then spins around and sashays back to her seat. *Well, that might just mess with my head for the rest of the day.* I put on my helmet, straddle my bike, rev the gears, and let her rip.

Chapter Eleven

Nate

THREE WEEKS HAVE GONE BY SINCE CHARLIE AND I started dating, and everything is seemingly going well. Even our friends are getting along great. We mostly do things as a group. However, there have been a few times when Charlie and I were able to get away by ourselves. Those times have been some of our best moments. Charlie has opened up to me about her expanding family, and her job as a Receptionist in a doctor's office. She's shared with me about being shy her whole life, and how she likes that I'm helping her break free of that. Even our groups of friends have helped to loosen Charlie up more. I don't want her to completely lose her shyness, though. It would mean losing a part of who she is, and I find that side endearing. It is, however, nice to see her opening up by joining in with the group instead of holding back.

I, on the other hand, haven't really opened up to Charlie in the way she has with me. I tell her as much as I can handle, but there's just one thing that I'm not sure I will ever be able to discuss in detail—with anyone, not just Charlie. I don't even want to think about it, as it makes my heart ache and miss her more. I hope that I've made her proud with my choices in life, in the things I do and how I live. Maybe someday the pain will subside, and I can loosen the hold that these bands have on me and how they affect me in certain aspects of my life. But for now, I choose to keep that part locked securely away.

The morning after Charlie had given me her number, I couldn't help myself and sent her a few text messages throughout the day. I felt like a different man; I'm not used to texting sweet words to a woman, or even checking in on one, for that matter. The only other woman I occasionally talk to is my sister. Otherwise, I haven't done that since Heather Morgan, my old college girlfriend.

Heather and I were in a committed, long-term relationship, with plans to marry, have children, and own a business that we could pass down to our kids someday. Then life happened, and all of that was ripped away. I'm not sure those milestones will ever be on my list of future goals again, but for now, I'm enjoying what Charlie and I have together.

Right now, work is keeping me busy, which isn't a bad thing. Mr. Cates is working us hard and showing us the business, in all its facets. I've made it over to see my family a few times since my last visit. Holt even came out with me the last time. I feel like everything in my life is in a good balance, between work, the home front, our friends, and my girl.

We're taking our relationship slow, and I'm definitely utilizing my right to hold her hand and kiss her in public every chance I can. She's still shy, sometimes, about the kissing part, but doesn't protest much. I know she secretly likes it. There's no pressure on us, which helps the relationship to work the way it should: fun and carefree, yet with an undeniable connection between us. We haven't labeled it, though. For now, she's my girl, and we date exclusively without defining exactly what we are. She hasn't said otherwise, and I'm happy with how it's all going, so why ruin a good thing?

Tonight, Charlie has one of her family dinners in

Sacramento to attend, and I've decided to head to the track, where I'll meet up with the guys, and their women, shortly. They've been spending a lot of time with Naomi and Halley. I'm curious as to where they will end up with those women, as none of us are long-term relationship kind of guys. I have a feeling one or all will eventually fall apart.

The question is, who's going to dive headfirst into forever?

Charlie

"Charlotte, when are you going to stop hiding this new boyfriend of yours and bring him home?" Mom asks me with a frown on her face.

My fork drops to my plate with a loud clatter as the whole table grows quiet. I look at my siblings and wonder who the culprit is. "All right, who spilled the beans before I could—and before I was even ready to?"

Of course, none of my sisters fess up. I'm pretty sure I only told one of them that I was seeing Nathan.

With a loud and long sigh, I face my mother and break the news to her. "Mom, he's not really my boyfriend. We're casually dating, and that's all there is to it. If it grows more serious, you'll be the first to know." I say while glaring at each of my sisters. Even my sister-in-law, Rachel gets the glare.

"Were you even going to tell me? You know you don't have to hide parts of your life from me. I'm your mother. You should want to share with me. Your father and I only want the best for you, honey. We're here to love you, and support you. You know that, right?"

"Mom, I know that. I just don't want you—or *anyone*, for that matter—to blow this up into something bigger than what it is. I don't even know that much about him yet. He's a really nice guy. He works in construction. He rides dirt bikes, and our groups of friends have a lot of fun together. It's only been three weeks since we've officially started something, and we're still in the getting-to-know-you phase. I promise, if it escalates, I'll bring him home to dinner." That's the best I can do at this point, because I know Nathan is a sweet guy and he treats me like a gentleman should. We have a great time together, he makes me laugh, and he has cracked my shell mostly open.

However, I can tell that he's holding back from me, and not fully letting go of his secrets. I haven't met any of his family, and come to think of it, I don't really know much about them at all.

"Sweetheart, she's still 21-years old. We have time with Charlotte, so let's not push her. She'll come around if and when the time is right," Dad tells Mom. "Won't you, Charlie?" He looks over at me, and I can tell he's trying to give me a little reprieve from my family's questions.

Grateful for his intervention, I give him a small smile to show I appreciate what he's trying to do.

"Why don't we talk about something else, like who's up for a round of Monopoly?" Dad asks us with a hopeful voice, but we all just let out loud groans or make excuses about why we can't stick around and play. I feel bad for my dad, but we can only handle his competitiveness in small doses. I know he's just trying to find ways to interact with us and hold the family together, like Mom does with family dinners. We don't actually mind playing these games, deep down. After all, we bet on the side to see who can beat Dad in the next game. It makes it more of a fun challenge that way. But tonight, it seems like no one's up for the challenge. So, my dad lets it go, and the conversation turns to weddings, babies, and work.

Sitting here watching my family interact, I can't help but feel the love and connection we all have with each other. It makes me think about Nathan and his family, and the fact that he doesn't talk much about them. It makes me feel sad for him, knowing that he probably doesn't have the kind of family that I've been blessed with. I do know that one day; I want to give him the chance to experience what I have.

Nate

I knew the minute I set foot on the dirt at the track that I would realize how much I've missed being on my bike. I haven't spent as much time as I would have liked over the past three weeks here, and I feel like a part of me is missing. I need to come out here and touch base with the track—*and myself*—more often.

Tucker and Holt should be here soon. They went to pick up Halley and Naomi. To be truthful, I'm glad Charlie was busy tonight. This is something I felt like I needed to do on my own, to free my spirit by knowing that no one is watching, judging, or distracting me. I don't think Charlie would ever judge me, but she would definitely be watching, which would serve as a major distraction in and of itself.

I know I need to bring Charlie out here more so she can become more comfortable with what I do. She worries a lot about me riding, as she feels this is a dangerous sport. And she's right, it can be dangerous, but I need to calm her fears by showing her that I know what I'm doing, and how awesome it feels to be here. Today just didn't feel like the right timing for that, though.

Today is just about me.

I'm geared up and pushing my bike out to the track when I see that the guys are making their way over to me, with the girls in tow. You can tell the girls are extremely happy to be here, just as much as the guys are to show off for them. Personally, I think Tucker isn't using his head, considering that he could run into Lisa at any given moment. I don't want his drama out at the track. The last thing we need is to make a big scene.

"Tuck, Holt. Ladies," I greet with a two-fingered salute as I continue on my way. I don't have time to sit around for idle chat. I'm losing precious riding time and daylight hours. Plus, I want to be home in time to talk to Charlie before sleep claims us, and the workweek overtakes our days.

Charlie

"All right, which one of you ruined it for me tonight at dinner?" I pointedly ask each of my sisters. We're on kitchen duty, so I take this moment to have a pow-wow with them, knowing it's safe to talk since Mom and Dad are in the living room, relaxing with the guys.

"Hey, don't get all huffy and puffy on us, all right? I was just excited that you finally met someone. I didn't know that blabbermouth over here would say something to Mom!" Bethany shoots Lindsay the evil-eye glare.

"Hey, don't jump all over me. I didn't tell her." Lindsay

looks at Jennifer, so we all turn our eyes her way.

"Oh, give me a break. I have better things to do than to run my mouth off to Mom." She fires back at us.

"That only leaves you, Rachel," Bethany says, looking her way.

Rachel shakes her head. "I swear it wasn't me. So don't go pointing your fingers my way, now. My only guess is Anson. He might have overheard us talking about it and mentioned it to your dad, who would have passed it along to your mom. Don't worry—I know how to make him talk. I'll be right back," she says as she walks out of the kitchen.

We all bust up laughing at that, knowing that if it was him, he's going down once Rachel gets a hold of him. I decide not to say anything further and start cleaning the kitchen.

"Well? That's it?" Jennifer asks.

"No. I'm waiting for Rachel to come back. I have plenty more to say, believe me!"

A few minutes later, Rachel is back with a sad-faced Anson. *Who knows what she promised to hold against him.*

"Look, I'm sorry I said anything to Dad, okay? He and mom were on me about a few things and I just let it slip, to take the pressures off of me. I'm really sorry, Charlie-bear. Forgive me?" He gives me a ridiculous pout that might have worked in the past, but right now, I'm not feeling so forgiving.

Well, not just yet, anyway.

"Here's the deal. I wanted what everyone else got—safe passage from the family before the subject was brought up. Lindsay got three months, if I remember right, and Bethany still has safe harbor with her *two* men." I remind them, cutting Bethany a look. *She seriously needs to pick one already.* "Why couldn't I be afforded the same rights? All I was asking for was at least two months. Do I not rank high enough for respect around here? Who's to say Nathan and I will even work out?"

"We're sorry, sis. We know it can be rough being the youngest in this family. Sometimes, the youngest is just easy pickings. I didn't purposefully set out to sabotage your need for space. It really just slipped out, and I'm really sorry. It was a defense mechanism—you know me." Anson both tries to defend himself and give me an apology, all in the same messed up sentence.

"I know this is a big deal. It's a big deal for me, too. But we're taking it slow. We're exclusive, but we haven't defined our relationship yet. He isn't used to having a serious girl-friend. I'm not even sure when the last time that was for him. So, let's not set the family up for false hope, in case it all goes down the toilet before it can even takeoff. I really like him, so I don't want to push and freak him out. I'm pretty sure I will send him packing if I invite him to dinner here. I haven't even met his family yet. We've only known each other for a total of four weeks. With three of those weeks spent dating, so it's still new and fresh. Just promise me that I won't be blindsided like that again, okay?" I ask all of my siblings and my sister-in-law.

"We can respect that." Lindsay says as she wraps her arms around me in a tight, squeezing hug.

"Careful there, Buff Armstrong. Save your strength to squeeze the life out of your man. Some of us here are fragile, you know." I smile at Lindsay before she lets me go, allowing the others in for a turn.

"All right, it's time to do what you women do best," Anson says.

Oh boy. Rachel is looking like she's ready to chase him with a fire poker from the fireplace.

"And what's *that*, babe?" Rachel asks—clearly waiting for Anson to make the right response.

We all know he won't, though.

"Cleaning," he deadpans. It takes him a second to remember that he's outnumbered before he slowly backs his way up to the entryway. However, for him, it's too late. Rachel starts making her way towards Anson, causing him to start running with her hot on his heels.

"When will he ever learn?" Bethany chuckles.

"This is Anson we are talking about, so my guess is never." Jennifer says, making us all laugh a little more.

"Once Rachel gets her hands on him, he's toast," Lindsay chimes in.

We're all laughing while turning back to our chores in the kitchen when we hear, "*Mom!* Rachel's being mean to me!"

"I'm sure you deserve every bit of it, too." Mom yells back, causing us to lose it again.

"Boys," I say through a big smile as I shake my head.

Nate

"Hey, hot stuff. How was your evening with your family?" I ask Charlie the second she answers my call.

"It went really well. What about you, cowboy? How was your time at the track? No injuries, I presume?" she asks with a hint of worry in her tone.

"No injuries to report, sweetheart. You can stop worrying yourself sick over there. You know the boys would have called if something happened. Anyway, it's exactly what I needed. I hadn't realized how much I was missing the track. I was thinking of taking you out there next weekend. What do you think?"

"Who could say no to seeing you in action again, looking

all hot on that bike!" She giggles into my ear through the phone.

"Charlie, maybe I shouldn't take you out there. That sounds like you're going to be one big distraction."

"I promise to be good. I swear." She laughs.

"Why don't I believe you?" I mutter in response, causing her to lose it.

"Oh come on! I'm the good one in the bunch, remember?"

"Uh-huh. Don't make promises you can't keep, little one."

"We'll see about that."

"So, what really happened at dinner?"

"Oh, the usual—Mom wanting to know what's going on in our lives, Dad trying to get us to play a game with him, and the siblings being troublemakers." She chuckles, describing her evening like it's one of many fond memories.

I wish I had that to offer her, but it will never be that way in our house again.

The spark of pain reminds me it's time for a subject change.

"I'm glad to hear you had a nice time. So, what's on your agenda tomorrow? Do you think you have time for dinner in your busy life?" I tease her, knowing her life consists of work, our friends, and now, mainly me. Every free moment we have is usually shared with each other.

"For you—any time, hon." She replies, shocking me into silence for a moment. Charlie has never used a term of endearment before, unless you count 'cowboy.' I can barely get her to call me Nate, like everyone else does.

"Well, if that's all I had to do to get you to call me something other than Nathan or cowboy, I would have taken you out to dinner every night for the past three weeks." I tease her, making her laugh.

"Oh, hush. Don't make a big deal out of it, or you'll

embarrass me more. Anyway, just text me the details tomorrow, and I'll be ready and waiting for your hotness to show up," she giggles.

I have to admit, I sure do love this playful side of her that's coming out more and more. I already can't wait to see her tomorrow.

"All right, sweetheart, it's getting late, so I'll let you go. Make sure you check in with Halley and Naomi tomorrow and ask about their dirt-coated adventures," I chuckle. "Goodnight, Charlie. Sweet dreams."

"Goodnight, cowboy. Dream of me." I hear her say before hanging up the phone.

I don't think tomorrow can come soon enough for this cowboy.

Chapter Twelve

Charlie

I MEET UP WITH HALLEY AND NAOMI THE FOLLOWING day during my lunch break from work. Of course, it can't be a girls' lunch since Holt and Tucker are with them. These two are clearly head over heels for my two best friends. Holt still seems to be in denial over this fact, but I know one day—it will dawn on him, and he'll wise up. Until then, there's no leading that horse to water unless he completely wants it.

"Guys," I address the group as a whole, as I flop down into a seat at the end of the table. "No Nathan?" I ask the two Stooges.

"Not today. He had to go out to his dad's house. Something's up with his sister, and he went to see what he could do to help out."

"Oh," I say, feeling dejected by this news. *Why doesn't he ever say much to me about his family?* Forming a smile, one that I don't genuinely feel, I look at my friends. "Well, his loss, right?" Everyone silently watches me, but wisely chooses to move on. They either know what's up, or they don't have to worry because it doesn't affect them directly. Clearly, it's time to move on.

"How was the track the other day? Nathan mentioned

something about you girls getting into a dirt-coated adventure?" I eye Halley and Naomi. "What's that all about? And please, tell me it's something good!"

"Do we have to get into this again?" Tucker complains from his end of the table, as he pulls Naomi into his side a little more securely. "I'm really over this chick. She's making my life miserable at the track, and she's definitely ruining it for Naomi as well."

I laugh at his expense—which seems mean, but I can't help it. I'm definitely in a bad mood, now. This is so unlike me, at least when I'm around my friends. My emotions are not in check at the moment, all thanks to Nathan and his lack of trust in opening up to me about his family—and essentially, his life. "Lisa is *still* bothering you? Doesn't she know you have a girlfriend?"

"She doesn't care what I want, or think, obviously. I've been the object of her obsession since high school, and I had no idea until I went out with her, how unstable she would turn out to be. I know she's not clueless. She was the smartest girl all throughout high school. For some reason, she doesn't seem smart in the guy department, though. Or at least not bright enough to take a hint. I can't believe I ever got mixed up with her," he groans.

"Hey, I'm pretty sure we tried to warn you." Holt puts his two cents in. *Which isn't helpful.* I give him the 'shut-up' face, but he studiously ignores me and keeps flapping his big trap. "And since when are you and Miss July over there," he nods to Naomi, as he uses an earlier nickname Tucker gave her when we first met them, "classifying your relationship? That's news to me." I know he's not trying to be a jerk, but he really could have used a little more tact.

"Well, Curly," Naomi enters the conversation, "am I dating you?"

"Touché. Still, are you guys straight up dating, now?"

"Why are we even talking about this? How did it go from Lisa, to my relationship with Naomi?" Tucker asks Holt. "For now, we aren't classifying anything, but we aren't seeing other people, either. It's just me and Miss July. Right, babe?" Tucker smiles fondly at Naomi.

"Right." She softly replies. He kisses her gently on the lips.

I still think they're in denial about their relationship, but since I'm in a foul mood, I'm not going to bring them down with me. Holt's doing a fine job of that for the both of us.

"So, Halley, is Kyle still bothering you? You really haven't mentioned him in a while." Halley's eyes bug out as her head tips towards Holt, before turning her laser beams back on me, trying to incinerate me on the spot.

"Who's Kyle?" Holt tries to ask nonchalantly, without being overly interested but making it sound as if he's only curious. Which I know is a big lie, but whatever.

"He's some guy who works with Halley. He seems to think she really wants to go out with him." I crack up, but I'm the only one, because Halley is really getting agitated, and the other two wisely stay in their own kissy-faced bubble.

"Really." Holt continues to carefully watch Halley, looking as if he's trying to decide something. "Woman, why didn't you say anything? I'm more than happy to help a lady in distress." He wags his brows at her. She rolls her eyes, and then turns her face back to me.

"Thanks a lot for that. The situation is under control, for the time being. Besides, he's too loaded down with work to have any interest in pestering me." She turns back to Holt. "And for the record, Curly, I can handle my own business, thank you very much."

"Halley, I'm serious. You ever need anything, you call me. You have my number. Please, use it day or night." His tone is serious, for once, and sincere. "I don't want one of my good friends to end up hurt."

Halley's face softens at his sentiment. "Thanks, Holt. That really means a lot to me. Trust me, if he becomes more of an issue, you'll be my first call for a rescue maneuver." He gives her a real, genuine smile that I can see knocks her off guard for a moment before she recovers. "So, where's our waitress already? I'm starved!"

I'm sorry, I mouth to Halley, and she waves me off. I know she won't forget, and we will certainly be visiting this subject later, without prying eyes and ears.

"Wait, no one ever did tell me what happened with Lisa!" I decide to re-open that topic, causing the whole table to groan. I give them all a sheepish smile, but forge ahead because I really want to know.

"She was trying to stake her claim on Tucker at the track the other day. Naomi and I are getting pretty sick of the show. It's no longer entertaining. It's really just pathetic. Naomi was snuggled up to Tuck, as she is now, and Lisa 'accidentally' bumped into her, causing her to fall out of the stands and into the dirt. She's a little banged up, but otherwise fine. However, Lisa and I had it out. No way was I letting her get away with that. I know she meant it maliciously," Halley explains to the table.

"You should have seen her, too!" Holt whistles. "She was a beauty, rolling around in the dirt, after mouthing off to Lisa." He gives her a sexy grin of his own. "Anyway, Lisa decided to trip Halley and caused her to fall, too. It wasn't a good situation, and it took me, Nathan, *and* Tuck to get the girls apart. I've never seen Halley so irate before. Remind me to never get on her bad side!"

"Well, I'm glad no one was seriously hurt. I feel bad that happened because Lisa has it out for me. I'm not letting her run me off the track, or dig her nails into Tucker. Karma always has a way of getting even with people. Sooner or later, hers will come knocking." Naomi calmly states.

"Dang. I keep missing all of the good stuff. I really need to get back out there. And even though I love the way Nathan looks all suited up, and in his element—it still makes me nervous watching him." I realize I'm starting to become a Debbie Downer again right when the waitress *finally* shows up. We place our orders and find our way back to a better topic, and leave the weight of the world behind us, along with my bad attitude.

It's been a few weeks since our lunch with the guys, and by the way, Halley did ream me out over my introduction of the Kyle topic. He's only bothered her a few times recently. But otherwise, all seems kosher on the home front, for now.

Tucker has been spending less time on his bike and more time cozying up with Naomi. I suppose this is a good thing. At least they won't have to run into Lisa as much. As for Nathan, we're spending a lot of time together still, but he has yet to open up about his family, so I'm still in the dark about the troubles of his sister—and he has never come up to my folks' place for Sunday dinners. But we're only seven weeks into our relationship, so I'm really not going to try and rock the boat. When the timing is right, I hope he feels comfortable opening up more. Though, I'm a bit hurt he hasn't mentioned his sister's problems to me. And since he's never brought it up, I didn't feel right about prying. I was actually hoping I wouldn't have to pry and he would volunteer it on his own, but he hasn't yet. He's been really busy and distracted lately.

Tonight was another Sunday family affair up in Sacramento, complete with dinner and board games. All of the family's usual suspects were there, plus Greg, Lindsay's fiancé. We had a few good laughs, and for once, no one tried to throw anyone else under the bus with their life's secrets.

Driving home from dinner on the I-80W freeway, I reflect back to the gathering, full of board games and laughter. I still can't believe my dad almost lost to Greg during one of the many rounds we played. The look on his face, when he thought he was about to lose—*priceless*. I wish Nathan had been there to share in the experience with my family. I think he'd fit in with everyone, giving as well as he gets.

I let the air in my lungs pass over my lips with a deep sigh as I approach the long stretch of road from West Sacramento towards Davis. I really don't like this segment. Once you're on it, you can forget about getting off for a bit, which reminds me—*do I have enough gas to make it home?* Quickly glancing down, I see that the gauge is half full, which eases my rattled mind. This is my least favorite part of the drive, from here to Dixon. It's dark out, and tonight, it looks like it's just me, the highway, and no one else. Yep, it's definitely time to kick the radio on so I can stay awake, but to also drown out the noise of the tires on the road.

It's that, or let my mind prattle on about why Nathan doesn't want me to know about his personal life. *Is he hiding something?* I don't really think that's the case, though I can't seem to figure out what his deal is. The darkness of the night seems to be never ending, especially while I feel like I'm on autopilot, and wondering how to bring Nathan's walls down.

"What the heck?" I'm suddenly pulled out of my musings by a strange noise. "What was that?" I frown, looking around the car before trying to inspect the hood out the windshield for any signs of—what exactly, I don't know. "*Great,*" I continue to speak out loud to myself, which is something I do when I'm alone and freaked out. "Please don't let anything be wrong with my car. I just want to make it home to my nice, warm bed." I say, as I immediately shut the radio off, and then lower my speed a tad. I realize I'm gripping the steering wheel a bit too tight. "It's just your imagination," I tell myself, in hopes of calming my nerves.

However, the further I travel, the more I'm sure my Honda doesn't feel right. My stomach starts to tighten as I realize that if my car breaks down, I'll be stranded, completely alone. *Maybe I should get into the other lane?* I know there's a shoulder coming up soon, where I can pull over on. Checking over my left shoulder, I flick on the blinker, then merge to the left lane. As I cross the white bumpy dividers, there's another loud sound, which seems like it's coming from the back of my car. *Why do I have a gut feeling this isn't going to go well?*

I get a little further down the freeway when my stomach drops, because the car is starting to shake. My fingers hurt from gripping the steering wheel so hard. "Please don't be a flat tire!" This is the last place I want to get stuck at. I'm basically in the middle of nowhere, alone, in the dark, without an exit for many, many miles.

If it is a flat, then I'm screwed. I start to panic, because I can't even change a tire. *Why did I never learn how?* "Why didn't the men in my life show me how to change a freaking tire?" I mutter, as I rest my head against the headrest for a quick moment, all the while praying I can make it far enough to find a decently lit place to stop, or to an exit. As long as it's not a dead zone for cell reception I'll be okay, because this area is pretty spotty like that.

"Well, thank the stars." Relief floods my body when I see that the freeway now has a shoulder to the road. "Should I pull over, or keep going?" I'm seriously freaked out that my tire will blow, but I know that this isn't really a good place to stop. Though, I might not have any choice in the matter.

My stomach muscles tighten again as I ponder on what to do, but I feel like I should try to go a bit further. It might be a stupid idea, though I do it anyway. I don't know how much further I go before the right back side of my car starts making a rattling noise. My stomach sinks, and I know something even worse is about to happen. I've been in this position before, and it wasn't pretty.

After another few minutes of driving, my car is shaking—hard. "No!" I groan. "Oh, come on! For the love of my life!" I really don't want to pull over on this creepy freeway. *This stinking car!* It feels like it's falling to pieces. "You can do it! Just a bit further. *Please, just a little further.*" I reach out and pat the dashboard.

Unfortunately, my pleas are ignored a few moments later, while I pull over to the side of the freeway at 11:00 at night. Driving along this route, I've seen no other traffic, coming or going. Concentrating on my breathing, I can do nothing but just sit here, trying not to have a panic attack—even though I'm scared to death.

Just as I start to calm down, I remember what a dope I am. I forgot that I have a cell phone! I swear, sometimes panic mode takes over my logic. Reaching over to the passenger seat, I snatch my purse up and start digging for it. Of all the times to just toss it in this bag! After I fish it out, I swipe the screen, but nothing happens. I start pressing the power button, hoping it was accidentally shut off. But still, nothing happens. "No, no, no, no!" I chant in the silence of the car.

"How could I have a dead phone?" I toss my purse back into the passenger seat, and open the center console, looking for my charger. Not finding it, I lean over and look in the glove box, hoping the portable charger is in there. But of course, it's not. Now I'm seriously ticked off at myself. I chuck the phone on the seat next to me, by my purse. "Why? Ugh, it's too late for this garbage!" I complain to myself, as I lean my forehead on the steering wheel, allowing the tears I was holding back to fall.

Of all nights for this to happen, it had to be when I was on a deserted road! This has to be my worst night ever. I know what I have to do, but I dread it all the same. My stomach feels like one knotted mess. I really wish Nathan had been more willing to come with me to my parents' house. So far, he hasn't been too interested in meeting them.

I really don't want to get out of my car, but I know I have to, so I can try to find an emergency phone. I say a silent prayer, steel my nerves, and climb out, locking the car behind me before I start a trek back to where I know the phone will be.

I'm scared. I'm cold. And I'm giving into my panic and letting my tears completely win the battle against any calmness I might actually still possess. "*You're fine. You're okay. The boogie man is not out to get you.*" I whisper to myself as I walk—for what feels like forever—to the yellow emergency phone.

I finally make it, and dial for help. I tell the person on the other end that I'm stranded, and I give the location to the best of my knowledge. The operator tells me to go back to my car and sit tight, with the windows up and the doors locked. She tells me to put the hazard lights on, and to wait for an officer of the California Highway Patrol to assist me, and not to allow anyone else to lure me out of the safety of my vehicle. My body shivers at the implication of that statement.

I didn't think I could be any more scared out of my skull, thank you very much Miss Operator! Now I have to walk back to the car after that lovely little chat.

And wouldn't you know it, as I walk back to the car, my mind starts to recall all the scary stories I've ever heard about people who hide in ditches and get truckers to pull over before they kill them. Putting a little pep in my step, I hightail it back to the safety of my car. Once I reach the Honda, I fumble with the keys, trying to hit the button to open the doors. I somehow manage to get in, where I settle into the driver's seat still freaking out and trying to calm myself down. I really need to stop listening to the news.

It seems like I'm waiting for eons before I see headlights coming my way. They start to pull off the road, which ratchets up my nerves even more. Hoping it's the police officer that's supposed to rescue me, I can't help but think, *please don't be a crazy person!* A few moments pass as I will the other person not to know I'm here, and to keep moving when the car's flashing red and blue lights light up the night around me, and someone exits the vehicle. As the officer walks toward me, I feel both relieved that my rescue party has arrived, but also nervous, as I remember the stories on the news about people using the app on their phone to impersonate the police. *See? I should totally stop watching the news.*

A tap against my driver's window causes me to jump a mile high, and it scares the life out of me. I look through the window and up to see an officer shining a light in my car. He yells through the glass that it's okay to get out, and that he was sent to help me get my car. He then tells me the name of the operator I was talking to, to verify the story.

I climb out on shaky legs, and with a wet face to boot.

"Ma'am, are you okay?" the officer asks with a great amount of concern.

"I am now. Thank you for coming to get me. I was pretty scared sitting out here all alone."

"I can imagine. I'm glad you stayed in the car with your doors locked. The tow company isn't far behind. I think it would be best if you wait with me in the back seat of the cruiser."

I nod my head in agreement, as I certainly don't want to be out here alone any longer. Though, I would be lying if I didn't admit to feeling slightly apprehensive at the same time. Still, I follow him back to his car, and he lets me in. He sits in the driver's seat and pulls up a computer, then starts asking me questions, filling out a report while we wait for the tow-truck. A short time later, the towing company arrives and hooks my car up. The officer gives him directions to a shop he can leave it at in my town before the man takes off.

"Is there anyone you would like to call, so they know you're okay?"

"Yes. Is it all right if I call my parents?"

"Sure, you can use my cell." He digs his phone out and hands it to me. I immediately call my parents and fill them in on what happened. They're distressed by the news, but glad to know I am safe. Though, my dad wouldn't be my dad if he didn't ask to speak to the policeman before he felt like he could hang up, even knowing I was okay. Of course, he asked the officer for his badge number, his name, the station he worked at, and his license plate number. You know, just in case we had a creeper on our hands, I guess. I'm glad my dad is overprotective.

Sitting in the back of the cruiser, I heave in a deep breath, and then let it go as I watch the tow truck take my Honda away, before the officer drives me safely home.

I wonder if Nathan is worried that I haven't checked in with him yet.

Nate

Holt, Tucker, and I are hanging around in the front room, watching ESPN, as we unwind for the night. I'm getting pretty tired as the night wears on, knowing I need to get to sleep soon, due to work early in the morning.

I couldn't help my frequent glances down at my phone as the time slipped away, looking for any signs of Charlie through a text or maybe a missed call. I can't help but wonder where she is, as I was pretty positive we were supposed to have a phone date. But, apparently that's not the case.

"What's up?" Holt asks, from across the room, in the best recliner we have in the house. "You've been checking your phone all night. Waiting for Charlie to throw you a bone? Someone's a little whipped!" he laughs.

"She was supposed to call when she got home from her parents'. She hasn't checked in yet."

"Shouldn't she be home by now?" Tucker frowns as he checks his phone for the time. "It's well past eleven. That seems a bit late to still be up in Sac-town for dinner with her parents."

"I know. I was just thinking the same thing, but thanks to you guys, now I'm going to worry even more." I sit back on the couch and stab my finger at the contacts list to pull Charlie's number up, and then touch her name so I can call her. I place the phone to my ear and listen to it ring, and that's all I get—more ringing, and then voice-mail. I shake my head at the guys and lean my head back against the couch, dejectedly.

"I can call Halley and see if she's heard from her," Holt offers.

"Yeah, I would appreciate it. Thanks, man." I feel a little bit better with the offer, hoping Halley will know something. It's not like I expect Charlie to have my number memorized. Though, I know it's in her phone, as I made it her number one contact a few weeks back while she wasn't paying attention.

"Hey, babe. Have you heard from Charlie tonight?" I hear Holt say, as I turn my head in time to see his brows furrow. "No, she hasn't checked in with Nate. We thought maybe she had called you, or maybe she was held up at her parents' place?" He shakes his head at me, confirming what I'd already gathered—Halley doesn't know anything, either.

"I'll call Naomi," Tucker quietly offers, so he doesn't interrupt Holt's call.

"Yeah, would you? Thanks. Call me back." Holt hangs up his phone and tosses it with a clatter on the side table. "She says she'll call Charlie's mom, and then she'll call us back."

I nod at him. "Thanks. Tuck is calling Naomi. Maybe she knows something." We both look over at Tucker, who is quietly speaking on the phone. He looks up and shakes his head in a disappointing confirmation. Sighing, I sit up and drag my hand through my hair, then down my face.

"Maybe it's nothing. Maybe her phone died when she got home and she's in bed now, not wanting to bother me so late."

"Would you do me a favor? Would you swing by Charlie's place really quick, and see if her car is home?" Tucker asks Naomi.

"No, don't have her do that. It is way too late for her to be out alone," I admonish Tucker. He just shakes his head at me.

Covering the mouth piece, he says, "Its okay, she was about to suggest it herself. She's a bit worried, and said this doesn't seem like Charlie at all." Then he goes back to his conversation.

"Well, nothing we can do until we hear back from Halley, anyway," Holt states.

"I'm going over there myself, even if I have to pound the door down, and her neighbors call the police. I want to make sure she's okay." I stalk down to my room and grab my coat, truck keys, and a baseball cap. I turn to leave the room when all of a sudden Tucker is standing there, leaning against the door frame.

"Why don't you wait until one of the girls' calls us back?"

"If this were Naomi, would you sit around and just wait for a call?" I raise my brows at him.

He shakes his head. "I would want answers, too. Though, I bet you're rattled for no good reason. Calm down and wait it out a few more minutes."

"I'm headed to Charlie's. You can come or you can stay, but I'm leaving in two minutes." I say, as I shoulder past him, and head back down the hall to the living room. "Any word from Halley?" I ask Holt.

"She says Charlie left her parents around 10 pm. But— there was a problem, which left her stranded on the side of the freeway." I start to panic before Tucker clamps his hand down on my right shoulder. "She's fine, Nate. She was able to get help and now she's on her way home. She should be there soon."

"Thank Halley for me, will you? I'm going to make sure she's okay with my own eyes. Are you guys coming, or staying?" I call over my shoulder as I walk towards the front door. "I'm sure Naomi and Halley will be there, too." I can't help feeling guilty for not going with her to Sacramento. She hasn't asked me to these dinners, directly, but she's hinted around a lot that I should come. If I had gone, then she wouldn't have been stranded on the side of the road, late at night, all alone. I feel like the biggest jerk at the moment.

I slam the door on my way out, ticked at myself for not being better to her. I know her car isn't in the best shape. I should have taken her there myself, in the truck. Shaking my head at myself, I unlock the door and climb into the cab of my Ford. Just as I start the engine, there's a knock at the passenger side window. Both Holt and Tucker are standing there. I press the unlock button, and they hop in.

"You won't do her any good if you go over there like a maniac. She didn't get hurt, or robbed, or anything else. Her car broke down, and she's fine. Just remember that." Holt says, though it's not at all helpful in lulling me into a sense of peace.

"Look, she was a woman traveling late at night on a dark highway, in a car that's not the greatest. I should have taken her myself. And another thing—even if she wasn't in a bad accident or other trouble, it doesn't mean I won't stop worrying over her wellbeing." I shake my head in annoyance at the guys, but mainly mad at myself. *They just don't get it.*

"You may think we don't understand, but we do. We may not be in committed relationships, and neither are you—if I have to remind you, but we would be worried if it were one of our girls, too." Tucker says quietly from the back of the cab.

"You sure have a funny way of showing it." I huff out, even more pissed off at them.

Ten minutes later, we pull into Charlie's apartment complex. I find a spot, close enough to her apartment, and then jog over to where I see Halley and Naomi. "No word yet?" I'm anxious for any bit of information at this point.

"Not yet, but I'm sure she's fine, and we're all overreacting. She's probably going to be more upset when she sees all of us when she gets here." Halley tells us.

"Tough. She'll just have to deal with having overprotective friends, and if she—"

I start to go off, but my words take a flying leap. At this

very moment, I see a CHP cruiser pull into the lot, and making its way towards us. We all stand here, waiting patiently, when really, I just want to rip the back door open and hug her tightly to me.

The car stops in front of where we're all standing, before an officer gets out. He eyes each of us, and then looks back at Charlie, who's sitting in the back seat of the squad car like a common criminal. She looks all wrong sitting there.

"Are you friends of the young lady I just brought home?" he calmly asks the group as a whole.

"Yes. I'm Charlie's good friend, Halley." She reaches out and shakes his hand. "Thank you for bringing her home. Her boyfriend," she nods at me, "was starting to worry. We called her parents in Sacramento when they told us she had car issues."

"Is she okay?" Naomi asks him quietly.

"Why don't you ask her?" he smiles at us, then let's Charlie out of the back seat. Before anyone can do, or say anything, I'm there faster than a heart can beat, hugging her with all of my strength.

She snuggles into my chest, and it feels like the weight of the world has been lifted off both of our shoulders in that moment. I kiss the top of her head, breathing in her scent. "I'm sorry, sweetheart. I should have gone with you tonight to your parents' house. Are you okay?" I ask, as I gently pull her slightly away from my chest, so I can see her pretty face.

"I am now." She smiles up at me, but I can see that she has been crying. There are dark circles under her eyes making her look worn out. She pulls away and looks at our friends. "What are you all doing here?"

"We heard you had car problems from your mom. We were worried, and called the girls to see if you had checked in when you missed your phone call with Nate." Holt supplies her with the answer she's searching for.

"I'm so sorry you all were dragged into this!" She ducks her head in embarrassment. I pull her back to me, hugging her around her shoulders.

"Don't even worry about it. This is what good friends do, right?" I wink at her. She shakes her head, and then lowers it against me.

"Thank you for the rescue, and the ride home." She tells the officer.

"It was my pleasure, and I'm glad it all ended well. It's good you have a nice group of good friends to come home to." He reaches into his car before handing over his card. "Here's my number, in case you need any further assistance. Don't forget to call the tow company tomorrow about your vehicle." He waves to the rest of us, and tells us to have a safe night, before pulling back out of the lot.

"Since you're all here, you may as well come in. I know you must be patiently awaiting the tale of my adventure." Charlie says, just as a big yawn over takes her breath.

"It's well after midnight now. I think we can leave it alone until tomorrow." I eye the rest of the group, but Charlie is shaking her head in protest.

"It's all right. Let's go in and get it over with. I'm so tired, I could sleep for days! I'll be in no shape to reminisce over my little journey tomorrow, either."

I gently tug Charlie's hand to pull her back for a moment, while the others climb the stairs to her apartment. I know they'll let themselves in, seeing as how the other girls' have a key.

"Charlie—" I start, but she stops the apology before it can form on my lips, with her index finger.

"Nate," she looks up at me with those beautiful eyes, and they get me every time. I'm a goner, and I don't even know how that happened. I can't believe I let it happen, but for now, I don't care. I just care that she's safe and I can hold her in my arms before I have to go home. "It's enough that you're even here. Thank you." She whispers the words, as she goes up on her toes, and I lean down the rest of the way to complete the kiss she's trying to bestow upon me. I relish her sweet kiss, wrapping my arms around her so I can feel her body pressed against mine. All too soon she pulls away and reaches for my hand to lead me up to the rest of the gang.

We're all piled into her living room as she explains about her tire blowing out on the freeway in the worst stretch of it, and being scared out of her mind all the while. Her phone battery was dead, hence why she didn't call me, or anyone else for that matter. She had to use the officer's phone to call her parents. I'm just grateful nothing major happened, and she was able to use an emergency phone to call for help.

Still, I should have been there. I get up and start to pace a little bit, while the others talk to Charlie for a few minutes more, before they all head home. I feel a hand on my arm, halting my next steps. I look up to see Holt and Halley watching me.

"It's not your fault, you know. You can stop blaming yourself. Charlie certainly doesn't blame you, either. We're headed out now. See you in the morning." He slaps my back while Halley squeezes my arm, then they walk out the door together. A few moments later, Naomi and Tucker leave, as well, officially leaving me alone with Charlie. That doesn't happen too often, and sometimes it feels a bit awkward to not have a bunch of others around.

I'm still facing the door, thinking of what to say to her when I feel her wrap her arms around my waist. She leans her head against my back and I feel my body lose a little bit of the fight it had pulsing within me. I lay one hand over hers, and give it a little squeeze, relishing this moment in her arms. It doesn't happen often, so I take it whenever she gifts me with it.

"You're going to worry yourself to death. Stop," she gently commands. "You're not to blame. Who could have predicted my car would have caused me such havoc? It was bound to happen, and I'm no worse for wear and in one piece. No bad accident." She squeezes my middle.

"I'm still going with you next time, and we won't be driving your car." I slightly shake my head at her. "I don't want to hear any lip about it, either." I firmly close any more discussion on the matter at hand. "Now, we should discuss you getting a backup phone, and another charger. I'm not pleased that you were stranded, without a way to reach me, or your parents, unless you had to leave the safety of your car. But that's a discussion for another time. It's one in the morning, and we're both shot. You need to go to sleep, little one, and I need to head out. Six comes too early." I spin around, knocking her off balance. She presses into me close, but I notice she doesn't say anything else about the car, dinner, or a new phone.

"I was so scared, with a lot running through my head— however, I remember thinking a lot about not being able to let you know what had happened. It's late, and I know you're exhausted, but it means a lot to me that you care enough to come over here in the middle of the night to check on me."

I kiss the top of her head, but don't say anything more. There's nothing left to say. I would do it again, in a heartbeat. Any guy would for their friends, or their best 'exclusive' friend.

And here's one perfect reason why I stay away from attachments. Tonight, she could have been seriously harmed, had there actually been a severe accident, with the possibility of death. Am I over-thinking this? *Yes*. But, with my experience, you can never be too safe, and if you aren't prepared, that's when life takes a bite out of you. She has me tied up in knots, and is forcing my possessive urge to take care of her. Let's not forget I felt the need to drive her to Sacramento the next time around and voluntarily agreed to meet her family. *Am I ready to take this relationship, as it is, that far?* That's something I need to ponder on, later—*much later.*

Pushing those thoughts to the side, I focus on what we have, right now—not what the future holds. "Give me a kiss so I can leave, or you'll end up with an overnight guest. I'm a terrible bed hog, too." She giggles, but does as she's told, and gives me a kiss.

"Who's to say you wouldn't end up on the couch?" she taunts me.

"Hey, I didn't imply you could sleep in the bed, too." I say, in mock outrage. "The couch seems good enough to me. I think you'll be just fine out here."

She pinches my waistline, shaking her head. Though, I see her trying not to crack a smile. "If it's good enough for me, then it's far better for your hulking size."

"Smart aleck." I snatch her up and toss her on the couch. "See? The couch *is* perfect for a little runt, such as yourself!" We're both laughing, and I decide to push my luck by tickling her. She tries to get away from me, as she's laughing pretty hard now at this point, but I keep at her for a tad longer before letting her up.

"That's it! You broke the sleep over rule." She says, even though she's trying to be serious, while pushing herself up into a seated position.

"I hate to break it to you, little one, but I don't play by the rules." I wiggle my brows at her. "Haven't you learned that yet?" I tease her.

"Don't you have a bed to find?" She's grinning at me.

"You wound me!" I give her my best sorrowful look. "Trying to kick your man out after he was so worried about you? I see how it is."

She leans over and shoves me back onto the couch, then props her elbows up on my chest, holding up her chin. "So, cowboy. What's it going to be?"

I intently stare into her eyes, searching her face, before I make up my mind, as I know this is not a good idea—*for the time being*. "As much as I want to see your hair looking like a ratted mess when you wake," I wink at her, "I think its best that I head home." She doesn't look sad or put out by my answer. We both knew what the final answer would be. I can see it in her eyes, and neither one of us is ready to go there, just yet.

She pushes off of me, and then reaches down and pulls me up and off the couch. I hug her one last time, needing the contact of our two bodies, even if I know being more intimate isn't where this is headed, before I force myself to leave. I give her a final kiss on her forehead, and then head out—stopping on the porch until I hear the lock click, before finding my way back to my truck.

I'm not sure what I'm doing, when it comes to pursuing a deeper relationship with Charlie, but I might need to get my priorities straight, sooner rather than later, I deduce before I point my truck towards home.

Chapter Thirteen

Charlie

"What do you think? Is this hot, or just okay? Or should I find something hotter?" Halley contemplates aloud, as she holds up a black and turquoise semi-modest bikini. *Is there even such a thing as a modest bikini? Well, modest for her, at least.* I admit to loving the two-tone color, but I wouldn't be caught dead—or alive—in it. *It's not my style.*

"It's definitely cute, and it suits you. I don't think you should break the bank on looking too illegal, though." I jest, chuckling at her pouty face. "I think you should go for it." I insist, while moving through the racks, trying to find something I wouldn't mind Nathan catching me in. I'm more of a conservative dresser than Halley is, and even Naomi, at times. She's the happy medium between the three of us. "I don't think Holt will be able to concentrate on fishing, or anything else for that matter, if he gets a glimpse of you in it."

"Was I being that obvious?"

I grin in her direction. "No, I just know how you operate. Don't over think it."

It's Wednesday evening, and right now, the girls and I are out shopping for clothes, due to an impromptu camping trip with Nate and his friends. It's been a couple of weeks since my car situation, and I have since learned it had a few issues besides the tire that needed fixing. In the end, I had to get new brakes, two new tires, and wheel hub bearings—which were not in my budget planning for the present to near future, so I ended up calling my dad to help bail me out.

"Oh, that's really cute, Naomi!" Halley exclaims. "Right, Charlie?"

Naomi's holding up a blouson-style tankini. The bottoms are black, but the top is made up of turquoise, purple, and lime green, with accents of white and black. It has an Aztec theme to it. "It's totally you, Naomi. I would put that in your buy pile."

I continue browsing down the row, looking for a suit I would wear. "Do you think Nathan uses our group activities to hide behind so he can keep me at an arm's length away?" I blurt, completely out of the blue. It's something I've been contemplating this for a little while now but too scared to put a voice to it.

Halley and Naomi stop their musings over shorts and tank tops to look at me with expressions of shock and confusion on their faces.

"What?" Naomi recovers first.

"Is there anything specific that would make you jump to this conclusion?" A baffled Halley asks. If she's baffled, then I'm probably imagining things. She's a good judge of character, usually. She would have been the first to point something out, if there was something at all.

"Never mind. I don't even know why I brought it up," I murmur, moving away from them and letting the conversation drop.

"Now hold on a minute. Was there something to make you speculate?" Naomi questions.

I give her a small shrug. "Nothing that he flat-out said, or even did, really."

"Then what's the matter? Obviously there's something bothering you," Naomi points out. She looks at Halley, whom gives her a little shake of her head.

"I think it's a bit strange that we have more group hang-outs than we have one-on-one dates. Not that I don't love hanging out with everyone!" I backpedal. "I just feel that Nathan is holding himself back from me."

"To be honest, I hadn't really thought anything was off, in regards to that." Halley admits. *Well, that surprises me.* "I think Holt has my radar all scrambled, sorry." She quietly grumbles.

"There's no need for apologies. Really, it's probably just me. I mean, I feel this intense connection with him. It's been three months, roughly, and I feel like I'm still in the 'getting to know you, but not quite know you' phase. He never opens up about his family. Why does he keep me in the dark?" I look to my friends, in hopes that they might have some insight.

Both girls give me a pitying look, but don't answer. *But really, if I can't answer it, then how can I expect them to?*

"Anyway, I don't want to put a damper on this trip. I don't even know why I blurted it out in the first place." I move to the last rack of swimsuits and start pawing through them. Halley and Naomi don't let me get away with shirking the conversation, though, as I look up and find them eyeing me over the rack.

I give them a pleading look.

"Fine. I don't like it, but just for this weekend, we will let it go. Right, Naomi?" Halley pointedly asks her.

I can see that Naomi wants to protest, but in the end, it dies out before it can form into actual words. She gives Halley and I a disapproving look, though. Not surprising.

"I know. I'm sorry. I promise we can dive into the deeper meaning of it all when we get back." I hold up my pinky so we can do the silly, girly ritual pinky swear. It's something we've done since we were younger, and, just like always, she gives in and lets the subject drop until a later date.

"Finally!" I semi-shout minutes later, while pulling a swimsuit off the rack and holding it up to my body for the other two to inspect.

I found a black one-piece, with one white strap sweeping across the top in a diagonal crossing where another piece twists around it and connects to it. There's a little peek-a-boo triangle cutout between the top of the suit and the strap that sits high over the left breast. I really like the gathering that encompasses the suit from the top to the hip area.

"Oh, Charlie! That's the one. You're buying it. There's no fighting it, either." Halley commands me, as if I had planned to protest against the idea.

"I wouldn't even dream of it." I can't help but grin from ear to ear. I may have my doubts about Nathan's heart, but at least I'll look and feel like a million dollars this weekend. "I think we only need a few tank tops, shorts, and sunscreen, right?"

We continue our shopping expedition, like my crazy thoughts hadn't spilled out, and get into the spirit of the exciting upcoming weekend.

Nate

It's been two weeks, and so far, I haven't been called upon to take Charlie to Sacramento for dinner with her family.

However, this could put a potential strain on our relationship if I don't make an effort to participate at some point. I know I'm being unfair to her, but I'm not ready to crack open my emotional baggage just yet. Up to this point, we've been enjoying ourselves, and spending a lot of time with our friends. I see no reason to rock the boat. If it can stay like this, then why make any waves? Hopefully, we can just continue on as we have been.

The guys and I decided it's time for a camping trip, as it's been too long since our last one. Also, I thought it was time to get away from the women, and do our own thing. That was the plan at least, until Tucker mentioned it to Naomi in passing. That wasn't smart, since we all know by now that once Halley catches wind of something, she barges her way in until it's a full-fledged group outing.

Though, the more I think about it, I'm not completely upset, or even opposed to the women tagging along, as it does give me full on access to Charlie, yet, we'll still have enough of an audience around that it feels safe to be alone with her.

Friday morning comes soon enough as the guys and I are making some last minute preparations for our trip, while waiting for the women to arrive. We decided that it was best for them to park at our house rather than Charlie's apartment complex, where the parking is limited for overnight guests.

I had just finished adding a few more things to the bed of my truck, and then checked to make sure everything is tied down when Halley shows up in her own truck. I let a whistle fly to the guys from the driveway, alerting them to the presence of the women as they start to climb down from the cab.

I see Charlie first, in her cutoff shorts, t-shirt, flip-flops, and a ball cap. She looks pretty sweet in her camping gear. She sees me right away and gifts me with one of her bright smiles. Once she gets to me, I lift her off her feet and swing

147

her around.

"Hey, Charlie." I kiss her right there, in the front yard, for the whole street to see. She giggles as she wraps her arms around my neck, hanging on. I get the impression she's not about to let me go, and I mean that in more ways than one.

"You're in a cheery mood, little one." I smile up at her, as I've yet to place her back on her feet. She wraps her legs around my waist, and keeps her arms loosely draped around my neck. She leans in and kisses me again.

"I had a handsome cowboy to see. Besides, I get him all to myself this weekend. Who could deny my excitement over that?" She winks at me.

"Should I be jealous of this so-called man?"

"Are you sure you're a man?" Holt slaps me on the back as he bypasses me to collect his own woman in a bear hug. We hear her squeak as he lifts her high off the ground in a similar fashion.

I shake my head and look back up into Charlie's eyes. I can see so much joy and happiness in them. I know that's all for me—there's no denying it. I let that feeling slide through me, and it might feel good, but it sure scares the life out of me. This weekend isn't for sentimental feelings, though. It's for fun and making crazy memories. I put Charlie back on her feet and tug on her hand to help me check on their luggage.

We round the back of Halley's truck just in time to hear Tucker whistle. "What did you women pack? It's just a two-day camping trip!" he exclaims.

"This is why women shouldn't be allowed on a man's outing." Holt shakes his head in disapproval as he eyes the truck bed full of the women's luggage.

"Oh, come on!" Halley protests. "We didn't bring that much, just the bare necessities. Stop being such babies about it."

"Woman!" I guess that sums up everything Holt has to say about the matter.

"Well, what are we waiting for? Let's transfer this to the other truck and get going!" Halley bounces on the balls of her feet with sheer excitement, reminding me of a little girl who can't contain herself, giddy on Christmas morning.

"You heard your woman. Stop being lazy, and make yourself useful." I biff Holt on the back of the head, and then duck before he can cuff me back.

Charlie smiles at our boyish antics, and moves to the side so we can get their stuff moved over. I jump into the bed of the truck first, and start handing everything out to any willing, and available, hands. Fifteen minutes later, we're all piled into my truck as I drive, with Charlie perched at my side. Holt claimed the passenger seat, while the other three climbed into the back cab. I flip on the radio, tune it to a favorite country station, and then we hit the road to *Lake Berryessa*.

It takes a little over an hour to arrive at our destination. I pull up to the gate of the Pleasure Cove Marina portion of the lake, and park. "I'm going to check in. I'll be right back." I give a gentle squeeze to Charlie's left knee, and then hop out to check in and grab our parking pass. About ten minutes later, I'm back in the truck, and we're all headed towards our campsite.

"Who knows how to pitch a tent, besides one of us men?" Holt has the audacity to ask.

"Are you insinuating that we women are clueless when it comes to camping?" Halley scoffs at what we know to be in true Holt fashion, when it comes to being a hotheaded male in all things outdoors-related.

"You're reading too much into my statement. It was an innocent question."

"This time." Halley, it would appear, can't resist to comment.

"So—" Naomi interjects, "what are the sleeping arrangements, anyway? I heard you guys were supplying the tents, right?"

"Don't worry, babe. We've got you covered." Tucker pipes up from the backseat. "We have all of you covered. We brought the eight-man tent. Just need some willing hands to help set it up, and then to load all of our gear inside. Once we get everything underway, we can worry about lunch. Maybe Holt wants to stick his foot into that statement?" Tucker chuckles.

"If he knows what's good for him, he won't tick his woman off any further, so the rest of us can have fun." I add to the conversation. Charlie leans her body up against my side and snuggles into me as we're just about to pull into our campsite.

"All right, everyone. Listen, up! All hands on deck, as soon as I park, for setup. No lip, either. Yeah?" I can feel Charlie shake with silent laughter next to me as the others roll their eyes and jump out of the truck once we've parked.

"That's one way to clear the truck. How about you lock the doors, and we stay here for some quality time on our own?" Charlie shyly flirts with me.

"I think you're an excellent mind reader. I love that you're willing to sacrifice them to do all of the grunt work, just so we can steal a few moments of make-out time. My kind of woman." I smirk as I lean in to nuzzle her cheek with my nose. Just breathing in her shampoo and lotion does all kinds of things to me.

"What have you done with my shy, innocent, little Charlie?" I whisper to her. I don't give her time to reply as I reach out and hit the button to lock the doors. I tilt her face towards me and gaze down at her for a moment.

"What are you waiting for?" she coyly asks.

I answer her by pulling her into my lap, allowing my hands to slide into her hair, and pulling her down so our lips just barely meet. I yearn to kiss her soft and slow—at first— then build it up with that sweet burn she gives me each time we kiss. I love the feel of her lips as they caress mine, and the taste of her tongue while she supports her body against my chest. Charlie wraps her arms around my neck, holding me firmly to her, and picks up the pace of the kiss while my right hand slips down her back and up again.

That's when we hear the *thump* against the window, breaking the nice illusion that we were all alone. Charlie buries her head into my neck, giggling. I don't even bother to acknowledge the person at the window. Instead, I take a few more moments to savor the feeling of holding Charlie on my lap, without any other outside influences.

I let her climb off of me, and then we both make our grand exit from the truck to whistles, hoots, and laughter.

"Yeah, yeah. You all were wishing you had thought of it first." I laugh, slinging my arm around Charlie's shoulders as we head towards the pile they made of all of our belongings.

"Next time we won't fall for it, when you try to issue orders." Tucker grins at me, sitting next to Naomi in one of the camp chairs we brought with us.

"Let's get camp set up so we can get lunch started," Naomi chimes in. "We want to check out the lake today before it gets dark."

So, that's exactly what we do. The guys and I get the tent all laid out and start putting it together while the women do whatever it is they're doing, away from us. I hope they're going through the food and getting something prepared for us. I know we're all starved.

"Don't you think they should come over here and learn how to put a tent up?" Holt questions Tucker and I. "If we plan on having them come with us in the future, it would be good to start teaching them these types of chores so they can help."

"I hadn't thought about anything beyond this weekend of camping. It's not a bad idea, though," Tucker admits. I nod in agreement.

"But, I'm too hungry to want to deal with it now. Let them fix lunch for us first." They look at me like I'm from outer space. "Wait. I didn't mean it like that. I'm just hungry, and they look like they're okay with making something for all of us. Don't give me those crazy looks. I'm not the one with the snarky comments," I pointedly look at Holt. He gives me his stupid trademark smirk.

"Whatever. I say we go figure out lunch, then we can come back and have them learn the ins and outs of setting up a tent." Tucker decides for the group.

"Seriously, you all are making a big deal out of nothing. It's just a tent. Anyone can read the instructions and figure it out." We hear Halley say as we turn around to catch her staring at the tent, then back to us.

"Don't worry, we fully plan on teaching you. But first, we're starving. What did you ladies make?" Holt asks her.

"Nothing fancy, since the pit isn't up yet—or any other cooking gear, for that matter."

"Well?" he asks again.

"Oh, just sandwiches, fruit, chips, and potato salad. Like I said, it's nothing fancy." She turns and walks back to the picnic table, then starts dishing the salad portions onto each plate.

"Who cares? I'm starving. Let's eat!" Tucker walks away, leaving Holt and I to follow in his wake.

After lunch, we teach the women how to properly clear the ground, lay the tent out, and get all of the poles, stakes and ties for the tent ready for assembly. We get it up in 20 minutes, and then add our gear to the inside of the massive space. It's a nice warm day so we take the women down to the lake and play in the water for a bit. Tucker brought a Frisbee and a football, so we have a couple of options for activities beyond playing in the water.

It's not until later in the evening, as we're sitting around the campfire, wrapped in blankets, that someone suggests we roast marshmallows and share ghost stories. You know—the typical campfire cliché. It wouldn't be a decent camping trip without creepy stories and roasted 'mellows, I suppose.

"Isn't this the Kodiac Killer's old stomping grounds?" Holt, donning his best innocent face, asks the group. I know what he's up to. He wants to scare the women with something that happened ages ago. Shaking my head and quietly laughing to myself, I play along. I can't help it. Everyone's heard of this guy, but still—it's creepy to speak of it, especially at night. *Isn't that when all of the real evil comes out to play?*

"You know, now that you mention it, I think it is." I look at Charlie, and she doesn't look too thrilled about this new piece of information. I watch as she draws the blanket around her shoulders a little tighter before she burrows into it.

"Yep!" Tucker decides to get in on the act, too. "He came out here to kill a college-aged couple."

"Right," I pick up the story. "They were out here one early evening, relaxing on a blanket at the shoreline. They noticed the tall, heavy build of a man in a strange costume approaching them, holding a gun. He claimed he was an escapee from a prison, and needed money and a car so he could get to Mexico."

"That's right, but he didn't take the money or keys the young man was offering him. Instead, he had planned to kill them." Tucker adds to the story.

"He tied them up with a plastic clothesline and started stabbing them. He stabbed the young woman like ten times, and the man six times," Holt continues on with the story. "After he attacked them, he calmly walked away. Eventually, the couple started screaming for help. A local fisherman heard them, came to see what was happening, then called the local park rangers. By this time, they had gotten themselves untied. She died, but he was only wounded."

"Well, that was ages ago. We don't even know that it was in this area of the lake." Halley says, looking over at Charlie's face and then back to us.

"Are you sure it was at *Lake Berryessa*?" Charlie's face is a bit pale as she whispers her question.

"That happened in the very late '60s, Charlie. There's nothing to worry about," Naomi reassures her.

"Good thing there's a big group of us, and I highly doubt we need to worry about anything crazy like that this week-end," she gives each of us guys a quelling look. "Besides, there are a lot of people around. You're just as safe here as you would be at home—*alone*." Halley tries to reassure her.

"Umm—do you guys mind if we don't talk about creepy stories?" Charlie quietly asks us, wrapping her arms around herself.

"What's wrong, Charlie?" Tucker asks. "We're just trying to pull your chain. That was the only incident from that crazy guy up here. It happened so long ago, no one even knows the details in our generation, anyway."

"I just don't like scary things. Real, fake—you name it. It just messes with me." She looks at me for assistance. I pull her into my arms and hug her closely to me.

"All right, little one. We'll change the topic," I assure her. "I wouldn't let anyone harm you, you know that, right?" I kiss the top of her head. She nods under my chin, and we move on from the scary stories.

As the night wears on, I start feeling horrible about scaring Charlie. She seems worried, and hasn't left my side—not even for the bathroom when the other women went together. Later that night, in the tent, Charlie makes me zip the flap closed, though we usually like to sleep with it open and watch the stars as we shoot the breeze. She also places her sleeping bag between me and Holt, making Tucker sleep at the ends of our feet. I can't help but smile to myself. *Who knew Charlie scares so easily?* That's okay with me, as it affords me all kinds of moments to hold her, both now and later down the road.

And there's that thought again, the one I need to shove out of my head so I can enjoy my weekend without complicating it with deep feelings or emotions. I feel a pang in my chest at that thought, but I'm not willing to explore it right now.

Charlie

Waking up the next morning, feeling the sting of the chilled air as it hits my face, just pushes me to burrow further into the warmth of my sleeping bag. And that's when it strikes me that I'm nestled between two hot guys. *Yeah—who wouldn't wake up happy?* I stretch out a bit, but then snuggle back down to get toasty again. It might be a warm month, but it's definitely cold in the morning up here in the mountains.

I can't help it, and decide to sneak a peek at the others. Looking to my left, I see the back of Holt's messy head of hair sticking up from the top of his bag. I quietly giggle, and then

155

roll over to look to my right, to check on Nathan, only to find him lying on his side, propped up on one arm with his head cocked into his hand. I can feel the blush stain my cheeks as he caught me checking him out. I give him a little sly smile, then bury my head into my sleeping bag, trying not to laugh out loud and wake up the others.

From deep under my shield, I hear Nathan chuckle before he peels the sleeping bag down over my head to uncover my face.

"Good morning, Charlotte." He says in a quiet, but rough, sleepy rasp. I look up to find him smiling down at me. "What do you say we share some body heat before we have to ditch this Popsicle stand?"

In the past, I would have balked at an idea such as that, but right now, I'm so cold, and it *is* Nathan, after all. I really don't want to be shy, or feel hesitant this morning. I'm still trying to break that boring shell I live in, though I still surprise myself at times with my boldness. Today, however, I don't have any shame. I inch my way to his side as he unzips my sleeping bag before unzipping his. He scoots closer to me, and we snuggle into each other, while he rearranges the covers and wraps his arms around me, hugging me to his chest. I let out a sigh of contentment while we enjoy the sounds of nature going on all around us outside of the tent, accompanied with a light snore coming from someone inside.

"What are we doing today?" I ask from the comfort of Nathan's arms.

"I thought we would spend the day on the lake. Maybe get a few hours of fishing in."

"Oh! I'm definitely in for swimming, or hanging on the boat. It sounds perfect, but not so pleasant with this morning's temperature."

"The mountains are good like that. Don't worry, as the

morning wears on, the weather will warm up." He runs his hand down my back, then back up to twist it into my hair. Tugging my head back, he places a kiss on the corner of my lips. "We can't have the brisk air ruining my fun of seeing you in a bathing suit, now can we?" he whispers into my ear, sending shivers down my body. "Cold?" He laughs.

"If I weren't in the position of getting chilled to death, I would smack you one," I laugh.

"I think it's time we all wake up and vote on someone making breakfast and something hot to drink," we hear a hoarse Halley grumble. "Though, just saying—that someone won't be *me*." I look up into Nathan's eyes to find the mirth playing in them.

"It won't be Charlie, or I. Whoever wakes up last is the lucky winner," Nate announces, just as Tucker rolls over and bangs his face into Nate's feet, as they're tangled into mine. I can't help the laugh that comes out of my mouth, sending Nate into a fit of laughter, too. Before we know it, Holt is lying on top of us, and then Tucker joins in on the dog pile—sore face and all, I'm sure.

"Punishment for Nate's big feet jumping out and attacking my face," Tucker grunts.

"*Boys.*" Naomi cracks up, and a moment later, I'm pretty sure she jumped on top of them to weigh Nate and I down even more. I'm laughing so hard, but it really is getting hard to breathe. I'm lucky Nathan has me cocooned in his strong arms, as he rolls to try and shove the human weights off of us.

"I'm not making food—unless you want me to burn it," Holt states.

"I knew your beauty outshined your intelligence." Halley teases him.

"I outshine in many ways, Woman. Just wait and see." He winks at her.

Eventually, everyone in the pile moves to get up and start the day. I don't even know what time it is, but I'm starving. Though, I'm not ready to truly brave the biting cold air just yet. But I know I don't have a choice the second I feel strong arms lift me up and sling me over a strong shoulder, eliciting a yelp out of me.

"I think Holt's asking for instant karma to smack him upside his big, hot head." Naomi laughs, as she crawls out of the tent.

"What? We need a cook! I'm enlisting this little camper right here."

"And if you swat her bottom, you'll find instant karma faster than you can count to one." I hear Nathan warn Holt.

"I wasn't really going to touch her fine behind. Fine, I'll save all of my caresses for Halley." I take that moment to slap his rear before I find myself being pried away and back into Nate's arms.

"Thanks, cowboy." I lean back into his embrace. "Was he really going to swat me?" I laugh, as I can't believe Holt would actually do that.

"Only just to mess with Nate." Holt chuckles, then climbs out of the tent right after Tucker, and immediately followed by Halley.

"Now you've done it, Curly," we hear her tell Holt as their voices get further away.

"You're not mad, are you?"

"Nah. I just like to bust his chops. Though, I don't want to see another man's hands on you, little one. Or yours on another mans." he levels his eyes on me then kisses my head, before he lets me go to exit the tent.

I end up helping Naomi and Tucker with a breakfast of pancakes, bacon, and fried eggs. After we clean up, we head to the bathrooms to freshen up and change. It may be 10:30

in the morning, but no one is ready to go swimming just yet. During breakfast we decided to take a bit of a hike and check out our surroundings before lunch. After lunch, the guys plan to fish on Nate's fathers' boat that they hauled up here too, while us women swim and lay out in the warm sun.

After the hike—which was filled with pretty scenery but basically uneventful, and a lunch of sandwiches and chips, we get the boat situated into the water and take off towards the middle of the lake. Once the guys have their poles set up, they crank up Tim McGraw on the radio, and the girls and I relax on the deck while trying to catch the afternoon rays. Before long, I feel a set of fingers feathering up and down my spine. It feels good, and I instantly know its Nate.

"Did you put any sunblock on, little one?" His voice is lazy, yet a bit of concern can still be detected in his tone. "I don't want you turning into a lobster."

"I had Halley rub my back down earlier." I yawn into my hand. My eyes are still closed, as I'm presently feeling too lazy to open them. "Though, I wouldn't turn you down if you wanted to massage in a little more." The sunlight I'm basking in is lulling me into a stupor, and the best thing I can imagine at the moment is a little rubdown from Nate.

"The little one gets what the little one wants." His voice is low and intimate. After a few moments, I feel his hands on my skin, massaging my shoulders with warm, coconut-scented lotion. "Tell me, Charlotte, does this feel good?" he whispers.

"*Mmm.*" It's all I can hum out as he molds my body into a formless state.

I hear him laugh. "Charlie, you need to either turn over so you don't burn, or take a dip in the lake. Though, just saying—if you turn over, I won't be able to contain myself." I feel his lips trailing over the back of my shoulders in light kisses. I can't even respond. All of this attention feels too good, so I just let it be what it is. It's sweet, it makes me feel special, and it's even a bit romantic.

"I don't want to move, though. This feels too good. You and the power of the sun combined is just pure bliss." I sigh, rolling over so I can see his gorgeous face. I manage a smile the moment we make eye contact. He lowers his head to brush his lips with mine.

I prop myself up on my elbows so I can get a better handle on the sweet kiss we're sharing. I feel like time has suddenly stopped, and it's just us two in this moment. He gently pulls away and winks at me before he suddenly jumps to his feet and scoops me up. We're racing towards the end of the boat when I realize what he's about to do. I let out a shriek right when he jumps off the boat and straight into the cold water.

I go all the way under before I crest the top of the water. I'm sputtering water out of my mouth as I try to stay afloat. Nate swims over to me and wraps his arms around my flailing body. I try to elbow him, but he holds me too tight, so I can't. I can only manage to scissor my legs to keep from going under again, just as I hear the laughter coming from the boat. Next thing I see when I look up is Holt and Tucker jumping off the boat, too.

"I thought cowboys were only able to buck broncos and heft a fishing pole," I tease Nate.

"I think I have a smart mouth over here, guys!" he laughs, right before he dunks me under the water again.

We end up horsing around for a while until we decide to dry off in what's left of the hot afternoon sun. The guys have taken to their fishing poles again, deciding to get more serious about it.

"I hope they're not trying to catch our dinner," I say to the girls in a hushed tone. They giggle as they lay on either side of me while we dry off on our backs. I definitely had enough of lying on my stomach. I wouldn't say that the boat deck is exactly comfortable, and now my body is starting to feel the stiffness from lying on it for so long.

"No worries, I saw extra food in the coolers. I think we're safe," Naomi assures us.

"What are you women whispering about?" Tucker calls out to us.

"About how sexy your butt looks in your board shorts!" Halley teases back.

"Why don't you do a little runway walk for us, so we can *all* check it out?" Holt razzes him. "And woman! *You* better not be looking." He frowns at Halley. She just laughs as she closes her eyes and settles back onto the deck.

"Are you threatened by my hotness? No woman can resist these sweet abs and buns of steel." Tucker says as he flexes for us. Nate and Holt groan and shake their heads.

"Don't hate!" Tucker wags his brows at the guys.

"Go crank on *Southern Girls*," Nate pushes him towards the cabin, laughing at him. "You have nothing on us, anyway. Though, if you want to prove you're a real man, we can take it to the track."

"I don't need to prove anything, but I'll see you on the track. That's a promise," Tucker replies with cockiness.

Pretty soon, we hear Tim's voice coming through the speakers on full blast. Nate comes over and pulls me to my feet to start dancing with me. I fan myself, because this boy is pure hotness when he dances. He makes my cheeks blush with his moves.

"I can't wait to get you back on the dance floor at *T.J.'s*," he yells over the music, causing an instant grin to pull at the corners of my lips. *I can't wait, either.*

The day turns into the evening before long, and we make it back to camp to clean up and fry up the fish the guys caught, though I politely decline. I'm grateful there are other things to choose from, as we settle around the campfire with plates in our laps, the night descending quickly upon us. We're all content to be with each other in the cold mountains on our last evening outdoors—where I get one more chance to sleep right next to Nate in my own sleeping bag—before we pack it up bright and early the next morning. I relax into my chair and watch my friends as they talk and tease each other. This is the feeling of really living, and I'm so glad I took a chance on *Texas Jacks*, for once in my life.

Chapter Fourteen

Nate

I T'S THE DAY AFTER THE LAKE, AND I'M ON MY WAY TO check in on Charlie. As it turns out, she came home with a nasty sunburn that kept her home from work.

After I finished work for the day, I stopped by the store to pick up soup, saltine crackers, and Coke, in hopes that she would feel better with something in her stomach. I also purchased aloe vera gel to help with the burn.

I pull into her complex parking lot and luckily enough, there's an open space close by her place. I pull in, grab my purchases, and then jog up the steps to her door. I have to knock a few times before she finally opens the door, and to my surprise, her skin is worse than I could have imagined.

"Charlie, wow. I had no idea," I regretfully say. I should have paid better attention to her the next morning as we cleaned up our campsite to leave. I knew she was moving at a snail's pace, and that her skin was beet red, but who would have known she had water blisters all up her legs? Shaking my head, I gently push her out of the way and walk into her living room.

"Little one." I say into her hair, as I kiss the crown of her head. "Go lay down. I'll warm up some soup and bring you some aloe." I head towards her kitchen to unload my goodies, and she doesn't complain, just does as I ask.

Ten minutes later, I'm pulling a kitchen chair up to the couch she's laying on. "All right, Charlie. Why didn't you tell me it was this bad, sweetheart? I would have gotten here sooner."

"You had work, and I didn't want you to worry. Besides, I didn't realize how bad off I was until this morning. I woke up not feeling well, and then noticed the blisters. I could barely get my sleep shorts and tank top on last night. I think I'm stuck in them for the next few days." She pushes her lower lip out in a pout.

"Do you have the air on? I just realized it feels like a freezer in here." I rub my arms for emphasis.

"I can't seem to get comfy, and the air feels great on my overheated skin. I called my mom—she says I need to lay low for a while, stay home from work, and rest, using plenty of aloe and fluids. You know, she tried to bully her way out here, and I had to make a convincing argument as to why I didn't need her help."

She gives me a fond smile over her mom wanting to help, and I wish I could bottle up the feelings she's wreaking havoc on me with—and she doesn't even know she's doing it.

"Well, I know I put sunblock on you, but Charlie, I'm sorry it wasn't enough. I feel bad you're in so much pain."

"No need to feel bad. You didn't do it. I did have a lot of fun, just so you know. This burn is totally worth the trip," she openly flirts.

"Remind me to have you repeat that in a couple of days when you're still miserable." I uncap the aloe, rub some on my hands, and forewarn her that I'm going to apply the green slime to her legs. "Be prepared, it's going to be cold, too!"

"I can do that. You don't want to touch my gross legs, and that aloe leaves your hands sticky when you're done." She tries to protest as I attempt to rub her legs with aloe.

"Charlotte, lay still and let me help you." I reprimand her as she finally gives up and lets me near her legs. If this were anyone else, they could do it themselves, but it is Charlie, so that's all there is to it. I would do anything for her.

"So, I have a question to ask you." She bites her lip.

"Keep that up and I'll kiss you. Right now, I'm trying to worry about your wellbeing and not your kissable lips." Her lip pops back out. "Why do you seem nervous all of a sudden?" I ask her.

"Well, I was wondering if you would like to take a trip with me next weekend." She starts twisting her hair as I continue to gently apply the goop to her left leg.

"Depends. If it's back to the lake, forget it. I'm not being held responsible for damaging your porcelain skin any further," I tease her.

"No, nothing like that. It's actually another family dinner in Sacramento. I'm inviting you to come with me." I look up at her and see that her face is full of hope, but she looks hesitant, too.

"In that case, I think I can manage a nice drive with my favorite person." I wink at her. I go to start on her right leg now in the silence of the room. Why she chooses now to be speechless, I haven't a clue. I'm confused, so I question her. "What?"

"I just didn't think you would want to go, that's all."

"Of course I'll go. I said you couldn't go back up there unless I took you, remember? So—of course I'll take you." She looks slightly crestfallen, and my heart breaks a little at the sight. "Charlie, sweetheart, why the long face?" I ask as I tilt her chin up. "I thought this is what you wanted? I don't understand." My brows draw together in concern.

"I wanted you to come because you wanted to, not out of obligation."

"I don't feel obligated. I really do want to meet your family," I immediately reply. This is tough. I do want to meet her family, at the same time that I don't. However, I can't let Charlie on to my mixed feelings about the matter. So, it's easier to give in—and I really don't want her on the road alone again late at night.

She gives me a small smile and rests her head back on the pillow. "I'm overreacting. Sorry. I feel out of sorts today."

"Charlie, there's no need to apologize. Now, be a good patient and let me finish with your legs so I can move on to your arms and face before you eat your soup. I'm not leaving until you do," I warn her. I see her mouth curve up into a grin, and I know I've changed her mood again. "That's better." I lean down and kiss her, which causes her to wrap her arms around my neck. I pull back a bit. "You're not being a good girl." I tease, and then go back in for a few more kisses.

I spend the rest of the evening caring for her, and just spending time with her. I ask her surface questions about her family, and who she thinks will be at her house. We put on the movie, *50 First Dates*, and watch it all the way through before calling it a night. I'm itching to hold her, but I know I can't, as I fear I'll make her body hurt more.

"Come lock the door behind me, little one." Once we get to the door, I lean in and whisper, "Even with a water-blistered, sunburned body, you're still hot." She rolls her eyes. "Now kiss me, so I can leave you to rest." She pouts but pushes up on to her toes so she can lean up to kiss me. We break apart all too soon, and I kiss the top of her head before leaving. I stay on the porch for two seconds more when I hear the locks click into place, and then lumber down to my truck and straight for my bed.

Charlie

"Nate is *finally* going to Sacramento with you?" I hear Halley's shocked voice in my ear, as I flounder around my bathroom, getting ready.

My body is on edge with anticipation of how tonight is going to go. Nate will meet my family for the first time, and I don't know how he's going to react. I'm not worried about my family, but more about Nathan. He's so closed off and secretive about his own family that I can't gauge what this will mean for him.

"Yes—finally!" I proclaim triumphantly.

"Wow. I can't believe he's actually going this time."

"Well, he did tell me that the next time he wouldn't let me go alone, and definitely not in the Honda. Though, I didn't believe he would seriously follow through with it. At the time, I could only hope that he was serious." I put the phone on speaker, so I can put the finishing touches of my makeup on and double-check my hair.

"Charlie, don't be so surprised that he would want to meet your family. You must know by now he has feelings for you, and only you. By heavens, he can't even take his eyes off you when we're all out somewhere. He's got it bad for you, in a good way. Why do you still question it?" She chides me.

"Halls, what would you think? He hasn't even brought me home to meet his family, let alone talk about them at all. I barely know anything, and it's been months! I feel like he's hiding behind our friends and good times, to safeguard his heart. Have you noticed we haven't had a lot of one-on-one time?" I point out, feeling irritated with her.

She doesn't say anything for a few moments, so I decide to speak up. I'm trying not to ruin my day with this heavy anvil I carry around with me constantly. "Anyway, I don't want to overthink it right now. I just want to focus on the positive. He's coming with me, and it's a giant step for him. So, I'm determined that all will go off without a hitch!"

"I'm sure whatever is lurking behind his barriers will come out soon. You just need to be patient. He's happy, and from what Holt says, it's been a long time since he's been like this. That means something, Charlie. Don't make it less than what it is. It's good, so let's keep the streak going."

All of the fiery heat I was building up with this conversation goes right out of me at that. "Right," I quietly admit. "He should be here soon, and I need to finish up with my hair. I'll call you later, or tomorrow, depending on when we get back tonight."

"Sounds good, Charlie. Have fun. Tell your family 'hi' for me. Maybe next time, Naomi and I will get an invite to the family table." She pushes with no subtlety whatsoever.

"I'll pass the word along, Halls. Why don't you go out to dinner with Holt?" I try to bring the man issues back around her way. Deep down, I want to be nosey and dig for a little more information about them.

"Maybe. I can't promise you anything. I can't even get him to promise *me* anything. It's—" she's cut off by an incoming call.

"Hey, that's my other line ringing. I need to take it. I call you later. Bye!" I don't wait for her reply, as I click over, knowing exactly who's calling on the other line.

"Hey—you're not getting cold feet are you?" I blurt out before he can say anything.

"Hey, little one. No. Why would you think that?" Nate hesitantly asks.

"Oh. Well—" I stammer, worrying my lower lip. "I thought you would be here by now, yet you're on the phone, calling instead."

"I'm calling to say I'll be a few minutes late. I had to stop by my dad's on the way over."

"Oh. *Umm*. So, uh—is everything okay?" I don't even know how to approach that topic, since I feel like I have no right to even ask.

"Yeah, all is well, I was just checking in on everyone. Nothing truly pressing or important, it just felt like I hadn't been there in while. So, hey, listen, I just wanted to say I'm on my way, and to see if you were ready yet?"

"I'm almost ready. Just last-minute touches. Just text when you get here and I'll come right down."

"Charlotte, there will be none of that." He scolds me. "I plan to come up to the apartment to get you. I better not find your cute butt downstairs waiting."

That makes me laugh into the phone. "Aye-aye, cowboy. I'll be good, and wait up here."

"Darn straight. See you in a few."

The line goes dead, and I slide the phone back to the counter. I finish up my hair in record time, and then brush my teeth again. I feel a little OCD at the moment, wanting everything to be just right. Not like my breath is a deal-breaker, but still, I can't help it. *I'm nervous.*

Not too long after, Nathan is at my door, pulling me into a hard, closed-lip kiss. Then we're locking my door, and walking down to his truck. He lifts me up into the passenger seat, and moments later, we're on our way.

Nate

"Slide over, Charlie." I gently order her.

She does, and makes herself comfortable next to me, placing her hand on my thigh. Right where I usually place it when we're together and she's in this same spot.

"Are you nervous?" She nibbles on her lip, looking up at me.

"No. Should I be? They don't plan to do any secret initiations, do they?"

She giggles. "No."

"No secret handshakes? No weird chants? No weird food to test out on me?" She just chuckles, and shakes her head. "No weird board game matches with your whole family?" She busts up laughing at that.

"No. Just my sisters, who will try to find out all of your innermost secrets," she teases.

"*Phew*! Glad I don't have to turn around and head for the hills, then."

She nuzzles her head into my arm, then reaches over to flip the stereo on. We drive to her folks' house in a relaxed mood, ready for whatever the evening has to offer.

Almost an hour later, I pull up to the curb at her parents' place, and help Charlie out. The minute we set foot onto the porch, the front door swings open, and an older version of Charlie reaches in between us to pull her into a hug. She then hooks me into a hug, as well.

"I'm Natalie, Charlie's mom." She says, as she steps back.

"Wow, *Mom*—" Charlie sounds embarrassed. "Couldn't

you have waited until we actually made it *through* the door?"

She winces as she turns to me with an apologetic look on her face. *Can she tell that the hug made me uncomfortable? That I haven't had a hug from any type of mom in eight years?* I give her a placating smile, and shrug my shoulders as if to say, 'it's okay,' and 'what can you do about it?'

"Sorry! I didn't mean to be so forward. I was just so excited to meet you. Charlie never brings *anyone* home." She gushes, and I automatically tense up. I hope Charlie isn't paying as much attention to my posture as she is to her mom overdoing the welcome committee routine.

"It's fine," I reply, so Charlie can relax and we can move on from this awkward moment. "How about we go inside so I can meet the rest of your family?" Charlie gives me a grateful smile, and we maneuver through the front door.

The minute we clear the entryway, Charlie shouts, "No one else better sneak-attack us, or I'm out of here!"

"Oh, don't be so dramatic, Charlie-bear." A tall, dark-haired guy a little older than me tells Charlie. "What? You can't be seen hugging your brother now?" He ribs her. She shakes her head but grins at him before she complies with his request. "Now, tell me all about *you know who.*" He mock-whispers in her ear.

She gives him a shove, but then introduces me. "Nathan, this is my big brother, Anson. Anson, this is my—" she stops and looks at me with raised eyebrows. "Uh, this is my *good friend*, Nate." She presses forward when I don't give her the right word she's looking for. We've never claimed to be anything but friends, even though we know darn well it's more than that. However, I'm not ready to admit it out loud just yet. It's still a subject I need to reevaluate—at a later date and time.

"Nice to meet you." I reach for his hand to shake. He nods

his head, and gives Charlie a weird look before the rest of the family joins in, and more introductions are handed out.

"Smells good, Mom!" Charlie praises her mom, as we sit down to dinner approximately 20 minutes later.

"Yes, it sure does. Thank you for the invite to your special family dinner." I wholeheartedly tell her parents. Here's another thing that I haven't done in ages—had dinner with my family at an actual table.

"All right, everyone dig in so we can get to the juicy stuff." Lindsay slyly smiles at us. I have a feeling this night is just starting to really liven up. Charlie reaches under the table and places her hand on my thigh, squeezing it for a moment. She releases her grip, though she doesn't take her hand away.

"No need to embarrass them." I let out a little air of relief, until Bethany continues, "Just yet, anyway. Wait until they start to stuff themselves on Mom's enchiladas." She wags her brows at Lindsay, who laughs in return.

"You women are horrible." The tall blond guy—*Greg, I think his name is*—says to everyone at the table then turns to me. "They're harmless. I've already been through the interrogations, and honestly, contrary to whatever you've been told, it's tame." He tries to reassure me.

"Honestly, Charlie led me to shark-infested waters on this one."

They all stare at her with a mixture of shock, surprise, and amusement. "What?" She defends herself. "I didn't want to scare him off! I'm not that stupid." She nervously laughs, and all the while, she won't make eye contact with me. So I reach under the table and give her hand a squeeze. Although, a shiver did crawl up my arms at her announcement.

"Don't worry, Nathan, it's not as bad as whatever has your face turning pale," she promises. "I just didn't want to give off a bad impression of my family. We can be loud and obnoxious, and I didn't want you thinking we were nuts."

"Geez! Now that's all you're doing, sis!" Anson chuckles at both of our discomfort.

"All right, stop trying to make matters worse. Your sister will stop coming to visit us if you keep ragging on her and her friend." Her dad intervenes at her siblings' so-called-teasing. "Nathan—or do you prefer Nate? I believe I've heard my daughter call you both this evening."

"Nate is fine, sir."

"Sir," he chuckles. "Please, just call me James. Now, where did you two meet? It would seem my daughter is pretty tight-lipped these days on the subject of her friends." He gives her a pointed look. She returns a weak smile to him before ducking her head and paying her plate far too much attention than it deserves.

"We met at *Texas Jacks*, in Vacaville. She was sitting all alone at a table, and I couldn't resist the pull to meet her." This time, she's watching me, wondering what will come out of my mouth next. I wink at her, causing her to blush.

"I see. So, a bar, then?" Her dad doesn't seem fired up about how we met.

"It's a dance club, too, Dad." She steps in before I can say anything further. "We were there to dance, not drink."

It would appear that even though Charlie is an adult, who is old enough to drink—but doesn't, her father would probably prefer her to say young for awhile longer, or not hear about such things to color his view of his sweet, innocent daughter.

"How long have you been seeing each other?" he asks, looking at both of us.

"Just over three months," I reply.

"Charlie!" her mother exclaims. "What is wrong with our children, James?" she says, turning to her husband before looking at the rest of the table. "Why do you all feel the need to hide who you're seeing from me? I'm getting old, here! My poor heart can't take it."

"Mom, cut out the theatrics." Jennifer shakes her head. "We are not going through this song and dance again."

"Oh, fine—but seriously, I thought we promised not to keep secrets anymore. Unless—" she trails off, eyeing each child as they squirm in their seats. Someone coughs, and it feels like the air is getting warmer.

"Sorry, Mom," a guilty-looking Lindsay speaks up. "We promised to give her space, until she was ready to share it with us."

Her mom solemnly nods her head, and then tucks into her dinner, allowing Charlie's dad to pick back up with his many questions.

We end up getting into a nice groove through the rest of dinner and dessert, as the family asks us a million questions. It's pretty easy to keep the focus on Charlie and myself, and off the topic of my family. Each time they mentioned them, I could feel Charlie tense up. I don't blame her—it's not like I've really shared anything on that subject with her. But I can see why she wanted me to meet her family. They're funny, love being together, and are genuine.

Charlie's dad does manage to eventually draw us all into a game during the course of the evening, to the siblings' dismay. Truthfully, I think all of their posturing is just for show, and they secretly love it. I even saw some side-betting happening amongst the players.

By the time we leave, I've made a promise to come back for a round of Backgammon and another dinner. I'm not going to lie; I think I'm biting off more than I can chew by agreeing to all of this. It scares me to death. I'm not as used to all of this family closeness now as I was in my youth. Even having a serious girlfriend has, by choice, not been in the cards for me. I'm not going back there again. As it is, Holt, Tucker, and now Charlie are the closest people I have in my life. And as far as my relationship with Charlie goes, I'm one hundred percent positive it has moved to the fast lane—granted, a lot of that was my doing. As much as I like her family, I need to apply some pressure to the brakes and slow us down.

"Thank you for coming tonight," Charlie brings me out of my musings as we drive along I-80 towards home. "My family really liked you." She leans her head on my shoulder and yawns.

"Tired?"

"Yeah. I'm grateful you're the driver tonight. I might have just crashed at my folks' if it had been just me there."

"Glad I'm good for something." I tease her, as she nuzzles into my side a bit more. "Preparing to nap on me now?" I laugh.

"Maybe," she shyly replies.

"Go to sleep, little one. I'll wake you when we get home."

If I get any deeper with Charlie, I just might drown, because I don't think I have any strength, when it comes to her, to stay afloat. I might let her take me down and hold me there. The fight is too real, and my heart isn't ready to go there completely. I went there once, until my life fell apart, and now—allowing it to happen after so long—I can't fathom it. I don't want to hurt myself again, let alone Charlie. Ultimately, that's probably going to happen, no matter how much I try to prevent it.

Chapter Fifteen

Nate

"**A**RE YOU CRAZY?" CHARLIE IS STARING AT ME, with her mouth agape.

"One lap."

"You know what? I think you've gone mental."

"I'll go slowly."

"Nope. No, way. No, how." She shakes her head at me.

"No one else will even be on the track. It's perfectly safe." Leaning against my bike, I gently pull her between my legs. "*I'll* keep you safe." I murmur, as I feather kisses up and down her neck.

"If you think this is working," she stops talking, and I can feel her body relax, giving into my devious whim. "Then you might be right." She laughs. "You dirty, rotten, scoundrel." I feel her arms tangle around my neck, and one of her hands starts to play with the hair at my nape.

"*Mm-hmm.*" I murmur against her throat. "You can't resist the powers that be." I tease her while brushing a few more light kisses against her throat.

"If you two are done making a spectacle of yourselves," I hear a snide voice, which once used to be sugary sweet.

Charlie stiffens as I pull my head up to catch Shelly scowling at us. Shaking my head at her, I look back down into

176

Charlie's eyes. I can see she's fired up to say something, so I lean down and effectively cut her off with a hard kiss.

"Caveman." I hear Shelly mutter under her breath in disgust. "Are you two finished?"

Charlie turns in my arms, so her back is now flush with my chest. I wrap my arms around her waist as she leans into me further.

"Is there something we can help you with, Shelly?" I ask, ignoring her previous comments, not wanting to give her any more reasons to be rude, or insulting, to Charlie.

"My car won't start. I was hoping you would be able to give me a lift home." Now she's back to being sweet, and studiously ignoring Charlie in every way possible. She's standing in front of us—wearing super short shorts, a tight tank top, and heeled boots, using her body in a flirtatious way. She's going for sexy, and hoping I'll jump on board with whatever she's offering, even though Charlie is clearly standing right here. Even if I didn't have Charlie, I wouldn't be tempted with her desperation in the slightest.

"Sorry, I can't give you a ride." I give it to her straight, not even feeling bad that I won't help. "I have a date with Charlie. Did you ask anyone else to see if they could give your car a jump start?"

"Of course!" she chides me. "Do you think I wanted to come over here, and see you two sucking face? *Please*." She scrunches her nose in disgust.

"Well, I don't know what to say. Call a cab?" I offer with a small grin.

"Did he ask you to take a ride on the back of his bike, yet?" She ignores me and looks to Charlie. "He promised me ages ago he'd let me ride with him, too. In fact, he offers all of the girls a ride once around the track before it shuts down for the night." She smirks at Charlie.

"Really? Do you honestly think I would believe anything that comes out of your mouth?" Charlie asks in a bored tone, not giving in to her snide remarks, or looks.

"You can believe whatever you want. It's still the truth. Go ahead, Nate. Why don't you tell her about how you've given me *plenty* of rides?" She challenges, daring me to deny it.

"Well now, look who's stirring up trouble!" Holt states as he walks up to our little group. "Shelly, are you the reason that Charlie's sweet lips look like the duck pucker pout?" he quips.

"Hey, sexy," she purrs in Holt's direction. She makes her way towards him, pushing her body up against his as she greets him with a hug. I can feel Charlie's body silently shaking. We both know that Shelly isn't into Holt. She's just trying to play her games, and using him as her newest pawn. "I was just asking my dear old friend, Nate, for a ride home." She pouts while latching her arm around Holt's waist.

"Oh my stars, he didn't turn you down, did he?" He winks at us, as he mocks her with his stupid comment.

"I know! I can't believe it, either." She exclaims. "What about, you? Do you have any plans tonight? Maybe you'd want to bring me home." She gazes up at him.

"Sure. I can give you a lift." He assures her. I watch as her face lights up, and she flashes me her sly smile, before turning her attention back to Holt.

"Thanks, babe. You're a life saver." She nuzzles into him a little more.

"Let's get out of here, and leave the love birds to do their own thing. What do you say?"

"You don't have to ask me twice." She shoots Charlie one last disapproving look, then turns on her heel and propels Holt towards the car lot.

"What was that all about?" Charlie questions, as we both watch them walk away. "I'm not thinking good thoughts about what Halley would say if she knew he just offered to bring her home."

"Don't worry. He's not fooled by her antics, let alone tempted to go there." I turn her to face me, once again. "But I can think of better topics I would rather be discussing." I kiss her gently.

"You're not going to give up, are you?"

I shake my head at her. "Just say yes."

"On one condition."

"Name it."

"You have to tell me if you really gave Shelly a ride on your dirt bike, and the answer better be a resounding *no*." she narrows her eyes at me.

"Mood killer." I sigh, knowing that I'll have to confess to this beautiful woman how I let a bike bunny take a ride from me a time or two around the track.

"*Uh*—why does that sound foreboding?"

"I cannot tell a lie." I start. She smiles, but smacks me in the chest. "Okay, fine. Yes, I did give her a ride a couple of times. But!" I hold my hands up in surrender, before she can whack me again. "In my defense, it was before I really knew her. I was just showing off, and trying to impress the ladies out here. It was a long time ago. I've since learned my lesson, and no woman has been on my bike since." I gaze down on her. "The only woman I want on the back of my bike, is you, *Charlotte*." I firmly tell her.

"I'm not happy that she had the first, and only other, experience with you. Though, in all fairness, I didn't know you back then. So, I really have no right to be hurt, or upset." She looks up at me a bit sadly, and I have a palpable feeling of understanding. I don't want to picture any other man with her, either. "Though, I am. Just saying."

"I get it, Charlie. I do. There's no changing the past. We

just have to move forward together and not let people like her get into that pretty little head of yours."

"Fine. You're right. I don't want her to have any other piece of our night." She pulls back from me and claps her hands, rubbing them together. "Let's do this!" she says enthusiastically.

"That's the spirit, little one." I playfully swat her on the butt. She rolls her eyes at me, but I can see the smile she's fighting, pulling at the corners of her mouth.

I grab the extra helmet I brought, knowing I was going to try and push my luck with her tonight. I help her with it, before assisting her onto the bike. I climb on in front of her, reaching back and pulling her arms tight around my waist. "Hold on tight!" I yell back at her. "Don't ever let go, sweetheart."

"I thought you said you were going to go slow?" she yells back at me.

"I am. Still, I want those sweet arms around me, and hey—I need to be careful out here with you. I don't need you winding up in the ER."

I push up the kick stand, start the bike, and rev it up really loud. It's unnecessary, but it's fun to do, and I'm definitely all about having fun with Charlie, tonight. She holds on a little tighter, right before I take off at a slower than normal pace.

I'm happy to have Charlie with me, but at the same time, it's bittersweet. I promised myself I would cool my jets, and doing this with her is far from that. Something about Charlie has me holding on, for a tad bit longer. Right now, I'm sharing the most important piece of my life with her, and she doesn't fully understand it. But I'm not going to explain it to her. For now, I'm enjoying the feel of her behind me, the bike underneath me, and the pull of the track.

Tomorrow is a new day. Tomorrow I'll start to pull back,

a little at a time.

Tomorrow.

Charlie

Spending time with Nate on the track last night was exhilarating. I can't believe I let him talk me into it. Watching Nate ride is already scary enough, but to be on the back of the dirt bike at the same time? I think I'm the mental one, now. Still, I can't deny how much fun I had. He did go slowly for me, and we definitely went around a few times, once I got over my fear.

I just got home from work, and already my phone has been beeping with text messages from the girls. The gossiping boys have already shared what Nathan and I did last night. I just set foot into my apartment when my phone rings.

"Who are you, and what have you done with Charlie?"

"Well, hello to you, too, Halley, my dearest friend." I laugh, as I shut the door and chuck my keys onto the table. Shuffling off my shoes, I toss my purse on to the couch as I walk into the kitchen to round up some food for dinner.

"Please tell me you just got home!"

"I'm home."

"Good. I just pulled into the lot with Naomi."

"Oh, goodie," I laugh. "I'll see you in a few," I tell her before pushing the *end call* button. I place it on the counter, open the fridge, and a few moments later my front door flies open.

"Are you crazy?" Naomi shouts at me.

"Want to calm it down, a bit?" I ask her.

"I can't believe you were on a dirt bike, and he took you on the track!" She's clearly freaking out. "Charlie, that does *not* sound like you. At all!"

"Oh, please. Pipe it down. It was fun, and I would even consider doing it again."

They stare at me in shock. "Says the girl who flips her lid every time Nate is out on the track." Halley states the obvious.

"Right. And do you both remember that I wanted to try new things and not be such a fuddy-duddy anymore? This was my chance to do so. So, I took it. Plus, you weren't there at the end. You missed all of the stupid drama with Shelly."

"Oh, we heard. Holt's in hot water with Halley," says Naomi.

"I can't believe he gave her a ride home! Please tell me she wasn't all over him." Halley pleads with me.

"Okay. I won't tell you." I turn my attention back to the fridge, trying to assemble something easy and quick for dinner.

"What?" she asks.

I sigh. "He was doing us a favor by trying to make her leave before she found herself face-down in the dirt, by yours truly. Yes, she tried to cast her net over him, but he wasn't falling into her trap."

"Right." Halley shakes her head. "Between her and Lisa, I'm thinking I'm done visiting the guys out at the track."

"Don't get so huffy now. He didn't do anything wrong. She was being ridiculous, and he was cutting off the drama before it came to blows. Cut the man some slack, will you? Besides," I look over my shoulder at her. "She's not even into him. She's was trying to goad me—and Nate—but we didn't fall for it."

"I know. She just makes me so mad. I can't help but be

crazy sometimes when she or Lisa plays these games."

"If anyone has a right to be ticked off here, it's me and Charlie." Naomi reminds Halley.

"She has a point," I turn my attention back to the task at hand. "So, let's not talk about either one of them, and instead move on to a better topic. Like—what are we going to do for dinner?"

"I vote for dinner, a movie, and you telling us all about that ride." Naomi plants her butt into one of the chairs at the kitchen table. "But not necessarily in that order."

"Right. I'm thinking we should order in." Halley confirms, as she pulls out my menu stash from a kitchen drawer.

"I'm so hungry, I'll eat from whatever place you decide to pick." I tell her, as I head down the hall. "But I'm changing first."

In the end, we ordered Chinese take-out, watched *27 Dresses,* and plotted ways to keep the guys away from the race track. Even though, they've been going less and less over the last month, or two, we still planned ways to keep them off for the rest of the summer, at least.

Nate

"What's going on with you, and Charlie?" Tucker questions me, while we work out at the gym two days after the track. It's Saturday, and I really needed this. I've been a bit neglectful of my work-out regimen.

"The same as you, Holt, and the girls."

"I don't know. I think it's a little more special with her than you're letting on."

"Possibly, but if it's special for us, then it's the same for you and Holt." I really don't want to hash this topic out with the guys at the gym, but it looks like that's the case, since I know Holt can't keep his mouth shut.

"You don't plan on breaking Charlie's heart, do you? I like to think of her as the sister I've never had." Holt voices his displeasure.

"I don't plan on it, no. I'm not a jerk, man."

"Have you even talked to her about your family?" I can hear the concern in Tucker's voice as he questions me.

"No. And I don't plan on it, either." I continue to lift the bar with weights over my head, then drop it back down to my chest and up again.

"Why?" Holt seems confused, but he really shouldn't be. He knows the score.

"That would imply that we're headed into forever, here. You know my rules on being fully committed. It's not a goal in my life."

Holt narrows his eyes at me, as he starts working out his biceps. "Seriously?"

"Look, I really like her, and if I were a man who could give her his heart, completely—" I quirk a brow at him, stopping him from saying anything else, "I would. But you know that's not me. Not after my mom. I just can't. If I could, I would have made it work with Heather."

"I think you should take a chance on her, man." Tucker pushes. "She would be good for you. Her family would be great for you, too, after what you said about your visit with them. And didn't you promise to go up there again?" he asks, while he works on his leg presses.

"Yes, but that's not going to happen." I tell them, as I sit up on the bench, and wipe the sweat off my face.

"I can't believe you right now." Holt shakes his head at

me, in a disapproving way.

"What?" I ask them both. "And hold up a minute. What about *you two*? What's the deal with Halley and Naomi?"

"That's a different story all together, and you know it. We don't have the same hang-ups as you." Holt replies in a clipped tone. "Don't even try to turn this around on us. We like the girls, and we'll take it to wherever it's going, but we're not in a race to the altar here." He looks to Tucker for back up. Tuck gives us a chin lift in solidarity.

"We're not trying to get up in to your business, or tick you off. And I know Holt didn't mean anything by the hang-up comment. Right?" He looks at Holt to assure us that he didn't mean to be a jerk about my issues.

"Right." he confirms.

"We like Charlie a lot, and we can see she's head over heels for you. I think she may even be in love with you." Tucker shocks the ever-loving life out of me at that.

"*Love*?" I falter in my steps, on my way to a new weight machine. It's nice and quiet here this early in the morning. We practically have the gym to ourselves.

"Uh—," he looks over to Holt, not sure in how he should proceed.

"You haven't caught on to that fact, yet?" Holt looks on in disbelief at me.

"No. Hence the reason I'm in shock over here."

"To be fair to Charlie, I don't think she fully realizes it, either. The way she watches your every move, and how she gazes at you? She's definitely in love with you, bro," says Tucker.

I feel dumbfounded by this revelation. "How did I not see that coming?" I ask, more to myself, than to them.

"You've been living in la-la land for the last few months!" Holt tries to lighten up the mood. "How could you not clue in to her feelings by now?" he wonders out loud.

"I thought that was the reason you haven't had many dates with her on your own." Tucker tries to reason why we've been hanging out more than normal, rather than me flying solo.

"Safety in numbers. You know how I operate," I remind them.

"Right, we do, but you've been different with Charlie. That's why we wanted to know what was going on. Now, I see we shouldn't have brought it up." Holt shakes his head and goes back to his bicep curls.

"No. No, this is good. I'm glad you pointed it out. You're right, I have been clueless. I mean, not completely, obviously. I know we have this pull with each other, but I've been trying to figure out a way to distance myself without hurting her in the process."

I hear them both groan, and Tucker lets the weights on the back of his machine drop with a loud *clang*. "Really? You can't be serious!"

"As a heart attack."

"That's just plain stupid," Holt replies.

"Didn't you just share a piece of your soul with her not more than two days ago? Why else would you continue to share your self and the track with her? Let alone take her out joy riding on the back of your dirt bike?" Tucker seems even more baffled, as this conversation goes on.

"You've only had one girl on the back before, and that was Shelly. I'm still trying to figure that one out, years later." Holt looks at me, trying to figure me out.

"There wasn't anything special to it at the time. I was messed up and being stupid back then, and you both know it. Have I let anyone else on my bike, since? No."

"See? That right there just proves your feelings for Charlie." Holt points out.

"Right. It does. It's also why I need to put the brakes on a little more firmly." They both look at me in dismay, but I know they get where I'm coming from. "Look, you both know that her anniversary is coming up, and how hard that time is for me, not to mention my family. It's going to be a rough week. It always is. I don't want Charlie to see that. It's best to start the process of pulling back now." I try to compel them with my arguments for this horrible idea. I know it's a bad plan, but it's the only one I have in my head at the moment. "Do you have a better solution?" I ask them.

"Yeah, actually, I do." Holt voices in irritation.

"Yep. I do too, and it's the same one as Holt's."

"*No*. I'm not telling her. She shouldn't be burdened with my sorrows year after year. You guys know how I get. How is that going be for her? I don't want to be a douche to her every flipping year. I'm already a big enough jerk to you, my dad, and my sister for a least a week."

"Right, but we're still here for you. You're not even giving her a shot to do the same. She's a part of you now. She's under your skin, and in your heart. You know it even if you want to fight it." Tucker states his case on the matter of my feelings.

"You know, Nate, it's okay to let someone new in. It's okay to let that person be Charlie. She can hold your hand and see you through your darkest days, and be your light at the end of the spiral you go into." Holt says, in a more hushed voice.

"You can't live like this, year after year. It's already been eight. Haven't you put yourself through enough pain? You need to start healing, brother. We love you, and you know we'll always be here, through thick and thin, but one day— you're going to need to let someone else be that shoulder to lean on. Just think about it being Charlie. She cares for you deeply. Don't push her away." Tucker gets up from his weight machine and walks away, leaving me speechless.

I look over at Holt. He's watching Tucker walk away before he sadly looks at me. He, too, gets up and heads towards the locker rooms. I'm left standing here wondering, *what just happened, and when did my life get so complicated*?

Chapter Sixteen

Nate

I T'S THE FOLLOWING FRIDAY, ALMOST A WEEK SINCE THE gym incident with the guys. All week long, I've been trying to push aside that conversation we had. Thankfully, it's been a busy week, so I haven't taken the time to examine their words too closely. I decided it was time to take Charlie out, one-on-one, as she deserves it. I haven't been fair, if I'm being honest with myself. However, I still stand firm on my decision that she doesn't need to be weighted down with my sorrows. *Why do that to a good woman, like Charlie?* Besides, I don't need the pity that I know I would see if I told her.

So, tonight it's all about Charlie. I'm taking her out, not only because I really want to see her, but to prove to myself, that we can continue to keep this going as it is, minus the personal and deep emotions. I've checked my baggage at the door, and so far, it seems she doesn't have any. I know I've been contemplating applying the brakes on us, though I've not done a great job of it. It's been easier to brush it off and enjoy what we have, even if it's mostly time spent with our friends.

"Where are we headed, cowboy?" Charlie asks, as we travel down the freeway.

"I thought I would take you to do something fun!"

"Every time we're together, I have a fun time." She softly admits.

"I'm glad, sweetheart." I give her a tender smile. "There's one small problem, though." Frowning now as I notice where she's sitting. I can't help it. I like the closeness of her body, and to be able to touch her hand as I drive. It goes against keeping certain things in check, however—it reminds me of my parents in years past, which is something I've always enjoyed, and wanted for myself. Until I decided it was too intimate. With Charlie, it feels natural to crave it, so I let it slide and push my limits every chance I can.

"Oh?" She looks perfectly perplexed.

"You haven't figured it out?"

"Uh—no?"

"You're in the wrong seat, little one." She gives me a sheepish look but slides over on the bench seat to sit right next to me, where I like her.

"So? Where are we off to?" she tries again.

"I thought we would head over to the airport. They have a decent selection of places to eat, though BBQ sounds good right about now. I figured afterward we could head to *Yogurt Zone* for dessert. We could even cozy up in the back of the truck bed to watch as flights take off and land. Though, just saying—I'm not opposed to the idea of shopping, if you want. There is one thing I really want to do."

"Oh? Did you want to learn how fly a plane or something?"

"One day, maybe. Though I prefer to keep my feet firmly planted on the ground. So, no. But I do want to play a game of chess."

"Chess?" She gives me a crazy look. "Uh, I hate to break it to you, but I only reserve board games for my family dinners." She gives me a disgruntled face.

"Trust me, this is one you'll want to play."

"Yeah, but I think I'll have to pass." She's settling in on being stubborn, I can tell.

"No, really. It's a giant chess board. The pieces are probably your height." She scrunches her nose at me. "What? I can't help that you're fun-sized!" she shakes her head, fighting like hard not to laugh. "Just let the laugh out. You can't deny it." I laugh myself, as I squeeze her knee, where I know she's ticklish.

"Whatever," she giggles, trying to push my hand away. "Okay. I could play one game with you, on two conditions."

I raise my eyebrow at her. "Oh, who's making conditions now? Fine, what will they be, your highness?

"One, you can't tell my family I played a game outside of the house." Now I look at her like she's nuts. "Trust me. I'll never live it down. And two, you can't take any photos of this event. I won't have any blackmail held over me!"

I can't help but laugh at her, and her crazy requests.

"I can't promise you anything. I might want to document this momentous occasion, for proprietary sake." She rolls her eyes.

"I'll hijack your phone if you dare take a photo!" I don't take any stock into her empty threats. She's too short to reach for it over my head anyway, not that I would tell her that. I don't need to anger the little beast any further.

I'm still laughing at her, and gently squeeze her thigh one more time, then lean over and place a quick kiss on her lips. Grinning, I turn my focus back to the road. "We'll see. I make no promises."

And I'm glad I didn't promise her anything, though I would probably give her whatever she wanted. I couldn't help but take a few photos of her on the sly. We had dinner, walked around the mall, and grabbed frozen yogurt. Of course, she had to lick mine. She just *had* to test the flavor to make sure she didn't want the same thing. Which, of course she didn't. Good thing I don't mind swapping spit with her.

We played a few games of chess—which I dominated every game. I couldn't even give her one, it was getting pretty sad. I ended up taking pity on her and quitting after three games. She was a good sport about it, and mostly laughed. I think there were a few times she was ready to jump me, and take me down like an angry wrestler. Now, we're sitting in the bed of my truck, warming up under a couple heavy blankets, as we watch the planes come and go.

It's a quiet crisp evening, except for the loud planes, as we huddle together under the blankets, trying to keep each other warm. We haven't spoken much. It's nice to enjoy just being here, with each other, and away from the hustle of people, and life.

"Thank you for tonight. I had a lot of fun, even if I wanted to pound you into the ground. I still think my dad could beat you at a life-size chess game." She chuckles.

"Bring it." I pull her into me a bit more, as I stare up into the night stars. "I had a great evening, too. I appreciate every moment we share. You make it easy to spend time with you. I love that about you, Charlie. You're so easy going, and I love your cute feisty side, and how shy you are, too. It's the best of both worlds when I'm with you."

I hear her sigh in contentment as she hugs my middle tighter. "It's you who makes it easy for me. I've not dated much, and I still feel new to the experience."

"I would have never guessed. You would think, being the baby of a large family, you would be the loud and crazy one. You certainly surprise me. In a good way."

"Well, sometimes it's the quiet ones you have to watch out for." She teases.

"Hmmm. I think I need to keep a closer eye on you, to

make sure you don't pull anything on me. Maybe I need a pow-wow with your brother. We guys need to stick together."

"No way! He would fill your head with every embarrassing moment I have ever had!" she practically shouts.

"Well, you have threatened violence in the form of WWE wrestling moves." I tease her. "Maybe I should have a care for concern when it comes to my well-being."

"I think I should warn you that Anson taught me all that I know. He used to practice on me. I was the perfect size to throw around." I can't help but to crack up.

"I think you probably had a crazy childhood." I smile into the night, thinking about the kind of life she had, knowing I had a really good upbringing myself.

"I can't say I threw my little sister around, but I sure did threaten every guy who tried to date her. I went as far as to tell them at school to keep away from her. She couldn't figure out why the guys didn't want to go out with her. She heard rumors that certain ones liked her, but didn't get why they wouldn't talk to her. She did find out later the real reason." I laugh. "She, of course, didn't laugh. She was ready to chase me with our dad's hunting rifle. Good thing Holt, and Tuck were there. They had to help me escape the house for a while."

Charlie's body is shaking with silent laughter. "You big meanie! I can't believe you did that. How did she even find out?"

"One of the guy's, who happens to be her boyfriend now, finally had enough. He figured he would be the brave one and take the plunge. He also figured she was safe, now that she's over 18, and that I had no ground to stand on when it came to scaring him off. He went for it, and told her all about my high school antics."

"I can't believe those boys fell for it. What a bunch of wimps." She laughs. "I'm glad my brother wasn't in school with me. It would have been a death sentence. Why do you think I live so far away? Yet, I'm still close. I need privacy from my siblings or they will forever be in my face. Anson would be beating the guys back at my door, and my sisters would be sending those same guys to my door. They think I lead a very mundane existence."

"Well, it's good you live out here, then. And there better not be any other men at your door, or I'll put a round or two in their backside with my pellet gun."

"Settle down, cowboy. It's only you." She nuzzles her head into my chest and darn if that didn't feel good to hear. Though, I already knew it. It makes the burn go deeper, and I know we're headed for choppy waters. I just can't stop it.

We stay in the back of my Ford for a little longer, talking, and stealing kisses in the stillness of the night with an occasional plane flying overhead. Eventually I gather up the strength to pull away and take her home, where I deposit her on her front porch.

We kiss for a little longer, until a few neighbors walk by, whistling and cat-calling so we give it a rest. I hug her and tell her I'll see her before Sunday. She goes into the apartment, where I hear her lock the door before I jog down the steps. I'm just getting to the truck when she yells out her window.

"You totally took pictures, didn't you?" I can't help the burst of laughter that comes rolling out of me. "I knew it!" She exclaims.

"Calm down, crazy lady. I won't post anything, and I won't even tell your family. See? Your secret is safe."

"You're so lucky I'm too tired to come down there and beat you with a broom!" She yells back.

"Keep yelling and someone else will come down and beat me with a broom." I call back. "I'll send you the photos when I get home. Sleep tight, short-stack!" I call out before climbing in my truck, effectively cutting off anything else she has to say. I laugh the rest of the way home, knowing she'll pay me back somehow, later.

Charlie

I've been dealing with tooth sensitivity off and on for a while now, but haven't done anything about it. Now, I'm so over it, so I scheduled an appointment for laser treatment. The dentist was concerned on my last cleaning about my gums receding. He felt like causing a scar on my gum would help, as well as stop further problems. So, that's how I'm spending my Friday afternoon. Instead of with Nate, or my friends, I'm sitting here—in the dental chair listening to the assistant, Chris, explain the procedure and how uncomfortable I'll be. *Lovely.*

I'm a bit nervous, as I've not had a shot in my gums in years. Just seeing the syringe is doing all kinds of things to my brain. I can list a hundred other things I would love to be doing at this moment, though I know this is important.

My dentist comes into the room, making small talk to ease my nerves a bit, until Chris has to wipe a cloth over my gums. Shortly after, I see hands, so I look down just in time to see the big syringe get close to my mouth before it makes its way to my gums.

I have just enough time to say, "Oh no! I had a feeling this was going to happen," before the syringe does its job, and goes straight into my gums.

"We could always do this without the numbing effect," my dentist jokes.

"No way is that going to happen!" I laugh.

After I'm thoroughly numb I have about 15 minutes to sit around, as I wait for my mouth to be ready for the laser procedure. At one point Chris comes in to swish water around my mouth, then she tries to suction it back out. Unfortunately, my mouth is too numbed, so I can't latch onto the hose, and the water dribbles out of my mouth, and all over my chin, and chest. *Well, that's just lovely*, feeling like the biggest dork ever. I laugh, as does Chris before she wanders away.

By the time the dentist comes back, I can't feel my mouth—or my nose. Chris warns me I'm about to smell a burning smell right when the dentist starts working away at my gums. I'm not going to lie; this wasn't as easy going as I thought it would be. By the time I'm done, and go to leave, I can't feel my nose, or my lips. I also have a killer headache, to top it off.

My mouth is in a lot of pain, and I realize I should have asked someone to drive me. I take a few pain killers once I'm in the car, already starting to feel exhausted from the pain, and the long bout in the chair. I can't fathom how I'll drive home in this condition, but I know I have no other choice. Why didn't I ask Nate, or one of my friends to come with me?

I had mentioned this appointment to Nate, telling him it wasn't a major deal, and that I would be fine to meet up later. *Boy was I wrong*! I can't remember the last time I was in this much pain after a dental appointment.

I decided to text Nate, before I pull out of the lot—though I wait for his reply before I leave.

Charlie: I'm headed home from my appointment and I'm pretty tired with a bad headache. Can we postpone tonight?

He responds immediately.

Nate: Sure little one, we can go out another night. Do

you want me to come over?

Charlie: As much as I do want to see you, I won't be good company. Trust me. I'll probably just pass out once I get in the door.

When I don't hear anything back, I decide to head home. I really need to lie down, and pass out pronto!

By the time I get home, there's a truck in my extra spot with one handsome guy leaning against it. He stands there with his arms folded across his chest. Secretly, I'm thinking how grateful he ignored what I said, and just showed up anyway. His concerned eyes take me in, as I get out on wobbly legs, yet he still has a smile on his face, happy to see me. I have to admit, I'm happy to see him too.

"You okay, Charlotte? You look exhausted." He watches me from his perch. "I know you didn't want company, but I was worried about you. I missed you and I needed to see you in person—just to know you were ok," he says, walking over to me, and wrapping his arms around me.

I love being wrapped up in him, as he provides me with warmth and the feeling of safety. I try to smile up at him and admit, "I'm actually glad you came over." I'm pretty sure that all came out slurred, because Nate's chest all of a sudden started vibrating against my good cheek.

"Are you laughing at me?" I ask.

"Come on little one, let's get you inside and taken care of," he chuckles, as he moves his arm around my shoulders, propelling us to the stairs that lead to my door. Once we reach our destination, he reaches over for my keys to unlock the door, letting us into the apartment.

He takes my hand into his, while flipping the light on with the other. He leads me over to the couch where he plants me. He crouches down to take off my shoes before heading in to the kitchen. Once he gets me situated with pain relievers, he stands me up, and walks me down the hall to my room where he helps me to sit on the bed. He starts searching my drawers, coming up with sweats, a t-shirt and warm fuzzy socks—which he lays on the bed next to me. He tilts my chin up as he leans down to place a sweet kiss on my nose. Gazing into my eyes for a moment longer, he finally let's go and walks out, shutting the door behind him.

I'm still out of it, due to the pain when I walk back down the hall to the living room, where I find Nate in the kitchen. He looks up and smiles at me with a warm smile that turns my insides into butterflies.

"Come here sleepy-head." He says to me. So I make my way into his outstretched arms.

"How about we get a blanket, snuggle on the couch, and put on a movie? Does that sound good?" He nuzzles my hair.

"What if I pass out? I'm tired, my mouth hurts, and I have a killer headache," I try to reply back, but it just sounds like a garbled up mess of words.

He shakes his head, grinning at me, as if I'm a goofball. "Don't even worry about that. I only had one thing on my list tonight, and that was to see you. So, we'll stay in. If you happen to fall asleep, then that's okay. I want to be here to make sure you're all right."

"If you're sure, then I would love to cozy up to you and a movie."

"On one condition."

"Oh brother." I groan, though a giggle escapes.

"What? I know how much you love my conditions. Besides, you don't get a choice on this one."

"What?" I act affronted.

"Hey, you're in no shape to talk back." He laughs. "You know you'll pass out, so this means I get full control of the remote." He waggles his brows at me, causing me to crack up.

"Stop making me laugh!" I smack his chest.

"What was that? Are you learning a new language?" he's having a lot of fun at my expense.

"I'm the one in agony." I pout.

"Stop gripping, and get your cute butt to the couch." He orders as he starts pushing me towards the couch. "You'll watch whatever I pick and like it." He gives me a lopsided grin.

"I'm so glad I'm about to pass out so I won't be subjected to horrible movies and a bossy man!" He shakes his head, but laughs as he smacks me on the butt.

"Sit down, Charlie, and don't hog the whole couch!" he winks, so I know he's playing around.

"If I wasn't in such pain, I would take you down, right here and now, WWE style."

I watch in fascination as his smile takes over his face and he belts out in laughter.

"Ahh, Charlotte," he smiles at me. "Sit down." He pushes me onto the couch.

I watch as he gets everything we need, and then sits down on the couch, where he rearranges me so I'm lying on his chest, before he pulls the covers up and over us. He turns the TV on and shortly after I pass out, completely missing the James Bond movie he ordered from On-Demand.

I wake up later to find Nate passed out under my cheek and nice big drool puddle on his chest. I can't help but snicker over it, though I'm mortified. I start to pull myself up, so I can go use the bathroom. When I look back up, I see Nathan is staring at me.

"Don't think I didn't notice you slimed me. Trying to make your grand escape?"

"I just have to answer the call of nature." I poke him in the chest, before climbing off the couch. When I come back out he's still laying in the same spot, with his head propped up on his hand.

"What?"

"Nothing. I'm just trying to figure out how long it will take me to beat you to the bed, so I can have it all to myself."

"Not very smart to give your secrets away. I have a head start."

"Yeah, but you're all doped up, with a slow reaction time."

"Yeah, yeah. I might be on pain meds, but I'm not an invalid."

"Get your butt back over here, so we can go back to sleep. I'm beat!"

I lay back down, on Nathan—my life size bed. We lay there for a while, trying to get back to sleep, but it's just awkward.

"Do you want to sleep on the bed?" I ask him. "You get your side and I get mine, and no funny business, mister!"

"I think I should just head home. I don't want to make you uncomfortable." He starts to push up, causing me to have to move, too.

"It's okay. I know you're tired. I'm not worried. Come on, don't make it a big deal. I won't make it one either."

"All right, shorty, get a move on. I'm tired and I need my beauty rest." He hops up off the couch, scoops me up in his arms, and I point him to the only room in the apartment. He sleeps on one side and I sleep on the other, with only our hands holding on to each other. Eventually his breathing evens out, then I finally let go and fall back into a deep oblivion.

Chapter Seventeen

Charlie

THE PAST FEW WEEKS HAVE FLOWN BY WITHOUT much excitement. The last exciting thing to happen was my dental appointment—when Nathan was really sweet to me. The group met up a few times at *Texas Jacks*, and we still see each other—it's just not as frequent as it has been for the last few months.

Halley, and I, had medical training seminars out of town recently, while Nate and the guys are working a lot of extra hours to finish a major project for their company. If they aren't working, then they're home keeping a low profile so they can recuperate. Unfortunately, my time with Nathan has been cut down to half of what it was.

Naomi's been around, but it seems like she's taking this opportunity to have one-on-one time for herself. She said she needed to reconnect with life outside of our group. I can understand that.

As for myself, I haven't had time to go home for family dinners, much to my family's dismay. I can honestly say that if I haven't been busy with work, or out of town for training, then I've been home—retreating to my old ways.

I feel so disconnected, not just with my friends—with

their busy schedules, but with Nathan as well. I can't pinpoint exactly what's going on with him, but I feel like he's pulling away. Ever since our last date, he hasn't asked me out again. Nor has he invited me out to the track when he's racing. I understand that his job is really demanding at the moment, but still, something's not right. I mean, it's not like we don't see each other, or call, and text when we can. It just feels off kilter, and I can't shake this feeling.

I think that's why I've retreated into my shell again. But this time, being around the family, isn't even enough to pull me out of my weird funk. I miss my family a lot, but I miss the connection I have with Nathan even more so. If I think on it too often, it sours my mood, making me less than a joy to be around.

It's Saturday night, and once again, I don't have any plans with a single soul. It's just me, and my DVD player. What a sad, lonely existence I've been living in lately. Thank heavens for work, which keeps me busy. My sisters, and mom, try to keep me up to date with the family, as for Halley and Naomi—they still drop in at random. I guess I'm not completely alone, it just seems like, for the past three weeks, everything has changed.

I pop some popcorn, put one of my favorite movies in the DVD player, and settle in to what I know will be a crying fest soon. I'm still hopeful Nathan will call and ask me to go out, or invite himself over.

About an hour into *The Notebook,* I hit pause to answer my cell. I've been lying in the middle of the floor, feet propped up on a chair while watching the movie.

"Hello?" I sniffle into the receiver, hoping like crazy Nathan will be on the other end.

"Are you watching that movie again?" *Go figure*, I can't even hide that I've been crying—with one clogged word, from Halley.

"So, what if I am?" I volley back, feeling bummed it wasn't who I was secretly wishing for.

"Get your butt up, right now! Go wash your face, and make yourself pretty. We're going out. I'm tired of our lame groups' existence lately. It's time for fun and for once, I don't want any of the Stooges tagging along."

"Halley, are you okay?" I sit up, snatching a tissue off the floor, amongst the mess of popcorn, to wipe my eyes and nose with.

"Why wouldn't I be? I'm bored. I'm *restless*. Work has kept me busy. So, I'm declaring this a girl's night out. *Is that a problem*?"

"No." I climb up onto the couch, getting comfortable with a throw blanket. "I'm bored, too. Though, I'm curious as to why the guys can't come along."

"Do they always have to?" she replies with irritation.

"Are you having problems with Holt?"

"Mr. Non-Commitment? Who, *him*? What's new there? Anyway, why can't a girl hang out with her two best friends, without inviting the guys?"

"Sorry. They don't always have to be with us. I just miss Nate, that's all." I heavily sigh. "I miss the whole group, in general. You know? We had a lot of fun together, before life got in the way and ruined it. Now, I'm back to being a fuddy-duddy again."

"That's exactly why you need to pick your butt up off the floor and get ready!"

"How did you even know I was hanging out on the floor?"

"A lucky guess. Now, quit stalling. Are you in or not?" she asks in matter of fact tone.

"Fine. I'll go get ready. What about Naomi?"

"We're both on our way to you now, actually." she laughs.

"Thanks for the warning." I huff. "I hope you're prepared to wait. I haven't even showered today. It's been a lazy, pajama day."

"Stop yapping, and get ready. We're almost there." She hangs up on me.

I stretch fully out on the couch one last time, then toss my phone onto the cushion next to me, before I head down the hall to start getting ready—knowing that when I get out, they'll be in my apartment waiting.

About 45 minutes later I'm all dolled up and ready to paint the town. I'm not completely feeling it, though. The thoughts of seeing Nathan still plague my mind. It's a good thing I'm getting out of the apartment. I know it'll be ten times better than sitting around, crying my eyes out. I've missed my best friends, and our nights like this before the guys came along with the added complication of feelings.

"I vote for *California Pizza Kitchen*!" Naomi smiles at me when I walk back into the living room.

"Nice! I second the vote."

"CPK it is! Let's go before something else happens in our lame lives." Halley mutters.

I lock up and make a beeline for her truck. I don't know about them, but I'm starving. Even popcorn wasn't enough to curb my hunger.

It takes us about 45 minutes to get where we're going. It's been a long time since we've been here, and I can't wait to dig into their BBQ chicken salad. It's one of my favorites.

"Guys suck." Halley pouts a bit later over a slice of pizza.

"Tell me about it," I mumble in agreement around a bite

of salad.

"What's going on with you two? You're acting like it's the end of the world. The boys have a life, too. It's not like they have to dedicate all of their free time to see us. So everyone's busy with work? It's okay to take a break from people sometimes." Naomi arches a brow at us.

"Stop making a case for them," Halley demands.

"Besides, it's not like they don't check in with us. Don't forget, we *have* spent time with them. In fact, it wasn't that long ago." Naomi point outs.

Ignoring Naomi, Halley asks me, "Do you think the Stooges have even clued in that they're breaking our hearts?"

"What?" Now I'm confused. "I don't feel like my heart is being broken. What's gotten into you, Halley?" Though, I do feel a sense of loss when it comes to Nathan which is something I'm not in the mood to talk to my best friends about.

"It's not like they don't have time to hang out with us, come on!" Halley practically leans across the table, looking between me and Naomi. Though, she gives Naomi more of her sour faced look. "I know we're all busy, I get it. But we've found time before to be together. Now, what? Holt's too busy to even call most days?" frustration runs deep in her voice. "Give me a break." She sinks back into her chair, folding her arms across her chest.

"Wait," I tilt my confused face towards Naomi. "I thought you said they at least called to check in?"

"Tucker does. We've gone out a few times." Naomi tells me, and then looks at Halley. "Seriously, Halley, you're making a big deal out of nothing. I think you're searching for something to hold against Holt, since the relationship you semi have—by the way, isn't going the way you want it to." Narrowing her eyes at Halley, "Why are you asking for borrowed trouble?"

Halley shrugs one shoulder in reply, refusing to voice anything further. I can tell that her irritation has a new target in the form of our best friend, Naomi.

"I admit that I miss the guys, too. Especially Nate."

"Are you two forgetting how much fun we had before they showed up?" Naomi arches her brows.

"Point taken." I smile at her, trying to appease everyone so the conversation doesn't get any more depressing. Also so they can't question me about why I'm missing Nate.

"We're just being silly, and it's probably for no reason at all. Right, Halley?" I look at Halley and in return, she scrunches her disappointed face at me.

"Fine. I'm probably being ridiculous for no reason," she concedes, though it's not convincing in the slightest.

"How about this, next weekend, we'll plan to meet the guys at T. J's. Agreed?" Naomi, the cool level-headed friend of our group, compromises. "Until then, we're not talking about them. We're having fun like we used to." She sternly looks at both Halley and me. "I mean it!"

My phone buzzes right when dessert arrives. Looking down, I see it's from Nate. I can't help the smile that spreads across my face when I look up at the girls. "It's Nate," I share with them before accepting the call. No way am I letting this go to voicemail. They shake their heads at me, Naomi with a smile on her face. Halley on the other hand doesn't look thrilled.

I decide to take the call outside for privacy, so I motion towards the doors, to them to let them know as I speak into the phone.

"Hey, cowboy!" I answer, stepping out into the warm breezy night air. I find a small curb to sit on while I take the call. It's silent for a minute, and I wonder if maybe Nate accidentally hung up on me.

"Nate?" I call into the phone.

"Hey, this is Charlie, right?" A woman asks. Furrowing my brow, I pull the phone away from my ear, and double check the number. Nope, it's not a wrong number. It's definitely his phone.

"Uhh, yes." I hesitantly reply. "Is something wrong with Nate?" I still can't place who this woman is, and I'm trying not to jump to conclusions as to why she's calling me from his phone.

"I was actually hoping you could come down to the house." She sounds apprehensive. "He's in a bad way tonight, and I think he needs someone other than me to take care of him." *Whoa. Who is this woman, and what's going on here?*

"Not to sound rude, but I'm not sure who I'm speaking with."

"Oh! Sorry. This is Nate's sister, Carianna." Well, colored me shocked. I've never spoken to her before. Of course, I've heard of her name in passing and a tidbit about her. Though, I had yet to meet her.

"Would you mind coming over as soon as possible? I'm a bit worried about him." Now I'm worried even more because of this weird conversation.

"Carianna, what's going on? Is he hurt? What happened?" I'm such a worrier and this cryptic conversation is doing nothing to ease my nerves.

"I'm sorry. I'm not at liberty to say what's going on. It's his story to tell. All I can say is that he's not okay, and he's needs more than I can give to him. The guys called me over, but I think he would want you here more than me. Do you think you can come over? I can leave the spare key under the mat for you."

Okay, what does she expect me to say, no? Not going to happen? Find someone else to take care of my man? Wait, *is he my man*? It sure feels like it, although we haven't officially declared ourselves to each other.

"Carianna, I'm pretty sure Nate wouldn't want me there." I quietly admit to her.

"He would. Trust me. He may act like he wouldn't want you here, but deep down he knows he needs you. He's too scared to admit it. This will be good for him." She tries to reassure me.

"I'm not sure you have the right of it." I try again.

"Then make it the right way." She quietly demands. "Charlie, trust me on this one. Nathan needs you."

"I hope you're right." I sigh. I know he's going to be so mad when he finds out his sister called me. "All right, I'm on my way. I'm up in Walnut Creek at the moment, so it'll take some time to get there."

"I'll stay with him for an hour then head out."

"By the way, where are Holt and Tucker?" I ask, realizing that they hadn't called me with worry over their friend.

"They took off to play pool, and to give Nate some space for a bit," she tells me. "I'm sorry we haven't officially met. Nathan doesn't bring anyone home to meet the family."

"Can you give me any clues as to what's going on?"

"I think it would be best if he told you why he gets like this once a year."

"That's not really helping."

"I know, and I'm sorry. It's the best I can do. I'm already meddling enough, and if he finds out you know, before he shares it with you, he will blow his lid. I'm already on shaky ground here as is, with phoning you."

"All right. Like I said, I'm not in town, so I need to get my friends and head back that way. And—Carianna, thank you for calling me. I wish we had met under better circumstances, even if it *is* over the phone."

"Me too," she quietly replies. "Thank you."

"I wish I could say you're welcome but to be honest, I'm scared here. If he won't even tell me about his family, and with whatever is going on, he's going to be ticked when he sees me."

"I know. I'm sorry, but thank you anyway. I truly believe it will all work out."

We say our goodbyes and hang up. I'm not sure this is a great plan, as I stand here, in the parking lot feeling at a loss for words. Eventually I get my thoughts collected, and return to the restaurant.

I get inside and head to the table where the other two give me questioning looks.

"So—what's up? Did he want to see you?" Halley inquires.

"It wasn't Nate."

"*What*?" They ask in unison.

"It was his sister, Carianna." I shake my head, still trying to make sense of what just happened.

"Uhh—okay?" A perplexed Naomi questions.

"I just had the strangest conversation with his sister. I can't make sense of it, but I do know that I need to leave so I can see what's going on with Nate. The others are at *Texas Jacks*. I bet if we leave right now, you can catch up with them."

"What do you mean it was strange?" Naomi asks.

"I don't know for sure. She said he was feeling really sick, and she felt like he needed me."

"Sick? I'm still not connecting the dots here. Also, why are you telling us we could meet up with the guys?" a very confused Halley asks.

"Something's going on with Nate. Apparently he gets like this once a year. What does that even mean?" I ask my friends, like they have a clue.

"What does that even mean?" Halley repeats.

"I don't know. She told me she wasn't at liberty to say. Apparently, he would be upset if she told me, rather than hearing it straight from him."

"It sounds like we need to get our check and clear out. We'll swing by your place to get your car, after we drop you off at Nate's on the way." Halley says, as she waves over the waitress.

After paying, we make a hasty retreat and Halley heads straight for the guys' place. Fifty minutes later, we're taking the exit that will lead us to his place.

"I'm sorry to leave you both in the middle of our girl time." I tell them apologetically as we wind our way through the neighborhoods.

"Don't even worry about it." Naomi assures me. "But please, let us know if you need anything while you're there," she offers.

"We'll reschedule our girls' night for another time, don't worry." Halley reassures me. "For now, we'll go check in with the guys, to make sure all is well with them. Maybe they can shed some light on the matter."

"Thanks. I'll text you when I know more." I say goodbye and hop out of the truck that's idling in front of Nate's house.

His truck is in the drive and the porch light is on. I head up to the door, lifting up the mat to find the key Carianna had promised to leave. Upon opening the front door, I realize she left the front entry-way light on for me. I make my way to the kitchen, flipping on the light when I enter the room, setting my purse on the kitchen counter with my coat on top of it, before taking in my surroundings. It doesn't seem like anything is out of the ordinary. I didn't even see Nathan when I came into the house. I take in a deep breath and call out to Nate. The last thing I want to do is scare the daylights out of him. When I don't get a response, I decide to take action by heading down the hall towards Nate's room, and get to the bottom of the mystery of what's going on with him.

I flip the hall light on, slightly pausing at his closed bedroom door, listening for any noises to give me any signs that he's even in there. It's silent so I reach out my hand and twist the door knob, not knowing what I will be walking into.

I step inside, but leave the door open so I can see what's going on from the hall light. Walking in as quietly as I can, I make my way over to his bed to find him resting. From what I can tell, everything seems fine. I don't see wadded up tissues, a barf bucket, or even a bottle of medication on his night stand by his bed. I'm not sure what his sister was worried about. He's lightly snoring, lying on his side. Though, he's not covered up. I start searching his room for a blanket, so I can go wait in the front room until he wakes up, or someone comes home, and that's when I see it. It's a bottle of Jack Daniels sitting on his side table by his alarm clock, that's on the opposite side of his bed.

I'm shocked, frozen like a deer in headlights, not sure what to do next. From what I know of Nate, he's not one to drink hard liquor or to get drunk. *What's going on?*

I slowly ease myself onto his bed, trying not to ruffle it, or startle him. Turns out that wouldn't have matter as he's out for the count. I take him all in, realizing he's lying in his pajamas on top of his covers. I slowly rise from the bed to go out to the hall linen closet to find him a blanket. Searching his room was a fruitless endeavor—though I didn't really look too hard, then head back into his room and lay the blanket over him. There's nothing I can do at this point, except get him items that will help when he wakes up. Deciding on my next plan of action, I go back into the kitchen to look for pain relievers. While I'm there—I get him a glass of water, and grab the garbage can, too. It may come in handy. I can already tell this is going to be a long night.

Before I head back into his room, I shoot a text to my friends to let them know that I don't know what's going on, but I will keep them in the loop when I get to the bottom of this. I wish them a good night with the guys, and then turn my attention back to the objects I need.

I gather up all the items from the kitchen and head back down the hall. I grab a towel from the closet, before returning to his room. I lay everything out where he can easily get to them, wondering if I should sit on his bed and wait this out, in-case he needs me? Or, should I just wing it, and crawl into bed so I can hold him? I'm not good at this, and I don't want to freak Nate out if I climb into his bed. *Or is it myself I don't freak out?* Though, we had a trial run at this the night he came over to watch over me. So, I guess the nervousness I'm feeling can take a flying leap.

As I'm lost in my musings, I feel movement on the bed, when I see Nate blindly reaching for the covers. I take over in his struggles, pulling the blanket higher up over his chest. He accidentally hits my hand with his hand, causing his eyes to fly open. At first, his eyes rapidly blink, and then go to squinting at me, trying to piece together who I am. When he finally recognizes me—he gives me a lazy smile. *Does he realize I'm actually here?*

He reaches out again, this time to grab my hand with his, and entwines our fingers together. "What are you doing here, little one? Please tell me I'm not dreaming, and you're really here in my room." He sounds so out of it. *How much did he drink?*

I smile back at him, trying to tease him. "Maybe this isn't a dream, and you're stuck in a nightmare."

He drunkenly laughs. "Heaven, I hope not." He looks up at me, then orders, "Stay with me."

I hesitate, "I'm not sure if this is a good idea, Nate."

"I don't know what I need, or how you came to be here. What I do know is that I need to feel you in my arms. I can't even describe it. I just have this sudden urge to hold you, Charlie. I need your arms around me." He says while tugging on my hand, causing me to fall onto the bed and slightly onto him at the same time. I quickly right myself, and then slide in to place beside Nate on his queen size bed. We lay there silently for a few moments just taking in the silence, wrapped in each other's arms.

Eventually he rolls us both onto our sides, then sighs out in contentment.

"Waking up to your pretty face could never be a bad thing. If I could wake up every day to your gorgeous face, I would die happy." His words warm my cheeks and cause my insides to get all funny. "Did she call you?"

"Carianna?"

"You know, it doesn't even matter that she did. It's enough that you're even here."

"Are you sure this is okay? You won't be mad at me tomorrow?"

"She would have loved you, you know." He suddenly, but quietly states into the darkness, ignoring my questions.

"Who?" I don't have the foggiest idea as to who he's referring to. It's not like he's given me many clues about his family, or past girlfriends.

"She was full of life, love, and just pure happiness." He continues, as if I didn't just ask him another question. "I wish you could have met her." He twines his fingers through mine again, resting them at my belly. "She was always there, cheering us on, you know? No matter what we were doing—winning, or failing—she was the biggest cheerleader you could ever wish to have."

I'm at a loss, as to who he's reminiscing about, but I realize that it's best to just let him continue on without speaking in return. I wonder if he will remember any of this tomorrow. Will he be mad that he told me these personal thoughts? Or will he feel relieved, maybe even free of the ghost that haunts him?

"She was always making us laugh, or volunteering for whatever school function she could. We were *that* house that everyone loved to come over to, and never go home from. She became like a second mom to Holt, and Tucker. Boy did we ever try her patience with our pranks. We were a bunch of teenage troublemakers, that's for sure. Staying out way passed curfew, dating too many girls, and not finding that one good girl to hang on to, stirring up trouble with our friends. Though, she was the one who taught us how to toilet paper houses." He chuckles. "You should have seen her with the three of us, and my sister. It was a riot.

"We used to tell her that there was no way we would settle with one woman. Where was the fun in that? Though, we knew it was more just to tease her, and that we didn't really believe we would be serial daters. She used to lecture our ears off about settling down with a good girl when we were older. She would remind us about how her, and dad, had such a strong love. 'Once you find the one, you will know it', she would say. She really believed in the theory of—'The one'. Their marriage really was a great example for us to learn from. It wasn't perfect, by any means. They just learned how to deal with their issues, and when to let go of a losing battle.

"She was so pretty, too. She wasn't much taller than you, with her shoulder length, black hair. I remember she would always pin her bangs up to the side, to keep them out of her eyes. And she always knew when you were up to no good. I don't know how she did it, and she never did get the chance to reveal her secrets to us. She was still full of life when she passed. Though, you could see the strain and exhaustion in her frail body, as it was ravished by cancer.

"She didn't want anyone feeling sorry for her. She did her best to keep up appearances, like she wasn't sick but still healthy. She tried her hardest to be involved with as much as her body would allow. Some days though, she wouldn't be able to get out of bed. It got to the point that the rest of us stopped going out. No one wanted to be away from her. Carianna and I would come home during school lunch breaks to check on her. Dad eventually started working from home. When we couldn't be there, due to obligations, we had friends and family stay with her around the clock. No one could bear to be apart from her, but sometimes you can't help it, right? Heaven, we hated those times we had to leave her, not knowing if we would come home to find her gone. It was pure agony and you couldn't concentrate on the tasks you had to accomplish.

"Even Tucker and Holt started staying over all the time. Luckily their parents understood, and knew how much she loved them, and vice versa." He stops, and I hear nothing except the white noise of the house, as he mentally collects himself. My eyes burn with tears, as does my throat—as it tightens a little more, not allowing words to pass my lips. Even if I want to speak, I know there's nothing I can say at this point, or that would penetrate his ears. I feel like he's talking to me, yet he's not. I now know that he's talking about a lost parent, one he had a deep love and respect for. One who was his whole life. The reason he no longer gives his heart away fully, just partially. The only thing I can do is just lay here, hold his hand a little tighter, and let him get it all out. I just pray he doesn't regret this by the light of day.

"I had a serious girlfriend at the time." He picks up the thread of the story again, with more new pieces of his life.

"Her name is Heather. We had these great plans to marry after high school, and be just like my parents. Heaven, we were so young and so hopeful that love lasted forever. We wanted to keep their example going so we could pass it down to our children. I was going to own my own construction company with the guys, have a few kids, and even get a dog. We planned to stay in town, so our kids could grow up around their grandparents. I guess that was all wishful thinking. Now? There's no way I can even think of subjecting anyone to that kind of pain. I can't even imagine having a child at this point. I don't want to imagine the day they would have to suffer the loss of a parent. How can life be so cruel, to take away a beautiful, vibrant woman? It's horrible to think about, let alone speak about." His whole body shudders. My ears are ringing from his words, my mind is going a million miles a minute, but all I can do is continue to lie still, and take his words in.

"You know my truck? It was hers," he quietly informs me with a deeper emotion in his voice, than previously. "She took such good care of it, like it was another child. The day she gave up the good fight, it was passed down to me." His voice hitches. "I didn't even want it, though she tried to talk to me about it closer to the end. I would do anything, trade anything, to have her back. I didn't want her stupid truck. I just wanted her." He curls into me more, holding on tighter. I listen as he silently sobs into my hair, but not daring to speak words I know nothing of to help soothe his soul. I can only be the person he holds, while he lets his past come to life in the late hour of the night.

We stay that way for a really long time until he eventually drifts back to sleep. His body relaxes, but I stay right there in the same spot, not wanting to leave. I don't think my legs would work anyway. My whole body feels numb from staying in one position for so long, and I am just so tired. I know I should probably get up and head to the couch, but really—I can't physically make myself do it. Instead, I just let my mind comb over his words until the darkness takes over and I fall asleep, with Nate wrapped around me for warmth and comfort.

Nate

I'm looking at one of the most beautiful faces I love to see, wondering how she ended up here, in my bed. I don't remember calling her. Maybe one of the guys' called her? I must have been really bad off last night for them to ask her to come over. I wouldn't have thought they would ever go there, but apparently they did. My mind is still fuzzy from the details of the previous night.

I feel like the worst jerk in the history of my life. The guys knew that I didn't want her to come over here to see me in this sad state. It's precisely why I didn't call her myself, in the first place. Apparently Holt, or Tucker, had other ideas, thinking they know what's best for me. They did try to tell me this the last time we all worked out together.

There's nothing I can do now, since she's already here. I might as well make the best of it. I pepper kisses down her nose, across her cheek, then up her temple before coming down to her mouth. I lightly kiss her a few times, praying my breath isn't disgusting from the Jack. She stirs, and I watch as her eyes slowly start to open.

At first she seems shocked to see me until she realizes where she is, giving me a timid smile. I'm not sure why she's being this way. *What did I say last night?*

"Come here, Charlie." I softy order her.

She still seems hesitant but rolls further into me, mumbling, "I wasn't sure what you were going to need, so I grabbed a garbage can, pain medicine, water, and a towel." she says with a shy hint to her voice.

Well if that isn't the kicker of all things grand. My girl comes to see me, I'm drunk and she's gotten all of the things she thinks will help me feel better. What do I say to that? But before I can even say another word, she's talking again.

"To answer your earlier questions, yes, your sister called me to come take care of you."

"Wait, *what*?" I don't recall anything about my sister being here. "What questions, and why was my sister here?"

I know it's the anniversary of my mom's death, but Carianna isn't usually around to watch me make a fool of myself. It's been years since she's tried to talk sense into my head. I was positive she had given up on me at this point.

"Last night," she shyly replies. "Umm—you know, when you weren't feeling good?"

"No, I honestly can't remember anything." I mutter, silently loathing the horrible Jack Daniels.

"Oh," she sadly whispers.

"I thought the guys had called you to come take care of my sorry self." I chuckle, not truly feeling funny. It's not a joking matter but I need to cut the tension she's starting to feel.

"I didn't even realize you had moments like this." She's states, causing my body to go rigid.

"Moments like this?" I try to keep the suspicion of what I know is coming out of my voice.

She doesn't respond, so I prod her along. "Did my sister say something last night, Charlie?"

"Not really." She falters. "Just that umm—," she starts

stumbling over her words, unsure of what she should say, apparently.

"What exactly did she say, Charlotte?" I never call her by her full name, unless I'm serious and need her to listen and pay attention.

"Just that once a year you get really drunk, but it wasn't her place to tell me why. She was afraid you would get mad. Like right now." I can tell she's lacking all confidence now in this conversation, not wanting to say something she shouldn't, or letting anything slip further that my sister's big mouth might have told her.

"That was it?" I cock my head to the side, peering down into her face, with as blank of a face as I can manage.

"Yes," she's reluctantly admits. "I promise, Nathan, she didn't say anything else. Please don't be mad at me, or her." She pleads.

I relax a little, changing my demeanor. *For now,* "It's fine, Charlie. Don't worry. I'm not mad at you." Smiling at her as best as I can manage.

"And your sister?"

"Don't worry about her. It'll clear itself up." *Eventually.* I silently reply. "Let's get up and get you fed. You must be starved. I know I am!" I roll us to a sitting position, kiss her nose, then hop off the bed, and make my way to the bathroom. I need to compose myself more, before she catches onto anything else.

I can hear the guys ribbing her about spending the night when I get back to the front of the house. She looks thoroughly embarrassed, red faced and all. "Ready for some pancakes?" I ask before cutting a look at the guys, letting them know to knock it off.

"I think it is best if I just go home," she says uncomfortably, though she still gives me a small smile.

"Are you sure?"

"She doesn't want your foul-tasting tongue in her mouth." Tucker crassly taunts.

"Seriously?" I'm not in the mood for his stupid jokes this morning.

"All right, everyone calm down. Stop with the taunting and insults." Holt surprisingly intervenes, while he watches Charlie's face closely.

I can tell she's upset. The balance I was trying to ride has tipped over, and I'm not sure where this will go after whatever happened between us last night. I can only guess at what it was. I know eventually my memories will come flooding back, and it might be too late to go back to what we were.

"I'll walk you to your car." I offer. She gives me a sad smile, but nods her head.

"Bye." She quietly tells the others, before heading out the door.

I look back to see the guys watching us, curiously, noting that Holt looks upset. "What did you do?" he asks.

"I have no idea. I do know that Carianna called her over here, and told her I get like this once a year then left us to ourselves. Take from that what you will." I turn on my heels, making a slow exit to all knowing eyes. I bet we all can figure out what happened. The question is—will she ask me about what happened?

I wonder how long it's going to take her, or if she's too scared. Only time will tell, and time is what I'm afraid of the most. I don't think I can allow this to go any further.

It will only save us both in the long run, for my sake, and hers.

Right?

Chapter Eighteen

Charlie

I T'S BEEN OVER A WEEK SINCE NATHAN INADVERTENTLY revealed his broken heart to me. He's been distant, to the point where we go days without talking, or communicating in any way. Right now, I'm looking at Nate, and I can tell something is going on behind those all too knowing eyes. I just haven't the faintest idea what's holding him back from me. I feel like this rift in our relationship is causing him to slip through my fingers, and I'm powerless to stop it.

I try to ask questions, but he brushes them off, like nothing is the matter—when I know that's so far from the truth, it's laughable. Honestly, all was fine until his incident with a bottle of Jack. That's when he rapidly started to change.

At the moment, we're at his house, trying to enjoy a relaxing evening. I feel like he's trying to pretend we're okay—to him or to me, I'm not sure. I know it's not for the guys' benefit. I can see the irritation in their eyes as I sit here, silently watching him from my place on the couch while he talks with them. He's completely unaware that I'm watching the way he acts towards me—or *doesn't* act.

I haven't brought up the night he spilled his guts to me,

nor do I want to. He was so upset when he thought his sister had told me what was going on. His demeanor towards me completely changed. So, I'm waiting for him to open up again, on his own terms, and while he's sober. I want him to actually remember our conversation. When he didn't remember it the next morning, I was crushed. It meant so much that he finally opened up about his family, only for him to be completely oblivious of it. I hate that he doesn't even know he told me about his mother. I want to talk to him so badly, but I know if I do, it will only push him further away. I'm definitely not enlisting the guys for help, either. They haven't even brought it up; though, I get the nagging feeling they want to say something. Instead, they stand firmly behind their friend and keep their lips tightly closed on anything Jackson family-related.

I don't know how much longer I can sit back and watch him destroy us before it's too late. But I do know this—only time will tell what will happen between us, and I refuse to give in, or give up on him.

The man who holds my heart in the palm of his hand. The man I know, without a shadow of a doubt that I love.

Nate

I haven't spoken too much to Charlie in the last week or so. It's a jerk move, I know, but I need space to dig deep into what we were truly doing. Or more like, what *I* was doing. I was breaking all of my self-imposed rules for one tempting, chocolate-brown haired, and blue-eyed beauty. We had an instant connection, and I let my heart run away with this little woman. It's not what I would normally do, but I couldn't resist the pull toward her.

The guys are at their own breaking point when it comes to this situation. They're trying to stay out of it, but I can see it in their faces. They really want to lay into me good, or get me into a boxing ring and pound it out of my head. That might be a real possibility at the moment, as I'm definitely going crazy.

I know I'm not broken. I'm just reserved in taking the plunge with a relationship. Though—I came really close to it with Charlie. That's precisely the reason I've been keeping a distance from her after the night she came to my drunken aid. *Am I ready to settle down?* I don't see why I couldn't be— as long as it came with a set of certain expectations. Can I go through the motions of growing old, and losing my love? *No.* Can I stand by and watch when she's in pain while she's sick, or having our child? *Absolutely not.*

After all we went through in losing the glue that held the family together, and seeing how it tore my father apart, it makes me reluctant to put myself completely out there for her. But then again, I honestly don't know if I could handle losing the woman I hold so close to my heart. I also could never dream of putting my children through that torture, either.

I know that I'm probably way too young to think along these lines, but you never know when fate wants to deal you a nasty hand. One minute, it's beautiful and all is well, but then in a moment, it all becomes darkness, and your life blurs from one day to the next, just going through the motions.

There is a part, deep down in my soul that wants to say yes, I can handle life lessons like that. But then, there's a bigger, louder part of me that can't dwell on the "what ifs", so I try not to go down that road. At the moment, though—I just feel so lost and torn up over Charlie. I want to stop being a jerk to her, *and* my friends. The question is—*can I do it, without giving in to the feelings that haunt me?*

Every time I see Charlie, she gets to me, working my insides over until I'm turned into knots. I know I'm on a collision course now, one where putting on the brakes at this point will completely wreck me.

I know I need to let go of the pain from losing my mother and finally let the grieving process run its course through my heart. The guys are right; Charlie can see me through this, if I choose to let her. But if I can't even deal with it, going on eight years now, then why would I want to put her through the motions with me? She deserves to be happy with a man who can give her everything she wants when it comes to a future life and family. Heaven knows I want to be that man. I just can't make myself do it, and I would do anything for Charlie. *Anything.* This is the one and only challenge blocking me. *So why hold her back?*

The images of her at her parents' house are seared into my mind. The love, laughter, and the closeness this tightknit family has hurts my heart in a bittersweet way. I want what she has. I used to have what she has. I took that for granted, and now it no longer exists. My father works like a well-oiled machine, leaving no time for my sister and I. We rarely talk anymore. We certainly never have a family night for food, togetherness, and laughter over silly games. He managed to lose himself in his work, once he lost the star that brightened his world. I know he will never recover from my mother's loss, and I certainly can't blame him for that.

As for Carianna, she didn't make good life choices for a while. I had to bail her out of many troubling issues, and show up for court-appointed hearings as my father's replacement. She lost her way, without a female role model to show her the ropes. I was her mother and father figure, and at the same time, trying to be her big brother, watching her back. Thankfully, she's better now, and she has Brett, her boyfriend, to fall back on.

We each seem to have our own mechanisms for coping with the loss of our loved one. Carianna got into trouble, my dad gave up and became more or less robotic, and then there's me—afraid of having a deeper relationship with anyone, but especially with the one who can crush me the most. *Charlie.*

I'm stretched out on the couch, playing these thoughts over in my head, remembering how much Charlie scared me the night she had car trouble, when my phone dings with a text. I snatch it up off my chest to find a message from Charlie, checking in for the day. I send her a reply, keeping it short, but semi-sweet.

My mind takes me back to the night Charlie saw me at my worst. Worst for now, at least, though nothing compares to the night I lost my mom. It took some time, but the longer I sit here, the memories slowly trickle in of the events that played out that evening in my room. It's the reason I've suddenly distance myself from Charlie. Thinking about everything that my loose tongue told her just drives me mad. I'm mad that I unloaded my burdens on her. I'm equally just as mad that she hasn't tried to talk to me about them, either. She now has knowledge of what happened, and not once has she even made an attempt to bring it up. It's not like I really want to dive into this topic, again. *But, what gives*? Why isn't she trying to save me for my own good, like everyone else? It's not what I want from her, but how do you not say anything? Especially when it's something as big as this?

I can't fathom it. She's my heart, my world, and I wanted that comfort from her. I'm hurt that she hasn't tried, in her own way, to break the barriers I set up. Instead, she just sat back and allowed the space to separate us. She was somehow able to let me be the kind of man I never thought I would be able to be again with a woman—which only shows how upset I am now that she hasn't tried to save me from myself. But most of all, I'm mad at myself for ruining what we had. I should have taken better care of it, and not gotten so stupid that night. I usually keep my faculties about me the week of that anniversary, though I'm not so easy to be around. But I *never* get obliterated like that. This year, I blew it with not only Charlie, but with myself and my closest friends. They lost her, too, and I became selfish, not bothering to accommodate for their pain, as well.

At this point, my friends aren't thrilled with me, or how I'm handling things. And then there's Charlie. *What to do about this sweet, young lady? Can I truly find that happy balance we once had?* I know I haven't lost her. *Yet.* It's just a matter of time before I truly push her away for good. Now, I just have to decide if that's really what I want. My heart and gut scream at me, telling me *no.* It's my head that says it's the right move. It's hard to keep up in this fight of what's right for her and what I selfishly want and how I want it.

I guess time will only tell which side will fall in the battle.

A few more weeks pass when I decide that I really need to find solace. And there's only one place for that to happen, so I take my bike out to the track. Thankfully, everyone else is too busy to pay me much attention, though I can see Shelly conspiring with Lisa over by the old snack shack. If she knows what's good for her, she will stay clear of my warpath. I have no patience for her or her antics today.

I'm relieved that I don't see Charlie's friends here this

afternoon. They're not high on the list of people I want to run in to at the moment. I can only imagine what they think, as I'm sure between Charlie and the guys, they've been fully briefed on my idiocy.

I'm about to push my bike out to the dirt course when I feel a hand on my arm. I look to its owner, only to find Shelly, who happens to be accompanied by Lisa. I look down at Shelly's hand then back up into her eyes with what I know is not a friendly look.

"I'm not in the mood for your games today, Shelly. Find a new bag of tricks, then try them out on someone else, for once." I brush her hand off my arm and start walking again.

"Well," she coldly states, "there's no reason for you to be nasty about it." She sniffs, while wiping her hand on her pant leg.

"If you're here to say something stupid about Charlie, or try to throw yourself at me, then you can move along. This fish isn't biting."

"I only came over to see why you were in a foul mood."

"And what do you know about that?" I eye her suspiciously.

"It's easy to tell. You're walking around with a scowl on your face, acting broody, and won't talk to anyone."

"How do you know?"

"I've been watching."

"I bet you have. I'm sure you were wishing Charlie would stop by so you can kick up more havoc in my life, right?"

"What's gotten into you? What happened to the one guy everyone thought was a gentleman?"

"Sorry to burst your bubble, but even nice guys have terrible days."

"I did notice that your girlfriend hasn't been around much." She's pushing for more information, but I'm not willing to give her any new ammunition.

"Don't worry, we didn't break up," I deadpan.

"Who says I was worried?"

"Are we done now? Or did you want something else out of me? More dirt on Charlie, or something else altogether?"

"Geez, Nate! I just wanted to see why you were upset. Honestly. I guess that was too much to ask for—one guy to be nice to loser Shelly." She turns on her heel and starts to walk away.

"Shelly," I call. "For the record, if you lost the attitude, dressed with more rather than less, and if you weren't so catty or all over all of the men, you would probably be able to find a decent guy." I turn back to the track.

I shrug Shelly off and spend the rest of the day riding, finding peace within myself. It's an exhilarating feeling—being on my dirt bike and back at the track. I'm regaining my balance here. Now, if I can just find a way to do that with Charlie, my life would be in such a better place.

Chapter Nineteen

Charlie

I FEEL LIKE I'M MARCHING TO THE BEAT OF A DYING DRUM, while life passes me by. Nate's still being distant, and now we go out even less. *If that were even possible.* He still calls and checks in with me, or sends quick texts to make sure all is right in my world, though I want to tell him so badly that it's not. That nothing is okay anymore. I know he's trying to hold on to what little of this so-called relationship is left. But the sad thing is—I don't even know what sent this sweet, loving, caring, and funny man in the direction that he has us on. He has one drunken episode, and the next day he starts putting me on the backburner? It doesn't seem like Nate. And, once again, I'm back to being a wallflower, suffering a lonely existence. I'm too depressed lately to do much of anything, let alone visit my family, and it's rare that I miss them for anything. I haven't seen much of the girls lately, either—though that's mainly due to my own fault. I definitely haven't chatted with the guys, as they are Nate's territory. No way do I want to step on a landmine in that house and watch it blow to smithereens.

I'm scared that soon, there won't be a 'Nate and I' left to pick up the pieces. He's put up a barrier between us, but there are still times when he's sweet and loving towards me. I know he has no true desire to hurt me, or be so mean through his actions, but he has changed, and he's not willing to share the reason why. I've finally come to the conclusion that it all centers on the night he unknowingly talked so openly with me. I know he doesn't remember what happened, though he thinks his sister talked to me about something secretive. But now? I'm starting to wonder if he actually recalls what was said, and he's angry that he let it slip. *I mean, what else could it be?* If he doesn't remember telling me anything, he wouldn't be acting this way toward me.

One would think he would eventually want to tell me about his family, and past. *Right?* I'm basically his girlfriend, even if I haven't been given the official stamp that says I am. I only know that I'm at my wit's end now. It's at the point where I can't sit back as the quiet mouse anymore. I know I have to do something to draw him out from this thundercloud he's living under. All I want to do is to be there for him like he's been there for me, pulling me out from my shell, and making me feel so alive.

And to make matters worse, for the last two weeks, just about every day when I turn on my car's radio, I hear these words coming out of my speakers: *"Say something, I'm giving up on you."* So today, when I get in my car to head home from work, it's no different, and the nagging words yet again flow from the speakers, bouncing around in my head.

My eyes start to water, and I wonder, is this what Nate is doing? *Is he finally giving up on us?* My heart races every time I hear these words, knowing the truth of them. I know the time is now or never to finally say something to him. *Wasn't he always there, prodding me along, and making me open up? Wasn't he the one who worried over me when my car broke down, when I had water blisters, or other medical needs? He's been my rock, and what have I've been for him?* I'm more like his quicksand, not holding out my hand to help once it was bitten the first time. I've quietly stayed in the background, giving him space and time to heal so he can come to terms that we are okay, but not questioning anything. I now know that was very wrong of me. I can't even use the excuse of little dating experience for my blunder. There is really no excuse at all.

At first, my mind had whirled with the age-old relationship questions of: *Is he not happy with me? Is he tired of having to pull me out from the recesses of my shy self?* I thought we were doing great, and I had opened up so much more to him than I ever had before. Now, I know better. I know it's not me that doesn't make him happy. I know for a fact that I do. I just need to find a way to ground him, and bring him back to me.

These are the thoughts I have on my mind when I pull into my spot at the apartment complex. I turn off the engine, pull the keys from the ignition, and lay my head back against the seat rest. I close my eyes and let the tears flow down my face, wondering when I'll see Nate next.

I don't know how much time has passed since I've been sitting in my car when I realize that the sun is going down and here I am, crying in the driver's seat for the whole world to see. I fumble for my purse on the passenger's seat and turn to unlock my car door to climb out. Just as I'm about to get out of the car, my phone starts to ring. I look at the caller ID and see that it's Nate.

I quickly dry my eyes on the back of my shirtsleeves and clear my throat, then answer the phone, trying to sound like I haven't been crying.

"Hi, cowboy. How was your day?" I greet him, feeling relieved that my voice didn't give me away. I decide that I need to help get us back to *us*, and invite him over so we can talk, have dinner, and work it out. I'm feeling wholly optimistic about the outcome.

"Hey, Charlie. My day wasn't too bad," he replies. "Just calling to make sure you made it home from work okay."

"Yes, I'm home. I was just getting ready to head in to the apartment," I tell him, and then realize here's my opening to see him. Closing my eyes and crossing my fingers, I ask, "Would you like to come over? I can make us dinner, and we chat for a little while—I miss you," I add at the end in a whisper.

There's a little bit of hesitancy on Nate's part before he tells me, "I miss you, too. I would love to come over tonight, but I already have plans to hang out with the guys."

My eyes start to water again, and I don't even try to hold them back. I let them silently roll down my cheeks and quietly say, "Oh. Okay." Then rush the rest out before I turn into a chicken. "That's fine. I hope you have a good time with the guys. Make sure you tell them hello for me."

"Charlie, are you—"

But he doesn't even get to finish that statement, because I cut him off and calmly keep talking. "It's okay, go out and have fun with the guys and be safe. Listen, Nate, I'm sitting in my car, it's getting late, and I really would like to get inside. I'll text you later to see how you all are doing. I've gotta go. Bye!" I quickly hang up the phone before he can even get one more word in.

I don't want to hear any other excuses, or suffer through the strain that will surely be mixed into our conversation now. Maybe I can't be the strong one in the group. I'm beyond tired and filled with worry, wondering what his problem is—though I now believe I know what the deal is. He won't talk about it when I try to, and it's getting exhausting. I'm starting to feel that it's up to Nathan at this point to let me in on the world's best kept secret, the one that's tampering with our relationship. I can make calculated guesses all I want, but I need confirmation. For tonight, though, I knew I couldn't sit there one more moment and listen to the awkwardness and lame excuses, let alone anything else he had to say. I need my sanity back. I want my happy existence back. I might even want my fuddy-duddy life back, the one I had before he came in and destroyed me.

I can't sit here any longer, either, with tears falling unchecked down my face. Taking a deep, calming breath, I get out of the car and walk up to my apartment. I barely get the door unlocked when I get a text. I look down and see it's from Nate. I don't even want to know what it says, so I completely ignore it as I walk into my place, shutting and locking the door behind me.

Once inside, I stand in the middle of my apartment, staring off into space. I can't really decide what to do at the moment. *Stay here and wallow in self-pity, or go for a drive and try to calm my mind?* There *has to* be away to fix us, even if Nathan doesn't seem to want that. My phone chimes again just as I decide it would be best to get out of here. Looking down at my phone again, I see it's Naomi, and I just don't have the heart to talk to anyone right now, so I push *ignore*, turn back around, and leave my apartment.

Nate

Charlie says goodbye on the phone and hangs up immediately, not even giving me the chance to say it back to her. I feel like a jerk, as I have for many weeks now. I know she's upset, but trying valiantly to hide it. I hate it when she cries; it always gets to me. Right now, I'm so conflicted. I want to give her my whole heart, and to think of our future, but at the same time, it scares me to death.

I decide that the best thing I can do at this moment is to send her a text, letting her know that I'm really sorry, and I'll call her later to see when she's free, then hit *send*. I wait for a few minutes but she doesn't reply, causing me to let out a heavy breath.

At this very moment, I feel like stomping on my own heart, or at least what's left of it. A part of me wants to tell the guys I've got something to do, and race over to see her. I want to scoop her up, hold her tight in my arms, and promise her it will be all right, and that we're going to make it.

But it's not what I do. Instead, I call out to the guys, "Get a move on, or I'm leaving you high and dry. I think you know Pete and Repeat, don't you?"

I hear a laugh, and someone throws his balled up, dirty socks at me from down the hall. I jump out of the path of the stinky ammunition coming my way, then head to the bathroom to shower and get ready to leave.

Holt and Tucker finally called a truce on their attitude towards me, and we're starting to get along. I'm glad it didn't last too long, though I know they secretly hide ill feelings towards me in regards to me dodging Charlie, and the whole mess of our relationship. I appreciate that they're more or less staying out of it, though.

It's an hour later when Holt, Tucker, and I all climb in my truck and head to *Texas Jacks*. We decided it was a good night to hustle some out-of-towners at the pool tables. Heck, *anything* is better at this point than thinking about Charlie and what she's feeling. I'm not trying to be a jerk, here. I just know that once I really start to think about it, my conscience will eat at me. Then I'll be hauling my tail over to her place and begging for forgiveness over distancing myself from her.

I let out an inward sigh and pull into the parking lot of our favorite haunt. We climb out of the truck and head to the doors, where I spot Dave. He's looking at me with narrowed eyes, and is definitely not too pleased to see me. I'm not sure what his deal is, or why he's looking at me like he wants to take me out back and kick the ever-loving stuffing out of me. I nudge Holt's arm saying, "If I go missing later tonight, look in the back parking lot. I'm thinking Dave has plans for me that I don't want to be a part of."

Holt looks over at Dave, then back to me, and lets out a small laugh as we get up close and personal with Mr. Snake Eyes himself.

"Dave, what's shaking?" Tuck asks. "It looks like you're about to incinerate my pal over here with that look you've got going on. Did he do something that warrants the death stare you're giving him?" Tucker decides to jump into the situation, in case Dave wants to blast me straight to heaven.

Dave just shakes his head at me and says, "If you don't know why I'm seriously pissed at you, then you're a bigger fool than I thought." Then he stamps our hands and tells us to get lost before moving on to the next group in line.

Well, that was interesting. What's his deal, anyway?

We make it past the doors and over to the pool tables when Holt notices Halley and Naomi hanging out at one of the tables by the dance floor. He decides to wave them over to hang out. When the ladies see us, they smile and get up to head our way.

"What are the Three Stooges up to tonight?" Halley asks Holt, giving me a narrow-eyed look.

"Just a few rounds of pool, my dear," he tells her as he wraps his arms around her, kissing the side of her temple.

"Care to throw down some of your own wages against us? We can play gents against the ladies."

"I think Naomi and I will sit back and just enjoy watching the game, while admiring the view." She gives him her best smug smile before she slaps him on the behind, which makes Holt grin like a fool, causing all of us to burst into laughter. Thankfully, they don't say anything about Charlie, and all move toward the pool tables.

"Hey, where's Charlie tonight? Is she joining you ladies later?" Tucker asks, ruining my moment of peace. I want to tell him to mind his own business and to take a flying leap somewhere.

Cutting my eyes to his, I try to catch his attention to shut him up with a shake of my head before anything else can come of it.

"I don't know. Why don't you ask your best friend where his lady is tonight?" Naomi replies sharply.

They all turn their eyes to me, waiting on my answer.

Well, doesn't that just beat all? Sounds like her friends are ready to crucify me. So far, I've been able to avoid them. *Great.* Putting on the best fake smile that I can muster, I try to throw off her sarcastic response with my own nonchalant one.

"*What*? She's at home. Tonight's a guy's night." I reply, looking each of the girls in the eye, daring them to say more. When none are forthcoming, I continue. "That's it. Nothing to get upset about." I mumble, as I turn to the table, trying to get it racked and ready to go. "So, who's up first?"

I know no one is fooled by that, but it's none of their business. They all know by now what's going on—no one's stupid. I just hate that we're all so tightly connected, my own hand-picked family of sorts, and that it affects us all. Tucker grabs a pool stick and starts chalking it up as I place the rack back on the wall, feeling like I'm lower than dirt.

About 30 minutes go by, and we're all having a great time, as best as we can, when Dave wanders over our way. I still have yet to figure out what his deal is.

"What's shaking, Dave baby?" Halley asks him when he stops next to her.

He gives her an easy smile and tells her, "Just checking out the crowd, making sure everything is running smoothly," before he heads over to the DJ booth, completely ignoring my presence as he walks passed me.

A few songs later, a familiar song starts to play by Great Big World. This song really hits close to home, and I decide to sit this new game out, as I focus on what's being said. Dave walks by again—looking at me with arched eyebrows—as he continues on his way past our little group.

Something is definitely up with Dave, and I'm getting tired of his looks. I decide to track him as he makes his way back to the front, but he surprises me when he heads straight to the bar. That's when I notice that he's making a beeline for a very beautiful woman who just so happens to also be mine.

Charlie.

What's she doing here? When did she arrive? And how did no one even notice her?

Sitting back in my chair, I keep my eyes trained on them, mentally promising all kinds of harmful maneuvers I'll use on Dave if he makes any moves on her. I know I have no right to say anything at this point, as I did this to us. I need to get my head on straight, so I let them be. *For now.*

And that's how the rest of my night goes. Me, brooding in the corner, while the rest of our friends are having a good time, and all the while, I keep a close watch on Charlie and Dave. I don't like it, but that's how it has to be. And boy does it kill me every time I see the sadness on her face, and the simple fact that she never looks directly our way, not once, the entire time we're both here.

After an hour, I can't take it anymore. Really, I should have given up twenty minutes ago. I know it's time to get out of here before I do something I'll regret, or to make Charlie more upset. And I really can't stand the fact that Dave hasn't left her side once since he sat down next to her. And wouldn't you know it? Charlie, who's clearly hurt and upset, has been drinking soda all night. I'm not a big drinker myself, but the one time I let my guard down, I got myself hammered, and it was Charlie who picked up the pieces. But tonight? It's not me she's crying with, and it's not me picking up the pieces. Instead, it's me who made her break, and it's me who sent her into Dave's all too eager, wide-open arms.

I'm completely ticked off at myself. I throw back the rest of my water, and decide it's time to make a hasty exit.

"I'm heading out. You guys coming?" I ask Holt and Tucker.

"No, we're cool. Halley can give us a lift when we're ready." Holt eyes me, then looks over to where my girl is sitting with the man I want to bounce right out of here. "Shouldn't you be over there?" he nods towards the pair at the bar.

"No. I'm the reason she's messed up to begin with. I can't stand watching him wrap his arms around her anymore. She deserves someone better than me. Anyway, I'm out. I'll see you guys later." I'm done with this conversation, and decide to take off before anyone else gets any bright ideas to confront me.

I walk past Charlie, but she doesn't even notice me as I go by. Dave sure does, though. He barely acknowledges me before cutting his eyes back to Charlie, like I'm a piece of dirt that he wants to brush off, or he'll become filthy from being in my presence.

Well, screw him.

I slam out of the main doors and into the parking lot, running into the one person I haven't seen in ages, and don't wish to now. Heather Morgan, my ex-high school sweetheart. If I thought the night couldn't get any worse, I was wrong. *Way wrong.* This isn't the time to make nice and play catch up. Too bad, though, because that's exactly what's about to happen.

Charlie

I've been here for a long time. So long, I can't even remember how long ago it was when I came into *Texas Jacks*. I know one thing for sure; I arrived before the guys showed up. Once they arrived, I made a beeline for the bar, planted my butt there, and haven't moved since. At the start of their night, they didn't even notice, but as time moved on, they slowly— one by one—started to notice me. Though, I will point out that none of them actually tried to come and talk to me.

I'm getting pretty sick and tired of sitting here, avoiding them. I'm also tired of crying and pouring all of my problems out on Dave. He's a great guy, but I'm in no mood to be consoled, and I really don't want to keep analyzing what's going on with Nate. I just want some peace and quiet. Why I thought coming here tonight was a good idea is beyond me. I should have stayed home and enjoyed the solitude, shutting out the world.

I even sent my friends away. They know me well enough to know when to leave me alone. Thankfully, they get it and

239

took off to hang with their guys. It really doesn't help that they're dating Nathan's friends, though.

I sigh, running a hand through my hair. I think I've done pretty well all night without looking in Nathan's direction once. I mean it's not like I couldn't see him. I had a good side view from my periphery all night, but there was no way I was letting him know how much he was affecting me.

As I'm sitting here, beating myself up, the song Blue by Keith Urban comes on. *Great. Just great.* First it was A Great Big World's song that I kept hearing on the car radio, now it's Blue? This is starting to get a little too depressing, even for me who already feels down in the dumps.

Dave jerks his head up all of a sudden, staring over my head at someone—who I'm pretty sure is Nate. I refuse to look, though. I'm not playing games, but I know he doesn't want to see me, or talk to me right now. He made this mess, and he obviously wants time away from me. If he wanted to fix it, he's had hours to do so tonight. Yet, nothing ever came my way from him. I didn't purposefully come here with the knowledge that he and the guys would be playing pool. I just got in my car, started driving around, and found myself sitting in the parking lot. That's how Dave found me, and learned what was going on. He took it upon himself to text the girls, letting them know what was up—causing them to make their way to the dance club, as well. We had a little chat, then they went their own way. Though, I'm sure they knew the guys would be here, too. Our two groups can't go anywhere without each knowing about it.

I throw a few dollar bills onto the bar and stand up, deciding it's time to head home myself. I look at Dave and give him a half-hearted smile.

"Thanks for being my shoulder tonight, Dave. It means more than you'll ever know. I really shouldn't have dumped everything on you, though. Sorry for that." I smile again, giving him a shoulder shrug.

He grabs my hand. "There's nothing to be sorry for. The only person who should be sorry, and didn't do a thing about it, is that sorry son of a gun, who broke your heart to begin with. Don't you go apologizing to me for his mistakes."

Okay. Apparently someone is ticked off—maybe even more than me. I'm just sad and brokenhearted, but Dave seems really riled up. Up until this point, he's been pretty quiet about it all.

"Don't worry, Dave. I'll be fine, eventually. I'm tired, though, and I really just want to be alone. I'm going to head out." I stifle a yawn. "Thanks for calling in a favor and getting someone else to man the doors tonight. I'll text you when I make it home safely." I lean in and kiss him on the cheek, then grab my purse.

"You do that, but I'm still walking you to your car. Don't even think about giving me any lip for it, either." He stands up and wraps his hand around my elbow, leading us down the steps from the bar area and out the front door.

As soon as we walk outside, we both stop dead in our tracks. I feel like a deer caught in headlights, as there stands Nathan and a tall, gorgeous redhead, talking to each other. She's got the biggest smile plastered on her face, and she's aiming it right at him.

I can't even move. I'm frozen in place as I continue to watch them together. I'm so confused and have no clue what's going on with them, or who this woman is, or why he's got such a fond look on his face. I don't want to jump to conclusions, but I'm so thrown off balance at the moment, I don't know what to think.

I feel Dave nudge me a little, breaking the spell I was trapped in while staring at Beauty and Charming talking to each other.

Turning my head, I look over to see Dave giving Nathan a hard look as he shakes his head. He squeezes my elbow before leading me away from them, and out to my car. I turn my head back one more time, to take one last look. I don't think I can bear any more tonight, but I have to see him just once more.

He looks right at me, and there's pain in his eyes, causing my own eyes to water before I duck my head and turn away from him and this woman who has just put her hand on his chest. I can't stomach any more. I thank Dave again, giving him a quick hug, before climbing into my car and taking off, not even daring to look in my rearview mirror.

Nate

Why did Charlie pick that moment to leave?

My muscles were locked up tight from the second I noticed her and Dave. I really didn't like his hand on her elbow, or that he was walking her to her car. That should have been *me* taking care of her. Instead, I stand here like I don't notice her or care, while Heather chatters on about how she misses us, reminiscing about the good old days, and about my mom. I really can't listen to any more of this, especially when she talks about my mom. It's too painful.

"Nate?" Heather calls me back from the rage-induced fog I'm experiencing over watching Dave with Charlie. I mostly checked out to whatever she was saying.

"Yeah?"

"Are you okay? You look like you're ready to cause some

bodily harm to the man who was just walking his girlfriend to her car. Do you know them?" she asks with a bit of concern and suspicion, all rolled up into one.

"Oh, I know them all right." But I don't bother going into more detail than that or correcting her mistake as Dave walks back towards us.

"Was that really necessary?" I ask him. My pissed-off meter is off the charts at this point.

"What do you care? You seem *occupied* to me." He gives a pointed look at Heather.

"What's going on here?" she asks us.

"Nothing." I don't want to give her unnecessary details, and I'm hoping Dave keeps his trap shut, if he knows what's good for him.

"Oh, it's something, all right. But that's for him to explain, not me. I'm not the idiot in this story." He scowls as he turns to walk away.

"I beg to differ." I taunt him. I'm so mad, I really can't stop to filter what comes out of my mouth at this point. He stops walking and turns back to look at me.

"You don't know what you're talking about."

"Will someone *please* fill me in?" Heather tries again.

Continuing to ignore her and focusing my attention on the man of the hour, I go on. "I'm not the one who sat on his hands, waiting for something to happen. You had plenty of chances to get in there, but you blew it. Now it's me who's in there, so back off," I warn him.

"I don't think you have any idea what you're doing to her."

"That's where you're wrong. I know exactly what it's doing to her, because it has the same effect on me."

"Bull. If it did, you wouldn't have let it go on this long. You would have done something about it the moment you noticed her at the bar. That's right, I clocked you the minute

243

you saw her. I've been watching you all night. You didn't make one attempt, so why should I believe you?"

"Stay out of it. It's none of your business. I don't need to explain myself to you."

"Nate's a good guy. I'm sure that whatever is going on, he will work it out when he's ready to. Not when he's being forced to." Heather throws down for me.

"And who are *you*, again?" Dave asks her a bit rudely.

"An old friend of Nate's, who can vouch for his character, which *you* are calling into question. And who might you be?" She eyes him up and down, finding him a bit lacking, before settling back on his glare.

"A good friend to the woman he just destroyed."

Heather turns to me, giving me a questioning look.

"I didn't destroy her. Broke her heart, sure. But her in general? Never." I'm confident in that fact.

"I will give you this," Dave starts, as he returns his attention back to me. "I did wait too long, and blew my shot with her. But, the moment she's over you, I will be there to pick up all of the pieces, and *I'll* be the one to glue her back together. Then I'll be the real man who treasures her, and I won't be letting her go." And with that final parting shot, he turns and walks away.

"Uh, do you want to explain what that was all about?" I hear Heather ask, as I stare daggers into the back of the man who just told me he's ready and waiting to steal my girl.

Shaking my head, I look back to Heather, not really wanting to bother with her any longer. I don't want to be a jerk. But what we had is long over, and it's never going to come back again. I know she's hopeful, but I have some things to work out, and when I do, it won't be her I'll be groveling in front of to take me back.

"It's a long story, and I really don't want to talk about it.

Look, Heather, it was great to see you again. But this really is a bad time for me to go down memory lane."

"I can see that. I'm sorry. I had no clue what I was jumping into the middle of when I saw you." She looks down for a moment, but then strengthens her resolve to carry on. "It's just that, when I ran into Carianna the other day, I couldn't help but remember what we had. I missed you. She never mentioned if you were dating anyone, so I was hopeful." She gives me her best breath-taking smile, one that used to do me in, but now doesn't have quite that power. "I guess." She shrugs, as she looks out towards the parking lot.

"How did you know I would be here, anyway?"

She looks back at me. "Carianna. She said you and the guys come here quite often. I had to take a chance in the hopes that I would see you."

"Heather, you've had years to seek me out, why now?"

"You."

"*What*?"

"Because it was you. I never got over you, Nate. I've always loved you, ever since I was a little girl. The time we spent together, they were the best years of my life. I miss that. I miss *you*. I want it all back. I gave you as much time as I could stand, which was really hard to do, and now, I want a second chance." Her eyes are pleading with mine to give in and take a chance on her. *On us.*

"Heather—" I gently say, running my hand down her cheek, like I used to do.

She latches on with her own hand, twining our fingers together. "Please, don't say no," she whispers.

"I'm not the same guy you dated back then. I've changed. My life took a different direction, and I've moved on. It may not have been a healthy change, but it was a change all the same. I really loved you, Heather. But that was then. This is now, and I have a complicated relationship—of all my own doing—and I need to fix the broken part in me first before I can move on with anyone, her or you."

She gives me the most sincere, hopeful look, just as I hear a loud noise from the crowd inside the club. I look up just in time to see our friends. They're staring at me with a mix of hard looks, disbelief, and disappointment. *Great.* Another moment that I have no doubt will be shared with Charlie.

When will this night ever end?

"Lucy has some 'splaining to do." Holt says in his best Ricky Ricardo impression.

Ignoring them, I look back to Heather, giving her hand a squeeze as I pull my fingers from hers. "I'm sorry, Heather. When, and if I ever get myself together, it will be Charlie's door I'll be breaking down."

"Charlie? Is that the woman who just left, looking like someone stomped all over her heart?"

"The one and only." I give her a small, sad smile. I'm silently wanting to berate myself for putting that look on her face, and none too pleased that Heather just reminded me of that fact all over again.

"You can't blame me for trying, Nathan. If your mother hadn't passed away, we would still be together. I truly believe that. I really believe we could make a second go of it, and be so happy."

"Heather, please don't bring his mother into this. That was a low blow. If it was meant to be, don't you think he would have tracked you down a long time ago, once he got his head on straight?" Tucker's now aiming his hard stare her way, clenching his jaw. My mom was like a mother to both Tucker and Holt. They don't like to be reminded of that sad time in all of our lives. Though the guys both have wonderful moms of their own, they really loved mine.

"Hey, Tucker. Holt." Heather says, smiling fondly at them. "It's been a long time since I've seen your mugs. And Tucker," she says, glaring at him, "I wasn't being a jerk to Nate, or blaming him for his mom dying and our relationship falling apart. That was never my intention. So, Nate," she turns back to me, "I'm sorry if it came out that way. I meant no harm. I can see now that my idea was a bad one. Honestly, you can't blame a woman for trying to get back the best thing she ever had. It was worth a shot, because Nate, you are worth it." She leans in and gives me a lingering kiss on my cheek, then pulls away. "I'm sorry to have shown up at a bad time, and for causing any pain for you, Nate. Or any of you," she amends, looking over at the guys.

"Heather, it's always a pleasure to see you. We miss having you in the guy's club with us, but Nate has enough on his plate at the moment. He doesn't need his ex-showing up to complicate matters further. Good thing Charlie left awhile ago." This comes from Holt. *Little does he know, the damage has already been done.*

"Well, I wouldn't say he got off scot-free with her. She saw me talking with Nate, which caused problems with some other guy, and honestly? I have no idea what that was all about. But I'm pretty sure this other guy is ready to take over Nate's place when he gets the chance." She not so helpfully fills the rest of the gang in.

"Oh, boy." I hear Halley say. *She can say that again.*

"It's late. I'm tired, and I feel a headache coming on. I need to head to bed and forget that this day happened." I turn back to Heather. "It was great seeing you again, Heather. You look beautiful, as ever. I'm sorry for how our story played out, but that was long ago. It's time for you to make your own story with someone who deserves a good woman like you. I'm not that man. And no, I don't blame you for trying. I just want you to be happy." I reach out and give her arm a light squeeze. No need to add more fuel to the fire of the glowing eyes of the two women staring my way.

"Thanks, Nate. You were always such a great guy. I really hope you make peace with yourself, and Charlie. It was good to see you guys again," she tells Tucker and Holt. We really did have the best group when we dated. The guys were sad to see her go, but a lot of time has passed, and we've grown up and moved on.

"Have a good night, Heather, and be safe in your travels." Tucker hugs her, then Holt follows suit.

"We loved seeing you again. Don't be a stranger in the future," Holt adds with a gentle smile.

"Goodnight." Heather says to our group, before walking back to her car and leaving the parking lot.

"Nate—" I hear Halley start, but Holt beats me to it.

"Not now, babe. Let it be. We don't know the full story. Give the guy room to come up for air. You can rain all over his parade tomorrow. I promise." He chuckles, but even I can hear the strange way it comes out.

"Thanks, man." I bump his shoulder. "I'll see you all back at the house. Ladies," I bid them farewell as I take my leave.

Bed. That's all I'm going to worry about now. It's too late to think about anything else.

Chapter Twenty

Nate

I T'S THE DAY AFTER OUR RUN-IN WITH HEATHER, AT T.J.'S, and I'm still conflicted. At the moment, I really want to jump in the truck, and go make-up with Charlie. There's a part of me that's scared out of my mind, for a couple of different reasons. One—I'm scared of the long lasting feelings, and second, I'm scared that Charlie is done with me. I'm slightly more confident over her taking me back than I am of my feelings.

I can't shake the thought that I've just let her slip through my fingers, though. And I'm not in the mood to take advice from Holt or Tucker, should I run into them. I'm doing what I do best—avoiding everyone. Instead, I'm letting the back-and-forth thoughts bog me down.

Even if I need space to just be me for awhile, I know I can't leave Charlie hanging with what went down last night. Rolling over on my bed, where I've been for the last hour—letting my mind get trampled on by my thoughts, to pick up my cell phone. I dial her number, and listen to it ring until it turns over to her voicemail. I frown down at the horrible device in my hand, not wanting to believe Charlie wouldn't answer the phone for me. Once again my mind travels over last night's incident, leading me to automatically think the worse.

Surely she's busy, or didn't hear it? I try her again, only to get her voicemail once more. Deciding that the whole 'third time's a charm' is the best way to go, I try her yet again, to my displeasure when she doesn't pick up. I hang up, without leaving a voicemail, and send her a text instead.

Nate: Hey, Charlie. Just checking in. Hit me up, when you get this message.

I chuck the offending piece of metal onto the bed, and flop back into the mattress, not wanting to get up or on with my day. I know I need to get out of the house for awhile, and away from the prying housemates. They're sure to come my way before the day is out.

The best medicine for all that's ailing me is the track, I decide, while rolling off the edge of the bed. It's time to put everything behind me and just give into the one thing I have left that keeps me solid, racing and head to the track.

Charlie

I see Nate's number pull up on my phone, but I can't find it in me to answer it. I'm not ready for whatever he's going to dish out. I thought I knew him. I thought we had something really great going, and I thought giving him space was the right move. Boy was I the village idiot in this play. I should have known he would never succumb to a deeper relationship. I thought we were making leeway, until the night he shared about his mother—when it started really going downhill. I could've lived with his conditions, for the most part, but to watch him have a tender moment with some woman I've never seen before? I felt as though he sucker punched me.

I bet he was calling to apologize and explain away who she was, but I'm tired of being jerked around with his wishy-washy ways. I never thought I would feel that way. After all, he's mostly been a perfect gentleman. Now, he can't make up his mind, and yet he's distant, too. I feel like I'm on a roller-coaster and I can't get off of the ride. So today, I choose to put a stop to it, and take back what I was giving away. Either he sits down so we can sort out his issues so we can get back to the us we were becoming, or we call it quits. I'm in love with Nate, and my heart can't take anymore up and downs.

I turn my phone off, so I don't have to feel guilty because I know I will miss more calls from him today, and decide to go the salon. I could use a hair trim, and my nails painted. It's an indulgence, but I really need to do something for myself and for once, I'm focusing on me. I need to find some joy in my day and I deserve a splurge day after all I've been through with my emotions, feeling like a wrung out rag.

Feeling good a few hours later, I take myself out to lunch and then a movie. I haven't had alone time like this in a really long time, and boy does it feel good. I got too wrapped up in one guy, it was nice, but I forgot to take care of myself in the process. I'm over being the fuddy-duddy but I'm not revert-ing back to my shell again. That part of my life is through. If there are a few things Nate taught me, it was to live and to love. I can't predict what will happen with our relationship, but I know that he needs a time-out, and I need to make my-self happy. That's exactly what I'm doing.

I hope in a few days' time, I can talk to Nathan and fig-ure out what's going on between us. I can't be strung along anymore.

I check my phone and see I've missed a couple of more calls from Nate, which I decide not to return right now, and walk into the movie theater fully prepared to laugh like crazy at some silly comedy. I think this is the best medicine to cure my needs for the time being. It won't take care of everything in the long run, but it sure feels good to live and do things without relying on Nate, or my friends. I have to wonder why I never tried this sooner.

Nate

I can't get away from my own thoughts today, so I decided to do laps out at the race track. It's the only way I could think of to get my mind free from the jail it's been in for the last few weeks. Not just the events from the other night. Trying is the keyword as my mind is plagued with all thoughts of Charlie. I'm still mad about Dave. I can't believe he had the nerve to imply that he's waiting in the background to catch Charlie when I break her. I'm not a violent man, but I really would have liked to have knocked him a good one, when he had his hands on her, or when he spouted his mouth off.

Hurting Charlie is the last thing I wanted to do. Not only am I hurting her, but I'm hurting myself, and everyone else in the process. I'm not proud of these facts, either. I have these strong feelings for Charlie, after the time and memories we shared, and they scare me. I want to be the man she needs. I'm afraid I'll fail her, or of losing her—which it appears to be happening, whether I want it or not. I've been a mess over this very subject, going back and forth on what I should do. Do I let go, and let it happen? Or do I hold close to my rules of never going the full distance.

I tried calling Charlie today, just to check in. I want to

know if she's okay, and explain to her what she saw with Heather. She never answers her phone, though and I didn't bother to leave a message, either. There's no point in trying to explain something this big over the phone, to someone who obviously rather not take my calls. I feel like she's hit me in the gut.

Charlie ties me up in knots, and keeps me on a ledge. I'm trying to teeter between her and my feelings, not wanting to let go, or let her be the one who falls and gets hurt. I'm screwed up, I know. I fight my feelings, and yet I give off the vibe that I'm all in, with the exception of personal family information.

Charlie was never supposed to be long term. It was all supposed to be fun, sweet, and romantic with the eventuality of letting go, and moving on. I knew the moment I saw her that my life was about to turn upside down, and hang me out to dry. Charlie is not one to be strung along, or just for fun kind of woman. She's meant to be the last woman you date. The last woman you give your heart to. The last woman you ever say 'I love you' to. She's supposed to be there for all of your trials and triumphs. She's supposed to be the kind of lady who gives you sweet smiles for no reason, holds your hand on your worst day, and gives you a new reason to let the light shine on you when she brings a child into the world.

Distractions! That's what Charlie is doing to me, causing one big distraction. I can't focus properly, and that's dangerous. It's in these moments that I miss her, and I'm mad that she invades my solitude.

I can't figure out what's wrong with me lately. I'm mad at myself, at Charlie, and yet I can't let go of anything. I want peace and solitude. I want to go back to my old ways, but at the same time I never want to go back to those places again. I really just want Charlie. I feel like I'm losing my mind with all of this back and forth madness. Will it ever stop?

Knowing nothing good will come from staying on the bike while Charlie controls my every thought, I realize it's time to call it quits and head home. I just finished latching the tailgate, when I see Shelly. She's hanging onto another guy. Thankfully it's not me, though I have to shake my head at her. I hope he knows what he's doing. I'm definitely not going to get into that mess. I'm in a big enough of one on my own. I give a chin nod to the guy then swing up into my truck and take off.

I'm a glutton for punishment, because I get the brilliant idea to stop by Charlie's place before calling it a night. I don't see her car in the lot, so I leave, not bothering to call her this time. If she wants space, I can understand that.

My phone rings the minute I step foot into the house. My heart races, thinking its Charlie, I answer without looking at caller ID.

"Hello?"

"Hey, big brother."

"Carianna," I say with less enthusiasm once I know it's my sister.

"I wouldn't want you jumping for joy over my call," she teases.

"Sorry, I thought you were Charlie."

"Oh? What's wrong? You sound like your down on your luck. Having woman troubles?" she inquires, but I can hear concern in her voice.

"I don't want to talk about it." I mutter.

"If you decide you do want to talk about it, I could lend my best listening ear."

"I know. Thanks. But like I said, I don't want to talk about it." I add with a little more force than I mean to.

"Look, I'm just going to go out on a limb and say it. I

think you're mad about something, and I have a feeling it's from the night you got hammered."

"You're right. I'm really ticked off. And now that you've mentioned it, I can't believe I didn't think to aim my ire at you while I've been kicking myself, and I've been mad at Charlie and Dave."

"What's Dave got to do with this?"

"He's trying to steal my girl!"

"What? So you're not broken up with Charlie?"

"*What? Of course not.* Who have you been talking to?"

"No one. I guess the vibe I'm getting from you, came off wrong."

I don't believe her for a minute. "Seriously, Carianna. Why do you think I've broken up with Charlie?"

"Oh, come on, Nate. It's not like you bring anyone home. You certainly never share about our mom, and her passing with anyone. I'm sure you pulled away from Charlie, as you certainly gave me the cold shoulder since the night she came over. What gives?"

"Are you trying to pick a fight?"

"No, but I've been waiting for you to talk to me about that night, and yet—you haven't. Don't tell me you aren't mad that I asked her to come over."

"Okay, fine. Yes, I was really upset that you would go behind my back and ask her to come over. I never wanted her to see me that way. Why do you think the guys didn't call her? She didn't deserve to see that. To top it all off, I feel like a jerk because I didn't remember telling her about mom the next morning. You weren't there, and it wasn't you who saw that face of dejection. I did, though. I saw how hurt she was by my actions which were exactly why I didn't want her over here in the first place!"

"Look, I was doing you a favor. When are you finally

going to grieve the loss of our mother, and let go? I would say you're definitely in the middle of the process, with how mad you are at everyone. Don't think I don't know you, Nathan. It's time to let the past go."

"Did I ask you to butt in? I can handle myself, Carianna. I don't need you to mother me. I haven't had one in a very long time and I think I turned out just fine."

"If you don't think anything is wrong with how you handle your relationships, or your family relationships, then you need a wakeup call. You might have had to pull me out of my own messes, and stepped in for dad, but you never did handle your own grief properly. Do you think Heather wanted you to let her go? She would have done anything to hold on to you. You don't remember much during that time, but I do. I remember how much Heather had to grieve you, as she did our mother. She loved her just as much as the rest of us. She loved you, to see you through to a good place in your life. Instead, you cut her loose. Now, you have Charlie. Why are you throwing something special away?"

"I'm not throwing anything away. I can't give myself to her one-hundred percent. I'm not even a whole man, I know. I'm not stupid, or blind at how I live my life. I know exactly what I'm doing. I just didn't plan for Charlie. She was an unexpected distraction."

"Really, Nathan!" she scolds me. "You're not this type of man. I know you're hurting and you're upset. But I'm telling you right now, if you don't make things right with Charlie soon, you'll lose her for good."

"Are you done trying to tell me how to run my life, and my relationship with my girl?"

"I don't know, are you going to listen? And is she even still yours?" and with that she hangs up on me. I throw the phone at the couch then throw myself onto the couch, too. I have no idea why that just all happened the way it did. I know she's right; I just don't want to hear it from her.

"Well, that was something." I open my eyes, to see Holt standing over me.

"Listening in on conversations now?"

"No. I can't help over hearing anything in my own house when someone's yelling." He frowns. "What's going on?"

"Just Carianna, giving her two cents about how to live my life and how to treat my girlfriend."

"Sounds like she hit the right nerve." He quirks his brow. "I didn't realize you decided to call Charlie your girlfriend, now."

I scowl at him. "I'm not in the mood for the inquisition."

"Of course not," he scoffs. "Good old Nate, using his famous 'avoids' tactic. Tell me, how's that working out for you?"

"It's not. Is that what you wanted to hear so you could gloat?"

"No, I just wanted to help my best friend out. Is that a crime? I don't want to see a sweet innocent woman be hurt in the process, nor do I want to see my friend spiral out of control like he started to on the anniversary of his mother's death."

"Don't bring my mom into this!" I yell, jumping off the couch.

"Whoa! What's your problem, man?" Tucker rushes into the living room.

"Nothing. I'm just mad, and I can't understand my own emotional state at the moment," I feel myself deflate and flop back onto the couch. "Maybe Carianna was right. Maybe I'm finally going through the grieving process. I don't even know what's going on anymore. I thought I had a good balance for Charlie and me but then I go and screw up, and now we're just a big jumbled mess to my own doing." I scrub a hand down my face. "I'm sorry I yelled." I give the guys an apologetic shrug of the shoulder. "I feel so screwed up. I can't seem to do anything right. I've gotten so off course from where I usually am that I don't know who this new angry person is."

"You need to get your head on straight, brother. But first, you need to patch things up with Charlie. I'm not saying you need to jump in with both feet, but you need to make common ground with her, and figure out where you two stand. She's going through a rough time herself." Tucker gives it to me straight.

"I know. I've been a real jerk lately." I sigh, looking down at the ground so they can't read the humiliation that runs through the course of my body.

"We all know this isn't like you. Just remember, you've never been in this situation with a woman before." Holt reminds me. "When you and Heather were together, you were just teens with endless possibilities before you. You both had a lot of life to live before you settled down. I can't say you didn't love her, but I will say this—it's nothing like what I've seen with you and Charlie."

"I think the pressure of keeping to your rules, yet trying hard to not fall in love, got to you, and you *did* let yourself fall. It's like, once you realized it, you messed up, and started spiraling after that. Holt and I didn't want to step in, but now? We wouldn't be good friends to you if we didn't do something. It's time to help you." Tucker gives me a look of sympathy, but I know he's right. I need them to be the support that holds me up.

"I suggest you cool your jets, and then go to Charlie in a couple of days."

"I don't know if she'll take me back, or listen to me. She won't even take my calls, let alone return a text. I even stopped by her place and she wasn't there. I think she's avoiding me."

"Can you blame her? You've been stupid with her, then she saw Heather and she still is clueless as to who Heather is. We haven't told the girls much either, but it wouldn't matter. She's not talking to anyone right now anyway. So, it's not just you, though you deserve it more than the rest of us." Holt mutters.

"I know. I'll straighten it all out with her, eventually. Right now, I feel a headache coming on and I'm afraid we'll start singing Kumbaya then you'll ask me to share more of my feelings."

Holt punches me in the arm. "No, we'll just sit on the couch, play video games, get mad at each other for cheating, while kicking your butt since you seriously suck when it comes to playing any team related games."

Tucker laughs, punching me in the other arm as he passes me by. "Now, if you're done. I'm grabbing a pizza and I'll be back in a bit. Be prepared to eat dirt!" he calls over his shoulder while he walks out of the living room.

"You couldn't even survive a Zombie Apocalypse. All of that preparation in game play was for nothing." I laugh, feeling a little bit better. I'm far from it, but these guys know how to handle me with their special brand of care. Thankfully I have them in my life to help me pull my head out of the sand.

My next big challenge will be to beg the woman who has my heart to hear me out.

Charlie

I've been avoiding everyone for the last few days. It's been nice, but now I'm lonelier than I ever was to begin with. Why did I ever decide that being a fuddy-duddy was lame? I would rather that then being yo-yoed with.

Halley texted me yet again, for the twentieth time, that they wanted to me to come hang out with them. Why does it have to be at the race track? I pray they're not trying to set something up. I thought I was ready a few times to sit Nate down and have it out with him. Now, I'm not so sure. If he wanted to talk to me, and work it out, he would have called me already. Well, fine that's not right. He has called, and texted, I just haven't answered. If he really wanted to make this work, he would have shown up at my door instead of lame texts.

I feel stupid, and like this is now becoming a game. One I never intended. I just don't know what to do. I want to fix this stupid issue, but I don't want him to take me back and hold me at an arm's distance anymore. I can't take it. I thought I could live with it, but I know that's a big horrid lie I keep telling myself I can live with. It's not happening. I want all of Nate, or—no, I can't even think about the other possibility. I wish I could call his sister, but I don't know how to reach her. And with my brilliant plan, not really, I've been ignoring his friends, and mine.

Halley's right, I need to get out and see everyone. So, here I am at the track, walking up to the bench. I don't see Shelly hanging on Nate. *Thankfully.* Surprisingly, it looks like she's found a new man to latch onto. Now, if only Lisa could get the hint. Poor Tucker and Naomi.

Stepping up to the bleachers, I see the girls hanging with the guys, but I don't see Nate. Frowning up at them, I look around but I don't see him elsewhere. But I do see someone else walking towards me. Oh boy, this isn't good because I see Dave making a straight-line towards me, and he's not slowing down.

"Hey, good looking!" he grins at me. "I didn't expect to see you here."

"That makes two of us," I mutter more to myself. "What are you doing here? I don't think I've ever seen you at the track before."

"I've come out on occasion, but the pretty girl in town I kept hearing about wasn't here." He winks.

"Oh?" Please don't be flirting with me. What if Nathan over hears him? I don't even know what we are right now, but I do know Nathan will blow his lid.

"Charlie, come on now. You have to know by now that I really like you." He slings an arm over my shoulder, causally resting it there. I try to slide out of his light hold, but he pulls me back in, but closer to his chest.

"I really didn't have a clue. Sorry." I'm embarrassed and feel like an idiot.

"Well, no matter. You know now. Anyway, I'm still your friend. I didn't expect anything to happen, for the time being. I just felt like you could use a good friend to be around right now."

"Thank you, Dave. I realized tonight that I really do need my friends. Hiding away wasn't a great idea."

"Anything for you, Charlie. Let's go see what everyone else is up to." He tugs me forward with him, leading us to my friends. We make our way up to the top of the bleachers, to looks of anger and confused faces. I give them a small, timid smile and a weak wave of the hand. I don't want to be in this position any more than they like seeing it. If they feel uncomfortable, it's nothing like I feel.

"Charlie! It's good you're here." Naomi is the first to recover, moving towards me to pull me into a hug. "We are so talking about this later." She quietly whispers into my ear.

"I have no idea about this either," I whisper back.

Halley leans over to hug me as well. "Nate is going to have a fit when he sees Dave with his arm or hands on you. Heck, just being here is going to cause issues." She whispers.

"Not my choice. I thought you all invited him?" I quietly respond.

"Nope! I don't even want to be here when he finds out." She sits back down next to Holt, who automatically claims her hand.

"Charlie. Good to see you're still alive and kicking." Tucker kisses my cheek. "Nate misses you, you know. I get the impression he wants to talk to you. Are you sticking around later?" he quietly engages me in conversation so it's not over heard by prying ears, and for my benefit since Dave is tagging along.

"I'm not sure this is the place to have this talk, Tucker. If he really wants to make it right, he knows where I live."

"Wow. You have more spunk in you then I gave you credit for, short stack!" Holt, who overheard us, laughs. "Good to know." He winks.

"Where is he, anyway?" I ask the group at large, turning my back to them to look once again for Nate. "I didn't see him when I came out."

"Oh, he's here. I'm sure he's already seen you, too." Holt not reassuringly shares.

"Are we going to have a problem?" Dave asks.

"Only if you let it be one, or if you don't keep your hands off his girlfriend."

"Last time I checked, they weren't labeling it, nor was he taking care of her properly."

I place my hand on Dave's arm. "That's none of your business. Please, let's not cause any trouble, okay? I'm out for the first time in a while with my friends, and I want to enjoy the evening."

"Charlie, you made me a part of this when I saw you at *Texas Jacks* and we had our chat."

"I didn't mean to drag you into it. Please, drop it. Don't stir the pot anymore than it has been." I warn him, dropping my hand. "Now, move your fat bottoms over, I want to sit!" I kick Halley in the foot with my own, so she will move over. I really don't want Dave here, or to sit by me, but I don't get that wish. He squishes in next to me. Right now, I feel really irritated and I want to push him off the end of the row. When did he get so annoying?

Nate

What's he doing here? I can't believe he has the nerve to show up, knowing I'll be here, hanging on Charlie. *Why is she even letting him do that?* This can't be right. I have to be imaging things, right? I've had Charlie on my mind for the last few days, and I've barely been able to sleep, let alone function. I'm torn up, and I'm ready to stop this madness. But now, this? Charlie and Dave? I see nothing in front of me, as I tear off around the track again. Everything is hazy and my mind is going a million miles a second.

Is this why she's been avoiding me? So she can see him? Has she decided we're done, and she would rather give Dave a chance? What, he won't break her heart? No. He wouldn't. Instead, he wouldn't give her enough space to breathe. I'm sickened by the fact that he has her undivided attention when I can't get a single second of her time. I know she didn't see me when she showed up, nor when she searched me out from the bleachers. I had to step back and hide myself, so I could see what was going on. Just watching him touch her, makes me see red. I want to pull him away from her, instead I'm out here skulking like a little boy.

I make it around the track again, slowing down to pull over to the side. I just happen to look over to where they are, where I can just barely make them out—still, I can see Dave sitting right up against her side, squished in by someone else. That's it. I decide that I can't take it anymore.

I slam on the brakes, and come to a dead stop. I jump off my bike, not really thinking about what I'm doing, but knowing I have to get to Charlie. I'm the only one for her, and I'm going to find a way to cope and lay bare to her my feelings—once and for all.

I start walking towards her, pushing my heavy bike along when the next thing I know, I'm airborne. I slam back into something, smacking my head. My body hurts, and I can't really move before the lights fade to black.

Charlie

There's a collective gasp in the audience, then a deafening roar of silence, before pandemonium breaks out. People start jumping up from the stands, pushing and shoving, while trying to get out of the bleachers and down to the ground.

"What's going on?" I ask no one in particular. I look back to the track, just in time to see a bike eat dirt. From there it's a domino effect. There are a few more crashes, or people jumping off their bikes so they don't crash into the pile-up that's already created.

"Charlie, I want you to come with me. Please." Holt says, taking me by my arm, gently.

"Why? What's going on? What happened?" I completely missed everything, but I recall hearing a distant screaming. I thought it was others here, acting up and having fun. I turn all around, looking at everyone in confusion. Some people are starting to look over at me, giving me funny or sad looks. I furrow my brow, and then it dawns on me.

"No." My nose stings and my eyes prick with tears. "No. It's not Nate." I look over to the guys, questioning them with my eyes. Holt looks at me with a tender smile, but Tucker can't even look me in the eye. He just gets up, and takes Naomi with him towards the track.

"It's all right; everything is going to be just fine." Halley reassures me, but I don't even know what happened. Not really. I push pass everyone and jump down from the stand of seats to the next one until I'm safely planted on the ground. Then I go running for the field. Someone tries to yell my name, and a few people try to grab me, but I'm good at evading and I pump my legs faster as I run towards the crash of men, and bikes.

I come to halting stop, when I can only see a tangle of metal and flesh. There's blood, and plastic pieces dotting the area. I still can't see Nate. He's probably not even in here. I didn't even see him racing, but by my friends' reactions, he has to be in this mess. I don't want to believe it, but I have a sinking feeling of what I will find in the aftermath.

"NATE!" I start screaming into the chaos. "Nathan!" I scream again, trying to look all over in case I miss him. Men start turning their heads my way, looking at me in pity as I continue to scream his name. My eyes well up, and blur my line of vision. I can barely see, but I know I won't find what I'm looking for.

"Get out of my way!" I yell at the onlookers. "MOVE!" I hysterically cry and scream at them. I start pushing and fighting my way through them, as I make my way to the center of attention. I see other men pulling bikes away, and men limping away from the scene. They clear the way to get to the people buried under the bikes, who are still stuck in the entanglement.

I stand at the front now, watching and waiting when I feel myself surrounded by others, who I know automatically, will be our friends. I can't do anything, but wait and watch. I know I can't get in the way of anyone. In the meantime, I randomly hear people reporting the incident to 911. The minute I realize this is bigger than life, I start to breathe in shallow little breaths. I feel the anxiety kick in, and I can barely pull air into my lungs. But I can't stop watching. People try to tug me away. Some try to talk to me but I feel like I'm in a tunnel and everything is drowned out. The rescuers finally get to the last one and I feel it. I just know it deep in my bones, that it's Nate.

The moment I glimpse the color of his riding jacket, and then see his special helmet, I lose it. I can't breathe. My chest hurts, and I can't pull in enough air because he's not moving. I lean over, resting my hands on my thighs, hanging my head down as I try to get oxygen into my lungs. I feel hands on my back, rubbing in a soothing circular motion, while someone speaks calmingly into my ear. It takes a few moments, but I start to barely pull myself together. The minute my lungs get enough air flow, I stand up—swaying with dizziness, then launch myself in Nate's direction. I make it to him and drop to my knees.

He's not moving, as I search him for any signs of broken bones, and to see if his chest is moving. His right arm is at an odd angle, and he's bleeding, but I can't see where it's coming from. No one removes his helmet, incase he's had trauma elsewhere that can cause more damage. I sit there, in shock, looking at this man who doesn't realize how much I love him, feeling helpless. I can't move him, and I certainly can't paw all over him to make sure he's not broken completely. Sitting back on my haunches, I can only stare and silently sob—while silently praying he will be fine in the end, and that it's worse than it looks.

A short time later, I'm pulled away so paramedics can evaluate him, and then move him into the ambulance. This is all going on while I'm going through the motions, not really connecting with anything, or anyone. I just can't tear my eyes off of Nate, fearing that if I do, he won't come back to me.

They ask me if I'll ride with Nate in the ambulance, but it's not my voice that answers them. I don't think. It certainly doesn't sound like me but it has to be because I find myself being helped into the back right before they close the door. I sit down, reaching out a hand to touch his face, his hand, and then laying it on his thigh, hoping those were all safe places to touch without causing more harm.

The ambulance starts up, the sirens begin to wail, and the paramedic starts asking me questions that I can't answer. We make it to the emergency room, but I'm in daze as they help me out of the back area, and then lead me with Nate into the automatic doorway. They start calling off information to others who work there, and someone leads me to the waiting room, sits me down, and then moves on. Our friends show up not too long after I arrived, and sit around me in opened chairs. They try to soothe me, but I don't hear a word they say. It's like I hear it, then it fades before it can stick.

That's the last thing I remember before I slump in my seat, in the waiting room, and cry my heart out before I succumb to the darkness that calls to me. My body, and mind are exhausted and the night wins the battle and pulls me under.

Chapter Twenty-one

Charlie

"FAMILY OF MR. JACKSON?" I HEAR SOMEONE CALL out into the waiting room. I automatically jump up from my seat to find the speaker, who happens to be the doctor we spoke to hours earlier.

"Yes, that's me." I anxiously await his prognosis with bated breath.

"Mr. Jackson is comfortably resting in his room now. You can come back with me, if you like. We can discuss his prognosis in privacy." He looks around the room at the rest of our friends, and I wonder for a moment if he's thinking of not letting me go back there. "I see you are all still here. Very well then. Let's move to a quieter area of the room so I can update everyone at once." He moves off to a corner of the waiting room, where no one else is hanging out.

"Mr. Jackson," he starts, looking at each of us, "is going to be just fine. He will have a long recovery, but didn't sustain any internal injuries. He's very lucky that he wasn't killed, and has no internal bleeding, especially after being crushed by the dirt bikes. He suffered a concussion as he slammed his head against the ground, or the objects crashing on him. Even with his helmet on, it caused some damage. I'm surprised he didn't suffer much worse. But, he did break the ulna in his right arm, and he broke a few ribs, and his nose. That's where most of the bleeding came from—the nose. He also has contusions all over his body. We will keep him in the hospital for the next two days, to monitor his head injury. We will then reevaluate his prognosis from there." He looks over at me, and then turns to leave. I follow him to Nathan's room. I'm worried about him, still. Even though the doctor said he'll be okay, I need proof. Thinking this, I stop and turn to look at our friends. *Should I be the one going in first?* I worry my bottom lip, wondering what I should do.

"It's fine, Charlie. You go in first. Carianna should be back soon with their dad. Until then, I know he would rather wake up to your pretty face over our ugly mugs." Holt softly smiles at me. I hug him, giving him an appreciative squeeze around his waist, then let go and continue following the doctor down to Nathan's room.

The doctor stops us at the door. "Don't worry, he won't look as bad as he sounds." He reassures me of this before opening the door and pushing his way in. I silently follow, dreading seeing Nate in that hospital bed. Once we clear the door and step into the room, I stop in my spot to take him in. I need to evaluate him with my own eyes, but don't trust myself to get too close to him yet. He might wake up and be mad when he sees I'm here. So I stay still, in one spot, just watching and waiting for what comes next. It all hinges on what Nate will do when we make eye contact.

Nate

Waking up *hurts,* and it shouldn't.

"Why can't I move my arm?" I groggily call into the emptiness of wherever it is that I am.

"*Where am I*?"

My vision is blurry. I can't move very well, and my arm feels weighted down. I try to sit up, but there's a burning pain and agony within my chest. Just breathing hurts. I look down and see wires and tubes coming out of my arms. I realize after a little more investigating that I'm in a hospital room, and I can't remember how I got here.

The last thing I remember is walking off the track to get to Charlie, before flying backwards as something hard hit me and threw me off my feet. And then it was lights out until now, apparently.

"Welcome back," I hear a deep, gravelly voice say as a shaft of light blinds me. I quickly squeeze my eyes shut, turning my head away from the brightness. But I have a killer headache, which causes even more pain to radiate through my skull. The new noises and light make me want to throw up.

"You're one lucky young man." The deep voice continues on, "I'm Dr. Johnson, by the way. I treated you for your injuries. Do you remember anything?"

"Just that I was walking towards my girlfriend, then something slammed into me. After that, I was knocked out. What happened to me?"

"As I was just explaining to your friends, and girlfriend, you've sustained a lot of injuries." I can hear him moving around, but I haven't opened my eyes yet. I prefer the darkness at the moment.

"You have a concussion, a few broken ribs, a broken arm,

and a broken nose," he continues. "With the injuries you sustained, and the type of accident you had, I'm surprised you didn't break your jaw, shatter your cheekbone, crack your skull open, or lose any teeth in all of that."

I can hear some rustling of papers in the background, and I'm presuming he's checking my chart, but I can also hear a faint crying noise to my right. I slowly turn my head that way, and open my eyes to find Charlie.

She sniffles quietly in her huddled space in the room. I try to hold out my hand, but it flops heavily back to the bed. I realize then that it's in a cast. I try again, and this time she comes over and, gently as she can, takes my hand into hers to hold.

"So, doctor," I say, turning my head back slowly his way. "How long will I be laid up?"

"Well, that all depends on how well your body heals up. Being a dirt bike racer, you well know how sore your body is after each time you ride. Luckily for you, you're still young, so it probably won't slow you down as much. For now, we want to keep you overnight. Technically, we plan to keep you for two nights, so we can monitor your head injury. From there, we will reevaluate how you're progressing, and then determine when we will let you leave, and what you should do for follow-up care. For now, I would suggest you lay off the racing for the foreseeable future. I've had plenty of men in here with injuries from this sport. Things as simple as losing their footing on a pedal, so their foot gets caught up and crushed. Or the ones who flip over their handle bar after hitting a muddy hole, and wind up fracturing their skulls. Some have had their teeth shoved up into their sinuses. There are all kinds of things that can happen out there, and I would hate to see you back here because of the sport. It's very dangerous."

I let out a groan from what he just told me, and the agony

my body is in. "Maybe we can share horror stories involving injuries when one, my body isn't trying to kill me now, and two—when my girlfriend isn't sitting here. I really don't want to terrify her more than she is already."

The doctor chuckles. "I'll send a nurse in with orders to up your pain medication dosage. You can have your friends visit, but not too long. You need some rest, but with that will come hourly wakeup calls. It comes with the territory of concussions, I'm afraid." He nods at me with a humorous grin, then to Charlie before taking his leave.

"Charlie?" I have to make sure she's really here.

"Yes, Nate?"

"Are you really here?" I quietly ask.

"Yes," she's just as quiet when she replies.

"Are you okay?"

She laughs, heartily.

"What?" I give her a sly smile, or as best as I can manage.

"You're the one laid up, broken and bruised, and you're asking me if I'm okay? That's the funniest thing I've heard in days."

She smiles sweetly down at me. "I've missed you, cowboy. But don't think you're getting off scot-free after the garbage you pulled."

"Charlie," I say in a serious tone, "maybe you shouldn't be here. I love that you are, but I don't want you stressed out because of me. Go home and rest." I rub her hand with my good one.

"No. No, you don't. And we're not fighting about this. Especially right now, while your body needs to be calm and rest. We can talk about this later." Her tone is sternly firm. I knew I would be in hot water with her. I don't want to push my luck, but I don't really want her wasting her time sitting here, babysitting me. I have to try one more time, though I selfishly want her here.

"I—" I start to say, until she kisses me, hard. I moan loudly, as my nose and head hate life right now. As much as I want to kiss her, the rest of me would rather pass out into a deep sleep until I can fully recover.

"Shut up, cowboy," she says against my lips.

I manage a smile against hers, right before she kisses me again. She pulls away just in time for our friends' to interrupt with a throat clear and a fake cough. I look up to find them gawking at us. "When did you hooligans show up? I can't believe they let just about anyone in here, these days." I try to laugh at my own joke, but end up in more pain than anything.

"You idiot! What were you thinking, man?" Holt chides me.

"'Hello' is how I usually start off my sentences when I see someone hurt. What about you, Charlie?" I ask, watching her fight a smile.

"Seriously, you could have been killed out there. You *should* have been killed. Racing is dangerous. Why do you think Charlie was always worried about you out there? Don't think we haven't read up on all of the crashes that have killed people, Mister!" Halley throws her full load of attitude and worry at me. "You're lucky you're in that bed and we can't beat you for your idiocy!"

"What happened out there?" Tucker calmly asks from his side perch against the wall, where he holds Naomi's hand.

"I wasn't thinking."

"That's obvious." Holt scoffs.

"Why did you jump off your bike in a crazy way, and then try to rush it off the track like that?" Halley questions.

"I saw Dave, and then I couldn't think or see right. I was raging, and saw red. I knew I had to get him away from Charlie, once and for all. That's what I was trying to do, when something slammed into me and I went airborne."

"Yeah, another rider hit you, which caused many others to crash. *On. Top. Of. You!* I still can't believe you were able to walk away with the injuries you have, and nothing more," Holt irately states.

"I know. I get it. I'm lucky to be here. I was distracted, okay?" I feel Charlie's hand tug hard to pull away. "And no," I look her in the eye, "you're not leaving me to heal on my own again. I want you here."

"Ouch. That was a low blow, don't you think?" says Tucker, rather than Charlie.

"I'm tired, my head is killing me, and you are all in here making matters worse," I say to my friends. "As for you, little one, I didn't mean it to come out that way. I'm going crazy over here without you, and I don't want to waste another day by being apart. I want you here while I recover." I give her a pleading look. "Please?"

"You're sure?" she timidly asks.

I nod at her question, trying to let everything in my eyes show her the truth of my words.

"I think she's still waiting for a few specific words, right guys?" Halley chimes in.

"Would you give it a rest, woman?" Holt grumbles at her. "We are all mad, scared, and wanting to kick some sense into him. But we aren't helping things."

"Thank you, finally!" I say, but it could be at Holt, or to the nurse who just walked in with my medication.

"I see it's a full house in here." She observes as she walks over to my IV stand. "Nathan's going to be groggy in a few minutes. So you'll want to say your goodbyes now, before he passes out." She smiles at my friends, and then administers the liquid medication into my IV. Once she completes her task, and checks if I need anything, she leaves the room.

"You heard the woman. Say your peace, and then get the heck out of here. I need my girl, and my beauty sleep."

"I don't know which one you need more, or which one will even save you." Holt taunts, making the others laugh. "Try sleeping for another thousand years. Maybe your Princess will see your beauty then," he continues ribbing me.

"Always the funny one, Curly." Halley laughs.

They all say goodbye and take their leave, leaving Charlie behind.

"Has anyone told my family?"

"Yes. Carianna was here earlier. She left to get your dad. He was working late, and she couldn't reach him. In fact, they should be back within the next 30 minutes, I would guess."

"I really wish they weren't coming by so late. I'm exhausted."

"You do know it's not in the middle of the night, right? I think it's closer to 8pm."

"Can I just hold you?"

"Is that even possible?"

"Anything is possible, if you let it be." I quietly admit.

She looks at me with so much love in her eyes, for a few moments longer.

"If I get in trouble for this, you're paying for it!" she scoots onto the bed and tries to maneuver her way into a comfortable position, though I know it's not easy. I can't move or help her. I feel like a useless gimp.

"You're not a useless gimp." She chuckles.

"How did you know I was thinking that?"

"You said it out loud. I think the pain meds are kicking in. Go to sleep, cowboy. I'll update your family, then send them on their way with a promise that you'll call them tomorrow."

"Thank you, Charlotte," I manage to say as my eyes start to get heavier.

The darkness and quiet, mixed with Charlie's light breathing and the beeping of a machine, start to lull me to sleep when I think I hear her say, "I love you, Nathan. Sweet dreams."

It's a nice thought, and I'm hoping and wishing that's what I really heard. I think it's more like my mind is playing tricks on me. Either way, I fall into a deep sleep for the rest of the night.

Chapter Twenty-Two

Charlie

N ATE ENDED UP STAYING IN THE HOSPITAL FOR A full week, instead of only two days. The doctors felt, with the head injury he had sustained and the broken ribs, that he could use more rest before sending him home. I think they were afraid he would try to do too much on his own. By staying there, he was forced to rest and take it easy. He will need to be off work for some time, which is unfortunate, as the accident happened during a crucial time for his company. I ended up staying every night with him, though I had to work in the day. His sister and dad took a more active role during that time, for once. It seems that his father had a wakeup call, where his family is concerned.

During his hospital stay, we didn't really get into all that had started to go wrong between us. It wasn't the time and place to worry over such things. We decided he should focus more on his recovery before diving into the arena of all the heartache we both suffered. Though, the first night I was there, I did tell him I loved him. I'm not sure he heard me, though, and it hasn't come up again—nor has he declared such feelings back.

He's been home for a full three days now, and we've

spoken on the phone, mainly. I'm trying to give him space to recover, without hovering. I'm also being a big chicken by purposefully not talking about our relationship. I know now at least that we are still intact. He seemed clear on that matter at the hospital, when he wouldn't let me go. The real crux of it all will be if he can come to terms with having a fully committed relationship, and if he can finally let me in the rest of the way. I'm tired of this back-and-forth that we have going on. He needs to be all in with me, or not at all. I can't continue the way we have been.

My phone rings, and I see that it's Halley. "Hey, lady," I greet her.

"What's shaking?" she asks.

"Not much."

"Have you seen Nate since he came home from the hospital?"

"I've gone over every day for short stays. Mainly, we talk on the phone about nothing of importance. I guess we're both pretty good at avoiding the big elephant in the room."

"You're going to have to be the one who man's up. I think he's scared, and isn't sure what to say at this point. Though, I know he does. He's said as much."

"It would be great to finally get to the bottom of our problems for the last month or so. He can't keep me at a distance anymore. I won't allow it. I deserve better than that, and so does he. I know where his problem stems from, but he has to know he can't continue to live his life with so many 'what if's', and not opening his heart up all the way to someone else."

"Well, if there is anyone who can make that boy sing like a canary—it's probably not you." She laughs. "I'm kidding. But I do think you have something special, and if he knows your worth, he'll do the right thing. For both of you. That I know for sure. He just feels like a jerk, and he's really upset with himself."

"How do you know all of this?"

"He's been spilling the beans to his friends. Or, it's more likely that they've not let up on him about what an idiot he's been."

"That's not right. They need to leave him alone and let him come to his conclusions on his own." I feel protective of Nate, and this is none of their business. If Nate wants to talk to me, he's a big boy who can figure that out on his own.

"Oh, don't worry about that. They really didn't have to pry much out of him. It's the same song and dance they've been having for a while now."

"You tell your man to butt out, Halley. I'm serious. I know they care for both of us, and they want this to work out. I do, too. But this is my relationship with Nate, not theirs. He will come to me in due time. I'm growing more certain of that the more we speak."

"Calm down, mama bear. They're not causing him any harm. Everything is fine with the guys now. It was strained for a bit, and he just hid that part from you. They called a truce for a while, but there was still tension between them."

"I plan to have the big talk with him by the weekend. So, what are you up to?"

"I was actually asked to see if you would go visit your favorite patient."

"Why didn't Nate just call or text and ask me himself?"

"You'll have to ask *him*. I was only asked to make contact with you and get you to say yes. I was charged to do anything necessary to get you to his house." She laughs.

"Well, gee—don't make me feel all special or anything." I sarcastically remark.

"Oh, relax. Go get ready, or you're going there in whatever you have on."

"A pajama party sounds fun right about now. We could definitely use a great distraction, one where fun and laughter are involved."

"Stop procrastinating and get off the phone already." She chuckles. "I'll be there in an hour. Oh," she says before hanging up, "and make sure you look really cute." Then the line goes dead.

I get ready in record time and am waiting for her when she finally shows. She takes me to the guys' place and parks in the driveway, then gets out.

"Where are you going?" I question her.

"To make sure you walk through the front door. Where else?"

"Okay, you can pipe it down already. I wasn't going to say no. *Geez*," I grumble.

We walk through the front door, and I'm immediately assaulted with the best aroma known to man. I'm not sure what they have in store, but the food smells fabulous. I walk in a little further and see that the dining room table is nicely set, and there are candles glowing. There are only two place settings, and I wonder who they are for. I look around for Nate, but don't see him. I only see Holt and Tucker with big smiles on their faces as they load the table down with what looks like delicious food.

"What's going on? And where is Nate?" I question the two men, who look like conspirators in a secret operation.

"Nate will be along shortly. He's just cleaning up. We're going to get ready and head out." Tucker says, without really answering my questions.

"Where to?" I inquiry.

"We have dates with two of Vacaville's finest women. Though, Charlie—no one is quite the cream of the crop as you are." Holt winks.

"Are you flirting with my woman?" I hear Nate say incredulously from behind me.

I turn to see that he's cleaned up, but still not looking any better since the accident. His bruises are yellowing, but his nose and eyes are still darkly discolored. His poor arm is in a thick, heavy cast. He walks a little further into the room, and I can tell his breathing is a bit labored as he gingerly makes his way over to me. I can only imagine the pain he's in. He wraps his good arm around my shoulders and reels me in to him.

"Hey, little one." He feathers a light kiss against my left cheek. "I've missed your beautiful face today."

I blush at his compliment and lean into him more, while trying not to hurt his ribs any more than they already do.

"It's good to see you up and out of bed, lazy bones," I smile up at him.

"Someone had to get up and fend for himself since his favorite nursemaid abandoned him." He pouts.

"Was that your plan, then? To get Halley to call me up and bring me back here for your daily routine? A little laundry, even?"

"You know me so well," he winks down at me.

"We're out of here, if you don't need anything else?" Tucker says, and I'm still left in the dark.

"No, we're good. Thank you, for all you've done." He looks to each of our friends. "Try not to get arrested while you're out getting into trouble."

Our friends head out on that cryptic note, which leaves me alone with Nate. He guides me over to a seat and helps me into it. "Be right back." He kisses the top of my head, and then leaves the room.

I hear the front door shut and the turn of the deadbolt before Nathan reappears and takes his own seat.

"What's all of this about?" I question him. I'm curious as to what he has planned, and what this all means.

"I thought I would do something special for my girlfriend, but obviously I'm a gimp this week and needed help."

"Girlfriend?" I raise a brow.

"You don't think you are?" He furrows his right back.

"It was mentioned in the hospital, but we haven't had that conversation yet. Even though we are exclusive, we hadn't ever labeled what we were. What we *are*," I amend.

"That's a topic I would like to discuss with you—tonight." He says sheepishly.

"Yes, we should talk about that, shouldn't we? I think we have a lot of ground to cover."

"You're right, and I'm sorry about that." He has the good grace to look ashamed.

I reach out a hand and place it on his, lightly stroking his fingers. "Well, you've got me here now, right? There's no time like the present. Unless, you'd rather have a nice dinner first, and then chat later?"

"That's my girl." He warmly smiles at me. "Thinking with her stomach, just like her man." He winks at me.

Shaking my head at him, I laugh. "You big dork."

My comment causes him to laugh, and breaks some of the tension I was feeling. My shoulders relax, and we start dishing up manicotti, salad, and mixed vegetables. The rest of dinner goes over smoothly, with light-hearted talk and teasing. After dinner, he leads me to the couch, where he serves chocolate pie.

"Okay, I have to say it. I know you didn't make this pie!" I laugh. "Though it is so dang sweet and delicious."

"Guilty as charged. I cannot tell a lie about food."

"So, do you want to start?" I hedge. "Or should I?" I try to ask with as much tenderness as I can.

"Let me say something first." He places his dessert on the coffee table, then takes my plate and does the same. He turns back to me and takes my hands into his. "I've been a real big jerk to you, and I'm sorry. I was only doing what I thought was best for my emotional wellbeing. It took me some time to finally come to terms with it. I wanted you completely, but part of me was frightened to give my whole self away." He gazes into my eyes intently. "You understand that, right? It was never about me not wanting you. I know you must have thought that for a while, and I apologize." I nod at his statement. "That was never my intention."

"I know that now. I know it even more so after the night you made your drunken confession that I was never meant to hear. Do you know how badly that hurt me? I was devastated that you didn't remember opening up to me the next morning. It only got worse when you started distancing yourself further. To be honest, Nathan, I would have never known anything was wrong or how unbalanced our relationship was until that drunken night. That's when we started going downhill. Sure, there were some hints that were red flags—like when you wouldn't talk about your family, which concerned me. But I was learning how to cope with that. What I really wanted was your heart—completely." I stare back into his eyes, trying to read the thoughts forming behind them.

"Don't you know, silly woman, that you've always had it? Even if I tried to pretend otherwise?" He caresses my cheek, willing me to believe him.

"I will admit, there were times I thought so, but other times told me to be cautious. Not to get my hopes up. I was learning how to handle things with what I knew about relationships, which wasn't much. But still, I had good role models growing up, and still do, with my family."

"Yes, you do, and you're blessed beyond measure for it.

What I wouldn't give to have that back in my own life. We had that once, what your family has. I miss it. It's one of the many things that drew me to you, though the seriousness of it scared me, and I wasn't sure I was ready to go back there again. I can't express how hard it was hearing about and watching the kind of family you have, and being reminded of my own when my mother was alive."

"Nathan, you shouldn't be scared to go back to something as good, loving, and wonderful as a close-knit family. In a way, you already have that with Holt and Tucker, and now with the girls and I. Don't you know that? We *are* your family, and we deeply care for you. You should never doubt or deny those feelings."

"You're right, Charlie. But when you lose the glue that holds your actual family together, the one who's the very light in your family's eyes, it's hard to get that feeling back. You can't replace it. You can only hope for something as close to it to come along, but then when it does, you wonder if it's a fairytale in your mind. Or if other families are truly that happy together."

"I'm sorry you lost her. I'm even more sorry for how I found out. I wanted to know things like this, but only because you wanted to tell me, and let me into your life. That's all I wanted, you know. To be fully allowed into your heart. After all, you've had mine from the start." I shyly tell him.

"You don't think I realized that? I've always known. I was just too scared of that knowledge, and the responsibility that would come with it. The last thing I ever want to do again is shut you out." He leans over and kisses my forehead.

"Speaking of hurting me, I really don't want to jump to conclusions, but we need to talk about the woman who I saw you with at *Texas Jacks*."

"I wish that hadn't happened. It was worse to see than you actually think it was."

"So? Who was she then?"

"Heather Morgan, my ex-high school sweetheart. We dated for a long time. Actually, we grew up around each other. We had big plans for our life together, until my mom got sick. After she passed, I broke up with Heather. I couldn't think straight, and I eventually made some unwise choices during the course of the period after, until I met you. Talking to you was the best choice I've ever made, to date."

"I love that you think that. But, can you tell me what she wanted? And why you looked like you were having a tender moment with her?"

"She was asking to come back to me. She missed me, and she felt like she had given me enough time and space to finally rekindle what we once had. I told her that the only door I would be knocking down was yours, Charlotte. I truly mean that."

"Thank you for being honest with me. I still don't like that she came back into your life, though, or the moment it looked like you two were involved in."

"How do you think I felt when Dave was around? I wanted to punch the guy, and I'm not a violent man. I thought for sure you had slipped through my fingers. I was so upset that day at the track. He was there, being too friendly in your personal space, and all I could see was this red rage. I'd had enough, and wasn't thinking straight when I jumped off my bike and started to exit the track. I was careless and blinded by jealousy. The likes of which I wasn't used to experiencing before, *ever*."

"Dave isn't *you*, Nathan. He's a friend, but not a personal, close one. I would never jump to another man when I have no clue where I stand with the one I love."

My eyes fly to his, and I'm in shock that I just admitted that out loud. It's how I feel, and I meant it when I said it to him at the hospital when he was sleeping. I couldn't stand the thought of rejection from him. It would sting if he didn't repeat the words back to me.

If his stunned expression is anything to go by, then I'm ready to hightail it out of here.

"Can you please repeat those words?"

I know I can't hide the feeling anymore, and I'm not about to play games. So I put on my brave face, and say it again. "I love you, Nathan. I have for a long time, now."

"Do you know how often I've imagined you saying those words? I thought I heard you say them in the hospital, but then realized it was only a dream that I thought was real."

"I did say it back then, too."

"Come here, little one."

I scoot closer to him so he can pull me into his arms. He leans us against the couch, as gingerly as he can. I lean against his good side when he kisses the top of my head. I shyly look up at him, wanting to know what he's thinking.

"Charlotte," he looks down into my eyes from his perch on the couch. I strain my head up more to get a better view. "I've been in love with you since the beginning, I just didn't comprehend what I was allowing to happen. I regret my actions. I should have told you months ago how I felt. Can you ever forgive me and my stupidity?"

"Nathan, how can I *not* forgive you? There is one thing that I need to ask of you, though."

"Anything."

"Can you forgive me for not trying harder to make you share your feelings? Can you forgive me for when I felt like I let you down after you told me about your mom? Here you've shown me a new part of life, and reached out your hand, holding mine the whole way, when I've let you down."

"Charlotte, I have to apologize here, too. I was so mad at you for not saying anything after my confession. Though, I didn't know it had happened then, and it would take days to remember it all. I blamed you for a while. I was so beyond mad at you, myself, Carianna—I should have talked to you like an adult following that night, and I didn't. I let it go the route it did and pushed you further away. I didn't mean to toy with your emotions, or to be so distant and hurt you. I was hurting myself. I had to go through the grieving process the rest of the way. I was mad. I was hurt. I was sad. I wanted to be alone. I just didn't know how to take in all of these emotions, or where to go with them. The guys really helped show me the light, but the kicker was when I thought I lost you. I realized that it was only my own doing."

"Even though you don't need it, I'll tell you that you are forgiven. I wanted you to tell me these things on your own, without the help of alcohol. I felt horrible for not reaching out in a better way. I think at this point, we need to let go of our mutual hurt and anger, and move on. Can you do that for me?"

"I want to do that, and I'm trying. It won't be easy, Charlie. I will still have setbacks. I will still get upset and feel lonely all over again, but never as lonely as I was, if we work on this together. I can make you a promise that I won't drink again like I did the night you found me. I've never gotten like that before, and I don't ever want to experience it again."

"I like that promise, and I can be your foundation. You just have to let me in when you have a hard day."

He leans down and kisses me softly, and that's how we end our evening. On the couch, cuddling, watching movies, and working out our past hurts, our future wants, and our lives in the present.

One and a half years later

Nate

I can't believe I've spent over a full year with Charlie. We're in a better place now than we were in the year prior. I'm learning to work out my issues by actually talking to her. She's been there for me on my hard days, and my best days. She encouraged me to make more time for my family, which is slowly coming back together, but still is a work in progress. We can't change who we are overnight. It takes time to work out the kinks. Regardless, it's been a great year, with several new additions to it.

We're not married yet, but I've already become a permanent fixture in the home of the Davenports. Greg and Lindsay were married. Jaxon and Jennifer had a baby. Bethany finally settled down with one man, and he treats her like she's his queen. Rachel and Anson had twins—both girls, to Anson's horror. We've had a few good laughs at that.

Tonight, we're celebrating our birthdays, Charlie and I, at *Texas Jacks*. We've invited our family and friends to come celebrate with us. It looks to be a promising evening with everyone we love, and all of the joy and laughter they bring us.

"Are you having a good time, sweetheart?" I bend to speak in Charlie's ear over the music. She wraps her arms around me and snuggles in closer.

"Yes, cowboy. Thank you for the best birthday to date. I don't know how you will top this next year."

"I'm sure I'll find a way, don't you worry." I lean in and

kiss her cheek, then up to her ear, where I nip it. "I'll be right back. I think I just saw Holt and Tucker head off to the pool tables. I want to see how much I can swindle out of them." She giggles, and I pull away to find the guys.

I clock them near the DJ booth. I'm heading their way when I spot Dave. We haven't exactly gotten past the Charlie-episode, as I call it, but we manage to coexist together, when we have to. Thankfully it's not that often. I give him a head nod and keep on moving to the two targets in my line of sight.

"Is it all set and ready to go?" I ask, the moment I get to them.

"That's an affirmative!" Holt salutes me.

"All right. Let's get to it then." The DJ hands me a mic and cuts the music.

"I would like the birthday girl to come out to the middle of the dance floor, please." I look through the crowd and spot Charlie. She looks at me, trying to guess what I'm up to. I don't think she has a clue. I hope no one spoiled it, at least.

She makes her way over, but does it hesitantly. "This beautiful woman standing before all of you tonight is the center of my life. She's saved me from a downward spiral. I want her to know how much I think of her. To me, she's the best part of me. I love you, Charlie. Happy Birthday."

She smiles at me, and I already know that if I were up close to her now, I would see how much it shines through her eyes. She's about to walk away, but I stop her again.

"Charlotte Davenport, I have a question to ask you."

Everyone is pretty quiet now, as I've got their full attention.

"Will you dance with me?"

Everyone starts to boo me, thinking I was going to pop the question. I can see her, and she looks like she's laughing, but pleased and happy all the same. I watch her make her way to me, and we start to lose the attention of the partygoers. Once she makes it to me, I take her hand and walk her back to the dance floor.

"You crazy man." She socks me in the arm, but I can hear the mirth in her voice.

I pull her into my arms as the slow song, H.O.L.Y. by Florida Georgia Line, comes on. Right as we start to slow dance, I stop and drop down to one knee. The music goes to a low hum, while I stare up into Charlie's eyes. Everything ceases to exist but her in this moment. I pull the mic back out from my back pocket and start to talking to the love of my life.

"Charlotte Davenport. From the moment I laid eyes on you here, in this very place, I couldn't stop. I felt a connection with you from the start. We had our ups and downs, but through it all, you've made me stronger. I've given you my heart, and then my love. Now, I want to give you one more thing. Will you do me the honor of taking my last name, and becoming my wife?"

Charlie's eyes are wet with the tears running unchecked down her cheeks. She stands there in a stunned silence. I pick up her left hand, and hold a ring out to her ring finger. I start to slide it on. I'm confident that she will say yes.

"Are you going to leave him hanging?" someone shouts from the crowd.

Charlie pulls out of the spell I cast upon her and slowly nods her head, whispering, "*Yes.*"

The moment finally dawns on her, and she beams the biggest simile on me before she jumps me. I almost fall over, but manage to save the day. I wrap my arms around her waist, resting my head on her soft belly, giving her an extra firm squeeze. She lets go and I stand up. I gather her back into my arms and kiss the daylights out of her.

"Ladies and gentleman, I would believe that's a yes." We hear the DJ say over his mic. "Everyone, please join in celebrating this fine couples' joint birthday—and engagement—out on the dance floor. Grab a partner and let's dance!"

"I can't believe you surprised me like this. I had no idea!" Charlie exclaims.

"It was a miracle that no one blabbed it to you. I'm shocked!" I laugh. I nuzzle her hair as we sway to the music. "Thank you, little one, for coming into my life. I love you."

"I love you, too."

We spend the rest of the night celebrating life with those we hold dear to our hearts. I won't say it was an easy one, as I had one important person missing, but I'm learning to deal with those hard times in a better way now. I have all of the support I need now. My mom would have loved Charlie, as I'm sure she does while she watches over us from Heaven.

Epilogue

Seven years later

Nate

I T'S A BEAUTIFUL, WARM SUMMER EVENING, AND I'M heading home from the track. I still drive my beloved truck that my mom left to me. It's the one thing I own that I won't let go of, and eventually our son, Jack, will take his first driving lesson in it.

You can just guess what we named him after.

I still go out to the track from time to time, but no longer feel the need to constantly. That pull to go there and block it all out is gone, thanks to my loving wife, Charlie. I no longer feel the sadness of losing someone all the time. What I feel now is an abundance of love from Charlie, our son, and our friends and family.

Now, when I go out to the track, it's to enjoy myself and to have a little time away from the hassles of work. Every now and then I can convince Holt and Tucker to meet me out there, and we have a blast laughing like old times and feeling the thrill of the race.

I know sometimes going out to the track worries Charlie, especially after our scare seven years earlier. But she knows there are times when I feel the pull, and need to go. I love that about her. She may worry, but she doesn't hold me back, trusting all will be okay, and that I will come back home safe and sound. Sometimes, I can even manage to get her and Jack to come out with me as well. Those are the days I get our friends out there, and they spend their time soaking in the rays of the sun, watching the children play, and enjoying each other's company.

I'm halfway home when I start reflecting back on my life and realize what a gift Charlie has been. She keeps me happy and sane. She fills my heart every day with her beauty and love, and then there's our son, Jack. He's such a little character, always going full steam ahead and loves to laugh. I look forward to returning home each night so I can see our family and listen to the joy of our son echoing off the walls of the house. He really is such a happy little guy, and he's by no means lacking in the love department.

Charlie is now a stay-at-home mom with our three-year old son. She's also very pregnant with our daughter, Savannah. She's got one more month to go, and she looks more beautiful than the day I first saw her on the dance floor at *Texas Jacks*.

Charlie and I are as happy as we can be. Our relationship is strong, loving, and solid. We have our bad days, like any couple, and we have lots of good days. We live every day one at a time, and take what life throws at us—or blesses us with.

As for the guys and I, we decided a couple of years back to try our hand at our own construction company. We got the business up and running, and things are going pretty smoothly. I love that I can be my own boss now, and that I'm home in time for dinner with my family.

I pull in to our long drive thinking how nice it will be to see Charlie and her beautiful smile. I really love her and our growing family. I'm thankful every day for taking a chance with my heart and handing it to her on a silver platter. I will never regret the events that led me to this point in my life.

I park the truck in the driveway and see that Charlie is sitting on the porch in one of the rockers. She's watching Jack play in the yard, chasing our black lab, Lucky.

I climb out of the cab of the truck and close the door. When I look over at Charlie, I see that she's turned her eyes and her bright smile on me. That warms my heart, and the love that I feel from the look on her face sometimes chokes me up. I want nothing more than to go over to her, gather her in my arms, and hold her tight.

I walk by Jack and Lucky first, so I stop and snatch Jack up and swing him around, which sends our little munchkin into a fit of laughter. Lucky runs around my legs while we spin in the yard for a few moments. I set Jack back down on his feet, but he's a bit dizzy and falls on his butt. This sends him into more laughter as Lucky starts licking his face. I reach down and run my hand along Lucky's black coat of fur before I take the porch steps two at a time to get to my wife.

She's still smiling at me when I reach her, and holds her arms out to me as I lean down and gently pull her up from the rocking chair. Charlie wraps her arms around me, as much as they will go with her belly in the way, and I pepper her face with sweet kisses before I gently fit my lips to hers. I pull away and look back at her with a gentle smile, and all the love I can possibly show her in my eyes. We hold on to each other and turn our heads to watch Jack and Lucky running around the yard, happy as can be.

At this very moment, I know I'm exactly where I should be. I'm the happiest, luckiest man on the face of the earth, and I know my mother is smiling down on me.

Holly Lane

Holly Lane

Amazon Bestselling Author
J.B. Morgan

EXCERPT

Prologue

3.5 years ago

THIS IS IT. *THE BIG MOMENT.* ALL OF THE EXCITEMENT and anticipation that has been building for months for this one day has finally arrived.

Ava Walsh, Jenifer Gustafson, and I were finally leaving high school in the dust of our rearview mirrors and traveling towards our futures, with the exception of a pit stop for a bit of fun in the sun first.

We've been the best of friends from kindergarten clear through high school, and now we have finally graduated together. Funny, crazy, and klutzy would sum us up in a nutshell.

Graduation took place last week, and this week is our final nod to high school and the last time we will all be together for a long time. Ava and Jenifer have ambitions to get out of this jolly town of ours and hit some bigger cities. They want to travel and live it up before heading to college, getting as far away from the busy-bodies of Holly Grove as possible. Then there's me, good old Hollie Reed, staying behind to attend a local community college and work at my parent's pharmacy. Overall, I was okay with where my life was headed. I loved Holly Grove, and saw no point in changing who I was or moving far away to live out a dream. *I was happy, end of story.*

But today… now today was something to be excited for. Today we were boarding a plane for the very first time in our 18 years of life. It feels as though there is a battle raging deep in the pit of my stomach, and my heart wants to jump right out of my chest. My brain wants to push its way into the fray, screaming at me, *why did you pick a flight that's over seven hours long to be your first flying experience?* I know it wasn't my brightest idea ever. But it is what it is, and it's too late to chicken out now.

The girls and I move up in the boarding line. It formed along the large glass window that allowed you to look out and see the giant airplane that will hold hundreds of people, flying over water for hours, and the vast majority of the flight. *Who wouldn't be scared?*

This is where the *crazy* comes into the group, because that's what we are. Or at least I am. *Why didn't I start off small, selecting somewhere closer to home and over dry land?* We inch our way along the window for a few minutes more until it's finally our turn to hand over our boarding passes to the lady at the gate. She takes Ava's ticket, then Jenifer's, and finally mine, where she scans the bar-codes, electronically doing a roll call for all of the passengers. *So why does handing over my boarding pass feel like I'm handing over my life?*

Passing the gate agent, we head down the ramp towards the plane in a slow-moving line, listening to excited voices and crying babies. *I really hope I'm able to sleep through most of this flight.* Not just because of the babies, but for my own sanity and nerves as well. Yes, my nerves were on pins and needles, and I hadn't even set foot onto the plane yet. *Will they go into hyper drive when I finally sit down?* I may need a horse tranquilizer by the time this trip is all said and done with.

It's a miracle when we get through the line to finally step over the threshold of the airplane's entrance. Ava, Jenifer, and I follow the other passengers like a bunch of lost sheep being herded into the cabin, and slowly make our way down the aisle to our seats. It's a relief to see that we have a small row to ourselves on the right side of the plane, as opposed to a large one in the middle. There are way too many seats next to each other over there, with little to no real legroom. There's no way I could last for seven-plus hours sitting next to some stranger, the side of my body pressed up against him. *Then again, who wants to sit next to a nervous, freaked out 18-year-old on her first plane trip?* I think that list would be two names long, consisting of my best friends.

We find our seats, and thankfully Ava and Jenifer let me slide into the row first, firmly planting my rear in the seat next to the window. On the bright side, I can lean my head up against the side of the plane and rest. Granted, the window shade needs to be drawn. *No way will I be looking out that window anytime soon.* The last thing I want to think about is plummeting to my death and... *Oh, great now that's what I'll be obsessing over next.* Letting out a sigh, I grab my seat belt and buckle up. I lean my head back against the seat's headrest, close my eyes, and grab the armrest, not even realizing at first that I'm white-knuckling it until Ava taps my left hand.

"You know we won't actually take off for awhile, right? We were some of the first to board, and there's a ton of people left who still need to enter the plane and find their seats," Ava helpfully points-out, like I didn't know this information already. I look over at her and give her a tight-lipped smile before turning my face to look out the window. Okay, I take it back; I can at least look out the window *now*, as we haven't actually left the ground yet.

"I know. I'm just preparing myself now," I tell both her and the window. "If I'm lucky, I'll be relaxed enough to pass out before we take off," I can only hope, while silently sending up a prayer to the heavens that this will come true.

"The more you tense up, the harder it will be to relax. You know that, so why don't you take one of the Valium's that Dr. Peters gave you?" Jenifer reminds me, seeing as how I had forgotten I even had any with me. "You'll definitely be sleeping, long before we even leave the ground."

I don't necessarily know whether Jenifer's statement is true or not, so I give a non-committal shrug, telling both of them, "We'll see," before returning to facing forward. I know they won't push me and will back off, giving me the space I need while they chat about the things they want to do and what to see during our week-long vacation.

Other students that we know board the flight, saying hi to us as they pass. Eventually the airline attendants give their spiel over the loud speaker, then execute a quick safety check of the cabin doors, luggage compartments, and lastly, check our lap belts before heading to their own seats to secure themselves for take-off.

The pilot comes on over the intercom and gives us an estimated time for our arrival to the destination, then gives additional instructions to the flight attendants. Next thing I know, our plane is moving, and I'm holding on steadfastly to the seat's arm rests. I've never been one for roller coasters or big, scary, heart-stopping, stomach-dropping rides, so being on a plane worries me. I pray I won't get sick, and that I'll have a lovely nap that will last for the rest of the flight.

It's our turn to leave the runway now, and it's finally hitting me completely, like a ton of bricks. *There's no turning back now.* I'm stuck right here, in my seat on this plane, with hundreds of people for the next seven or so hours. This isn't a dream anymore; it's definitely real. I can't believe I'm about to fly over an ocean, leaving Holly Grove behind me for a week. This will be the longest and furthest trip away from home for me, and hopefully also a memorable one that will last a lifetime.

Here we go. Our plane is starting to pick up speed as it heads down the tarmac, preparing for take-off. Everything feels surreal at this very moment, and I know that my adventure is just beginning.

Hawaii, ready or not, here we come.

Chapter One

Present day

Iᴛ's ᴛʜᴀᴛ ᴡᴏɴᴅᴇʀꜰᴜʟ, ᴍᴀɢɪᴄᴀʟ ᴛɪᴍᴇ ᴏꜰ ʏᴇᴀʀ, ᴡʜᴇʀᴇ anything can happen, and children's dreams come true. It also happens to be my most favorite time of the year, but maybe I'm a little biased, since I was born only a day before my favorite holiday, Christmas.

Since I had the day off from work, I decided to take a stroll down Holly Lane, the main street in Holly Grove, before I met with my friends. The air is cool and crisp; people are trying their best to stay warm, bundled up in sweaters, scarves, hats, and gloves. The sidewalks and streets are covered in snow, while the sun hangs low in the sky this late morning. Everywhere you look, you can see Christmas decorations in the window fronts of the town's shops, and in the middle of the town square, there's a very large, decorated

Christmas tree, ready and waiting for the annual tree lighting ceremony to take place.

Holly Grove is a small town with a slower pace of life, not in a hurry to catch up with the rest of the world. My love for this town has grown over the years. While the rest of my classmates and friends were eager to get out of this town and explore the world, I was content to stay here. I've never felt that strong need to leave, so here I am. This is where I'll stay.

I continue my walk towards *Noelle's Café*, where I plan to have brunch with my two best friends, Ava and Jenifer. They both came home this year for the holidays, and I can't wait to catch up with them. It's been nine months since we've seen each other last. They're so busy with their own lives that communication has become like an art form these days. Both girls are still in college, have boyfriends, and work odd jobs in the summer.

As for me, I'm currently single, and mostly content with life, living in my own apartment, and still working at my family's pharmacy. Sure, I'd love to have someone special of my own to be with. I miss the hand holding, shy smiles, the kisses, and just being around the one you truly love. It's been a year since my last relationship, and my heart still hasn't picked up the pieces of its shattered self. I know it's going to be a long time before I'm ready to find someone again, so I just take every day one step at a time. Eventually the pain will lessen, and I'll finally get to the point where I can actually move on. It doesn't mean that it will hurt any less than it does now, but I know that I can't dwell on the sorrow of my loss forever. It's best that I get off this topic, or I'll be in a melancholy mood for the rest of the day, and who wants that when I have a brunch date with my two best friends to get to?

Pushing my thoughts to the side, I enter the café where the girls and I are meeting. This month it's decorated with a Christmas theme. Noelle, the owner of the café, has hung decorative ornament balls in the front window, with white lights lining the outside of the window, which will be turned on later in the evening. There's also an elaborate-looking holly wreath hanging on the door, with a giant red bow at the top in the center, with little berries, ribbons, and gold jingle bells intertwined throughout the wreath.

Inside the café, there's a small Christmas tree sitting in the corner. Every year, Noelle puts the tree up and adds name tags to the branches. This tree represents the giving tree. Everyone is encouraged to draw a name tag and buy a present for the unknowing recipient who is in need of some help during the holiday season. Usually the names are of children whose parents can't afford much, or the elderly in our town who have little to no family around to give them something to put smiles on their faces. I can hear faint Christmas music playing through the speakers in the ceiling as I survey the tables, where Mason jars are filled with colorful candy canes sitting joyfully in the center. The jars all have garland bunched up around the bottoms, with little red bows attached in a few places.

I immediately recognize Ava and Jenifer, and make my way further into the café toward them. They both have big smiles on their faces, and quickly get out of their seats for a round of hugs. It's so good to see their beautiful, happy faces, and to hear their voices again.

"Hey! It's good to see you ladies. I was beginning to think I was Casper the Friendly Ghost these days," I joke.

"Yeah, sorry about that. I've been so busy with school this term, then finals, and finally meeting Jay's family. Life has been such a whirlwind lately," Jenifer says with a dreamy look. Just seeing her face brings a slow smile to my own. She's happy, content with what she's doing, and more in love than ever.

"Well, it looks as if this relationship just got more serious if you've already met Jay's family. Does that love struck look on your face and all of the stars in the universe shining from your eyes mean that you got the stamp of approval from his parents?" I tease her.

"Yes! They were great, and we had a wonderful visit. I can't wait to go back up to their home and spend some more time with everyone. I feel like I really fit into his family. Jay will be here in a couple of days to meet my family next. Since we did Thanksgiving at his house, we decided he would come here for Christmas. My parents are eager to finally meet him, and I feel like it will go smoothly. You know how laid back my family is," she gushes at us. *I think someone is on cloud nine, and the high she's on isn't just sugar, but bona fide love.*

"Well, this is good news, then. Maybe we can have a get-together with all three families before you leave. I think maybe we should have a birthday bash for Hollie. Let's keep up with the Christmas Eve birthday party tradition, but invite all of our families to come." Ava says, overly excited. I want to join her in that feeling, but I don't know if I'm happy about it. *Celebrating just isn't the same anymore, not ever since—*

"Oh, that's a great idea, Ava!" Jenifer exclaims, jolting me out of my thoughts. Turning toward me now, she continues, "We can coordinate with your mom."

Sighing, I say, "Yeah, sounds like a plan. Just tell me when and where, and I'll be there."

Yeah, right.

Hmm, it looks like it's time to turn the spotlight toward someone else.

"And what about you, lady?" I eye Ava with a quirked eyebrow. "What's your lame excuse for the lack of communication? Other than you leaving a voicemail telling me that you two crazies were coming home for Christmas."

"Well," she says slowly, with a grin, "I've got some important news I wanted to share, and I knew if I called you, I wouldn't be able to tell both of you at once."

"You're pregnant! I knew it. Of all of us, it had to be you." I throw out at her with a grin on my face.

"What? No!" she feigns exasperation, but laughs right along with Jenifer and I, knowing it's the furthest thing from the truth. "And keep it down. We don't want the town gossip-mongers out spreading that to my parents before I even leave the café. *Yeesh!* Can you imagine?" she laughs, and sadly, we can all imagine. This is a great town that we love dearly, but there really are some incredible gossipers around here.

"You're getting married. Are you trying to beat me to the altar?" Jenifer punches Ava in the shoulder.

"Okay, Miss Violence. And no, it's not that—well, at least not yet. I do have my suspicions that Sean is planning something before the year is out." *I just hope she isn't getting her hopes up too high if it's not what she's expecting from him.*

"Anyway, what I was trying to say when you two chatty Cathy's couldn't put a cork in it, was that I have some exciting news. I wanted to tell you both in person. Sean got a job offer from *Mentor Graphics*!" she excitedly shares with us. "And guess what?" she asks without waiting for our reply. "It's here, in Oregon. Isn't that exciting?" She beams at us.

She's extremely happy, but I don't know why she couldn't share that with us over the phone or individually.

"Okay. And what does that mean exactly?" Jenifer asks.

"It means that Sean has asked me to move back to Oregon with him, and I'll be semi –closer to home. I've already checked out the schools where he'll be located, and I can transfer all of my credits to one of them. He made a trip out to meet the team of people he will work with, and has already found us a nice apartment close to his job. Isn't that exciting?" *Okay, maybe the girl does know what she's talking about, and Sean will be proposing sometime soon.*

"Wow. That's just—wow. What do your parents think about it all?" I ask her.

"Well, they weren't happy at first. It will be a big change, as well as a pain to move and get all of my paperwork for school done and things fixed and all of that jazz. But, they are slowly accepting it now. I don't see how they can't be happy, though. I'll be closer to home, after all."

"Don't you think you're a bit young for such a big step? Why not stay at school where you are and finish out the year? Give yourself time to prepare. That would give Sean a chance to settle in, make friends, and get to know the area before you go out there to meet them." Jenifer, the sensible one of our trio, rationalizes. Or at least tries to, with Ava.

"Sean and I have been together for 12 months now. We are happy, and we know what we want. We are both on track, with his career and my education. This is an awesome opportunity, and Sean wants to share it with me. Why wouldn't he? And why wouldn't I want to go? I don't want to be separated for another half of the year," she says with a frown. "Don't you think we've been separated long enough?" she asks before she automatically realizes her slip. "Oh, I'm so sorry, Holls! That was very insensitive of me."

"Its okay, Ava. You didn't mean anything by it. No need to worry." I assure her. "And we are excited and happy for you and Sean. We just want to make sure it's the right decision for you. But if you feel this is a good thing, and you're positive, we will do our best to support your choice," I say, reaching over and squeezing both of her hands with my left hand, while giving her my best smile. "It just means we will see you even less than we do now, and will probably hear less from you, too." I add with a little pout. "You know how much we love and adore Sean. Please don't think we meant anything negative about him."

Just then the waitress comes over with waters, a plate of Noelle's homemade pumpkin bread, and our menus. We set about slathering the warm bread with butter and watch it melt quickly. My mouth is watering, and all of a sudden, I'm starving.

"Good morning, ladies. It's great to see you three. It's been awhile since you've all been in here together. Do you need a minute to look over the menu or do you already know what you want?" Jinger asks us enthusiastically.

"No menus for us. I'm pretty sure we will all want our usual order." Jenifer eyes Ava and I, to which we both nod, and she turns back to Jinger. "We'll have three mugs of pumpkin spice hot chocolate with whipped cream, and three orders of pumpkin chocolate chip pancakes. Along with three sides each of sourdough toast, bacon, and the cheese and onion scrambled egg mix." Jenifer tells her.

I hand Jinger back the menus, and thank her with a polite smile, before returning my attention back to my friends.

"Okay, if I wasn't hungry earlier, or after my walk here, just listening to that order is making my mouth water," I tell the girls as Jinger walks away with our ticket.

We hear a *ding*, then Jinger shouts, "Order up, Jerry!" *Here's hoping Jerry isn't a slow poke, and we'll see our food sometime this year.*

And just like that, we fall back into our old habits and catch up with each other, laughing and joking while I update the girls on the recent gossip that's been spreading around town. That always gives us a good laugh or a few tears, depending on the news.

Jinger comes back over after about 20 minutes to deliver our scrumptious-smelling food, and we all dig in. *Who cares who's here watching, this is too good to not tuck into right away.* A little while later, one of the girls decides to be the brave one and bring up *him* in a roundabout way. Well, Ava did semi bring up the subject a bit ago, but I should have known I wouldn't get out of this café without a little interrogation on the status of my own love life.

"What's going on in the fabulous and exciting life of Hollie Reed?" nosey old Ava asks.

"You already know all there is to tell. We just sat here for the past 45 minutes, hashing it all out. What's left to discuss? Zip, really." I try to change the subject, but before I can think of a topic to start in on, Jenifer jumps into the conversation.

"Really? Nothing? No good looking new guy in your life?" she asks, like she knows something I don't.

"Umm, honestly? I have no idea what you're getting at with this line of questioning."

"Oh." Ava says, shooting a furrowed look at Jen.

"Oh?" I ask her curiously. *Is there some new rumor in town going around that even I hadn't heard about yet?* "What's this about? Have you heard something that I haven't?"

"Oh, no, it's nothing like that. We just thought for sure that you would have met someone by now," Jen says, peeking over at Ava again before continuing. "We just think that it's time you start to move on and find your own happiness. That's all. We didn't mean anything else by it Holls, really. We love you, and we're just trying to be here for you and look out for you." She reassures me with a smile, but I can see the unveiled sympathy in her eyes.

"Thanks, I appreciate it. I know I need to jump back into the dating world. It's just hard after—after—" I let out a deflating breath. "I'm sorry. I still have a hard time talking about it."

"We know. But it's been a year since you last heard from

him. You don't know where he is, or what's happened to him. He hasn't even tried to contact you that we know of. I hate to be the bearer of bad or unwanted advice, but you have to let him go," Ava says as she wraps an arm around my shoulders for a one-armed side hug.

"Well, I really should go see if my parents need extra help today." I say as cheerfully as possible. "Thank you for meeting me for brunch and catching up. I've missed you both so much! It was so good to actually see you and talk with you. It's been way too long. Keep me posted on the birthday party, and when Jay gets to town." I tell the girls then swoop in to give them each another hug. I really do miss them. They're like sisters to me.

"Okay. We'll give you a shout when we know what our plans are for the rest of the holiday vacation, and so on," Jenifer promises.

"I better be off, too. I need to check in with Sean before he heads out to his family's house and we miss each other. See you ladies later." Ava waves to us before heading out into the semi-warm day.

"I guess I'd better go, too. I need to check with Jay and see exactly what time his flight arrives and then get the guest room set up. I'll keep you posted about Christmas Eve, and Hollie?" she turns to me with a warm look on her face.

"Yes, Jen?"

"Ava and I, we both love you." She hugs me then walks away and continues right out the door, leaving me standing by our table, alone. *How did that happen?* I was trying to escape them first, not the other way around. *They know me too well*, I think to myself, before walking down Holly Lane to *Reed's Pharmacy*.

The sun is a tad higher in the sky now. The weather is still pretty cool, and the sun is trying to warm the town up as best as it can this time of year. I take in my surroundings again, noticing for the first time today that all of the light poles have garlands wrapped all the way around from top to base, with red ribbon mixed in. I make a further assessment of the Linden Trail and notice all of the white, twinkling lights interspersed throughout the trees.

Linden Trail is a nickname that the town has for a cobblestone walkway that is lined with linden trees that were planted really close together. The trees form an archway-like covering over the path that leads down to the town square, on the other side of Holly Lane. I had forgotten how beautiful the trees could be in winter, when the leaves turned all white before they started to fall off. It's a gorgeous sight, and one that I often take for granted, even though its beauty greets me each new day.

And with that hope, I believe I can find it in me to pick up the pieces of my heart and start to mend them back together again. I'm excited to see what the New Year brings my way. Until then, I'll allow myself a little more time to mourn the one that got away.

Chapter Two

June, 2013

"J EN," I TUG ON HER SHIRT, TRYING TO GET HER attention while she's yapping away with Ava about wanting to get to the beach as soon as possible. "Look behind me, without being overly obvious about it, and tell me if you recognize anyone." I say with a slight, tilted backward nod, trying to be nonchalant about getting her to follow my directions, without appearing obvious myself.

"Oh my gosh," she breathes, bugging her eyes out at me.

"You see them too, right?" I ask. *Because I really want her to verify I'm not seeing things.*

"Who? Who are you two talking about?" Ava butts into the conversation, way too loudly. I give her a big *knock it off,* wide-eyed glare, but she's either clueless or doesn't see what I'm trying to do as she keeps trying to look around us on her tippy toes.

"Knock it off, Ava." Jen scolds her. "I believe I see Mr. and Mrs. Frost straight in front of us, behind Hollie's back. But, why are they here and how come no one mentioned they would be here at the same time as us?" Jenifer wonders aloud.

"They're probably here on vacation, like the rest of us. So, what's the big deal? It's a free country. Come on," Ava pulls on Jen's left arm. "Let's go say hi to them. Maybe they want to have lunch or dinner with us one day while we're here."

I bug my eyes out at her, like she just said 'The aliens have landed, the aliens have landed!' "Are you crazy? We can't just march up to the president of *Frost Bank* and say, 'excuse us. We would love to share a bit of food with you.' That's just nuts. He probably has better things to do than hang out with some teenagers. Plus, he's here with his wife. Maybe they're having a cozy, romantic getaway from all their nosey neighbors in Holly Grove?"

"Oh, don't be so dramatic. The Frosts are actually pretty nice, mellow, and down to earth people. You know that. They wouldn't turn their noses up at us. Stop being silly, and let's go." Ava says with an air of authority to her voice. *Who does she think she is, my mother?*

"Are you taking over the role as my mother while you're here?" I ask her, echoing my thoughts.

Rolling her eyes and sighing heavily, she asks, "Seriously Holls, did your fun gene take a vacation, too?" This cracks her and Jen up, and they start making their way over to the Frosts, leaving me to trail after them alone.

"Hi Mr. and Mrs. Frost!" Ava enthusiastically calls to them with a wave. "What a pleasant surprise, running into you all the way over here. What are the chances?" she says, holding out her hand while going in for a handshake with Mr. Frost.

"Well, it's sure lovely to see you three wonderful ladies. It surely is a pleasant surprise to see you here as well. We didn't realize this was the week of the graduation trip," Mr. Frost replies.

Yeah, I don't know how, since this is a big deal, and it has been talked about all over town.

"Oh dear, I hope you all don't think we're here to keep tabs on you for your parents, do you?" Mrs. Frost frets, earning her a shoulder pat from Mr. Frost.

"Nonsense, don't be silly, dear. They know better than that, right ladies?"

"Yes sir." Jenifer replies, showing off her good manners.

We shake hands with the Frosts and exchange a few more pleasantries before Jenifer says, "We would love to have lunch with you while we are all here. If you would like to, that is."

"That sounds like a grand idea, dear." Mrs. Frost replies with a warm smile that brightens up her whole face. *I think we just made her day.* Maybe when we return, I'll go around to their place once in a while to say hi.

We exchange cell phone numbers, and decide on a day to meet before parting ways. Once we are alone again, Ava says, "See? I told you so. You were worried for nothing. I'm actually excited to see them. We may get homesick, and by the time we meet up again, we'll be put at ease seeing two adult faces we know. It's good to have them here. You never know if we'll need some 'parental' help."

"Okay, now let's forget you just said that, because I'm thinking someone just sucked some fun cells out of *your* brain. Let's get our luggage and skedaddle out of here before we get left behind," I remind them as we head over to the baggage claim area.

"Who even says *skedaddle,* anyway?" Ava asks.

"Me, that's who. Now shut it, and march like a good

soldier over to our bags." I command as I head over to the carousels.

"Well, someone just took over the role of being 'mother hen' for this trip," Jen giggles, earning her an eye roll from me.

"No thanks. I'm here to have fun, not play mommy dearest to you two." I tell her over my shoulder while trying to locate our bags. We find them a few minutes later, and head out to find our group so we can all take the same mode of transportation to the hotel, and so no one gets separated, or lost. We eventually find our school friends shortly after exiting the airport, and we're automatically slammed with the warm humidity of the day.

"I'm all for changing into our swimsuits and hitting the beach as soon as possible." Ava says as she fans her shirt in and out to cool herself down.

"I second that," Jen says.

"And I third it."

Jude, a boy from our graduating class, walks over to us and addresses the group. "Hey guys. The airport is going to shuttle us all over to our hotel with some big, ten passenger vans, so we'll take two over there, and then maybe we can come up with a game plan. Let's all have a fun but safe trip while we're here."

Now, why isn't Jen dating Jude? He would be perfect for her! *It's like Papa Jude and Mama Jenifer have taken all of their kids on vacation.* But I don't say that out loud; I just nudge Ava in the arm and she secretly shares a smile with me, knowing we are on the same wavelength, as always.

"Sounds good, Jude. Thanks for doing that for us," Jen smiles over at him. He smiles back at her before turning away and making his way to where all of the luggage sits. He and some other guys start to load everything into the vans.

Ava and I give Jenifer a look, and she just shakes her head

and walks off in a huff at us, causing us to crack up. Yep, she totally knew what we were thinking about, which makes me laugh even more before heading her way to climb into one of the vans. I can't wait to get into my swimsuit and jump into the ocean. I've seen picture after picture of the green-blue, almost clear water. *It's beautiful.*

After we checked into the hotel, met with everyone in the lobby, and made a safety plan, we went to our rooms and prepared for the beach. That's where we find ourselves now, enjoying the sun on the beach and relaxing. I'm thinking about nothing while enjoying the cool sand between my toes as I keep digging them in and out repeatedly. Ava and Jen have gone down to the water with some of the guys from class, while I hung back with a few of the other girls. I know them, but we aren't that close, and I don't mind the nice, quiet solitude we have going on here.

I've been people watching for the last 30 minutes, and it's starting to get a little scary with some of the clothes, or lack thereof, I'm seeing here. If my eyes aren't deceiving me at the moment, there's a woman walking towards the water with no top on. *Say what? Is that even allowed?* I don't know, and I certainly don't want to find out anything else, so I quickly avert my eyes as a shiver runs down my spine. I'm glad she's down a bit further on the beach, as that was a scary sight to behold. I think it's time to get off of this towel and head towards the water myself. *Just not in the same direction.*

I walk a path in-between beach goer after beach goer, as I find my way down to the ocean and start to wade in, taking my time to adjust to the temperature. Finally, I'm warm and brave enough to venture further out. I eventually spot my friends quite a ways out, playing in the waves. They're trying to jump up before the wave hits them, but each time one builds up higher, then crashes down on them, making them all laugh as they get carried away or pulled under by the waves. It looks fun, so I make my way out there, not realizing that there are sandbars between their location and me.

After a few jaunts of walking on sandbars and dropping off into the ocean for a quick swim, I make it over to the group.

"Hey! You finally made it out here. We were placing bets on how long it would take until you were bored to death by people watching. Do you want to know who won?" Jen asks sourly.

I think she's trying to throw me off with that look. "Let me guess—" I pretend to look like I'm thinking really hard. "You," I finally say.

"Nope, not this time," she frowns over at the boys. "It was actually Jude, if you can believe it." She says under her breath, so no one but she and I can hear. *That is a shocker.* Jen is normally the best at this game, and Jude's not one to make bets. *I wonder why he did that.*

"Really? That is a surprise. How much do you owe him?" I laugh at her pouty face.

"I don't owe him anything," she says, which confuses me. "I have to take him out to dinner," she mumbles.

Okay, what? Does Jude like her after all? What the world is going on here? I'll find out later, but as for now, I want to see how far I can tease her before she cracks.

"What's that? I don't think I quite heard you right. Can you speak up a little louder? With all of these waves, it's making me a bit hard of hearing." I lay on the innocent act. I want her to have to say it louder, and watch as her face blushes a brighter shade of red. Sometimes I think she has a secret crush on him, but refuses to admit it.

"Oh, you heard me, big ears! I'm not repeating it." She huffs and puffs, and I think she's about to tackle me. However, she decides to splash water in my face instead, and it gets in my eyes and mouth.

"Hey, it's on, now!" I shout before diving towards her, causing her to scream and laugh while trying to escape me, but she can't swim away fast enough. I manage to get to her and push her head underwater, then swim a bit away from her. She comes up for air, sputtering out water while trying to wipe her eyes. She looks around, and spots me before diving my way, causing me to freak out because she's good at payback and no way do I want to be near the ocean when she gets her revenge. The boys are egging her on while laughing at both of us. I swim to the nearest sandbar and get out on it as fast as I can. Pretty soon, the boys and Ava have joined us as I try to run away from Jen, looking like a crazy lady while cracking up. I'm laughing so hard that I end up tripping as I step wrong and go down for the count.

Next thing I know, it looks like we've started our own WrestleMania match before someone shouts, "Let's play chicken!" If that doesn't get the boys' full attention, then maybe that topless lady down the beach will do the trick. *Seriously, did you have to go there?* I scold my brain, causing my arms to form involuntary goose bumps. *I'll have a nightmare about her tonight, that's for sure.*

By the time we crawl out of the ocean, flopping onto the sand like beached whales, our waterlogged bodies are exhausted. The skin on my face feels hot and tight from the sun, and my limbs are all like limp noodles. My brain has given into fatigue, and no one dares to move from our spots. But eventually we do get up and make our way back to the hotel.

I'm not sure how we even managed to get back to our rooms without dropping dead on the way up, though.

I'm lying on the bed, when suddenly a pillow smacks me in the face, eliciting much laughter from two people at my expense. "Oh, so mature," I laugh with them, because I'm too tired to care or do anything else. "Let's just stay in tonight, rent a movie, and order in our dinner." I say, right before Ava pegs Jen on the side of her head, which makes me laugh so hard. But I'm so tired that I can't move to join in on the fun.

"Hey, watch it, woman! I have a sunburn, and geez, that hurts." She laughs then quickly winces when she feels the stinging of the sunburn hitting her at full force. I'm not sure why, but right now this makes me laugh like a hyena. *I can't help it. I'm so exhausted that everything is funny, I suppose.*

"Are you high?" Ava eyes me suspiciously.

"Are you even playing right now?" I ask her, cracking up. "Oh my gosh. Why would you even ask a stupid question like that?"

"I don't know. I figured you must have gotten a contact high after being in the elevator with all of the potheads from the floor above us. Can't you smell it?" she asks, rolling her eyes at me.

"How do you even know what that smells like? I know nothing about it, and plan to keep far from it. So there's your answer. I'm not high," I state as I roll onto my side so I can pull myself up to a sitting position. "So, what's the plan for dinner?"

"I know we're tired, so maybe we can rest for an hour then head out and find food after?" Jen hopefully asks both Ava and I.

"Sure. A nap would be nice. How about we all take turns in the hot shower to rid ourselves of this saltiness, and then nap off our drunken, sun-induced state before heading out.

Sound like a plan, Stan?"

"Why do you always look at me when you say 'Stan?'" I ask her.

"I don't always look at you," she says as she heads to the bathroom to shower first.

"Whatever. Just go shower, Joe Schmo, so we can all get this nasty salt off. I'm closing my eyes for a bit until you're both done." I say as I flop back down onto the mattress and relax.

The next thing I know, I'm waking up with salt on my body, sunburnt skin, and a roaring headache. I look over and see that no one else is in the room with me. I feel slightly dazed and just plain rotten. I take a glance towards the sliding glass door and see that it's visibly later in the day, so I climb out of bed and head to the bathroom. I'm sure the girls are off visiting others from our school. I decide to hop in the shower and get ready before they get back so we can eat soon. I'm starving, and my next meal is as far as my brain can really let me think about.

About 45 minutes later, I'm ready, and I hear people at the door. I pop my head out of the bathroom, where I was adding the last touches of makeup, to find that the girls are back, along with some guests. I eye them with brows raised, doing my best to give them the 'mom look,' while crossing my arms over my ample chest.

"We have company," Ava cheerfully states the obvious, a bit too late.

"I can see that, smart-aleck." *Oh my gosh, I just sounded like my mom right then.*

"So, this is our friend, Hollie." Jen says, trying to dispel the embarrassing moment.

"It's nice to meet you, Hollie. I'm Jason, and these guys are my friends, Chase and Evan." Jason says with a slight nod toward his friends.

"We're actually your upstairs neighbors. Our room is directly above yours," Evan states.

"And how did you all meet, exactly?" I look to Jen for the truthful answer.

"Oh, see, earlier while you were sleeping, the guys were goofing off and dropped a shoe over the edge of their balcony, and it landed on our patio. So, we threw it back up to them. Then we got to talking, and they invited us up to hang out until you woke up." Ava explains, instead of Jen.

"The guys were just talking about ordering a pizza and hanging out here. They were tired of being around all the smoke on their floor," Jen fills me in.

"And once again, how do you know about this drug?" I wonder aloud, for the second time today.

"We've never tried it, as you should know, but we've heard about it around school. You live in a bubble sometimes, and you don't always realize what's right under your nose," Ava chides me a bit.

"Mom? Did I remember asking you to come on this trip with me?" I say to her, reminding her to check her *mom-a-tude* at the door.

"So—anyway, what do you ladies say to pizza?" Jason asks hopefully, while giving Jen his best charming smile.

"I think it sounds good. Though, we should get out of this hotel and find a place to eat at. I know I could eat a whole pie on my own. I'm *that* hungry right now." I embarrassingly blurt out. *Oh well. It's not like we'll see these guys again after this week is over.*

"Awesome. There's a *Round Table Pizza* right across the street," Evan shares with us. We all end up easily agreeing to it, as it sounds to me like the best possible plan at the moment.

"Follow us, boys," Ava says in her best flirty voice. I roll my eyes over at Jen, then go to grab my purse and hotel key before heading out the door.

Once outside of the hotel, we make our way across the street, enjoying the late afternoon weather. I'm glad I put on shorts and sandals, as it doesn't seem like it will cool off any time soon. *This weather is nothing like Holly Grove, that's for sure.* One could get spoiled by this weather every day. *It's perfect.*

Over pizza, the girls flirt to their hearts' content, and the guys eat it up like it's ice cream. They just can't get enough. They joke around and tease us, and in the end we all have a really good time. Even if I was a grump at first, and didn't feel so great, I'm really enjoying myself now. These guys are pretty funny, and have turned out to be a lot of fun to be around.

After our late lunch or early dinner—because I honestly can't decide what that just was—we get up from the table and head out of the chilly restaurant and into the pleasantly warm air. I sigh with relief upon exiting the doors. My body went from freezing to warming up instantly.

"So, the guys and I were talking earlier today about renting mopeds. Would you want to come with us?" Jason asks, giving Jen a hopeful look. "It's supposed to be a lot of fun. We may even be able to double up."

"Sweet, that sounds like fun. Let's totally do it." Ava excitedly says to me and Jen.

"Sure, why not? We did say we wanted to do all that we could while we are here. I'm down for it." Jen says, which makes Jason seem happier.

Jason *is* a good-looking guy with his dark hair, amber colored eyes and tall, toned form. But I still think Jen and Jude would be the perfect match. They would make cute babies together, all with blond hair and blue eyes and creamy pale skin. I feel an elbow in my ribs before I realize I've been caught daydreaming about my much too young friend and Jude making cute babies.

I blush with embarrassment, even though they have no clue what I was thinking. "Umm, sure that sounds like fun. I'm in." I manage to get out.

The guys are happy, and Evan shares a smile with us. "Awesome. Okay, let's go rent some mopeds and explore while there's still daylight."

I sure hope we know what we're getting ourselves into. We don't even know these guys, and here we are being extremely trusting. But as we make our way towards the moped rental place, we see other kids from our school headed in the same direction.

And oh look, there's Jude. "Hey Jude!" I call out, just because I can. For some reason, I want to giggle. Jen gives me a sharp look. *Oh boy.* Someone doesn't want me to rain on her happy little parade with Jason.

"What are you doing?" Jen hisses quietly at me.

"What?" I ask with my best innocent look. Ava and I crack up quietly, so the boys don't know what in the world we're up to as they walk slightly ahead of us, yammering on about sports.

"You know what. I don't have a secret crush on Jude. He's cute, nice, and just not my type," she says in an annoyed tone.

"Sure, whatever you say." I laugh then pick up my walking speed to catch up with Jude and the gang.

"Hey Hollie, what's up?" he asks as soon as I make it a few feet over in his direction.

"We're on our way to the moped rental shop. What are you guys up to?"

"We were actually headed that way, too. Cool. We can all ride together."

"Perfect! I'll tell the others, and you can meet our new

friends." I smile over at Jen and Ava as they catch up to us. "Guess what?" I say to them, fighting a smile.

"I don't know. What?" Ava plays along.

"Jude and the guys are headed the same way we are, and said they would love to ride with us. Isn't that great?" I make my voice sound overly excited.

"Yes, great it is, indeed." Jen says coolly. I know that later, she will exact revenge on me.

"Good. Let's introduce all of the guys together, and get this party started!" Ava shouts.

Jason, Chase and Evan make their way over to us and I make the introductions. Then we set off to *Honolulu Moped Rentals*. It's about a mile-long walk from our hotel, and it feels good to walk off the greasy pizza we just ate. It's also a good way for the guys to get acquainted, and to enjoy the sunshine in a leisurely way. One thing I can say about Jason and his crew is that they are efficient with information and directions. They told us at the restaurant that they had mapped out everything that there was to do here that morning. They wanted to try as much as possible, and didn't want the hassle of being lost or taking excessively long routes around the island. They scouted the area out, and asked a lot of questions at the front desk. They also have a map of the area, highlighted and scribbled on. They would make great boy scouts, which makes me wonder if they ever were.

We had a blast riding on the mopeds, and bringing Jude along was a great idea. We drove all around the area, making sure we didn't end up on the highway to the North Shore. After all, we did have a time frame to have the mopeds back by.

After walking us to our hotel room, the guys say good-night to us, then head down the hall. However, we notice that they stop in the middle of the hall and put their heads together, talking quietly for a few moments. Then they look back at us with grins on their faces and make their way back over. Jason nudges Chase in the ribs.

Clearing his throat, Chase says, "Tomorrow, the guys and I are planning to take a trip to see *Diamond Head* and the *Polynesian Cultural Center*. Do you ladies want to join us for the day?"

"Oh, that sounds like a lot of fun!" an enthusiastic Jen exclaims. "I want to get out, see the sites, and learn more about the island we're on."

"Well, you just said the magical words," Ava laughs out loud. "Jenifer loves history, and here's her chance to explore. And hey, it helps to tag along with three good-looking guys." She winks at the three guys. "We're not sure what we're doing tomorrow. How about we talk about it, and then give you an answer? We'll just yell up to you from our balcony, so leave your sliding door open."

"Sounds like a plan. Talk to you ladies later, and hopefully we will see you tomorrow, as well." Jason says before they turn back to the elevators and climb to the next floor for the night.

We walk into our own room, and I throw myself onto the bed, while Ava shuts the door. Jen flops down next to me. Shortly after that, Ava claims the other bed. It's been a long day, and we are all definitely worn out.

"So? Do we want to tour with the guys tomorrow?" I ask, but already know the answer. "I know you want to go, Jen, so why didn't you just say you would?" I question her.

"We *do* want to go, but we can't just jump at every invitation they throw at us. I like them a lot, and had a great day hanging out. However, we don't want to seem too eager," Ava says.

But it's Jen who points out, "We should figure out what else we want to do and make sure we have back up plans. We should also bring our own ideas to the table, too. We can't just rely on them to come up with everything. There could be a day we don't want to do what they have planned. I just know that it's good to do some things on our own and make memories with just the three of us before we split and go our own ways after the summer."

"Okay, mood killer. *Yeesh*, we don't need to get all serious up in here." Ava tries to lighten the mood. "I want to have fun memories, and we can make those no matter if we have extras with us or not. But, I know what we can do. How about this? We tell them we'll hang out with them tomorrow, and then invite them to go snorkeling with us on another day?"

"That's a great idea. That way it doesn't look like we just want to mooch off of their ideas. Great plan. I like it," I say. "Jen, since Jason seems to like you so much, I nominate you to share the wealth of news with the boys upstairs. You can act out a scene like you're Juliet and he's Romeo." I crack myself up, which only earns me a pillow to the face, causing Ava to join in, and soon we're in an all-out pillow fight. That is, until we hear a thumping at the sliding glass door, which makes us all scream and jump over the side of the bed, freaked out. Ava, who seems to be the brave one of the group, sticks her head up and starts laughing before jumping up and running towards the door.

"Are you crazy? What are you doing? It could be some peeping tom. What if he has a knife, and he wants to do us harm?" Jen shouts after her.

"Seriously, Jen? Why would she laugh and run for the door if a killer was on the other side?" I say before jumping up myself. "Oh look, it's Romeo on the other side."

That has Jen up quicker than if I said her favorite singer was here.

Ava unlocks the door then slides it open before Jason walks through.

"Are you crazy? I can't believe you climbed down to our balcony. What if you had gotten hurt?" Jen fusses over Jason. *Wow, that's not a case of instant like, nope, not at all.* I grin like a big loon over at her.

"The guys and I heard some yelling and banging noises, so I was selected to come check it out. The quickest route was going over the edge. So, here I am. What were you all doing in here, anyway?" Jason looks at us curiously.

"Oh no! Sorry we were being so loud and crazy in here. I was getting ready to yell up to you, before we got sidetracked." Jen says with an embarrassed expression on her face that soon gives way to a grin.

"Oh, and just what were you doing?" he asks her, giving her his own charming grin.

"We were having a pillow fight," she laughs.

"Oh dang, and you didn't invite us? You break my heart!" he feigns being hurt, while putting his hand up to his chest.

I roll my eyes at Mr. Cheese and toss a pillow at his head. He totally didn't see it coming, and it gets in a good *whap*, causing us all to laugh.

"So, what's the verdict about tomorrow, now that I know you're all safe and I couldn't be the white knight to save the day?"

"Yes, we would love to come out with you guys tomorrow." Jen tells him.

"Great!" Jason says excitedly as he fist pumps the air before a faint red hue washes over his cheeks. He gives us a sheepish smile then heads back to the sliding door and steps through it. Once outside, he yells up towards the sky, "She said yes!"

We hear some whooping and hollering before he comes back through the door and pulls it mostly closed.

"Well, as you can hear, the guys are excited about tomorrow," he laughs. "We have to be up early, as it's a long trip and takes up most of the day. Are you okay with that?" he now sounds like he thinks we may change our minds, knowing that we have to wake up before the sun. Or at least I assume before the sun.

"I guess if we're getting an early start, then that means you, my dear Romeo, must bid Juliet and her ladies farewell so we can get our beauty rest," Ava teases the poor guy. He looks a little embarrassed, but we all know that he's clearly infatuated with Jenifer.

"Yeah, you're right. Okay then. So, I'll see you all tomorrow? We'll swing by your place at 7:30 tomorrow morning, then head down to the shuttle bus together." Jason says, making sure that we know the game plan and when to be ready as he starts heading back to the balcony.

"Uh, I'm not sure that's the best way to exit the premises safely. Why don't you try using the door like real live boys do, and not fake boys, like Spiderman or some super hero like that?" Ava says, pointing out the obvious escape route.

"Oh, yeah, right. Good idea. Well, goodnight, ladies. Sleep tight and we will see you bright and early in the morning." Then he makes his safer escape, leaving us erupting into a fit of giggles over his embarrassment.

"He sure is cute when he's all flustered and embarrassed," Jen says.

"Someone's got it bad. Or should I say two some ones'?" Ava giggles, and this time I take a pillow off the bed and whap her with it before she tackles me, causing us to fall on the bed, laughing. All of our noise causes a great big thump on the ceiling that makes us laugh even harder.

Jen closes the sliding door and locks it, drawing the curtains closed while she's at it. Then we get ready for bed, and turn in for the night.

Thank you to:

Lindsay, who helped me with the final push I needed to write this story two years ago. Thanks for reading along as I slowly worked on this project. Thanks for all the late night chats, emails, suggestions, corrections/editing, making the cover, and helping me write out the synopsis, making me laugh, and over all, your moral support, your friendship, and especially for your time.

S.R. Grey, for your support as an author and friend, and for all of your help with the right tools I needed to get this book off the ground. Thank you for your help when it came down to final touches of the synopsis and being a cheerleader on the sidelines.

Amy, for beta reading, and for your awesome feedback that put a big smile on my face. I also appreciated all of your suggestions. But mostly, for being with me from start to finish, and being my friend. You took a long journey with me, and I'll be forever grateful.

Amanda- for beta reading, for your thoughts, and suggestions. I'm happy to have made a new friend.

Anna- thank you for being a friend and saying yes to beta reading for me!

Bethany, **Jennifer and Rachel**, for letting me ramble at you with my ideas when they first formed, putting up with my text messages and giving your opinions on the cover ideas. Thanks for your friendship and moral support. Thanks for cheering me on and checking on me as I went through this process, and beta reading when you could.

To my **kids** for their encouragement and sharing my experience.

My **family, friends and extended family members** for your support, encouragement and to those who read my story.

Thank you to those who don't know and will probably never know that you were the inspiration for this story.

An additional big thank you to all of those I've mentioned, as you were there from the beginning, you helped me push through this project, dealt with my texts and emails about anything and everything to do with this book, and over all were my biggest base of moral support.

About the Author

Author J.B. Morgan writes sweet romances with a good dose of humor, sensible heroines, good-decent guys, realism, and happily ever afters. After all, don't we read to escape reality? So why not read what makes us feel good on the inside and puts a smile on our faces? This is what she strives to put into her novels.

Her debut novel, Holly Lane, landed her as a bestselling author in the Coming of Age genre, and her newest release is titled, Nate (A Texas Jacks Novel).

Growing up, she would dream up hero-rescuing stories in her head, revolving around the boys she had crushes on at school. Later in life she decided to try her hand at writing where she could get some of those ideas out of her head. She's definitely in love with the idea of love.

J.B. grew up in California, but now resides in Oregon where she's a wife, mother, author, chocolate lover, and a Yankees fan. She also loves traveling the world. When she's not writing, she can be found carting her kids everywhere, busy with volunteer work, or trying her hardest to read—without interruptions.